THE

MISTAKEN

Nancy S. Thompson

Sapphire Star Publishing
www.sapphirestarpublishing.com
Sapphire Star Publishing trade paperback edition, October 2012

ISBN: 1938404130
ISBN-13: 978-1-938404-13-9

Cover Image by Thomas Voss

www.sapphirestarpublishing.com/ssp/nancysthompson

Dedication

To my husband, Eric, and my son, Brandon,
for standing by me when I had this crazy idea to write a book.

Acknowledgements

I'd like to give a huge hug of thanks to Amy and Katie, for believing in me and my story, and for giving me the opportunity to see my dream come true.

Big thanks to Diego Vargas, who graciously read my very first draft, and though it held every error a first-time writer could possibly ever make, he always believed I could do it and never failed to cheer me on.

I'd also like to thank Jeff O'Handley, a fellow writer of immense talent, for pulling words out of me I never knew existed. Your critical eye enriched my story more than I ever could have on my own.

Thank you, Carrie Butler, for being a wonderful friend, for believing in me at a time when I needed it most, and to Jenny Hillier for all her advice and sage words of "writerly" wisdom.

My greatest thanks go out to my best friend and writing soul-mate, Lisa Regan. Lisa and I met through a writing forum. We were strangers looking for critique partners, but we became so much more than that. My book is a product of her love and devotion as a both a friend and a writer. Quite simply, I wouldn't be publishing if it weren't for Lisa. I adore you, girlfriend.

And lastly, my most humble thanks to Eric and Brandon, for putting up with my obsession and for always believing I would make it someday. I love you more than words can ever say.

Prologue

I don't know how I missed it, that moment I changed, when I somehow became a different man. I'd lived my life — all thirty-three years of it — by a certain credo, a doctrine of conduct that made sense of everything. It defined who I was and kept me on the straight and narrow, and when I looked in the mirror, I saw a good man, decent and honorable. One who followed the rules and stayed within the boundaries of the law, of common decency. My brother often accused me of being too perfect: the perfect son, the perfect brother, the perfect husband. Always the straight arrow, he'd say. To be honest, it's what everyone saw in me, and I had to agree. That was exactly how I defined myself.

But what if what truly defined a person was stripped away through deceit, stolen by greed, or destroyed by the malice of others? What then?

I certainly never saw any sign that somewhere down deep inside me lurked a monster, an abomination, a bitter man so broken and lost that vengeance seemed the best course, the only road left to follow. I never saw any potential for madness when I looked myself in the eye.

How could I have been so wrong?

Chapter One
Tyler

God, I didn't want to do this. Just thinking about it had my gut tied in knots, but I was out of options. My brother had given me no choice. I was tired of his promises, sick of his attitude, of everything always being someone else's fault, never his. While my fiancée, Jillian, and I had discussed what I should say to him, I continued to rehearse, point by point, during my short commute home. But who was I kidding? I knew damn well, no matter what I said, my brother would throw every word right back in my face, like he always did. But I didn't care anymore. After four long weeks, he had overstayed his welcome, and now it was time for Nick to leave.

The confrontation loomed only minutes away, and I was dreading it. And if that wasn't enough, there was the fog. Cold and persistent, it clung to the road like a drowning man to driftwood. It was the one thing I'd never grown accustomed to here in San Francisco, the summer fog burning off each afternoon only to reappear a few hours later, denser than ever. Add to it the waning twilight and you couldn't see much at all, just indistinct shapes of black and grey. I could barely make out the colorful Victorian facades standing shoulder to shoulder along my street. The painted ladies simply faded into the mist.

I pulled into my driveway and shifted into park, a long sigh escaping at the thought of what waited for me inside. As I grabbed the roll of blueprints next to me, a movement outside caught my eye, a dark shape on the sidewalk a few doors down, writhing about in the murky shadows. I strained to see what it was, an injured animal perhaps, though it seemed too large for that, at least in this part of The City. Golden Gate Park maybe, but that was blocks away. I snatched my keys from the ignition, shut the door to my truck, and ambled up the front walkway, my gaze fixed on the squirming silhouette. There were no noises or crying that I could hear, but then again, the fog had a way of deadening all sound. After wrestling in the dark with the deadbolt, I shot one last glance over my shoulder then pushed through my front door.

"Nick?" I called out, my keys jingling as I worked them from the lock. "Why are all the lights off?" I switched on the hall light and kicked off my shoes as I waited, but I heard no reply, so I tried once more, only louder. "Nick, you hear me? Where are you?"

A disturbing silence hung in the air, uncomfortable and creepy. Unexpected since my brother was supposed to be home, day and night, no exceptions. He'd recently gotten himself into a heap of trouble, and now there were some large men gunning for a little payback. Par for the course for my little brother. He was always getting into one scrape or another. But this time was different. Nick was scared. Really scared. Scared enough to ask if he could hide out at my place while he tried to straighten out the mess with the men he'd crossed, a gang of Russian thugs from his neighborhood in the Outer Richmond District here in The

City. One wrong step, like out the front door, and Nick might not see the light of another day, or so he told me.

I glanced upstairs, but it, too, stood dark and quiet. Something definitely wasn't right. The hair pricked on the back of my neck, and the knots in my stomach morphed into a swarm of butterflies, all battling to escape. I threw down my keys and blueprints and walked through the house, turning on lights in my path.

"Nick, answer me! Where the hell are you?"

I don't know why I expected a response that third time. Maybe I was just praying for one instead, but the silence was all the answer I received. I stood still, deep in thought, worried about what might have happened. *He wouldn't have left the house, would he?* I turned toward the entry hall. *Oh God, no.* I dashed back out the front door, pausing on the porch as I scanned for the dark form. It was still squirming on the sidewalk, but it appeared even larger now.

The streetlight out front was just beginning to dance to life. Sporadic bursts of pale pink light illuminated two feet as they kicked and twisted in the hazy air. The single shape expanded into three distinct forms — all human — one prone on the ground and two bent above, their arms sawing up and down and back and forth with hands clenched tight into fists.

"Oh, God. Nick!" I sprinted toward them in a panic, anxiety blossoming into fear.

"Tyler!" he wailed, but his cry was cut short by pounding thuds.

The other two men — both built like bulls and panting in exertion — stood up straight. They turned toward me with their fists pulled back. And as the streetlight overhead finally flickered on for good, the one inside my head flashed bright then flamed out.

...

The rhythm of the monitor was comforting. Static like a metronome, its unnatural droning allowed me to close my eyes in the semi-darkness without worrying I might miss some small sign that Nick was slipping away. His sea-green eyes, a gift from our mother, lay dormant beneath purple, swollen lids stretched taut into slits above the bruised planes of his face, a younger, boyish version of my own.

I perched along the edge of a molded-plastic chair, slumped over my brother's bedside, with his hand in mine and my forehead pressed against it. My other hand lay draped across Nick's bare waist, bathed in the warmth of Jillian's soothing embrace. Nick felt too cold, his breathing shallow and ragged. Drugs dripped steadily into his IV line to keep him still and calm so the pain wouldn't hinder his recovery. *Would this be another long one, like the last time?* I prayed not. More like pleading really, bargaining with God, making promises I knew I could never keep. But at the moment, it was all I had. Desperation had me on my knees.

My thoughts drifted; I was exhausted after two sleepless days and nights at his side. Sharp odors and urgent sounds weaved their way into my bleary thoughts, clouding my mind as I recalled sitting at Nick's side in the same hospital, but at another time, nearly a year ago. The story was the same, though. My brother was fighting for his life yet again.

I jumped as the monitor chirped a disturbance in the steady cadence of his heart. My head popped up, my eyes scanning his nearly unrecognizable face for any sign of pain.

Jillian squeezed my hand, and I peered over Nick's shattered body into the comforting depths of her warm, brown eyes.

"Relax, Tyler, it was nothing. He's all right. Go back to sleep. You need the rest."

She smiled reassuringly, but my heart refused to settle back down. I shook my head and rubbed the grit from my eyes, wincing as I brushed against my broken nose, the only remaining sign of my altercation with Nick's assailants. With a tired sigh, I stood and stretched the stiffness from my back and shoulders. Other than taking the occasional break to alleviate the pressing needs of my body, I had not moved from Nick's side since he was brought into the Intensive Care Unit at San Francisco General Hospital.

I focused back down and examined his body. It lay riddled with carefully stitched cuts and vibrant bruises, striations of black, purple, red, and yellow that crisscrossed haphazardly across his lean form and gangly extremities. Coated wires leashed his body to the equipment behind his bed, each one blinking or clamoring in a discordant fray, and clear plastic tubes filled with oozing red and amber liquids drained into transparent bags hanging from hooks along the side rails.

"What's going to happen now, Jill? We're right back where we started, square one, only worse. *He's* worse. For God's sake, look at him."

"No, Ty, not really. I know he *looks* awful. His face took the worst of it." She ran her finger across his brow, pushing a lock of sun-bleached hair from his battered eye. "But all things considered, he's not hurt nearly as bad as he was last time."

Oh God, the last time. I held my hands over my face. My eyes burned; the rims red and angry after so many hours of uncertainty. An earlier glance in the mirror revealed two vivid crescent-shaped bruises, which only further punctuated my exhaustion.

Can he live through this again, I wondered. I dropped my hands, let my shoulders sag, and sighed at both the doubt and memories. Turning away, I walked over to the window and stared out into the darkness of The City beyond. The lights shimmered just as they always had, as if nothing had changed, like the world hadn't tipped, spinning wildly on its overturned axis.

Jill smacked both palms against her thighs. "Come on, Ty, relax already. You heard the doctor. He said Nick would recover."

I snickered in doubt. "Recover, sure, but at what cost? We're here now *because* of what happened before, and he barely survived that. I can't imagine what his life will be like now."

"Well, he did survive, and I know he can do it again. We'll help him through. We'll all do it again."

I bowed my head and drifted back over to Nick's side. With a deep sigh, I looked her in the eye. "No, Jillian. That's just it. I don't think I *can* do it again. God help me, I don't."

Chapter Two
Tyler

One Year Ago

The door had nearly closed behind me when I heard the land line ring inside. I turned toward Jill, her lithe form stretching at odd angles as she warmed-up on the sidewalk in front of our house.

"Hey, hold up," I said. "The phone's ringing."

"Just leave it, Ty. I want to go." With her long ponytail swaying back and forth, she jogged in place, anxious to get started on our morning run, a warm-up for a race held later that morning, likely the last we'd be able to make for quite some time.

"It might be my folks. I forgot to check their flight status this morning."

I ran back into the house and grabbed the phone off its base. The caller ID indicated my brother, and I huffed in exasperation. The phone chirped as I answered the call.

"What is it, Nick? I'm in a hurry."

A stifled yawn greeted me, then, "Hey, brother," said a voice thick with sleep. Nick always called me brother, a habit he picked up from his friends back home in Australia. "So

8

uh...don't get all bent out of shape or anything, but...I don't think I'm going to make it this morning after all."

I remained silent, my lips pressed together.

"Ty, you there? You hear me?"

"What is it this time, Nick? Lost your keys? Run out of gas? Abducted by aliens?"

"Ha ha, yeah, you're real funny."

"Well, what's your excuse this time? I'm just dying to know. Really."

"For God's sake, Ty, get off my back. I'm tired, all right?"

"And why is that? Out partying all night again? I swear to God, Nick, if you tell me you're hung-over..."

"No! Well...yeah...I guess. A little. Just got a bit carried away, that's all." A chuckle of embarrassment followed, fading quickly over the hiss of the open line.

I sighed. "That's brilliant. We just talked about this yesterday, remember? You knew you had to go to the airport. Why would you stay out all night drinking?" I don't know why I was surprised. I should have known Nick wouldn't actually listen to me. When did he ever?

"Yeah, I know, and I'm sorry. If it makes you feel any better, I'm paying for it now."

"Well, that's your problem, Nick. I was practically out the door when you called. You're going to have to take care of it on your own. I'm not bailing you out this time."

I was determined to hold my ground for once, for I knew exactly where the conversation was headed. My brother had a sorry track record of never following through on his promises, and, quite frankly, I was sick of it. If he looked up to me as much as our mother said he did then he should learn to be responsible and live up to his commitments, just as I had. At twenty-one, Nick was well past the age of accountability.

"Come on, Tyler. Please?"

Another huff of impatience. "What, are you still drunk?"

"No. I'm just...tired. Come on, Ty, you guys are already up. Why can't you and Jillian do it?"

"Because you promised me, that's why. You swore you'd pick them up. You knew Jill and I had plans. Besides, they're staying with us for the next six weeks, for God's sake. This is the least you can do."

"I know, but—"

"Forget it, Nick! Get your lazy ass out of bed and down to the airport now. I don't want them wandering around looking for you, especially after eighteen hours in the air."

He sighed and swore under his breath. "Fine, but don't expect me to be a tour guide while they're here," he said then hung up.

I cursed in return and threw the phone on the sofa then headed out the door.

Jillian and I took a short warm-up run into Golden Gate Park, stopping at the registration table near the music bandshell before commencing the race, a quick 10K up Martin Luther King Drive and back down JFK to Stowe Lake. The number of participants was light so Jill and I each placed respectably well. We rewarded ourselves afterwards with scones and tea at our favorite sidewalk café in the Haight Ashbury. The fog had burned off early, and thin wisps of sun filtered through the trees. Their shade offered us a pleasant respite from the unusually warm temperature for San Francisco in early June.

Jill and I discussed our plans to take my visiting parents and sister to every tourist spot in The City: the Golden Gate Bridge and Fort Point, the Embarcadero and Fisherman's Wharf, Lombard Street and Coit Tower, even Alcatraz if the weather stayed warm enough. We plotted as much of our course by cable car as possible, a special request from my mum. She imagined jumping aboard the moving cable car like she had once done on the old Routemasters back in London when she was a girl. I didn't have the heart to tell her it wasn't permitted. She'd find out soon enough.

With everything mapped out, Jill and I were gathering to leave when my mobile phone vibrated against my leg. I pulled it from my pocket and scanned the display. UNKNOWN CALLER, it read. I wouldn't normally have taken the call, but my folks were flying in from Melbourne. Although Nick had texted me when he had everyone and their luggage loaded into his car, when it concerned my brother, I'd come to expect problems along the way.

"Tyler Karras," I answered, hoping to hear a client's frantic plea instead of Nick's, but it was an unfamiliar voice that addressed me.

"Mr. Karras, my name is Joanne Weaver. I'm the patient liaison at San Francisco General Hospital. We have your brother, Nicholas, in the emergency room. He requested we pull your name and number from his cell phone."

My heart skipped a beat. "What happened? Is he all right?"

"I'm afraid he's been in an accident. I see this is a local number. Are you in the area, by any chance? Could you get down here anytime soon?"

"An accident? What do you mean? In his car?"

I glanced up at Jillian. Her worried eyes scanned mine for an explanation.

"I'd prefer to speak with you in person, if you don't mind. Just come on down to the emergency room entrance and give the triage nurse your name. I'll see you when you get here."

"Whoa, wait a minute! What about my parents and sister? They okay?"

A silent pause followed. "In person, Mr. Karras. We'll talk about everything when you get here. I'll see you then." And the line clicked dead.

Alarmed, Jill and I flagged down a taxi and raced to the hospital, only to find out from a nurse at the triage desk that Nick was in the middle of emergency surgery. We were ushered by elevator to the surgical unit six floors up and escorted into a small room where we endured a tortuous wait with endless pacing, interrupted only once for an update by another nurse. Three other families came and went in the time we spent staring blindly at the muted TV mounted high in the corner. Instead of reading the tattered, months-old magazines, I rolled one up and then another, drumming each impatiently along the outside of my thighs. Jillian balanced on the edge of a well-worn vinyl chair. Her eyes swept back and forth as I paced in front of her. After several hours, a woman dressed in business attire and a doctor in scrubs finally entered the stuffy room. Jill jumped to my side, her hand on my arm.

"Mr. Karras?" she asked, and I nodded in return. "Hi, I'm Joanne. We spoke earlier. I'm sorry it's taken me so long to see you. We had several emergencies come in all at once." She gestured to doctor beside her. "This is Dr. Manetti."

Jill and I shook both their hands. "My fiancée, Jillian," I said with a nod in her direction. "So what's going on with Nick? We've been waiting forever, but nobody's told us anything. And I can't find my parents or my sister."

"There was a car accident on the 101. Apparently, your brother fell asleep at the wheel. His blood-alcohol level was elevated, though within legal limits. Luckily, he was wearing his seatbelt," the doctor said, "at least that's what the bruising indicates. He sustained a moderate concussion and several broken bones, including a compound fracture in his right tibia," he explained with a touch to his lower leg. "An orthopedic surgeon is repairing it as we speak using small plates and screws. But at this point, we're more concerned about the injury to his spinal cord. Though Nick has responded to pain stimuli, there's still considerable swelling, and he's experiencing some partial paralysis."

I closed my eyes and turned away, a heaviness weighing in the pit of my stomach.

"Right now, nothing appears to be life threatening, but we'll need to keep a close eye on him, especially his liver for a seatbelt injury. Only time will tell. And he may need a considerable amount of it for recovery," the doctor added. "He should be taken into the recovery room soon. Once he's set, you can visit, but only for a short time. All right?"

"Okay but...what about their parents and sister?" Jill asked. "They were all in the car together. Are they all being treated here? We haven't heard anything."

I turned back for the answer, worried yet hopeful.

The doctor motioned toward his colleague. "Joanne will help you with that. I'm only on Nick's case right now. I should get back into surgery. It was nice meeting you both." He gave us a tight smile and stepped out of the room.

The woman moved forward with a sorrowful expression. "Yes, your parents, well, um... I'm very sorry, but the police reported two older victims—late fifties perhaps—both of whom died before the first responders even arrived on scene. I can certainly check for you, but it's likely the coroner has already moved their bodies to the county morgue. You'll need to go down there anyway, to make a positive ID, so..."

I just stood there and stared, as if that would somehow make it all clearer. "And my sister, Kim?" I asked.

"Yes, she's here. She survived the crash and maintained a heart rhythm for a short period of time, but...her injuries are rather extensive. Your sister sustained a life-threatening head injury. She's had a CAT scan, as well as an MRI, both of which show considerable damage. I'm afraid Kim is currently on full life-support."

Joanne took a step closer, her eyes full of concern.

"Now, I can take you up to see her," she continued, "but...you should be prepared. Her doctors have declared Kim brain dead, meaning there is no activity at all. Again, I'm very sorry, but...there doesn't appear to be any hope for recovery. And um...well... There's just no easy way to say this." She paused and looked me in the eye. "You'll need to decide how long you wish her to remain on life-support."

I stared at her open-mouthed, my heart skipping beneath my chest.

Joanne reached forward and gently grasped my forearm. "While I realize this is all very...difficult for you, I've been asked to discuss possible organ donation. Whenever you're ready, of course."

Too stunned to respond, I yanked my arm away. I couldn't allow my head to go there yet. It was too much for me to process all at once.

After asking to see my sister, I was escorted to her side in the ICU. I barely recognized her, though it was less about the changes she'd undergone since I last saw her three years ago when she was only twelve. Kim's face, her entire head it seemed, had ballooned. She barely looked human let alone like my baby sister. Her features were swollen, stretched, and exaggerated; the skin rippled like citrus fruit, and colored to a deep purplish-black. And her hair was still bloodied and matted against her skull. I wondered why they hadn't yet bothered to clean her up.

I forced myself to breathe as I reached down and lifted Kim's hand. Her skin was warm, her veins bulging blue beneath the translucent skin. I cupped her hand to my face and whispered as I stroked the inside of her wrist with my thumb, urging her to open her eyes and turn toward my voice. But she didn't. She couldn't hear me. She couldn't feel me. And she never would again. Her brain was dead, and no amount of medicine or surgery would ever reverse that. It was hopeless. But I didn't have it in me to pull the plug. Not yet. I just sat there, rocking back and forth, crying as a mélange of guilt, shame, and despair washed over me like a storm cloud entombing a mountain.

For the next eight days, I shuttled like a zombie between Nick's bedside and Kim's. After several combative consultations, Kim's doctor finally persuaded me to terminate her life-support. I sobbed as the hiss of the machine — the last tangible sign of her life — fell silent, and Kim's body stilled. I'd never again hear her chatter of boys and school dances, of her plans to follow me and Nick to the States. Her dreams, like her life, disintegrated, like fog in the warm afternoon sun.

Afterwards, I existed in a foggy limbo. My parents and sister were gone. Their deaths devastated me, but with Nick so gravely injured, I had little time to mourn them properly. The guilt and shame, however, dogged me every minute of the day, like hounds nipping at my heels. If I had only listened to Nick and given in to his request, they would all still be alive, and I wouldn't be pacing at his bedside, worried he might never walk again.

Nick's injuries proved difficult to recover from, and he spent the next few months in rehabilitation. Jill took time away from her photography studio, and I practically shut the doors on my contracting business so we could work closely with Nick's physical therapists. It was our mission to help him regain his strength and mobility, which he ultimately did with great effort. But the pain was a constant torment, and the guilt he carried over the deaths of our parents and sister made his recovery even more difficult.

I don't know which of those contributed more, but within four months, Nick was addicted to his pain meds then later to booze. I found it difficult to accept that Nick would want to live that way. He was the epitome of life itself, always living on the edge, one adventure after another. That he would accept a life mired in addiction—chained to something over which he had no control—confused and angered me. I urged him to clean himself up. I even put him in drug rehab, but it didn't stick. Over the next six months, his addictions took priority. All I could do was watch as Nick drifted further and further away.

Jillian tried to help. She and Nick had enjoyed a playful relationship before the accident, flirtatious even, but afterwards, he ignored her. We rarely heard from him at all, and then only when he was in trouble. He couldn't keep a job, and he was even caught stealing a couple of times, which landed him in jail, but somehow he always managed to skate on the charges.

To fuel his habits, Nick attempted an armed robbery close to his home at a liquor store in San Francisco's Outer Richmond District, an area notoriously controlled by the Solntsevskaya Bratva, a highly-organized crime family originally from Moscow, now firmly rooted in San Francisco's Little Russia. They knew my brother well and didn't take kindly to him robbing a store under their costly protection, especially with the owner screaming for Nick's blood. My brother realized they were mere hours away from taking justice into their own hands. Panicked and frightened, he called me and confessed his careless error in judgment.

"Careless?" I said, taken aback. "For God's sake, Nick, are you insane or just dumb?"

"I know it was stupid, Ty. I don't need you driving it into the ground like you always do. But I do need your help. I need a place to stay until I can smooth things over with those Russian pricks. I can't go back to my flat now. They'll come looking for me there."

"Yeah? And what happens when they come looking for you at our place? You'd put Jill at risk to save your own neck?"

"No way, Ty. They don't even know about you—or Jill—so they sure as hell don't know where you live. It'll only be for a few days, I swear. Please, brother, I wouldn't ask but I don't know what to do. I have nowhere else to go."

Though I resented always being put in the position of bailing Nick out of trouble, I relented and gave him one week to clear up his mess, but one week turned into two, then three and four. A few days ago, he assured me he was close to a resolution, but in the end, he let his habits get in the way, and when he ventured out to replenish my depleted bar and score some OxyContin, he was attacked, beaten, and left for dead on the sidewalk, with me unconscious beside him. And here I was again, back in the hospital at Nick's bedside, fixated on the monotonous rhythm of another bloody machine, grateful that he had made it through one more night.

I bounced back into the moment when the door to Nick's room swung wide. The ping of the elevator and drone of TVs rushed in, along with Nick's doctor, a tall man in his early forties dressed in green scrubs and blue Crocs. A harried nurse's aide followed. She rattled off notes from Nick's chart then handed it to the doctor. After checking his IV, she took his vital signs and turned back to the doctor who mumbled instructions, rapid-fire. With a nod, she left in a flash of faded pink cotton. The doctor walked over to my side, his eyes glued to the chart. I remained seated in the chair with my elbows leaning along the edge of Nick's bed.

"Your brother took quite a beating," he said without looking at me, "but he'll recover. His injuries aren't nearly as serious as the last time he was admitted."

He paused and scribbled notes then signed his name in a grand flourish before returning the chart to its proper place. He slipped the pen into his pocket and looked at me for the first time since entering. I wondered what he thought of my two black eyes and freshly aligned nose.

"No need for rehab this time. He should be up on his own within a few days and out of here in a week. His nurse will be back soon with his new meds. She'll call if there's any change, but I think Nick will be just fine. He was very lucky this time. Any questions?"

I shook my head and held out my hand. "No, Doctor. Thank you."

"Sure thing." He shook with a firm grip and headed for the door.

After he left, I settled back down and focused on the monitor's measured pattern. Nearly an hour later, Nick's nurse returned with his meds and asked Jill and me to leave. I placed Nick's hand back at his side then stepped away, the steady chime of the monitor fading into silence behind me.

Chapter Three
Tyler

Five times I watched the dense summer fog march in and retreat outside the hospital window, five long days of prayers and pacing before Nick was moved out of the ICU. At last he was conscious. The swelling around his eyes had eased, and he could finally see me hovering about his bedside. He was in good spirits, alert and talkative, though he hardly wanted to hear what I had to say once the staff left us alone. I'd waited long enough. There was no easing into it.

"I'm glad you're feeling better, Nick, but…that was pretty stupid, leaving the house like that. I don't understand. Why would you do that? I let you stay with us to keep you safe, and you leave to score drugs? What were you thinking?"

He glared hard at me then looked away, his eyes lost in the bags of bruised, swollen flesh that still hung around them. "Bugger off, Ty. I don't need your shit. I've suffered enough as it is."

I bobbed my head. "Right. And what about those Russian blokes? Will they agree? Or are they going to come back and finish what they started? And what about us? Did you even consider Jill…or me, for that matter?"

He turned his palms to the ceiling. "What was I supposed to do, Ty? I need those pills. I can't get through the day without them."

"That's bullshit. You've never even tried. It's just easier for you to rely on those pills and the booze than to man-up and face what's happened."

"Oh yeah, right, like you would know. You've never been messed up like I've been. If you had only listened to me in the first place, I wouldn't be here, and they wouldn't all be dead. It wasn't *all* me, Ty. Admit it. You played your part. You need to accept your share of the blame, too."

His words were like a slap in the face, because the truth of it rang so loudly in my ears. And the fact that I had always known yet never admitted that truth made it all the more difficult to accept now. But although Nick's words had been a long time coming, I was still stunned by his outright accusation. With a guilty conscience binding my tongue, I threw him an angry glare and headed for the door, but his voice pursued me, halting my escape.

"No you don't, Tyler! You can't run away from me. We need to talk about this, once and for all. Work it all out."

I stomped back over to face him, my anger defying the remorse I felt. "And just how do we do that, Nick? You disregard everything I say, and do whatever the hell you want, damn the consequences."

"Oh, yeah? Well, what about you, huh? You refuse to bend, even just a little. Everything always has to be *your* way, the *right* way, the *only* way." He shook his head. "I have to live my own life, Ty. Make my own mistakes. Why won't you just let me—"

20

"Look what your mistakes have cost us, Nick!"

"Because you wouldn't listen to me! You *never* do! I tried to tell you, but you didn't hear!" He drummed his ear with his finger. "I admit my part in all this. I was wrong, yeah, stupid and foolish. I get that, I do, but…what about you, Tyler? You had a hand in this, too. You know you did."

He looked at me as if daring me to refute, but I could not, because Nick was right. I never bothered to listen, not really. I always assumed I knew better, that simply being older, having more experience, somehow made me wiser. I tried to force Nick to live up to my expectations, by my rules. He warned me when he didn't think he could. Yet I ignored him. I couldn't even look him in the eye now. He held quiet while I wrestled silently with both my pride *and* my conscience. Finally, I sighed and nodded in acceptance for my role. It was about time.

"You're right. I *am* at fault. I *do* shoulder some of the blame. And I'm sorry I never let you see that. I never held you solely accountable, Nick. Never. Truth is, that accident was more my fault than yours."

He shook his and started to protest, but I held up my hand.

"No, just listen. I need you to hear this. All of it." I settled into the plastic chair with my elbows on my knees and my head in my hands. "You haven't said anything I haven't thought of a thousand times myself. Yes, I could have helped you out. Yes, I should have realized you weren't in the best shape to drive. You were a kid, and you liked to party. I knew that. I should have backed down. I'm sorry I didn't. More than you know."

It was difficult admitting my part, knowing full well that I could have prevented everything: his pain, our guilt, their deaths. I could have saved everyone.

"I was selfish. I can see that now. I didn't want to give up any of my time with Jillian. But, in my defense, we hadn't known each very long, and for the first time in my life, I was in love. Maybe I handled it wrong. I don't know. She just...consumed me."

"Yeah, Ty, I remember. That's when everything changed. Especially you."

I looked up at him. "I'm sorry, Nick. Really. You deserve better. I don't know what else to say."

He smiled, just a little. "It's okay. You don't have to say anything. I get it." His grin grew wide, stretching clear across his face. "She's damn hot."

I chuckled and peered back down at my feet. "Yeah, she is."

I shook my head, caught up in memories of our early days together. I'd never believed in love at first sight, at least not until I met Jillian Demetrio. I'd been set up on a blind date, but the girl I was to meet skipped out and sent her friend, Jillian, instead. It was serendipitous, to say the least.

"I remember when I first met her. She was the most beautiful woman I'd ever seen. I just sat there like an idiot, staring at her. All that hair, her gorgeous smile. And her eyes, God, I got lost in them, right then and there. Not usually my style, you know."

"Well no, Ty, I didn't know. Not then anyway. That's why I followed you here from half way 'round the frickin' planet, to be with you, get to know you again. But then *she* came along and you just...disappeared." He snapped his fingers. "Shut me out."

I hung my head, disappointed in myself. "I know. I'm sorry. But there was something so different about her, at least from the girls back home in Melbourne."

He snorted. "How would you know? You didn't stay around long enough to find out."

His sharp tone put me on the defensive. "Well, I didn't fit in like you did. You weren't even four when we moved. I was already twelve. I had to leave all my mates back in Maida Vale and St. John's. I was never happy in Melbourne. Nobody there seemed to get me."

"Maybe they would have if you'd tried to fit in. But you never did, Ty. Not once."

"I wasn't like you, Nick. You were practically born there. Or you acted like it anyway. Always the wild one, taking risks and pushing limits with no regard to the rules, just like the rest of your friends."

He blew once on his fingernails and buffed them along his chest. "Yep, that's me: fearless." His serious expression gave way to an ear-to-ear grin.

I snickered. "Yeah, you always were."

Nick's smile faded. "Why did you come here, Tyler, to the States? I always thought you'd head back to London."

I nodded. "Yeah, me, too. But Pops was adamant I not return. Said I needed to stay with the family. He was kind of weird about it. Said it wasn't safe, but he wouldn't explain why. Kind of rubbed me the wrong way, like he thought I couldn't take care of myself." I shrugged. "But even though I resented his interference, it was hard to disregard his wishes. So I decided to tour America first then maybe return to London later. But I ended up here. I like the cool weather. Reminds me a lot of London. For whatever reason, I've always felt at home here, and Jillian is a large part of that."

I tried to explain what drew me to San Francisco and what kept me here, but what I didn't share with Nick was that Jillian was the first person to truly get me, now more than ever.

She understood my dilemma with my brother, having her own tenuous affiliation with The City's underworld through her father, Jack.

Jack's brother, Joey Demetrio, was a long-time resident of North Beach, The City's Italian hub. He boasted of nebulous mob ties, though he operated only along its periphery. Jill's father kept his wife and daughters as far from his brother's influence as possible, but Jillian still had wild stories to share of her Uncle Joey's time with Jimmy Lanza and La Cosa Nostra. Unlike her father, she felt comfortable enough with the image to laugh about it. I, on the other hand, wanted nothing to do with the Russians or the Italians, at least the ones who called themselves Mafia. Yet I found myself connected, however casually, to both.

"I know you don't get it, Nick, but...have you ever loved or even wanted someone so much you didn't want to live if they weren't there right next to you every minute of the day? Well, that's how I feel about Jill. I'd do anything to be with her. She doesn't just talk a good game. She actually makes me *feel* loved. And that's a first for me."

"But, God, Ty, she's kind of high-strung. And moody. And the way she teases you. She's fucking relentless. Any one of those would bug the shit out of me."

"Yeah, well, apparently my 'stuffy English upbringing' bugs the shit out *her*."

Nick rolled his eyes and laughed. "Gee, I wonder why?"

"What is it with the two of you? Rules are made for a reason, you know, to be followed, not bent. So I choose to obey them. What's wrong with that?"

"Well, let's see," Nick said, holding up one finger and then another. "It's anal and annoying as hell."

"Yeah, well, Jill doesn't care, not really. She loves me for who I am inside, not some trophy to showcase before her bloody friends."

Nick laughed again. "Oh yeah, like that's been a real problem for you, huh?"

"Yes, it has, several times!"

"Oh, poor baby!" he replied as he hurled a pillow at my head then groaned at the pain it caused him.

I caught it with a grunt and faked a hard pass back, stuffing it instead between my head and the wall behind me. "Hey, enough of that. Your doc said to keep still and get some rest. I'm kind of tired myself. Been here five days straight waiting for your lazy ass to wake up."

Nick fanned his hand in front of his nose. "Yeah, smells like it, too," he said then laughed.

"Just shut the hell up and go to sleep, will you?" I replied as I nestled my head back into the soft pillow.

I closed my eyes and let my mind drift, quite easy on so little sleep. It returned straight back to those early days with Jillian. I recalled one night just before Nick's accident, when we were sitting together on our living room sofa as I read the paper and she watched TV. I raised one brow and smiled at her, knowing full well the kind of response it would provoke, as it always did. She did a comical double take, her hooded eyes settling on mine and her finger scolding me as it twitched near the end of my nose.

"Don't smile like that, buster, not unless you mean business," she warned playfully.

I twisted a make-believe mustache between my fingers and snickered dramatically like a vaudeville villain of old. "Ah, but I have only a few weapons in my arsenal, so I use them when

I must. I know how much you like it, that look, the way my eyes wrinkle. And my accent...hmm... You love that, too, don't you?"

I leaned over and pushed her down to lie back against the soft cushions as I hovered above. She laughed then looked at me with a provocative smile as she coiled her arms around my neck.

"Well, of course," she admitted. "All American girls love a man with an accent, especially that lovely up-speak way you have about you." She raised her head then and captured me in a seductive kiss.

I can't even count the number of times she had said those exact words to me. Apparently, it was what she loved most about me, that and my crow's feet, and she never missed an opportunity to tell—or show me, as the case were—just how much.

Jill's blood heated quickly as I moved my lips from her mouth and trailed them slowly along her jaw line and down her neck. She writhed beneath me, her hips undulating in silent need. I pulled back and opened her blouse then ran my hand over the curve of her breast before my mouth followed suit. It left a glistening trail to her nipple which stood erect beneath the lazy ministrations of my tongue.

She moaned and ran her fingers through my hair, pulling at it in her excitement. When she could take no more, she pushed up on my shoulders and pressed me back against the sofa. In one swift maneuver, she straddled my lap. Her hands worked deftly at my pants, unfastening the snap and sliding the zipper down. She found me ready and wasted little time on foreplay. Jill bunched up her skirt, worked her panties out of the way then slid down on me in one fluid movement. My head fell back against the sofa and I sucked in my breath.

"Oh God, Jill!"

With her head tipped back and her eyes closed, she moaned and rocked her hips into mine. I held her loosely at the waist as she worked over me. The discarded newspaper crinkled rhythmically beneath me as her efforts drove me closer to the brink. When she finally accomplished what she needed for herself, she tipped my head back and leaned over me with her hands wrapped around the back of my neck and her thumbs pressed against my throat. Her lips hovered a hair's-breadth above mine as she panted into my mouth. With her eyes half closed, she stared into mine, focused and methodical, until I could hold back no longer.

It was moments like that that took my breath away. I'd been waiting my entire life for a woman like Jill, and I made damn sure I wouldn't lose her. After the first six months, I asked her to move in with me at my Noe Valley rental, to live in sin, I joked, and she eagerly accepted. Afterwards, our lives intertwined in every possible way.

After living together for well over a year, I suggested we buy a house, perhaps in the Sunset District, a vibrant neighborhood that overlooked Golden Gate Park and the glittering, blue Pacific. Jill's eyes gave her away and, at first, she appeared excited by the idea, but as the hours ticked by, she grew quiet, and I realized something was bothering her. I nestled up next to her that evening as she absently watched reality TV.

"What's wrong, love? You seem troubled. Have I overstepped? Wouldn't you like to buy a home with me?

She tilted her head and pondered how best to respond, probably in a noble attempt to answer without offending me. "No, Ty, it's not that. It's just…well… Don't you think it's kind of…I don't know, backwards…buying a house together without, you know…being married first?" She lowered her head, nervous of my reaction.

I raised her chin with my finger and looked at her with narrowed eyes. "Why Miss Demetrio, are you proposing to me?"

With a tiny smile, she gasped and batted my hand away. "Absolutely not! It's not *my* place to propose."

I laughed. "No? Well then, I'm not quite sure what to do with this ring, that is, if you don't intend on marrying me." I pulled out a light blue box and tipped the lid back.

Jillian's chin dropped as she stared transfixed at the large, square-cut diamond glistening in the soft light. Her gaze snapped up to mine.

"Marry you? Oh my God! You really want to get married?"

I laughed again. "Well, of course. What do you think I've been working toward all this time? It's only natural for a man to want a wife, children, and a home. Don't you think?"

"Yes," she answered solemnly.

"Yes? Yes what exactly?" I wondered aloud.

She giggled, her grin mischievous. "Yes, it's only natural."

I raised one brow. "Anything else?"

"Yes."

I huffed at her stubborn sense of humor. "Yes what?"

This time, her response was little more than a whisper.

"Yes, Tyler, I'll marry you."

Chapter Four
Tyler

Looking back now, I could see that I was too absorbed in my relationship with Jillian and had excluded Nick to a certain degree. Of course, he was right, and I was relieved to have finally taken my share of the blame for his accident. But when I came to the States, I came to live out my dream, alone and unencumbered by my family overseas. Then Nick followed me, and I tasted bitter resentment—that he should intrude on my ambition, on my dreams. And when it fell on my shoulders to constantly pick up after his messes, I grew angry and even more contentious. In deference to my selfishness, I had learned a hard lesson in the end. Like it or not, my brother, Nick, would be forever at my side. Knowing now how close I had come to losing him, twice in fact, I decided to put all that bitterness aside. He was the only family I had left, and I loved him.

When I opened my eyes, I turned toward Nick. He was rolled onto his side with his palm cradling his cheek, staring at me. It still felt like an ocean lay between us, but with all the unspoken words and resentment now out in the open, I felt sure we could close the gap.

"I'm sorry, Nick. A whole year gone. I regret not saying something earlier. Guess it was just too difficult to admit. I hope someday you can forgive me." I stretched out my hand.

He gave me a lopsided grin, made more so by his fat lip, but it was still the same foolish smirk I'd known my entire life, a little something he borrowed from our father. "It's already forgotten," he said, accepting my apology with a tender handshake. "I'll always be there for you, brother."

I smiled. "Well I'm glad to hear that because…I'd like you to stand up for me at my wedding in the fall. Would you do that for me?"

Nick looked genuinely surprised, happy even. Then a shadow fell across his features. His brow knitted together as he dropped his eyes to his hand fidgeting with the bed sheets.

"Um…well…I'll have to think about it, if you don't mind," he said as he peeked back up at me. "I have a few things I need to take care of as soon as I get out of here. I'll give you my answer then, if that's okay with you."

I was stunned. I thought this was something he would jump all over. He was always bugging me to do things with him. It concerned me that he didn't accept right away, and I was curious what things he was referring to, but he rolled over and laid his head back with his eyes closed.

"Right," I replied. "Whenever you're ready then."

I excused myself and walked down the hall for a much needed cup of coffee. Jill called my mobile and told me she was on her way, so we met in the hospital cafeteria for a quiet lunch. She showed up, bridal magazines in hand, and shared all the pages she had dog-eared with a bright light glowing in her eyes. I smiled, but only half-heartedly, and told her what Nick had said when I asked him to be my best man.

Sadness replaced the glowing spark, and her bottom lip pouted. "He'll turn around, Ty. Nick just needs a few weeks to recover, that's all. He's had a very difficult year."

I agreed with a solemn nod and kissed her cheek as she left for an appointment. I felt a slight grip of loneliness tighten about my heart as I watched her leave. Sighing tiredly, I lifted myself from the chair and left to return to my brother.

As I walked down the long hall, stepping around the busy nurses and technicians as they scurried between patients, two men I didn't recognize walked out of Nick's private room. One was tall with a massive build, the fabric of his sport coat stretching tautly across his broad shoulders. The other was older with thick silver hair, a slight build, and impeccably dressed in an expensive, well-cut European suit. The older man turned back toward Nick's open door with a two-finger salute and a genial *dasvidaniya*. A chill ran through me as his unmistakable Russian accent registered in my fatigued brain. I picked up my pace and called out to him.

"Hey you, stop! Who are you? What do you want? Stop right there! *Stop!*"

Both men turned their heads in my direction, but proceeded briskly toward the open elevator door at the end of the hall. They turned back to me as they boarded the lift. The old man caught my eye and smiled while the giant jabbed repeatedly at the elevator's buttons.

"Wait!" I called out again, but the doors hissed closed, and they were gone.

With concern fluttering in my stomach, I rushed back to Nick's room, bumping into another technician as he wheeled a loaded cart past the open door. Nick stood near the window, staring down onto the busy street below. He didn't turn as I entered though I knew he must have heard me shouting out in the hall.

"Who was that?" I asked. "What did they want?" But he continued to gaze out the window without responding. I walked up from behind and rested my hand along his forearm. "Nick, did you hear me? Who were those men?"

His expression was wistful but resigned. "Just some mates. New friends of mine. No one you know."

"Since when do *you* have Russian friends? What the hell did they want?"

Nick sighed, his brow furrowing for a split second before he turned and looked me in the eye. "Not much. Alexi and I… Well…we've finally worked out a deal, that's all. Everything's been taken care of."

"Who the hell is Alexi? And what does that mean, you've worked out a deal?"

He stalled for a moment and rocked his head from side to side. "Well, he's kind of like a manager, I guess. Said his boss was willing to give me the…opportunity to pay him back, that's all. No worries." He jabbed me with his elbow. "You can relax now, Ty."

But relaxing was the furthest thing from my mind. That flutter and my lunch roiled together in the pit of my stomach.

"And how's that work, Nick? Huh? How are you supposed to pay them back? You don't have any money. You don't even have a job."

He looked me in the eye for a long moment then broke away to stare out the window. "Yeah, well… It looks as though I have one now, brother." He turned and shuffled slowly back to his bed, grimacing in discomfort as he pulled himself up under the covers.

I stared after him with my mouth slack. "What have you done, Nick?"

He lay there silently, his eyes closed against me.

I grabbed his shoulder. "Godammit, you tell me what you've done!"

He jerked free, his face twisted in an angry scowl. "What I had to, Ty!"

I shook my head. "You're insane. Who do you think will have to pay to get you out of this mess when you fuck it all up, huh? Who, Nick? I'll tell you who. Me. That's who. It's always me, Nick. Always."

He snorted and rolled his eyes. "Is that what you're worried about? The money?"

"No, it's not, but let me remind you that I just paid off the last of your medical bills from your accident. That's thousands of dollars, Nick. And now I'm going to have to pay for this one, as well. You never think about things like that. You never think about anything but your own selfish needs!"

"You're wrong this time. I've thought everything through. Everything. And this is the only way it will work."

I barked a short laugh and threw my arms up. "Oh, that's bloody rich! Tell me, who exactly is this supposed to work out for? You? Me? What about—"

"This is *my* life! *My* choice!" he yelled, startling me into silence. He shook his head with a look of tired resignation, but to what, I didn't know. "I *need* to do this, Tyler. And you need to back off and let me."

"Please tell me you're not serious. For God's sake, Nick, you can*not* run with those…those…thugs. They're nothing but a bunch of thieves and cutthroats. You'll end up in jail, or worse, get yourself killed!"

He snorted at me again. "And just what do you think will happen if I *don't*, hmm? Have you even considered that?"

Finally, I saw it, the motivation behind his decision. He stared hard at me, fear registering in his eyes, his mouth a thin, rigid line of frustration.

I shook my head. "No. Uh-uh. You can't do this, Nick. I won't let you. I won't."

"Yeah? Well, Dmitri Chernov and his man, Alexi—that guy who just left with his own pet gorilla—they won't let me *not* do this," he countered. Then he laid his head back and closed his eyes.

Fresh anger coursed through my body. "We'll see about that." I turned and headed for the door.

"No, Tyler, stop! You stay away from them! You hear me?" Nick pulled himself up in bed. "I'm not the only one they're threatening. They know about you now." He paused and pressed his lips together again. "And they know about Jillian, too."

I stopped in my tracks, anger coiling into fear, and swung back around. "What did you say?"

"You heard me, Ty. Stay out of my business. Let me handle it. This is more complicated than you know. And there's nothing you can do about it now anyway. So just keep clear. Got that, brother?"

I stood there for a moment, my eyes locked with his. I shook my head one last time.

"No. Uh-uh. No way. This isn't over, Nick. Not by a long shot." I glared hard at my brother then walked out.

But my resolve to quickly rectify the situation wavered when I considered Jillian's safety, as well as Nick's, for I knew these men well, or at least their kind. Working as a general contractor for so many years had brought me in contact with numerous labor unions and the bosses who ruled them like feudal lords over their fiefdoms. They were one and the same in the circle of The City's underworld. Ruthless and brutal in their methods to maintain absolute control, they routinely squeezed the builders and contractors for unfair advantage in gaining profitable contracts. They certainly didn't mind cracking a few skulls in the process, or eliminating the competition altogether if they saw fit. So instead of running carelessly into the lion's den—Dmitri Chernov's Little Russia—with hunting rifle in hand, I spread word throughout the union halls that I was looking for Alexi Batalov, Dmitri's mouthpiece and top diplomat, and now, apparently, Nick's new boss.

I wasn't sure what to expect, maybe some dark assignation in a back alley, or perhaps being snatched off the street, forced into the backseat of a waiting car, its windows glazed dark against the observant passerby. Just like in the movies. But it wasn't as sinister as that. It was actually rather ordinary, considering who I was dealing with, but unnerving nonetheless.

As I was eating lunch in a neighborhood café—my neighborhood, not his—Alexi Batalov, shadowed by another one of Dmitri's brutishly large men, sauntered in and sat down at my table. He had that same presumptuous grin he wore at the hospital, all confident and easy going.

"Thank you for the invitation, my friend," he said, carefully articulating every syllable.

His English was perfect, clear and precise, barely marred by his accent. I had the feeling it was something he was quite proud of, and I was inexplicably irritated by that, as I was by his dress and mannerisms, both executed with impeccable taste and deliberate propriety. But to me, it felt like he held himself in the highest regard, and I was but a nuisance. It caused a hot flare of acrimony to ignite deep within my belly.

"I wasn't aware I'd invited you," I replied as casually as I could, though I was rattled that he'd located me, choosing a crowded public venue for a confrontation.

"No? Then what is this I hear about you wanting to meet with me?" he asked.

I swallowed hard and glanced up at the man who loomed over Alexi's shoulder like a praetorian guard. Alexi raised an eyebrow, clearing his throat as he leaned in to gain my full attention.

"Yes, well...I just, uh...wanted to...discuss my brother, Nick. With you, I mean."

Alexi eased back and continued to stare at me, his pleasant smile belying the cocky flash of impatience that lingered in his eyes.

When he didn't reply, I continued. "Look, whatever he owes you or your boss, I'll repay myself. In full. With interest, if you want."

Alexi chuckled and rubbed his hands together like a devious cartoon character ready to unleash his fury. He leaned over the table in my direction, speaking softly, yet precise.

"Tyler... May I call you Tyler?" he asked, then proceeded without waiting for a response. "Make no mistake, this is not about money. This is about honor and integrity, neither of which your brother currently possesses. So you may consider this a lesson in both. He will work for a cause. *Our* cause," he stressed, his creased brow shooting upward, "and earn respect in the process. You will no longer have to support him, or his pathetic habits, and he, in turn, will no longer be indebted to you. This is something for which I think you will both be grateful. No?"

Alexi sat back in his seat and waved his hand as if to find the right words. "And besides, your brother has a certain boyish charm I find…advantageous, you might say, at least in particular circumstances. He is well known in the neighborhood, and I am quite certain he will prove to be a useful asset to us."

As I soaked in his words, discarding the charm of his eloquent speech, that flare in my belly kindled to a torch. It burned slow yet intense, despite the anxiety twittering alongside it.

"Well, Alexi… May I call you Alexi?" He gestured with a nod and an even broader smile. "What if I don't want my brother working for your cause? Or to be an asset to your organization? That boy has suffered too much already. Nick's been through hell this year, and I don't want him getting into any more trouble, especially *your* kind."

Alexi's grin remained, but the gleam in his eye was anything but friendly. "First of all, my friend, what *you* want is of no concern to me. Furthermore, you are wrong. Nick is young, yes, but a man fully grown, and deserves to be treated as such. *You* hold him down and treat him like a foolish boy, so why should he act like a man then?" He drew his fists up before his chest. "If he is treated as a man, he will step up and act as a man. Can you not see that, as his wiser, older brother? Or are you too stubborn and selfish?"

With a pause, he looked at me sideways. He poked his finger at the table between us and leaned in even farther, as if we shared a conspiratorial secret.

"I think you do not want him to be a man. I think you like your brother just as he is, under your thumb, always in your shadow, never good enough. Eh…my friend?" He leaned back again and crossed his arms over his chest. "Now, I commend your *brotherly* affection, your sense of familial responsibility. A most…admirable quality, likely inherited from your father," he emphasized with contempt, "but you do him no favor always sticking your nose in where it is not wanted. Nick has agreed to our terms. He knows what he is getting himself into, so I suggest you step aside and let your brother choose for himself exactly which path he wishes to follow: yours or mine."

The torch inside me blossomed into an inferno, blazing with the fuel of Alexi's words. My chair screeched loudly against the tile floor as I jumped to my feet. Alexi's man marched a forceful step in my direction and glared down from nearly a foot above my head. He raised his hands to my chest and pushed with little effort. I tripped backwards and knocked over my chair.

Alexi barked out a sharp command in Russian as the curious attention of nearby patrons turned in our direction. He laid his hand against his bodyguard's side with two quick pats. Like an obedient dog, the man backed away and resumed his stance behind his master. His impatience barely concealed, Alexi turned back to me and shook his head.

"There is no cause for belligerence, my friend. We mean you no harm. But you must respect the position we are in. On top of everything else, Nick has broken our laws and must now serve us in penance, both as repayment, as well as to teach a lesson to others who might seek to do the same. If you become difficult and offer us no alternative, we will have no choice but to defend our honor as a family."

I snickered in contempt. "What honor? You haven't a bloody fucking clue!" I threw money on the table to cover my bill then pointed a finger toward Alexi. "I'm warning you. Stay the hell away from my brother, or so help me God…" I threw his man one last glance then walked out of the café, my nerves so rattled my hands shook.

Three doors down, I had to stop and lean over with my hands on my knees just to catch my breath. I paced in small circles with my hands atop my head, trying my damnedest to douse the flame in my belly. I looked back over my shoulder and caught Alexi and his man as they were leaving the café. We shared another glance before Alexi broke away. He whispered into his bodyguard's ear then smiled, saluting me with two fingers—more fuel for the fire, igniting it all over again. Then Alexi turned away and climbed into a waiting black Mercedes.

As I walked back to my car, my eyes kept darting around, suspicious of every man who walked near, nervous that someone might slip a knife into my back. On the drive home, I decided I wouldn't share those ten minutes with Jill. It would frighten her, and worse, she'd be angry—at me, at Nick, even at Alexi. Jill could be moody and was often high-strung with a blistering temper, and while it was rare, I worried she might act out impulsively if she were to hear about the position Nick and I found ourselves in. The last thing we needed was a confrontation between Jill and Alexi, though Alexi would no doubt find that amusing. And I didn't want her to run to her Uncle Joey either. A war between the Russians and Italians would be a powder keg in this city, and I didn't want to be the spark that set it off.

For the next five days, I kept looking over my shoulder, afraid of who might be out to get me. I gradually lowered my guard, however, feeling confident I had made my point and would suffer no consequences. I'd just returned home from the hospital, where Nick and I had discussed his doctor's plans to release him at the end of the week. When I stepped out of my truck, a man rushed me from the shadows. I barely saw him in the dark, and had little time to defend myself before he raised a metal pipe high above his head. He swung a wide arc and landed a glancing blow to my head as I ducked away. I stumbled back into the open door of my truck while blood trickled over my forehead and down into my eyes.

When he came in for a second blow, I kicked him hard between the legs. He dropped his weapon and doubled over in front of me. I scrambled for the pipe and swung an uppercut to his chin. I heard a noise like crackling cellophane and felt his jaw crumble. Broken teeth flew through the air, and blood spurted from his nose and mouth as he screamed, clutching at his face. He stumbled off to a waiting car across the street, yelling at the driver who sat alone inside smoking a cigarette. The car sped away with its tires squealing in the quiet of the night.

Relieved but dazed, I dropped the pipe and clutched at my truck's open door before my knees wobbled and gave way. I collapsed slowly to the pavement, and stared unfocused at the starlit sky as a dull ringing began in my ears. I heard Jill call my name. It sounded muffled and distant as the ringing grew louder. Her worried face suddenly appeared above mine. She spoke to me; I saw her lips move, but I could no longer hear her words, only the resonant chime in my head as it continued to swell. I tried to focus on her eyes and keep mine open, but her face was swallowed up by darkness, and all I could see was a pinprick of light at the end of a long tunnel. As the ringing grew sharp, the tunnel walls began to collapse all around me. I blinked once then twice.

Then I saw nothing at all.

Chapter Five
Tyler

I winced as the young intern stitched up the deep laceration on my head. "Ugh! Bloody hell!"

He cringed but remained focused on his work. "Sorry about that, Mr. Karras. Almost finished. Just let me tie this one...last...knot," he said then chewed on his bottom lip. "Okay...good. There you go." He removed the sterile drape and sat back, smiling at his handiwork.

I raised my hand and fingered gingerly around the wound. Jillian swatted my hand away.

"Leave that alone," she scolded then carefully smoothed my hair back over the cut.

The attending physician walked into the room. He was an anxious chap with keen eyes that darted back and forth behind his frameless spectacles. He held my films in one hand, pushing them up to the wall-mounted light-box. With the other, he swirled a pen around the colorful images.

"We've taken a look at your images, Mr. Karras, and frankly, there's not much to see," he said, smiling at his own stab at humor. "No concussion. No swelling. Nothing at all to worry about. You're very fortunate to have such a hard head." He tossed the films onto the exam table next to me and winked at my fiancée. Pulling on a pair of latex gloves, he turned his attention back to me and examined my wound. "Looks like Dr. Matson's done a bang-up job sewing you back together. Hmm, yes, very good," he said and stepped back. "Okay then, once you're done with your paperwork, you can leave, but if you experience any nausea or an increase in pain or disorientation, I want you to come right back in. All righty?" He held two thumbs up and flashed a smile. "Awesome. Dr. Matson will help you finish up."

He peeled off his gloves, threw them away, and left just as quickly as he came in, before I even had the chance to thank him. Jill and I were left sitting there with our mouths open at his brusque manner, but grateful that I was all right. We turned our quizzical stares back to the young intern.

"Yeah, he's always like that," Matson said with a shrug. "Now, if you'll follow me, there are some gentlemen here to see you. When you're done, we'll just need a few more signatures." He pulled the door open and motioned for us to precede him.

The gentlemen he referred to were cops, two uniformed officers waiting as I left the suture room. They asked a lot of questions, most of which—pleading ignorance—I chose not to answer truthfully, something that went completely against my nature, but I couldn't risk involving Nick. He already had a criminal record, and I didn't want to get him into any more trouble, especially since I would likely end up having to bail him out.

"I really think this was just a random mugging," I explained.

42

"You've been attacked by strangers twice in the last two weeks, Mr. Karras. Why do you think that is?" the older of the two officers asked.

I waved my hand, like it was an everyday occurrence. "Yeah, well, the whole neighborhood's gone to hell. You guys should really do something about that."

He drew his lips into a smirk and threw me a look, like he didn't believe a word I said. His hand dipped into his pocket and pulled out a card. He reached forward and handed it to me.

"Just come down to the precinct and swear out another statement, will you? We expect to see you soon."

I accepted his card and agreed with a nod and a handshake. "Right. Sure thing. Thanks for coming, Officers. I'll be sure to make it in later this week."

"Please see that you do," he said then tipped his head at Jill. "Miss Demetrio."

An hour later, when all the necessary forms were filled out and signed, I was released. With her hand at my elbow, Jillian walked me back to her car, belted me in, and drove me home. She cringed when she stepped out of the car, spooked by the black pool of blood spilled across the driveway, and my assailant's broken teeth lying in its midst, like stars in a constellation. Jillian sprayed water from the hose and washed it down the gutter before the neighbors could ask questions. Afterwards, she helped me into the house and demanded I share the story I had refused to divulge earlier.

I told her everything, about Nick and his new friends, and my confrontation with Alexi and his goon. Jillian didn't take it very well.

"Oh my God, Ty! Are you crazy? You could have been killed! What the hell were you thinking?" she howled.

I bowed my head and looked up at her sheepishly. "I was thinking I needed to keep them away from my brother. I don't think he can survive them, Jill."

"Oh Tyler, I understand you want to protect him. It's a natural reaction. I would do the same for my sister. But you can't live his life for him. And I don't think you're doing him any favors. If Nick's ever going to grow up, he needs to learn there are consequences to his poor decisions."

"And if the consequence is death, Jillian? What lesson is there to learn then?" I asked, knowing full well there was no good answer.

She looked at me with a sorrowful smile and cupped her hand to my cheek. "I'm afraid you can't fix it for him this time. You're only putting yourself in serious jeopardy. Trust me, Ty. I know a little bit about these kinds of people. They mean business, and they don't care who gets in their way." She nudged closer and sat down on my knee, her arm resting along my shoulders. "What am I supposed to do if something happens to you? Our life together is only just beginning. Please don't risk it on something you can't possibly win."

It was uncomfortable having Jill be the one to talk straight, to calm me down, and spell out the repercussions of ill-made decisions. I was usually the one to do that while she bristled under my logic. And it was hard to admit there was nothing I could do. Being attacked drove home the seriousness of my situation and the consequences of getting involved on Nick's behalf. I didn't want any more of his indiscretions to affect Jill, so I caved in to her request. We had so much to look forward to that it would be foolish to pursue the matter any further.

Two days after my second attack, I wheeled my brother out of the hospital. Alexi and his ever-present army of thugs were there to greet us outside the front entrance. Nick stood from his wheelchair, looked me in the eye, and shook my hand.

"Thanks for everything, brother," he said with his lopsided grin and a gentle fist-bump to my shoulder. "You don't need to worry about me. Really. It'll all work out. You'll see."

He wrapped his arms around my shoulders and patted me roughly on the back. Then he turned away without a second look and jumped into Alexi's Mercedes. I took a step toward the car. I wanted to reach in and pull Nick out by his collar, slap him upside the head or shake some sense into him, anything to get him away from these monsters, but Alexi slid in behind him and rolled the tinted window up halfway. With his typical wry smile, he turned and offered me another two-fingered salute, his eyes twinkling in victory. As I narrowed my eyes and pressed my lips together, he leaned back, and the car drove away.

I rarely saw Nick after that, though we spoke occasionally over the phone. He said he would try his best to attend the wedding, but he was noncommittal about being my best man, explaining he was busy with new responsibilities. I guess I knew now what "few things" he'd been referring to back in the hospital when I first asked him to stand up for me, though there was nothing I could do about it at this point. Nick had made his choice. And it obviously wasn't me.

The wedding plans took shape quickly over the next few months. I gave my opinion only when it was requested, which thankfully wasn't often since there were moments when Jill exhibited signs of a frenzied bridezilla. In between our jobs and working our way through the list of last minute things to do, we were still looking for a home to buy. It proved more difficult than I had imagined. We looked at everything in the Sunset District within our price range, but had yet to find the perfect home. So we put our search on hold until after the wedding.

Guests began arriving a week before the big day. Jill, her sister, Megan, and the rest of her bridesmaids drove up north to the wine country in Napa for a bachelorette party weekend at a fancy spa and golf resort. Jillian called twice a day with a detailed report of their adventures. They enjoyed lounging by the pool, tasting wine, and getting facials and massages. Jill returned, relaxed and glowing. While she was gone, I spent a bit of time getting drunk with all my old mates, something I was not altogether accustomed to. Nick showed up on the last night and joined the festivities. He pulled me aside and promised to stand up for me.

From there, everything fell into place, though there was a tense moment at the rehearsal dinner between Nick and Jillian's Uncle Joey, who knew precisely where Nick's ambitions and loyalties now lay. The wedding itself was picture perfect. Jillian was stunning in her dress, of course, but it was her face, glowing with pure joy, that made everyone stare, especially me. I couldn't take my eyes off her, from her first step down the aisle to the moment we finally fell asleep in our suite at the Four Seasons, exhausted and still a little drunk.

For our honeymoon, I took Jill to Florence, Italy then to Bologna, Venice, and Rome. Our trip ended on the Amalfi Coast and Naples, where her father's family emigrated from over one hundred years ago. We spent two glorious weeks together and had the time of our lives, but it was time to get back to our jobs and settle into reality. When we arrived back home, hundreds of gift-wrapped boxes filled the living room, and we spent several evenings opening them together. As I waded around on the floor unwrapping all the gifts, Jillian sat at the dining table writing down the names so thank you cards could be mailed out. It was a painstakingly long process, and I wondered aloud what we were to do with all the items we had received. Jill was unconcerned as she sorted through the parcels.

"Well, some of these are things we already have," she said, glancing around the room. "We can return those and exchange them for something else we might need."

"What else could we possibly need, Jillian? I mean, come on. Look at all this stuff."

"Well, we could use a few things like...um...a crib, for one, and a changing table, a rocking chair, some baby clothes, and maybe a stroller, you know, like the jogging kind...and a car seat and maybe one of those diaper thingies and—"

"Whoa, wait a minute! What are you talking about? We don't need that stuff yet. You're jumping the gun a bit, aren't you?"

"Actually, no. I'm not," she said, staring boldly. I must have been staring back with a stupid look on my face because Jill shook her head and arched her eyebrows upward as if to say, "Duh!"

"What?" I asked. Besides Jill, a family was the only other thing I ever wanted for myself. There was no greater gift she could ever give me. "You're pregnant?" I asked again, and she nodded once. "Are you sure? How long have you known? How far along are you? Does anyone else know? When were you going to tell me? Are you sure...I mean...really, really sure?" I stopped, my mouth suddenly dry.

She laughed. "Okay, well...um...yes, I *am* pregnant. Yes, I *am* sure...really, really sure. I think I'm about seven weeks along. No one else knows except for you, and my doctor, of course. And lastly, I've wanted to tell you since Rome, but I wasn't sure, so I thought I should wait until I could see my doctor. And now that I have, I'm telling you." She beamed a radiant smile. "I'm pregnant, Ty."

I stopped breathing for a long moment and grew light-headed. My arms and legs started to shake, and my belly tingled. The walls seemed to spin then expand outward. With a shake of my head, I crawled over to Jillian. I knelt at her feet and grabbed her wrists, pulling her down onto the floor and into my arms. My tears left dark stains along the fabric over her shoulder. Jillian tried to pull back, but I refused to let her go.

She sighed. "Are you happy, Tyler, or do you think it's too soon?"

"Yes," I whispered, my voice tight.

She laughed again. "Yes? Yes what?"

"Yes, Jillian, I'm very happy!"

Chapter Six
Jillian

The aroma of freshly brewed coffee and bacon wafted down the hall and into our bedroom, pulling me inch by inch toward consciousness. Before I even gave it much thought, I breathed in deep and filled my nose with the delicious scents. My eyes fluttered open, worry overwhelming me as the strong odors permeated my brain. I peered over at the saltine crackers I always kept on my nightstand, ready to cram them in my mouth as soon the nausea hit. But for once, it did not. Relieved, I smiled and allowed myself the simple pleasure of enjoying the decadent fragrance.

I'd always loved Sunday mornings. They were lazy and relaxed, and, after making love, Tyler would pamper me with a big plate of scrambled eggs and bacon, with toast and jam and a steaming mug of coffee on the side. But the last few weeks had conspired against me as morning sickness flooded through me the moment I woke up each day. I was worried when the malady struck more than halfway into my first trimester, concerned that the change might signal some problem, but my doctor assured me that I was fine, that the baby was doing well—right on target, she said. I ran both palms over my gently rounded belly and sighed in relief.

I rose slowly and padded into the warm kitchen, my eyes settling on Ty as he threw a dishtowel over his shoulder. He whistled tunelessly and pushed a mound of scrambled eggs around a well-greased cast-iron pan. I approached him from behind and wrapped my arms around his waist. He stiffened in surprise then raised his arm, twisting around to greet me.

"Morning, love," he said with a smile and a kiss to my forehead. "How do you feel? Do you have an appetite?"

"Mm, yes, surprisingly, I do. It smells so good. Seems like forever since I enjoyed the smell of food in the morning." I snatched a crispy piece of applewood-smoked bacon and stuffed half of it into my mouth. "Not to mention the food itself," I mumbled.

Tyler chuckled. "Well, you go sit down, and I'll serve you a plate. I made you some decaf, unless you want to join me for some tea instead."

I gave my head a firm shake, my mouth too full to speak as I savored the thick slice of heaven.

"All right then, coffee it is. And the paper is right there. See what you can dig up."

With one foot tucked beneath me, I sat down at the kitchen table. "Ty, this would be so much easier on the computer, don't you think?"

He placed a plate of steaming food on the table before me. "Perhaps, but not nearly as much fun." He kissed the top of my head and pressed a prescription bottle of pills into my hand. "Make sure you take these before you eat." He gave me a stern look and moved back to the stove where he served himself a generous helping of food. "If you're up to it, I'd like to hit as many as we can before dinner."

I looked over the bottle's label and sighed. *Wellbutrin.* "Did you fish these out of the trash?" I asked.

"That's where you left them."

"And that's exactly where they belong. I don't want to take these anymore."

"You don't have a choice, you know that. No more Paxil. It's too risky for the baby. And Nardil is too dangerous for *you.*"

I groaned. "But this stuff makes me even more nauseous than the morning sickness, and it keeps me up at night. Besides, I feel fine. I don't need it. I haven't had any problems for a long time now."

"That's because you're taking the Wellbutrin," he insisted. "And it's the only one that has no side effects for the baby."

"But I've been losing weight when I should be gaining. That can't be good."

"Jillian," he said firmly, "you have enough issues with your moods as it is. This pregnancy will only make it worse. You can't afford *not* to take that stuff."

I pouted and pushed the steaming eggs around my plate. "I thought you said you loved my moods. Fire. Isn't that what you called it?"

"Yes, well, I can wait a few more months until the baby is born. Now eat up. It's getting late. We need to get moving."

With a petulant sigh, I nodded and popped one small pill into my mouth. Like a patient in a mental ward, I opened my mouth and stuck out my tongue, proving that I had swallowed. He gave me a bright smile, his eyes crinkling at the corners. With a shake of my head, I dug into my food and opened the newspaper.

Though it might seem archaic in the age of the Internet, it had become a weekly routine to spread the San Francisco

Chronicle out on the kitchen table as we shared Sunday brunch. We would circle every open house ad we could find in the Sunset District, Twin Peaks, and even occasionally Russian Hill. Then we would tour as many as we could fit into the day.

I loved Ty's little house. It was charming with large bay windows that framed a spectacular view of The City, and original millwork that fascinated the master builder in Ty. It was also chock full of wonderful memories that spanned the last few years. But at well under a thousand square feet, and with two separate businesses run out of the den, it was far too small to raise a child. With all the new furniture, toys, and clothing we were accumulating, the space was quickly becoming cramped and disheveled—not very safe for a baby. And it was a rental. Tyler and I both wanted a home we could call our own. So after I shared the news of my pregnancy, we threw ourselves back into finding a larger home, one that could accommodate our expanding family.

Feeling comfortably full, I showered and dressed for a busy day of house hunting. We ventured out into the chilly early winter weather armed with the well-marked newspaper and a map. We ran from one open house to another, dodging fat raindrops as they fell sporadically from the sky. If we didn't find the home to our liking, we simply crossed it off our list. But if we thought it had potential, we spent time discussing what we could do to make the house fit our needs.

After five hours of running around, searching for a parking spot, then touring each home, we had finally reached the end of our list, exhausted and rather discouraged. The last house was up on Russian Hill, a district normally out of our price range. But the homeowners had entered into a short sale agreement with their lender which could allow us the opportunity to enter the market in an otherwise unaffordable neighborhood.

As I entered the foyer and walked through the well-appointed space, a charge of excitement coursed through me. I looked back over my shoulder and saw Tyler's face light up as he ran his hands over a display of intricately carved moulding. The home was beautiful and well-designed. The kitchen and bathrooms were tastefully updated with the original millwork well-preserved. It had the right amount of bedrooms to allow us more children, as well as space for each of us to maintain a home office. And as I stood in the middle of my favorite room, I couldn't help but think that the house was meant to be ours.

"Look, Ty, the wood floor is in perfect condition. I love that dark cherry color." I walked over to the large bay window and pulled up on the built-in window seat. "Hey, there's storage under here. All it needs is a cushion and some pillows on top." Then I pointed high up at the wall near the ceiling. "It has beautiful crown moulding, too. And a chair rail. This would make a perfect nursery, don't you think? I could put a wallpaper border up at the top and a painted striped wainscot below the rail." My mind spun with a burst of energy at all the possibilities. I turned to Ty, anxious to hear his opinion.

Much to my surprise, he didn't even look at the details which had captivated me. He stood in the doorway, his well-muscled shoulder leaning against the carved wood trim and his arms crossed over his broad chest. He smiled at me with amusement dancing in his eyes as I twirled about the room.

"I like it, too," he said, his eyes pinned on me in my excitement. "You can see the spires of St. Peter and Paul's from the living room." Leave it to Ty to focus on the surrounding architecture.

"I figured you'd like that. And what about the kitchen? Did you see that range? It's one of those professional kinds. And, you know, my parents are only a few blocks away, plus there are a couple of parks within an easy walk. Oh, Ty, it's perfect but...can we afford it?"

While the house was a little above our limit, I didn't think he would have agreed to see it if he didn't think we could afford it. My photography studio was booked solid, and Ty had remodeling jobs lined up through the end of the year. We were in great shape.

"I think we can swing it," he replied. "We'll never know until we put down an offer."

I jumped up and down, squealing in delight, then threw myself into his arms. High heels clopped down the hall in our direction, and a head popped in through the doorway. The seller's agent whooped in embarrassment and recoiled with a polite apology back into the hall. Ty held me tight and spun me around once before lowering me to the floor and kissing me breathless.

Everything moved pretty fast after that. Since we had already been pre-approved, we put an offer down, which was accepted after a month of tense negotiations. After all the inspections were completed, it was just a matter of time until escrow closed. We filled it with shopping, packing, and reading baby books. We tried numerous times to contact Nick and share our good news, but he was nowhere in sight, and rarely returned our calls. So we focused all of our attention on preparing for the move, my pregnancy, and our baby.

"Guess what, Ty?" I asked one evening as we filled and labeled moving boxes.

He looked up, his wrinkled brow easing as he threw me a brilliant smile. His eyes sparkled as blue as the South Pacific with enticing little creases that blossomed at the corners. I gazed at him and lost my train of thought, as I often did. We'd been together for several years, but the sight of his smile and the lilt of his adorable accent continued to capture my attention, as they did most women.

Tyler was oblivious to the women who ogled and stared after him, young and old alike, and even some men. And it wasn't just his face that turned their heads either. His body was perfect, and in my mind, rivaled that of any Greek god ever carved out of marble. I was constantly catching women giving him the once over before settling on his backside. Some turned away in embarrassment as I caught their eye, but most slid me a look that seemed to say, "You lucky girl!"

I admit, I was proud to have landed such a spectacular specimen of mankind. What woman wouldn't be? But when it came right down to it, it was the pureness of his heart that captivated me most, and it didn't hurt that he loved me, even with all my flaws.

Ty waved his hand in the air. "Hello…Jill?" he called out.

I snorted, embarrassed to have been caught daydreaming yet again, even after all this time together. "Sorry, I was just thinking. You know, I'm well into my second trimester now. I think it's safe to tell everyone about the baby. My parents and sister. Maybe Nick. I don't think they've noticed. I haven't gained much weight, and I've been wearing a lot of loose clothing."

He dropped the load of books in his arms and walked up to me. "You must be relieved. I know you were worried, especially about your meds. And all for nothing. See? Told you so." He spooned me from behind and nuzzled my neck. His arms snaked around my waist, his hands splaying over the bump in my belly. Then he rocked me from side to side as he whispered in my ear. "So how long will it be, until I can feel her moving inside you?"

I spun around in his arms and pulled back. "Her? What makes you think it's a girl?"

He shrugged. "I don't know. Wishful thinking, I guess. I keep picturing a little girl with long, dark curls and eyes that melt my heart. Man, will I be in trouble with two of you."

I couldn't help but smile, but then I shook my head and ran my fingers along his brow. "Well, I think it's going to be a boy with eyes the color of a summer sky. Just like his daddy." I pressed my lips to his and curled my arms around his waist.

He pulled me in tight and returned the kiss. I felt a slight flutter deep with me, as I often had over the last week or two, but then suddenly, I reared back with a gasp as a firm kick poked me from inside.

"Oh my God! Did you feel that?" I asked.

"Feel what?"

I grabbed his hand and pressed it to my belly. After a moment, another jab startled us both. He gasped this time, his eyes round and wide.

"I felt *that*," he exclaimed with a huge grin. "Wow! That's...amazing. Thank you." He leaned in and kissed me again. "I love you. You know that, right?" He cupped my face and pulled my forehead to his lips. "You're the best thing that ever happened to me. Ever. I couldn't live without you." He smoothed his palm over my belly. "Either of you."

We stood there smiling at each other like idiot teenagers, a quiet moment of deep bonding, but it was interrupted by his cell phone's *God Save the Queen* ringtone. He pulled it from his front pants pocket and checked to see who was calling.

"Ah, it's David Sharp. Let's hope he has good news. Escrow should be closing any day." Excitement danced across

Ty's face as he drifted away and received the call from our mortgage broker. But his smile, so enthusiastic when he first answered, faded away quickly. His mouth drooped open and his brow knitted in concern.

"What? You're sure? And there's nothing we can do?" he asked David after a long silence. He stood and listened for a moment longer then his shoulders sagged as he dragged a hand over his face. "Right. I understand. Well, I guess we'll try again in a few months then." He paused again and looked me in the eye. "Right. Okay, we'll talk to you then. Yeah, thanks David." He ended the call with a sigh and a shake of his head.

"What's wrong?" I asked as a nervous flutter rolled through my stomach.

"David said the bank ran a final credit check on us yesterday. He said it's routine just before escrow closes, to make sure we haven't run up any undisclosed debt."

"Yeah, so. Why would that be a problem? We don't have any large balances."

"Well...it seems we do. Or at least *you* do."

"What? No way! I only have the one credit card and I only used it once up in Napa right before we got married. That charge was for less than a hundred bucks, and I've already paid it off. There is no balance."

"Not according to your report. Apparently, there's an $18,000 balance as of two weeks ago."

"$18,000!"

The flutter in my stomach rolled higher as bile rose up into my throat. Thundering down the short hall, I raced for the bathroom and vomited. My arms and legs shook as I knelt on the floor and gripped the toilet. Tyler followed in behind me and held back my hair, his palm swirling in slow, comforting circles along my back.

"Easy, Jill. There's no need to make yourself sick over this." He filled a cup with water and held it out to me, along with a towel. "Here, drink this. Take a few deep breaths. Everything will be just fine."

"We've lost the house, haven't we?" I asked, breathless after gulping the water.

With his lips pressed together, Ty gave me a sad look that answered my question. I started to cry. He pulled me up and wrapped his arms around my shoulders, rocking me gently as he stroked my hair.

"Maybe not, Jill. We'll need to make some calls in the morning and see what's going on. I'm sure it's just a simple mistake. That's all. It'll all work out. You'll see."

We stood in the middle of our tiny hall bathroom, his arms braced around my shoulders as he comforted me with soothing words, but I couldn't shake the feeling he was wrong.

Chapter Seven
Jillian

I made a few phone calls in the morning and my worst fears were confirmed. Someone had indeed run up a large balance on my card. I called the bank and demanded an explanation as to why they had never contacted me when the unusual charges were made. They informed me that they had called, citing an incorrect cell number, one digit off. They had even sent a certified letter last week which I found unopened in a box on my desk in the den. They provided as much information as they had on the purchases in question, none of which were mine.

It was a new card with a high spending limit for my business. I hadn't lost it, and the only place I had ever used it was at the spa, so someone up there must have duplicated it or stolen the numbers. The bank assured me the charges would be reversed within sixty days, but the damage had already been done. Taking both our small business loans into consideration, our mortgage lender would not relent and loan us the money until my card's balance was cleared. And since the house was under a short sale agreement, the homeowner's lender refused to wait while other qualified buyers were still interested. So they backed out of the deal, and we lost the house.

I filed a fraud report with the bank and major credit agencies then called the Napa police to report the theft. They asked me to come in and swear out a formal complaint. The investigator assigned to my case was a bookish young man named Mike Tucker, who, with his boyish face and horn-rimmed glasses, looked more like a computer programming student than a cop. He sat down with me and explained how cases like mine usually worked.

"See this, Mrs. Karras?" he said as he held up a narrow, palm-sized plastic box with a deep groove down the center. "It's a skimmer, easily attainable over the Internet. Thieves simply swipe a victim's card through it to store the stolen account numbers. Then they use the security code on the back of the card and any additional information they can glean from the victim as a means of creating a new card, as well as a new identity, either for themselves or, most often, to sell to a third party. We see it all the time, but the crimes are hard to trace and difficult to prosecute. So at this point, there's really nothing you can do except close the account and dispute the charges."

"I've already done that. Now I want to find out who's behind this, who did this to me."

"Well, unfortunately, that's very unlikely, but, if by chance we get a hit somewhere, we'll be sure to let you know."

I looked at him in confusion. "A hit?"

"Yes, if someone tries to use your card where there is video surveillance, we can get a photo and try to match it up to known offenders. If it hits on one, we'll call and see if you can identify him. Or her, since you think you know who it is. Your ID isn't required, but it would help your case considerably if we could tie the perpetrator to you in some physical way. Until then, there's not much else we can do. I'm real sorry." He reached into his inside jacket pocket and pulled out his card, handing it to me with a pleasant smile. "You can call me with any questions or if you just need an update, okay? Now, if you'll excuse me."

With a nod, he turned and walked away. I was left standing there with my mouth open. I ran after him and reached for his arm.

"Hey, wait just a second, will you? I told you, I know where my card number was stolen from, where this woman works. I might not know her name, but I can certainly identify her. Or you could send someone up to the spa with my description, maybe ask around, and get her that way."

He pressed his lips together with his head tilted to one side. "Mrs. Karras, we don't know for sure that your card was appropriated at that spa. Or, if it was, if the person you're speaking of is the one who made the charges. But we'll look into it. I promise you that. We just need some time, and your patience."

Patience? I had no time for that, nor an inclination. I was keenly aware of the slow pace with which most police investigations progressed, even with the most high-profile of cases, and mine was of little consequence, at least to them. Officer Tucker's promise carried little weight.

"So, what? I'm just supposed to wait for someone to investigate this? Like whenever you or someone else *might* decide to get around to it, right? That how it works around here?"

He huffed in response. "As I've said, we need a little time. Please understand, Mrs. Karras, the resources for this type of crime are thin right now, so you'll need to be a bit more patient and let us do our job, okay? I promise to call if anything at all turns up. Now I really need to get back to work."

So that *was* it. Our dream of buying a home was ruined, and we were helpless to fix it. We would not be able to buy any home in time for the baby. And once the baby came, I would likely be too busy to house hunt, let alone pack up and move. I needed this all to be taken care of *before* I was too far along, before the baby was born. But apparently, that was not going to happen. Frustrated and angry, I unloaded on Tyler the moment I got home.

"God, I could kill somebody," I railed as I paced around our tiny kitchen. "And I'll start with that woman. I should go back up to that spa myself."

"No you don't, Jill. The cops asked you to stay out of it. Just let them do their job."

I pounded on the kitchen table with both fists. "But they *won't* do their job, Tyler, that's the point! Don't you see?"

"Come on, Jillian, take it easy. Have you been taking your pills?"

"Oh for God's sake, Tyler. Yes! How many times do I have to say it already?" I couldn't believe he was bringing *that* up now.

"Well then, you need to mellow out. It does no good to lose your temper. You need to stay calm, for the baby, at least."

"God! You just don't get it, do you? I'm telling you, that's precisely *why* I'm doing this. For the baby. We need a bigger house for the baby, a safer one. And we need to have all this taken care of *before* he's born, before I'm too busy to even take a shower, let alone find a house and move. What are we supposed to do now?"

"Listen to me, Jill. It'll all get sorted out, in due time. You aren't responsible for those charges, so just relax."

"I can't relax. And it's not about the money. Someone out there is screwing with my life—with *our* life— and apparently there's not a damn thing I can do about it." I stomped my foot and covered my face with my hands.

Tyler wrapped his arms around me as I cried for the hundredth time.

Chapter Eight
Jillian

The next morning, I got to work trying to find out who might have compromised my identity. I was sure the problem could be traced back to the spa up in Napa, but proving so was more difficult than it should have been. I attempted to get help from the resort, but they had no answers except to ask who assisted me with my purchases. I told them I had been helped by only one employee—a woman—but I didn't know her name. Even though I described her to the manager, he was reluctant to name anyone specific, but I think he knew exactly who I was talking about and was only out to protect his employer's interests, and possibly his own job.

I resisted going back up to the spa and confronting that woman. God knows I wanted to, but Tyler had made me promise otherwise. It was one pledge I was determined *not* to break. I had already broken my vow to keep taking the Wellbutrin. I just couldn't tolerate the nausea and sleepless nights one minute longer, so I stopped cold turkey. So far, I was feeling all right, but there were times I had to work at keeping my cool, especially when it concerned this case. It was easy enough to blame the pregnancy.

For several weeks, it seemed as if nothing was being done. But then I received news of a break when Mike Tucker, who'd been working closely with my bank, informed me that they had videotape of someone attempting to make a purchase using my account. He asked me to come in and see if I could identify the suspect in a photo lineup. I drove up right away and sorted through a stack of still shots taken from surveillance videos. They were pasted neatly along white cardstock, three to a page, five pages in all. There was no mistaking the woman from the spa, the one who had assisted me with my purchases. My heart raced the moment I recognized her.

"That's her...number fourteen," I said as I tossed the sheet at Tucker.

I tapped my finger on the center image. He picked it up and removed my selection, nodding once as he held it up to the reflective glass along one wall in the small room.

"Positive ID," he said aloud to someone I couldn't see.

A voice thick with years of nicotine abuse broke over a speaker mounted high up in the corner of the room. "Thank you, Mrs. Karras. That'll be all for now. We'll let you know if we need anything else."

Tucker stood and collected the pages of photographs scattered across the table.

"Wait a second," I said to the mirror. "Don't just dismiss me like that. I want to know who that woman is. Do you even know? Am I allowed to know?"

Tucker looked over at the reflective glass.

"Yeah, sure. Go ahead, Tuck," the gravelly voice said.

Tucker nodded and turned back to me. "Okay then. Her name is Erin Anderson. She's been busted three times for check fraud but has never been convicted, at least not yet. She's still employed at that resort you visited last September."

I clapped my hands and rubbed them together, freshly energized with hope. "That's great! Now what? Do you arrest her? Will she go to jail? Stand trial? What?"

"No, not yet. We'll continue to gather evidence for the District Attorney's office. He'll determine whether Ms. Anderson should be brought into custody or not, but you shouldn't get your hopes up, Mrs. Karras. As I told you before, these cases are difficult to prosecute and are not high on his list of priorities. We'll send somebody up there to question her, but it could be a while, so..." He finished with a shrug, scooping up the stack of pictures and brushing by on his way out.

But I reached for his arm to stop him. "You've got to be kidding me! That woman has made it impossible for me to buy a home before my child is born, and now you're telling me I have to sit and wait for the DA? My case has nothing to motivate him. That is so unfair, Officer Tucker. Who the hell is looking out for *me*? This isn't just about a few credit card charges. That woman has affected my entire life. She needs to be held accountable."

"I agree, but it's out of our hands, Mrs. Karras. I'm sorry, really, I am. The minute we hear from the DA's office, we'll let you know, but you need to be patient. The process is complicated, and the DA won't prosecute if he doesn't think he can secure a conviction. Now if you'll excuse me, I have some phone calls to make." He tipped his head then walked out of the room, leaving the door open behind him. He stopped in the hall and turned back to me. "I can walk you back out, Mrs. Karras."

I grabbed my bag and left the room, stomping rather childishly down the hall. *Fine*. If the police wouldn't help, I would take care of it myself. I didn't know how, but I wasn't going to let this case fall through the sizeable cracks of a broken legal system.

...

For the rest of week, I wracked my brain trying to figure out a way to get the District Attorney's office to prosecute, or somehow coerce that woman to confess. I was frustrated that there didn't seem to be anything I could do. I tried to stay calm for my own health and the sake of the baby, but it continued to eat away at me for days on end. There was no way I could just let it go. Tyler acted sympathetic, but he was also patient enough to wait for the prosecutor's office to follow through. He was a stickler for rules, something I found particularly irritating at times. After two weeks with no progress, I decided to push the issue.

"So I've made a decision, Tyler," I announced one evening as we cleaned up after dinner. "I'm going to meet with the DA. If I put a face on the victim, give him a little sob story or whatever, maybe he'd care a little more. Or perhaps I should talk to one of those TV news investigators. You know, the ones who embarrass deadbeats on the air. I'll tell him all about the DA not doing his job." I turned from the sink and faced him, my eyes narrowing involuntarily. "I bet a little public humiliation would get him off his ass. Don't you think?"

He sighed. "You already know what I think, Jill. You need to let this go. It's not good for you or the baby to obsess about it *all* the time." He stood in front of me with his hands around my arms, stooping to catch my attention. "Look at you. You're a bloody wreck."

I wrenched free from his grasp, feeling like a scolded child. "I can't just let it go, Ty. I'm so freaking pissed. And you should be, too, for God's sake! That woman belongs in jail."

"Relax, love. She will be...eventually. It won't change us having to take the time to clear things up on your end though. You need to be patient."

"Ugh! I'm so tired of hearing that," I said as I paced the floor. "What are we supposed to do in the meantime, huh? There's not enough room for us here. We're already bursting at the seams, and it's just not safe with all this clutter. We need a bigger place, Tyler, and I won't have the time or energy to deal with moving *after* the baby comes. Don't you understand that?"

"I understand you're a bit overwrought right now, love. All those pregnancy hormones are wreaking havoc on your emotions."

My chin dropped. "So because I'm taking those goddamn pills, this is just me being hormonal, is that it? Like I don't have a legitimate reason to be upset about all this, huh? Let me tell you something, if someone was messing with *your* perfect world, you'd be pissed, too," I said, poking him in the chest, but then I pulled back. "Oh wait, I'm sorry, I forgot. Mr. Law-Abiding-Citizen here is content to just sit around and wait for that chucklehead DA to get off his ass and do his job. You'd never think to stray outside the rules to see to my interests, would you? Hell, no! And God forbid I should wander from the straight and narrow either, right? Tell me, Ty, do you ever get tired of being so self-righteous? God knows I do." I pointed my finger toward the door. "That bitch is ruining my life, my reputation. But hey, it's no big deal, huh?" I waved my hands at him. "Whatever."

My tone was mocking and flippant. Hell, it was downright mean, but Ty just stood there with his hands on his hips and let me rant, never once retorting with a biting reply. His patience made me hate myself even more, but I couldn't seem to control my outbursts. I knew it was probably time to get back on the meds, that I should muscle through the side effects, but I couldn't stomach the idea of months of sleepless nights and endless nausea. And I didn't want the baby exposed either, even if there were currently no known risks. You never knew what would be discovered in the future, and surely, a little anger and frustration was preferable to exposure to chemicals.

"Okay, look," Ty said. "I can move our desks out of the den and that can be the nursery for now. I'll get a storage unit and clean out the entire house, make it safe. It won't be forever, Jill. I promise. It'll all work out, you'll see. And if that's not enough, maybe we can just rent a bigger place until we get a loan approved again. All right?"

I rolled my eyes. "And keep flushing our money down the toilet? Yeah, that's a great plan, Ty. Terrific."

"Come on, work with me here. It won't take that long, only a few more months or so. In the meantime, I need you to focus on the baby, on staying calm. Okay? For me?"

I groaned in reply, but nodded for his sake. I'd already tried it his way, to let it go, to make the best of a bad situation, but that didn't work for me anymore. I wasn't going to just accept it and wait for things to get better on their own, or worse, wait for the cops and DA to get off their collective bureaucratic ass. I would figure something out on my own, and God help that woman when I did.

Chapter Nine
Jillian

I lay in bed all night thinking, staring into the darkness, but the solution to my problem was elusive. I thought about asking Uncle Joey for help. He would love the opportunity to demonstrate his influence, to bang a few heads together for the benefit of a loved one. But my father complicated that idea. He barely tolerated his brother. It was all I could do just to get Uncle Joey invited to my wedding. My dad was embarrassed by his brother's entanglement with "the family," a nefarious organization that had been operating in the neighborhood for countless generations. He believed it endorsed the Italian-American stereotype he tried so hard to disprove through honest, hard work.

My father had seen up close and personal just how Uncle Joey and his associates operated, several times from what I remember. I'd heard my parents arguing over it when I was little. My dad worried endlessly that my mom, sister, and I would be exposed to such a dangerous element, so I knew he would be disappointed if he ever found out I had used Uncle Joey to work around the law. And I couldn't delude myself into believing that Uncle Joey wouldn't take the first opportunity to tell my dad either. It was a matter of pride between brothers. Uncle Joey always wanted to show his worth, to give credence to his value and choice of lifestyle. That his brother's daughter would come to him for help, instead of her own father, would provide years of bitter resentment and conflict. So, as tempting as it was, Uncle Joey was definitely out.

Then there was Nick. I was very reluctant to involve him, as well, but at least it wouldn't get back to my father if I did, though Tyler was a different story. Just like my dad and his brother, Ty would never approve of me involving Nick. After everything that had happened and the choice Nick had made, there was no way Ty would accept his brother sticking his nose into our business. But I couldn't think of a better alternative.

Always the one to follow every rule, Tyler was unwilling to do anything but wait, and the authorities would likely sit on my case for months. I couldn't just accept that someone out there was screwing with my life, that she could steal our dream of owning a home. Next, she would likely take the very food from our mouths. That was unacceptable. The stress and frustration of doing nothing consumed me. My stomach blazed with it in constant irritation. And though I burned through too many bottles of Tums to count, I still wasn't willing to start back on my anxiety meds. Surely dealing with and solving my own problem was far healthier for me and the baby than relying on drugs.

After turning over every detail and possible scenario, I finally decided to call Nick in the morning and at least ask his advice. Besides Uncle Joey, I didn't know anyone else who associated with criminals, and the way I figured, who better to deal with one felon than another? So after Ty left for work in the morning, I called Nick and invited him over for coffee. Half an hour later, he was knocking at my door.

"Hey Jilly. You look lovely, as always," he said, greeting me with a kiss and a bear hug. "God, I've missed you."

His green eyes sparkled, and he beamed his signature grin. Save his eyes, Nick's face was the very image of his brother's, only younger, but he stood nearly two inches taller, all bones and wiry muscle, like he hadn't quite grown into his body yet. Whereas Ty's close-cropped hair was dark, Nick's was a dusky, burnished gold, bleached in the blazing sun of his youth. It hung in long, thick waves across his forehead and over his collar, brushing the black leather jacket that fit snugly across his shoulders. He looked both playful and dangerous all at once.

But it was his speech that exposed the greatest difference. Nick's twangy Australian accent was considerably sharper than Tyler's, which, true to his Anglo roots, sounded more British, though even that had softened and was now slightly nuanced with an American timbre. Ty was twelve when his family moved from London to Melbourne. Nick was so young — not quite four years old — that his speech was more affected by the move. And Nick hadn't been in the States as long, just over four years compared to Ty's ten. But stranger still was the clipped tone Nick had taken on lately, which I assumed was due to time spent with his new Russian friends.

"Thanks for coming over, Nick. I really appreciate it."

Though he seemed reluctant to let go, I backed out of his embrace and looked into his eyes. He stared back with a curious longing I had never seen before.

"Sure, sweetheart. It's never a problem. You know that, don't you?"

He reached out and, with remarkable tenderness, tucked a stray lock of hair behind my ear. Then his fingers traced along my jaw before his hand fell back to his side. The gesture felt intensely intimate, even for Nick. I stuffed my hands into my pockets and took a step back, dropping my gaze to the floor as a warm flush swam through me. Nick sighed, but it sounded like frustration to me. I peered back up and tried to smile.

"So, what's all the drama about?" he asked.

"Well, I um… I have a problem, and I can't figure out a way to fix it. I was hoping you might help me out somehow."

"Yeah? What's wrong? Ty not treating you right?" His tone was light-hearted, but I picked up on a subtle signal that he was only too willing to step in and save the day, should I ask.

I waved my hand. "No, everything's good there. My problem is with someone else."

I took a few minutes and told Nick about the house Tyler and I had found, and how we'd lost it. I explained Erin Anderson's role and the DA's unwillingness to move forward. He acted just as sympathetic as his brother, but unlike Ty, Nick didn't just leave it at that.

"And what would you like me to do about it?" he asked, his posture as forthright as the unspoken word in his eye that told me he would do whatever I asked.

But I wasn't quite sure *how* to ask, because I really didn't know what I was asking for myself. I stammered, unable to find the right words, and embarrassed that I would stoop to begging for his help when all he'd ever received from me and Ty was harsh judgment for his poor choices. It felt hypocritical, to say the least, but I felt I had little choice.

Nick closed the gap between us and captured my hand. "Spit it out, Jilly. There's a reason why you asked me to help and not Ty."

"That's the problem right there. Ty won't *do* anything. He won't even try, and he doesn't want me to either. According to him, I'm just supposed to suck it up and wait for the authorities to take care of everything."

Nick chuckled. "Of course. You know Ty. A regular Dudley Do-Right, that one." He rolled his eyes and shook his head. "Can't say I expect anything different."

"*I* can. I expect him to help. I am his wife after all."

"Well, *I* would do anything for you, Jilly. You only have to ask. You know that, right?"

I could only nod silently.

"So, what'll it be then? You want me to talk to that woman, straighten her out a bit?"

He had a hard glint in his eye, easily considered mean if you didn't know him, and I wasn't so sure I did any more, so it even made me a little nervous. But I suppose that was exactly why I had called Nick in the first place.

I bit my lip, unable to keep my eyes level with his. "Well, something like that, I guess. I mean, I'm not really sure. I just want her to admit what she's done, you know. I want her in jail where she belongs. And I want my life back," I said, throwing up my arm.

He snickered. "I don't know if I can manage all that, but I'm sure my friends and I can scare the holy hell out of her anyway. Not sure what good it'll do, but I can try, if you'd like." Nick winked and pulled my hand up to his lips. "I'll do whatever you need me to, Jilly." He stroked my cheek with the back of his fingers.

I attempted to snatch my hand away. "Nick, come on," I scolded. While I was used to his casual flirtations, his latest effort had ticked up considerably, and it was making me very uncomfortable. "I'm serious."

"What? You think I'm not?" He dropped my hand and smoothed over the hurt look in his eyes. "Okay, I get it. Message received, loud and clear."

I reached for his hand. "No, Nick, that's not what I meant."

He raised both hands in the air. "No, it's okay, really. I understand." He wagged his finger back and forth between us. "This is business, right? Well, I'm your man, whatever you need, sweetheart. I'll just go pay Ms. Anderson a visit and see if we can...work something out. I'll let you know how it goes. Good enough?"

I nodded once more, feeling guilty, but oddly relieved.

"Good. Now come here." He held his arms out wide. "I promise not to bite."

I walked forward and Nick folded his arms around me once more. He placed his chin on top of my head like I was his kid sister, though the way he rubbed my back felt much more intimate.

"I'll take care of everything. You'll see." He kissed my forehead, slow and tender.

"Thanks, Nick. I knew you'd help." I rested my hands along his waist. "I've missed you, too, you know. So has Ty."

He snorted in disbelief. "Yeah right." He clamped his arms down around my expanding belly and started to tickle me around the ribs.

My initial giggling quickly turned into sharp squeals as I twisted to escape his arms. We were both laughing hard when the door to the garage swung open and Tyler burst into the room. His eyes shot back and forth between me and Nick. His look of surprise morphed quickly into suspicion as his eyes narrowed and his lips pressed together. He didn't look too happy to see Nick, especially with his arms locked around me. I tried to break free, but Nick tightened his grip, smiling at his brother with a greeting.

"Ty, old man. How the bloody hell are you?" Nick pushed me back at arm's length and winked before turning to Ty with a wide grin splitting his boyish face.

"Nick," Ty acknowledged dryly as he shook his brother's outstretched hand. He shot me another suspicious glance before he turned back to Nick. "It's been a while. What brings you here?"

"Oh, come on, do I really need a reason to see my big brother and his lovely bride? Actually, I just wanted to see how fat little Jilly was getting," he explained as he rubbed his palm over my extended belly. Nick laughed when I slapped his hand away. "I think the old girl is filling out quite nicely, don't you, brother?"

Ty stepped toward his brother. "Nick," he replied as a warning.

Nick raised his arms up in mock surrender. "Apologies. Didn't mean to offend," he said, but there was a sulky twist to his lips, and mischief twinkled in his eyes.

Tyler turned toward me. "Jillian, what the hell is going on here?"

He had a short fuse when it came to Nick, always distrustful of his brother's motives. I opened my mouth to speak, but Nick interrupted, his eyes darting from me to Ty.

"Relax, old man. Jilly's just been filling me in on the house hunting, that's all. No worries. Sorry to hear it's gotten so...complicated."

Tyler stared at him for a moment before raising his chin in understanding. He was instantly in Nick's face, pointing his finger in warning.

"You stay out of it, Nick. I mean it. This is none of your business or your concern."

Nick pushed his brother's hand away. "I'd be careful if I were you, brother. I'm no longer that weak boy who followed you around like a lost puppy."

Tyler reacted swiftly, surging forward and pushing Nick back against the wall. His lips were pressed together in an angry line and he spoke through clenched teeth.

"You stay the fuck out of my affairs, you hear me? And stay away from my wife! She doesn't need your kind of help."

They stood facing each other, nose-to-nose. Ty's face twisted in anger, but Nick looked unfazed, even amused, a smirk pulling up along one side of his mouth.

"Funny, Jillian doesn't seem to agree with you," he countered. There was a defiant challenge in his eyes as he stared unafraid at his older brother, a new level of confidence for him. A reward of standing toe-to-toe with the Russians, I would bet.

"Nick, Tyler, please. Stop this!" I squeezed my hands between their bodies and tried to separate them.

After a long, tense moment with Nick still pressed against the wall, Ty took a step back and held his arm out toward the door. "Nick was just leaving. Weren't you, Nick?" he said, his eyes still locked with his brother's and his jaw ticking in agitation.

"Yeah, right." Nick stood still, his eyes unwavering and locked onto Ty. Finally, he stepped away and gave me a quick peck on the cheek. "G'day, sweetheart. We'll talk soon." he said, his voice sweet once again. "Remember what I told you," he added in a soft whisper. He took another step and glared hard over his shoulder before he walked out the door.

Tyler turned toward me, his face red and his eyes blazing with anger. "You keep him out of this, Jillian. Do you understand me? Under no circumstances is Nick to be involved. Everything he touches turns to shit and you know it." He pointed his finger at me, just as he had done to Nick. "You let this go, once and for all, you hear me? You let it go."

He stared at me for a few seconds more then walked past me into the den. He retrieved some building plans and left the house without another word, slamming the garage door behind him.

I clenched my hands into fists and heaved a sigh, trying in vain to cleanse the frustration from my head and the acrid burn from my stomach.

"Oh well," I murmured in resignation, "Guess I'll be taking care of this one on my own."

Chapter Ten
Jillian

Tyler and I didn't talk about Erin Anderson again. Nor did we discuss Nick, the police, or the District Attorney. My case was off limits now. He thought a warning was all I needed to let the whole thing go, to accept what fate had decided best. But as he slept beside me later that night, I continued to lay awake, silently working on how best to approach Erin.

The following evening, we had another huge blowout, and I spent the night alone while Tyler slept on the sofa. During those long hours apart, I decided I would just go ahead and do what Nick had been planning. I would talk to Erin, scare her a little. I'd tell her the cops knew about her and were going to arrest her soon, and if she just confessed, they would go easier on her.

Better yet, I would tell her about Uncle Joey and even Nick and his Russian friends, explaining that there were many who wouldn't mind putting the screws to her if she didn't step up on her own. It wasn't altogether a lie. And the message would be the same, just a different messenger, since there was no way Nick would ever cross his brother now.

I had no intention of telling Tyler. He'd just worry. What's worse, he'd be pissed. He'd never allow it, and I really hated when he'd tried to control me in his self-righteous, paternal way. I could handle him even if he did find out. I'd take care of everything on my own and be back before Ty came home from work. I worked through all the things I would say to that woman during the hour-long drive up to Napa. If I confronted her at the spa where there were other people—guests and fellow employees—I could use the threat of embarrassment to keep her calm and force her to listen. It seemed like the best plan, for now anyway. I didn't know what else to do, but I did know I couldn't just let it go, no matter what Ty had ordered.

I parked out front of the spa and entered the spacious lobby. Erin wasn't at the concierge or reception desks where I had seen her on my last visit. I walked up to the check-in counter and smiled a pleasant greeting.

"Excuse me. Do you know where I can find Erin Anderson?"

"Oh, you just missed her. She left on her break," the young woman said, but then she glanced at her watch. "But it's only been maybe five minutes. You might be able to catch her out back in the employee parking lot." She swung her head toward the rear doors.

I hooked my thumb over my shoulder. "Back that way?"

She nodded as she answered a phone call. I waved a silent thank you and took off.

I returned to my car and drove around back until I located the lot designated for employees. I was lucky and found Erin as she was unlocking her car door. I pulled into the empty spot next to her car, rolled my window down, and called out her name.

"Ms. Anderson? I'm sorry. May I speak with you for a moment, please?" I shut off my engine, climbed out, and walked in her direction.

She narrowed her green eyes as she tried to figure out who I was. It disgusted me that she couldn't even remember her victim's face, and the rage started to boil up inside me again. I clenched both my teeth and fists to keep myself from clawing her clueless eyes out.

"Do I know you?" she asked, one finely groomed eyebrow cocked up at an angle.

I took a deep breath to chase away the butterflies and ease my fury. "Yes, you do. *Very* well." I looked her in the eye, willing her to recall my face, but all I got back was a blank stare, both auburn-tinted brows now raised in question.

"I'm sorry, I don't recognize you. Are you a guest here at the spa?"

I slipped in between the cars and stood in front of her with my hands placed on the vehicles on either side of me, corralling her as best I could. I bit my lip to keep myself from hurling names and accusations at her. Though her mystified demeanor rankled me, it would all come out in good time.

"I was here, a couple of months ago," I admitted. "You might recall my name if not my face. I'm Jillian Karras. Jillian *Demetrio* Karras. Do you recall that name, Ms. Anderson?"

An uncomfortable flash of recognition sparked within her eyes before she smoothed it over with a false smile. "No, I'm sorry, I don't. Now you'll have to excuse me. I have an appointment I'm already late for, so if you don't mind..." She turned to open her car door.

I took a step closer, forcing her to retreat a step. "Well, I do mind, Erin. You see, I know what you've done, and the police do, as well. And you're about to face the consequences for it." I smiled to punctuate the threat.

Her jaw dropped. "I don't know what you're talking about. Now please, get out of my way." She advanced and pushed me, but I held my ground and shoved her right back. "You'd better get out of my way before I call security," she warned.

I swung my arm wide and gestured toward the building behind us. "Oh, please, by all means, call security. I'd love for them to know what you've been up to while in their employ."

"I've done nothing, you crazy bitch, now back off!"

"No, *you're* the bitch. You've cost me everything. I lost the home I was trying to buy, all because of you and your sleazy greed! But you're going to pay, even if I have to drag you to the cops myself."

I reached for her arm, but she pushed me backwards again, hard. I stumbled. With both arms wrapped around my belly, I fell in between the cars. I knocked my elbows against the hot metal then rolled onto my side, my arm grinding into the gravel and asphalt while Erin maneuvered forward and opened her car door.

"Watch it, you lunatic! Can't you see I'm pregnant?"

Erin jumped into her car and looked down at me as I lay on the pavement. "Well then, you better get the fuck out of my way before I run you *both* over."

She slammed the door shut as I scrambled to get out of her way. She started her car and raced the engine in warning, glaring at me through the closed window. I pounded on the glass as she pulled out in reverse. I jumped back so my toes wouldn't be flattened by her tires.

"You won't get away with it!" I screamed. "I'll make damned sure of it."

She gave me one last sneer, flipped me off with her French-manicured finger, and threw the car into drive. Her tires squealed against the pavement, spraying me with loose gravel. While she sped away, I scrambled back into my car and took off after her.

Erin drove like a mad woman with me hot on her tail. I could see her glaring back at me in her rear view mirror, her mouth spewing what I could only assume were obscenities. I hurled them right back. She gunned her engine and pulled away, barreling at breakneck speed down the country roads toward the busier city streets with me still close behind. As she entered the downtown area, Erin turned from one street onto another in an attempt to shake me. She hardly slowed for stop signs or red lights.

My fear grew at her recklessness, but my fury overrode any instinct that told me to slow down and back off. I drove onward, pushing the car even harder so I wouldn't lose sight of her. I turned left and swerved sharply to avoid other cars and pedestrians. I pulled back when my car fishtailed; barely missing an older couple who'd entered the crosswalk. They called out after me as I squealed past, their fists raised in anger.

I glanced back over my shoulder to make sure they were unhurt, but kept my foot on the gas. As I turned back around, I saw Erin run through a red light. I didn't even have time to slam on the brakes before I pushed into the busy intersection. I barely caught sight of the large SUV as it slammed into me from my left.

Glass shattered and metal screamed. The air bags exploded in my face. My thoughts flew to my baby and Ty as the heat from the SUV's engine rushed against my side. My breath was expelled violently from my body in a loud whoosh, and I felt myself snap from within.

Then everything went quiet. And all I could see was black.

Chapter Eleven
Tyler

With an active business to run, my mobile phone rang often during the day, and I answered every call, even if I didn't have time to talk. I didn't want to miss a call from Jillian, especially after our last argument and the scene with Nick at the house. I'd been waiting all day for that call, the one where Jill would say how sorry she was. Every call that came in I answered hoping it would be her, knowing just from the number alone that it wasn't. But it was already mid-afternoon, and I hadn't heard from her yet.

Jillian and I hadn't spoken much in the last two days, though when we had, we sparred in anger. When I returned home from work last night, she stood in front of me with her arms crossed over her chest, obviously still stewing. She was upset that I had intervened with Nick, and embarrassed that I'd found out about their plans. The calm had ended, and the storm was about to be unleashed.

"I'm not angry at you, Jill. I'm just worried. You must realize that," I explained as I reached for her, but she stepped nimbly out of reach. I rested my hands on my hips and turned around after her.

She shook her head and narrowed her eyes, a sure sign she was about to have one of her tantrums. She never saw reason when she was angry, and her pregnancy seemed to make matters worse.

"You could've fooled me," she said then pointed her finger in my face. "*'You let this go. You hear me?'* " she mimicked. "I don't know about you, Ty, but to me that sounded an awful lot like you trying to control me, and you know damn well I hate that."

"Oh, come on, Jillian, stop twisting this around. Yes, I am angry that you went behind my back, but this is about Nick. After everything that's happened, you still don't seem to understand how serious it is to get involved with him and his friends. How dangerous it is to be indebted to his boss, even through a tenuous connection. For God's sake, don't you remember what they did to me? You know better. *You* were the one to warn *me* off."

"Well, I can take care of myself. And besides, this was something between Nick and me. Not his boss *or* his friends. He would never let anything happen to me."

"That's bullshit! Nick can hardly take care of himself, let alone you, especially where those people are concerned. What, you don't think they'd love to have another reason to keep Nick under their thumb? Or me, for that matter? For God's sake, Jillian. What the hell are you thinking? You're pregnant. You have a responsibility. How could you even consider taking that chance? This is not just about you any longer. You're putting our baby at risk. Do you even get that?"

She hitched her hands up on each hip. "I'm not a child, Tyler, and I don't appreciate being treated like one."

"Then stop acting like one, godammit!" I roared.

I regretted the words as soon as they came out of my mouth, even more so when the hurt flashed in her eyes, but Jill needed to know how serious I was about staying away from Nick and letting the police and District Attorney's office handle the situation. With a stare that could have frozen hell over in an instant, she stormed off, slammed the bedroom door, and locked it. I followed, knocking quietly on the barrier between us.

"I'm sorry, Jill. I shouldn't have yelled like that. Let me in, okay? We need to discuss this."

"Go away, Ty. There's nothing more to discuss."

I slammed my fist against the door. "Come on, Jillian, if you want me to treat you like an adult, I expect you to act like one. Stop pouting and come out here so we can talk about this."

From inside the room, I heard her crying. "You said everything would be okay, but it's not. You told me you wanted a wife, a child, a home. Well, this is part of that, and that woman has taken it away, but you won't even stand up and defend it. You won't defend *us*. I am so sick of always playing by the rules. Well you know what? Screw your rules, Tyler, and screw you, too. You can sleep on the sofa tonight."

I rested my forehead against the closed door. "Jillian, come on, don't do this." I called out again and again, but she refused to say another word, even after I threatened to kick the door down.

She unlocked it in the morning, but when I tried to approach her before I left for work, she closed herself in the bathroom with the excuse she wasn't feeling well. So I left without so much as an "I love you" or "goodbye." I knew I'd have the opportunity later when she cooled down.

Although Jill and I rarely fought, I learned early on that it was better to just leave her alone than try to talk things out before she was ready. She wouldn't stay angry for much longer, and I wanted her to approach me. She had to know that, in this case at least, I was the one who had the right to be angry. After all, putting risk aside, she went to Nick behind my back. That in itself was a serious betrayal.

Still, I was surprised at how long it was taking her to call. Jill wasn't the belligerent sort. In fact, she often apologized even if she was right, just so we could get over it and make up. I bargained with myself, agreeing to be patient for another hour at most before I called her. I'd been waiting forty-five minutes when my cell finally rang, but it wasn't Jill, nor was it a number I recognized.

"Yeah, who's this?" I answered impatiently, not wanting to tie up my line.

"Tyler Karras?" the voice asked urgently.

"Yeah, this is Tyler. Who are you?"

"Mr. Karras, my name is Officer Matthew Reynolds. I'm with the Napa Police Department. Are you the husband of Jillian Karras?"

"Yes. Why? What's wrong?"

"Sir, I regret to inform you that your wife's been involved in a serious car accident. She's sustained significant injuries and has been taken by helicopter to the trauma center at San Francisco General." He paused. "I'm very sorry."

It took a few seconds to absorb what the officer had said. A strange skittering cantered up from my feet and settled in my chest. It was déjà vu, all over again. In an instant, my whole life constricted to a single pinpoint in time, a moment of dread down deep inside, as if I were about to be swept over a waterfall. I stood silently, my senses too stunned to reply.

"Mr. Karras? Are you still there?"

"I don't understand. Jillian was in an accident? In Napa? Are you sure it's Jillian Demetrio Karras? She drives a red Camry and has long—"

"Yes, I'm very sorry. You should probably get to the hospital as soon as possible."

"Is she...um...you know...?" I couldn't get the words out. I felt strangled by a thickness caught deep in my throat. "Please, tell me...she's not...dead, is she?"

"I honestly don't know. She was alive when she left the scene, but her injuries appear to be severe. You really should get to the hospital. Again, I'm very sorry."

"Right...right...okay. Um...thank you," I said and ended the call.

My feet were like dead weights anchored to the floor. If I moved, even an inch, I would be that much closer to a future I dared not face. I sucked in a large breath and willed myself forward. I ran to my truck and sped off to the hospital up on Potrero Avenue.

After abandoning my vehicle near the emergency room doors, I stumbled into the hospital and called out my wife's name. My voice rose in high-pitched hysteria as tears pooled up and clouded my vision. A nurse jumped in front of me and pressed her hands to my chest, an ineffective gesture to halt my progress. She shushed me like she would a child and asked if she could help, retreating backwards against my forward momentum. I tried to step around her when she blocked my path, but tumbled into a loaded cart left in the hallway. I fell, careening through the medical paraphernalia I'd scattered across the floor. At least dozen faces turned to stare, some concerned, others annoyed.

I scooped up what items I could and held them out to the nurse. "I'm sorry."

She pressed her lips together and relieved me of the contaminated equipment, depositing the packages into an empty bin. She returned, touched me at the elbow, and pointed back toward the front door.

"Sir, you need to take a seat out in the waiting room."

"No, I can't. I'm looking for my wife, Jillian Karras. She was in a car accident. The police told me she was brought here by helicopter. I need to find her, please, please."

She pressed her lips together and looked me up and down. "All right. Come with me."

The nurse directed me to a small office by the triage desk and motioned for me to take a seat. She asked for the spelling of Jill's name and checked the computer for an entry while I drummed my fingers against my thighs. The nurse mumbled to herself as she read the display then finally looked back up.

"Yes, Mr. Karras, your wife is being treated in trauma three. I'll go find out how she's doing. Please wait here."

As soon as she was through the door, I jumped from my seat and followed after her. She stepped into a trauma room filled with doctors, nurses, and technicians, all dressed in various shades of blue and green. I peered in from outside the large glass doors where I shifted from foot to foot, stretched up on my tiptoes, searching through the maze of bodies.

Several pieces of equipment were wheeled toward the center, and wires were hooked up to the patient still blocked from my view. Urgent alarms of various pitch and pace began to wail all at once. Fingers sheathed in latex gloves snapped impatiently as orders were called out. Three members of the crew quickly cleared a path.

And there she was—Jillian—lying on a narrow padded table in the center of the room, covered in blood. My heartbeat surged, and a hissing blast exploded in my ears. I couldn't catch my breath, and spots danced across my vision as the world tilted. I reached for the wall, trying to suck air into my lungs. The doors swung wide and crashed into my back. I straightened up and forced myself to focus back into the room.

It was in total chaos with questions and orders being hurled about simultaneously. The staff dashed about, each performing a critical task. A young doctor delicately weaved a narrow tube down into Jill's throat, while an older one fingered a hole he'd cut into her side. He shifted his feet around as blood poured out from the wound. Then he shoved a thick tube through the incision, allowing the blood to collect in a large, clear plastic bag hanging from a hook on the side of the table.

Multiple drugs were injected into an IV line attached to Jill's arm. The young doctor who had intubated Jill moved over her chest. He placed one hand on top of the other in the center and pushed in rapid succession as he counted out loud. A nurse worked the respirator at Jill's mouth, pumping air into her lungs at a pace steady with the doctor's count. After a minute or two, a new alarm sounded.

"Crash cart," an older doctor ordered.

As soon the nurse pushed the rig within reach, the doctor grabbed the paddles.

"Okay, charge to one hundred," he commanded as he laid them against Jill's chest. He waited for the machine to reach full charge then called out, "Clear!"

Jillian's upper body tensed, lurched off the table, then settled back down. Panic shot through me like tendrils of electricity slicing through my limbs.

"Nothing. Let's try again, two hundred this time," the doctor ordered. He waited and watched then shouted, "Clear!"

Again she jumped. Again no response. My heart rattled at a clipped speed, pitching wildly against my sternum. I felt like I was going to be sick.

"One more time. Charge to three-sixty. Okay...clear!" Again, nothing. "How long has she been down?" he asked a nurse.

The nurse looked up at the clock on the wall and replied, "Fifty-three minutes."

The young doctor returned to chest compressions, again and again, over and over.

I held my hands to my head. The roar inside was already deafening and getting louder.

"Asystole," a technician called out as the monitor sounded an even wail.

The young doctor performing chest compressions looked at his colleague. "What do you think?" he asked, so breathless he was panting.

The older doctor returned the paddles to the cart and shrugged. "Blunt force trauma like this, could be tension pneumo, aortic dissection. Take your pick."

"We can't shock her now. Should we try to get a chest x-ray then send her up to surgery?"

The older man glanced at the blood collecting in the plastic bag and all around them on the floor. He blew out a long sigh. "She won't even make it to the elevator."

"Richard," the young doc warned as he nodded in my direction.

The older man turned and caught my eye. His brow came together with a deep crease scoring through the center. He spun around to one of the nurses. "Let's push another amp of epi and see what happens."

The nurse was so fast she practically had the drug administered before the order was given. Everyone worked silently for another ten minutes, each dedicated to their part, but no matter what they did, nothing changed. The young doc continued to work over Jill's chest, his scrubs soaked through with his sweat and her blood. The elder one shook his head again.

"Still asystole. How long?" he asked the same nurse as before.

She checked the wall clock again. "One hour, five minutes, Doctor."

The older doc pursed his lips, deep in thought. Then he waved his hand above Jill's body. "All right, that's it. I'm calling it." He looked up at the wall clock and said, "Death at sixteen-fifty-two."

He stepped from Jill's side, steadying himself as he slipped in a puddle of her blood. With a snap, he removed his gloves and tore away his gown and goggles. He slammed everything into a tall, lined bin then signed a chart held out by a nurse. With a frustrated kick to the swinging doors, he left through a side entrance. He was gone without a backwards glance. I stared after him, praying he would return, but knowing full well he would not.

It was over.

Oh God, no! I banged on the glass. "No, don't stop! Bring her back! She's not dead! She's not dead!"

The nurse who had been helping me earlier stood in the middle of the room. She turned and spied me through the window then hurried over and proceeded to console me, but I couldn't hear a word she said over the keening that seemed to reverberate off the glossy tiled walls. It was me, wailing.

I clamped a hand over my mouth, and tried to focus back into the trauma room. I stared at Jillian's lifeless body lying on the table with all the tubes and wires still attached and her blood splattered on the floor. A nurse disconnected the respirator from the tube still stuck in Jill's throat. She shook out a long sheet and pulled it up over my wife's head.

"No!" I screamed and barged into the room. I pressed myself around the nurse and pushed her out of the way. "Jillian! Oh God, no!"

I yanked the sheet away from Jill's face and ran my hand over her forehead. Hands pulled gently at my arms from behind me, but I jerked free. I bent over and kissed the side of Jill's mouth.

She's still so warm. This is a mistake. It has to be. This can't be happening again. She cannot be dead. Please, God. Please!

"Oh my God, Jillian, no...no!"

The remaining staff backed away when the nurse told them I was the patient's husband. I bent over my wife and pulled her bruised hand out from under the sheet. I held it up to my open mouth and cried. My hand trembled as I placed it over her womb.

My wife, my child, both gone.

I tipped my face up to the ceiling and screamed, sobbing with more anguish than I had ever felt in my entire life. "God, how could you do this to me again? How?"

Then a new panic began to overwhelm me, tightening across my chest. Jill must have been terrified. She must have felt so alone as she lay dying. I wasn't there for her. She died believing I was angry with her. I wanted her to know that I was here for her now, for all the good it did.

"I'm here, love. Right here. No worries. I'm here."

Then it hit me, like a bag of bricks to the face. *I'm too late. She was in Napa, probably doing what I had forbid Nick to do. This is my fault! Jill is dead because of me. Because I did nothing. She begged for my help, and I did nothing! Oh God, no! What have I done?*

"Oh God, Jill, I'm so sorry. I'm so sorry."

With my hand still at her womb, I laid my forehead against hers and sobbed. All the sounds around me faded away and everything went still. I don't know how long I stood there. It could have been thirty minutes. An hour. Maybe two. It seemed like an eternity had swallowed me up whole. But at some point, I was finally pulled from her side, and I thought that eternity was not nearly long enough.

Chapter Twelve
Tyler

For the next three days, my home was constantly filled with people — friends, family, colleagues — but it didn't matter. I felt alone. And while I appreciated their collective efforts, I would have preferred to actually be alone. With Nick at my side, I made the obligatory rounds, accepting their apologies, their sympathy, but while I looked them each in the eye and nodded, I didn't speak, not to anyone. I didn't eat the food they brought. I didn't stroll in the backyard when they tried to maneuver me out of the house. I just stared and nodded, completely numb.

Finally, I retreated to my room where I sat with the door shut and the blinds pulled closed. Sitting there in front of me was Jill's purse, its contents scattered across the bed, including a prescription bottle for Wellbutrin. It was dated nearly two months ago, yet it was full. I counted. Not one pill was missing. Not one. I stared off into the darkness, wondering how in God's name I could have missed that.

I heard my in-laws in the hall outside my bedroom door, their voices raised, calling out my name, concerned for my well-being. But I didn't care anymore. My only goal was to make it through the next few hours, until the funeral was over and everyone went home to live their own lives and leave me the hell alone.

"Tyler, honey, Jack and I are leaving for the church now," Jillian's mother, Lily, spoke through the closed bedroom door. "Are you sure you won't come with us?"

Her voice was rough, constricted, as if she were choking back her tears. I imagine she stood outside the door for a few moments, waiting for me to respond, knowing that, after three days of brooding silence, I probably would not. I heard her and Jack talking to my brother. Nick assured them he would get me there soon then closed the front door behind them. He knocked on my bedroom door before he entered. He walked over, stood in front of me, and knelt down when I wouldn't look up. Nick's eyes were trained on my face, but I stared blindly past him as I sat motionless in my chair.

"Tyler, it's time to go. The funeral Mass is scheduled to start in less than an hour. It's important for you to be there. You'll never forgive yourself if you don't go." He paused, waiting for a reply he knew he wouldn't receive. "I know how it feels. I didn't get to go to Mum and Pop's funeral, or Kim's either. It's hard to move on when you don't get the chance to say goodbye." He placed his hand on top of mine. "You need closure, Ty."

He stood back up, yanked my suit jacket off the hanger, and held it up for me to pull on. He shook it and looked at me expectantly. I regarded him sullenly but complied. Hours earlier, Nick had managed to push me into the shower, but I hadn't shaved for days, nor had I slept, and the combination made me look like a strung-out zombie, not that I cared. I'm sure I was a fine sight, but no one said anything about it. It's not like it was an affair where pictures would be taken. Who really cared what the poor widower looked like, right? As long as he was there to grieve properly for his dead wife.

Nick pushed me out of the house and into the black Town Car idling at the curb. The driver took us to the same Catholic church where Jillian and I were married a few short months ago. I sat where Nick put me, next to Jillian's parents and sister in the front pew. I listened to all the beautiful stories everyone shared about Jillian, how much they all loved her, how much they would miss her. They cried through their speeches, and wiped their tears away with tissues and shirt sleeves. I listened to the Mass, my ears pricking when the priest spoke about God's will, and that through His forgiveness, we would all be saved.

I snickered in contempt. Saved? Ha! What a load of shit!

The priest looked over at Nick and nodded. He turned to me and indicated it was my turn to speak. I stared numbly at him for a long moment then stood up and walked slowly to the podium. I scanned the crowd and saw how they all looked at me. Their pity was palpable, filling the church with a silent dirge that clawed at my ears. Many cried as I stood there looking so mournful. I hadn't cried since leaving the hospital. I simply existed, grieving inwardly, angry with myself. I looked at the congregation and tried to speak, but the words stuck in my throat as the tears I'd been holding back for the last three days spilled unheeded.

I stared down at the photo of Jill I'd been carrying around. It was taken on our wedding day. Tremendous joy radiated from her. I could almost feel the warmth of it emanating from the paper itself. It made me smile to look at it and remember her that day. I gazed at the photo and, with a shaky breath, gathered myself to speak.

"I want to thank you all for coming." I paused while I scanned the crowd. "It would have meant a great deal to Jill." I stopped again, momentarily unable to continue. I chewed on my lip and tried to recover. "I'm sorry...I..." I shook my head, took another deep breath, and started again. "Most of you know how much Jillian meant to me, that she was my whole life. I know how much she meant to you, as well. So...so I want to say to each of you who loved her that I'm...I'm sorry." I paused a third time, my chin quivering with the effort it took to remain standing up there. "And um...while I know Father Kenny spoke to you all about forgiveness, you should know that...that this...was...my fault..."

Nick jumped up from his seat and was at my side in an instant, cooing softly as he tried to pull me away.

"No...don't," I insisted, twisting my elbow from his grasp. I turned back to the congregation. Many had their hands drawn up to their mouths while others dabbed at their eyes. I scanned them all, looking each in the eye as I continued.

"I did this. Me. Not Jillian. I deserve all the blame for taking her from each of you. I don't deserve your forgiveness. Or God's, for that matter. So, please...don't pity me. I don't deserve that either."

I looked back down at Jill's picture and smiled weakly once more before I turned to Nick. I pressed her photo into his hand, stepped down off the altar, and walked out of the service without speaking another word. With the Town Car idling slowly behind me, I wandered aimlessly through the neighborhood streets.

I did attend the grave-side service a couple hours later so that I could honor all that was good about Jill. I wanted to look into her family's eyes and apologize directly. They didn't seem to want to hear it, but I insisted all the same. When the service was over, I asked them all to leave, so I could be alone with Jill.

99

Everyone drove back to my in-laws' house where they held a wake, which I would not be attending.

I stood looking down into the dark hole that contained Jillian's casket, knowing that she lay cold and stiff inside, our child still nestled deep within her. Due to her extensive injuries, her casket had remained closed during the visitation and Mass. I never saw her again after I was pulled from her side at the hospital. That was the very last memory I had of her. The last image I had of her face. I would never forget what she looked like, all bruised and broken, her flesh pale white and her blood spilled all around.

I would carry that image with me forever. I deserved it. I was responsible. It was a burden I would keep close to my heart, always...right next to the place that ached for retribution against the only other person besides myself who held some accountability for Jillian lying cold and alone in that dark hole. I recalled the Bible verse where God said, "Vengeance is mine," and I sneered with derision.

"Well, fuck that," I said aloud. "It's mine. And I'll be damned if I don't find some way to have it."

I turned to walk away but thought of the last time Jill and I had spoken, and what I regrettably hadn't said to her. I pulled a single white rose—Jill's favorite and the sign of eternal love—from one of the arrangements nearby. I added a purple hyacinth to beg forgiveness and a pink carnation to let her know I would never forget her. And lastly, a red rose. I threw them all down onto her casket.

"Goodbye, Jillian," I whispered. "I love you."

Then I walked away.

Chapter Thirteen
Tyler

I locked myself in the house for five weeks after Jillian's funeral. I kept the blinds and drapes pulled tight and shut the world out as best I could. Client calls went unanswered, construction jobs left unfinished. Friends came by from time to time, knocked on the door, and left when I didn't answer. They often left food, hoping I would at least eat. It rotted where it lay.

Lily stopped by every day for the first two weeks. She talked to me through the door and reminded me of what Jillian would want. I thanked her for her concern, but told her I didn't want to see anyone yet. When she continued to drop by, I stopped responding to her pleas, praying she would just stay away. It worked eventually.

Nick was next. He called every day, but after three weeks, I finally stopped answering. Frustrated, he pounded on my front door. It shook and rattled under his fist as he called out my name.

"Ty, if you don't open this door, I'm just going to let myself in."

He waited silently for a full minute.

"Tyler, I know where you keep the hidden key. Jill told me. I'm going to use it."

He waited again.

"Tyler!"

He fumbled around on the front porch then worked the lock and pushed his way in.

"Ty?"

He couldn't see me sitting in the dark, or all the junk that lay scattered about the floor. The house was a complete disaster, a victim of my rage. I had no other way to discharge it except to throw whatever I got my hands on across the room. The dining chairs were first. Two lay in shambles, half their legs now useless posts protruding from the walls, and the seats shredded, padding and all. The pages of two dozen books, mostly my own design texts, littered the room like New Year's Eve confetti at Times Square, as did a month's worth of newspapers, all my building plans, and Jill's old photography magazines. Art work, old pictures, wall sconces, all of it a mangled mess strewn across the living and dining room floor.

Then there were all the things Jill and I had bought for the baby. When I first spied the large pile neatly arranged in the den, I sorted through it, one item at a time. Until I unearthed Jillian's jogging stroller. That was the proverbial straw. I triggered the mechanisms and allowed it to collapse, as designed. But then I picked it up like a club and began hammering it against the floor until it was nothing but a tangled jumble of metal spokes, plastic shards, and frayed canvas. The rest followed: the still boxed crib, the freshly painted rocker, the partially assembled changing table. Even the tiny infant clothes.

The house looked like Banda Aceh, Indonesia in the aftermath of the 2004 Boxing Day tsunami. The screams that accompanied these episodes probably sounded similar, too. I was left panting and sweating, but mostly sobbing as I surveyed the home Jillian and I had shared for the last four years. But still, I could not come to terms enough to clean it all up. Nick stumbled over the mess as he walked into the dark foyer.

"What the fuck?" he said as he fell to the floor. "Bloody hell, Ty. What is all this shit?"

He reached for the switch and turned on the light.

"Turn it off, Nick, and get the hell out," I warned quietly.

He kicked the debris to the side and found a path in my direction. He crouched down in front of me as I sat in the living room chair, resting his hands on my knees.

"Whoa, Ty, you look like shit. And your house..." he said as he scanned the room. "God, it's a wreck. We need to get you, and this place, cleaned up." He examined me closely, tensing his eyes and his head shaking in disappointment. "Ty, come on—"

"Get out, Nick."

He stood up and looked around for a moment then started picking up the mess that lay around us. "This is disgusting, Tyler. Jillian would be as mad as a cut snake if she saw the house like—"

I pounded my fist on the armrest. "Don't talk to me about Jill!"

Nick stood in front of me with his mouth open. "Ty, come on. Jillian wouldn't want this. You have to know that. She would have wanted you to—"

I sprang up off the chair and lunged at him, knocking him down as he tripped backward over the detritus. "I said don't fucking talk to me about Jillian! You didn't know her. You don't know what she would want for me. You don't know a goddamn thing, so just leave me the fuck alone." With my hands on his collar, I knelt over him, straddling his chest, pinning him to the floor.

Nick held his hands up in submission and gaped at me like I was crazy. I suppose I was—crazy with grief, with loneliness, and most of all, with intense, overwhelming guilt that burned through every cell of my being hotter than the Devil's anvil.

"Just go, Nick, please. Leave me be." I raked my hands over my face and pushed off, rolling onto the floor beside him. "Please, Nick, I...I can't. I can't stand to...to talk about her, to...to even hear her name. Godammit, it's bad enough I can't stop thinking about her."

Nick pulled himself up and sat cross-legged beside me. "Ty, you loved her. She was your wife. Why in God's name would you want to stop thinking about her?"

I covered my eyes with the heel of my hands and rocked my head from side to side. I beat them against my forehead, trying to erase the last image I had of Jill. All the tears in the world couldn't wash that vision away, though I tried futilely to do so. It burned through me on a slow, steady path, desiccating every happy memory I ever had of Jillian.

"Because...I don't... I can't...remember her...like that!"

"Like what, Ty? I don't understand. What are you talking about?"

"At the...hospital. She was so...so...broken and... Oh God, what...have...I done, Nick? What...have I done?" I hyperventilated as I rolled on the wood floor.

Until now, my grief had been contained, held back in anger. But now it rolled over me like a tidal wave, pushing me back and forth, unwilling to allow me to get my feet beneath me. I couldn't speak. I folded up onto my knees and laid my head in my hands on the floor, sobbing uncontrollably. I scared the hell out of Nick, no longer the stoic rock he'd always known. He stared at me silently then laid his hand on my back.

"You want to forget. I get that, Ty. I understand that, more than you could possibly know." He jumped to his feet. "You wait here. I'll be right back. I know exactly what you need. Just...just wait." He ran out the door, slamming it shut with a bang.

I wore myself out crying while he was gone. It didn't make me feel any better though. I thought venting would release some of the pain, but my culpability never failed to focus it right back where it belonged, squarely on my shoulders. Even vengeance seemed somehow out of order, unless there was a way to punish myself.

Nick wasn't gone for very long before he burst back through the door. He carried two paper grocery sacks filled with clanging glass bottles. He placed the bags on the dining table with a loud thud and pulled out his purchases, placing them on the table in a neat row. It was a variety of hard alcohol: vodka, whiskey, and tequila. I sat on the floor, leaning back against the side of the living room chair. I ran my sleeve over my eyes and stared at the bottles of varying shapes, sizes, and colors. Then I looked up at Nick, wondering what he was up to. He turned to me with his hands on his hips.

"You didn't understand when I started drinking after my accident," he explained, "when Mum, Pops, and Kimmy died. Do you remember how you scolded me? You preached to me, told me to man-up and all. I knew you were disappointed in me, which, of course, only made me feel worse. I couldn't explain it to you then, what it felt like. You never would have understood. But now... Well, now I think you do. Don't you, Ty?" He towered over me and nodded. "Yes, I think you finally understand."

He knelt down in front of me and looked me square in the eyes.

"Let me explain something to you, Tyler. There is nothing...*nothing*...that will ever make it better. That pain...it never goes away. It's a lifetime of shit, of frustration and guilt. Time may dull it, but it'll always be there, kind of hazy in the background," he explained as he twirled his finger around the side of his head. "And when you sleep, it awakens. And it pursues you — relentlessly — so that no matter how hard you try, you can never truly get away from it. But..." He stood up with his index finger raised.

Nick stepped over to the dining table and selected a tall, clear bottle of vodka. He looked it over deliberately before presenting it to me like Vanna White on *The Wheel of Fortune*.

"This, brother, will push it to the darkest corners of your mind, if for just a little while, so you can breathe again."

He grabbed two crystal tumblers from the china cabinet and poured us each a double shot.

"Here," he said, handing me a glass. "Bottoms up." Nick tilted his head back and swallowed the liquid in one swift gulp.

I stared at him open-mouthed before I turned my attention to my own glass. I studied the silver elixir as it swirled malevolently around the cut crystal, noting how it distorted my reflection and everything else around me. I was reluctant to go there, to that dark place I knew Nick had escaped after his accident. To me, it never seemed to do him any good, just an easing of the gravity that held him to the earth, a disembodiment of his grief, his capacity for being held accountable. But I was an outsider then, with no clear understanding of his pain, of the rage he felt at being left alone to carry the load made heavy by others, of the exhaustive guilt that consumed him.

That is until now. I understood it all now.

I copied Nick and swallowed the vodka in one shot, grimacing at the caustic burn as it slid down my throat. I was

106

glad it hurt. I deserved every ounce of that pain and much more. With a shake of my head, I blew out a sharp breath, my mouth finishing in a tense and perfect O. I deliberated over the empty glass then held it back out to Nick. He refilled it, as he did his own, and handed it back to me.

"May we both forget," he toasted bitterly with his glass held high in the air.

We slammed our shots together this time. Nick brought the bottle with him and joined me on the floor. I held out my glass and he filled it once more. I didn't wait for him this time. I threw it down my throat as fast as I could then silently requested another. And then another.

Soon, a fire burned inside me, its warmth radiating from my stomach and swirling into my limbs. It left my fingers and toes numb and my ears ringing. The thoughts and images that played mercilessly in my head blurred and moved about incoherently. I couldn't remain focused on anything for very long before I forgot it altogether. The tension in my shoulders eased. I welcomed both the comforting release from tormenting thoughts and the soothing of my frayed nerves. We continued until the bottle was empty, another piece of trash littering the wood floor around us. Nick crawled to the table to select another.

"Eeny meeny miny mo," he sang as he ran his finger down the line of shapely vessels. He grabbed the bottle where his finger landed, a square one filled with an amber liquid. Jack Daniel's. Nick turned to me and laughed, that stupid crooked smile twisting his lips.

"Hey Ty, would you like to meet my friend, Jack?"

When I nodded, Nick crawled back toward me, careening head first into my side. I shoved him away and he rolled around on the floor, searching for the lost bottle of JD. We both laughed like we were children again, playing in the sunshine without a care in the world. It felt good to laugh, even though it had the bitter aftertaste of a long-gone happiness. I was glad that it was with Nick. I felt as though he was the only person who could possibly comprehend the range of emotions that seemed to flicker and flash through me at light speed.

Nick and I shared the entire night together on the floor. Johnny Walker, Jack Daniel's, and José Cuervo were our constant companions. After a time, I couldn't hold my head up any longer, and Nick lay snoring along the edge of the area rug beneath the dining room table. I found my way to my bedroom, fumbling noisily through the empty bottles that rolled across the floor in my path.

I fell into the middle of the king-sized bed and moved immediately to my side on the right where I lay gazing toward Jillian's vacant spot. We had spent so many hours here together, making love, playing games, talking about our baby, and planning our life together. Tonight, for the first time in weeks, the good memories seemed easier to recall than the bad.

As I stared toward Jillian's side, an assembly of transparent colors oscillated above the bed, indistinct shapes quivering in the dim light. They merged and separated in constant flux then slowly coalesced into a translucent apparition. She smiled at me, her dark eyes sparkling brightly from an unseen source. Her long, dark hair danced around her shoulders like magic.

I blinked once, holding my eyes closed for a brief moment. Then I opened them, hopeful my delusion would remain. And she did. A single tear rolled into the inside corner of my eye and pooled up before it spilled over. I reached out to her.

"I miss you, Jillian. So much," I murmured. "I love you."

THE MISTAKEN

Then, though I was unwilling and fought like hell against it, I closed my eyes and let oblivion consume me.

Chapter Fourteen
Tyler

The days and weeks after that first evening with Nick followed suit in pretty much the same manner. I don't remember much of the passing of time except for the changing of the outside light to darkness then back again. Nick was right. The booze helped me breathe again for small increments of time. The pain and guilt always remained, but they were pushed to the outer reaches of my alcohol-soaked brain. I still felt it, but I could also ignore it, for a short time anyway.

When I was too drunk to drink anymore, I usually left Nick snoring on the sofa while I stumbled back to my room to say goodnight to Jillian. In bed, before I slipped into the welcome embrace of senselessness, I conjured up images of Jill that made me happy. I looked forward to seeing her and talking to her every night. Afterwards, my mind remained in limbo for only a few short hours until the effects of the liquor eased. Then the dreams would begin.

Sometimes they were simply pleasant memories that replayed in my head: the good times I shared with Jillian, our wedding, our honeymoon. But mostly I dreamed of the last time we spoke at length, our fight, Jill lying broken on the padded table with all those tubes and wires, a blood-soaked sheet enveloping her from head to toe. Maybe if I hadn't recalled those images, I would have recovered faster. As it was, those dreams were what made me get up every morning and pour myself another drink.

Sometimes Nick was there when I faltered out of bed, but often he was gone, and I was left alone to cope with everything I had pushed neatly aside the day before. It was during these first moments of each day when I often wished Jill hadn't become everything to me—maybe then I wouldn't have been so completely destroyed by her death. But that was just the pain talking, like a devil sitting on my shoulder, whispering evil thoughts into my ear. Most days Nick would return with breakfast, or lunch if the hour declared, and we would share a quiet meal before we returned to the bottle.

I consumed more and more alcohol as my tolerance grew and the dreams became unbearable. Nick stayed with me most days though he didn't try to keep up with me anymore. He looked amused at my drunken antics with one brow raised, his wry grin set askew. I suppose I was the inebriated loser now. It was amazing how the tables had turned. Having slipped into a dull state of apathy, I really didn't give a damn one way or the other. But Nick grew concerned and suggested I back off a bit. That wasn't about to happen any time soon though, not while I continued to feel the same way, day after day.

As time passed and I grew accustomed to the intensity of my pain, I spoke to Nick about Jillian, about how much I missed her, how empty the house felt without her. Nick and I eventually straightened out the place after he reminded me how much Jill hated a messy house. It once again looked as it did when she and I lived as a couple, but it certainly didn't feel the same. The

emptiness tormented me. Everywhere I looked there was
something that had a memory of Jillian connected to it, especially
her photographs which still lined the walls, and what remained
of all the things we had bought for our child which lay refolded
and untouched in a dark corner of the den.

It was just too much for me to see every day. My guilt and
loneliness gradually evolved into bitterness and rage, the venom
of each so pungent and sharp it soured my only refuge, my
treasured nightly sojourn with Jill's haunting apparition. My last
solace was gone, betrayed by the very bitterness that corroded
my soul. That was when I first seriously considered suicide,
contemplating the effectiveness of different methods. But there
was one thing that held me back. Once I'd read the police reports
and ascertained the extent of Erin Anderson's role in Jillian's
accident and death, I knew I couldn't leave this world with her
still in it, especially when the cops refused to arrest and charge
her.

Whereas I once spoke to Nick about Jillian—my memories
of her and our life together—I now shared my fantasies about
gaining revenge on the woman who had provoked Jill into such
reckless behavior. It soon became a favorite pastime to lie drunk
around the house and spin wild tales of vengeance against Erin
Anderson, the bane of my existence, the core of my deep-seated
hostility.

They started simple, as visions of setting her house on fire
with her trapped inside, or perhaps I would run her car off the
road and down into a steep ravine where she would lie
immobilized, entangled in the wreckage, unseen from the
roadway far above. I had an endless reservoir filled with
pernicious scenarios. I found that when I fantasized about a long,
tortuous death, I felt a greater sense of vengeance and a
considerable awareness of relief, as sick as that was. And I knew

it was sick. But I didn't care anymore. I wanted Erin to suffer for a long time before she died. Or maybe...maybe she shouldn't die. Maybe she should just suffer. Forever. I could think of many ways to make that woman suffer forever.

At first, it gave me some relief to savor the vision of retribution. Yet, I always woke up the next day with the realization that Erin Anderson was still alive and well, walking the earth, enjoying her life, enjoying her family, while my wife was not, while my child lay eternally buried in Jillian's cold womb six feet beneath the heavy earth, a tiny speck of immeasurable possibility heartlessly quashed into nothingness. I spoke to Nick about this train of thought and how crazy it was making me, how utterly enraged I felt, powerless and impotent.

"Tyler, do you think if you were to somehow get even with her that you would actually feel...I don't know...better? Relieved maybe?" he asked late one afternoon.

"Hell yes," I admitted. "Most days, it's the only thing that keeps me from drinking until I just fucking die." I shook my head, disappointed in myself, far removed from the man Jillian once loved.

"Well then, maybe we should do it," he suggested. "Get revenge. Go Old Testament on the bitch."

I snorted and rolled my eyes. "Don't get me started, Nick."

"Why not, Ty? I mean, we could probably do it, figure out a plausible way to really get back at her, to completely ruin her life. How hard could it be?"

"Nick, as good as that sounds, I don't think I'm actually up to killing someone. Even that rotten whore."

Nick walked around with his head down, his finger drumming absently along the sharp edge of his jaw, deep in thought. He turned to me, rather excited at the plan forming deep within the dark confines of his mind.

"We wouldn't have to kill her, Ty. Just make her wish we had. What's the worst thing you can think of to do to a woman, especially someone like her, to make every day of her life a living hell?"

I thought hard for a minute then snapped my fingers, leaving one raised in the air. "I've got it. We could sell her to the Taliban." I snorted with derisive laughter and took a long pull on a bottle of beer.

"What? Come on, be serious, Tyler. The Taliban? That's ridiculous."

I rocked my head from side to side. "Right. Okay well, maybe not the Taliban, but you know what I mean."

He shook his head. "No, actually I don't. Enlighten me, brother."

"Haven't you ever read those stories out of Afghanistan or Pakistan? Women under the Taliban have no life of their own. The men lord over every aspect of their miserable lives, and when they break some tiny rule, those sick bastards set them on fire, or cut off their nose, or beat them with a stick, right out on the street for everyone to see. And no one does a bloody thing about it." I gave him a drunken smirk and took another long drink, draining the bottle. I sighed then expelled a loud belch. "I saw it on the news once.

"God, I'd love to see someone beat Erin with a stick," I continued. "I'd love to see someone snuff out the very essence of who she is. She could be a fucking slave for all I care. That bitch deserves to live in misery for the rest of her insignificant life."

Nick stared at me in disbelief. He'd never heard me speak that way before. Neither had I for that matter. Nick had always thought of me as the perfect son, a brother who was hard to live up to, who could do no wrong. He'd told me so a thousand times. And maybe I was before, but Jillian's death had changed me. I was bitter beyond reason, and I knew it. But I didn't care anymore. I'd played by the rules my whole life, and where had it gotten me? It was my turn to be bad, to ruin someone's life like mine had been. Vengeance seemed the best course of action for me. But what did I know of that sort of thing?

I stared at Nick who returned my look fixedly. He smiled at me, and I smiled back with a careless shrug. He obviously had something in mind. I was just waiting for him share his depraved idea. But for all the twisted things I had ever dreamed up, I still wasn't prepared for what Nick had in mind.

"What are you thinking, Nick?"

He shook his head and waved his hand. "Nah, forget it. You'd never go for it."

"Try me."

"All right then. What would you say if I talked to Alexi?"

"Alexi? For God's sake, why? What could he possibly do?"

It was no secret that Alexi was an evil bastard, as was Dmitri, but I didn't know the extent of their operation. I'd like to believe that Nick would never be involved in the sort of things I'd been fantasizing about, but perhaps he had knowledge of others who were, like Alexi Batalov and his boss, Dmitri Chernov, the reigning czar of Little Russia.

"Dmitri caters to a lot of important men. He provides certain…favors and entertainment, and has a rather large stable of, uh…ladies who work for him," Nick explained. "Occasionally he buys and sells them to a few of his foreign clients, wealthy Russian oil barons, businessmen from the Middle East and such." He glanced up at me for my reaction. "Perhaps he might find a useful occupation for our little friend, Erin." Nick smiled at me as if this was the answer to our prayers. "It could be the perfect solution, Tyler. You get your fill of sweet retribution and that bitch gets what's coming to her."

But as much as I enjoyed fantasizing about torturing Erin, I didn't think I actually had it in me to follow through. It just wasn't in my nature. What I wanted and what I was capable of doing were two different things entirely, and I was a little shocked that Nick might actually feel differently.

"For God's sake, Nick. That's a bit much, don't you think?"

He snickered. "Says the man who wants to see her beaten with a stick."

"Come on, Nick, that was just a…a daydream. What you're talking about, that's brutal."

"Brutal? Are you fucking kidding me? Ty, she's the reason your wife is dead. She's the reason you drink yourself into unconsciousness every goddamn day of your pathetic life." He shoved his nose in my face and tapped his finger against my temple. "Why you can't get the image of Jillian's broken body out of your fucking head.

"Remember Jill on that hospital bed, brother, the way they pounded on her chest, shoved tubes down her throat, and needles into her arms. You said it yourself. She died alone and afraid. *That's brutal,*" he said, poking me in the chest. "How can you *not* want to be brutal right back? Fuck that bitch! I would see her sold to a butcher if I could." Nick paced around the room, looking at me with anger and disappointment. "Now who's the one who should man-up, Ty? You bloody fucking coward. *She was your wife!*" he screamed, his face crimson with indignation. "Or perhaps you've forgotten what that means yet again," he added cruelly.

It struck me then that Nick was as angry about Jill's death as I was. I had never considered that her death might have affected him so deeply. I thought that he was merely here to support me. But Nick appeared driven by similar demons. He seemed bent on revenge just as much, if not more than I was. Nick made me feel like I was letting him down as much as I had let Jill down. I was torn. That part of me that always followed the rules and stayed within the lines warred with my baser side, that rabid part screaming for revenge.

"I know, Nick. You're right. It's just that...what you're suggesting...it's dangerous and illegal. Hell, it's insane. I don't want to spend the rest of my life in prison because of her."

Nick stood before me and shook his head, his face twisted in disgust. He was quiet now. His shoulders slumped downward like a defeated boxer who'd just lost to a bad call.

"It never should have come to this. You should have let me help Jill to begin with, and then maybe none of this would have happened. But you were always the straight arrow, weren't you, Tyler?" He laughed bitterly. "You know what, brother? You have no fucking balls and you can't say that bitch took them from you, too. You've always been that way."

Deflated, he walked out of the house, quietly closing the door behind him.

Alone now, I sat back in my chair with a full bottle of tequila and drank. With my mobile phone in hand, I played Jill's last voicemail message on an endless loop, over and over, until I could recite it perfectly, word for word in pitch and tone. I thought about everything Nick had screamed at me, every accusation, about every sordid little plan we had ever dreamed up for Erin. I thought about what Nick had suggested doing for real, selling Erin to Alexi and Dmitri. She'd be gone forever. She'd lose her freedom, her identity, and her humanity as countless strangers raped her into madness. The more I drank, the more reasonable it seemed.

God, I wanted to do it, but how could I live with the decision? Wouldn't I be compromising my own humanity, as well? Jill would be ashamed and disappointed if she knew what I was thinking. But then again, she was gone. She would never have the opportunity to live out her dreams. She would never see our child born. Everything that ever gave me reason to live had been stripped away, carelessly ground under the heel of a ruthless stranger. My humanity seemed insignificant compared to that.

I was all too aware that life wasn't free, that it costs us each something, but I had already paid more than my fair share, giving up what gave me incentive to live in the first place. Life had cost me everything. I had nothing left to lose.

So with that, I decided that I *could* carry the burden of guilt and remorse, but only as long as it was because of Erin, not Jillian. If I had only acted when she'd asked me to, if I had been the man she'd expected me to be, if I had only considered her well-being instead of my own blasted rules, then Jillian would still be alive. We would still be anticipating the birth of our first child. But I had done none of those things. I had failed her. I had failed my child. And now it was time for me to pay the price. It was the least I could do for Jill, for our baby, considering how I'd let them both down.

I rang Nick on his cell. "Do it," I ordered. "Call Alexi. Tell him I want to meet, and that I'll deliver the girl to him myself."

I ended the call and opened another bottle of tequila, taking a long pull directly from the top. I didn't even feel the burn any more, just the poison as it destroyed what little was left of the man I used to be. I was past numb, a ghost of my former self.

THE MISTAKEN

I swilled the liquor around the bottle then took another long drink, draining more than half a pint in two swallows. Jillian once complained that tequila turned me into a mean drunk. If that was the fuel I needed to see the deed done, then so be it.

Chapter Fifteen
Hannah

It was nearly impossible to lay in bed, pretending to be asleep, as my husband, Beckham, climbed in beside me. I was furious with him, but, coward that I was, I was simply too afraid to show it. He hadn't called me once while he was away on business in Las Vegas. He was still stewing over our last argument, as was I. Our last exchange of words kept replaying over and over in my mind. I squeezed my head between my hands in a fruitless effort to stem the flow. But I still could not keep them at bay.

"Damn it, Hannah," Beck had yelled. "You know I can't entertain my clients here, not the same way. It's too cold and damp. How am I supposed to negotiate million dollar deals if they aren't happy? They want to be somewhere warm, somewhere sunny. Someplace they can relax and get away from all this godforsaken rain."

"Well, so would we," I reminded him. "Conner and I would like to get away from the rain every once in a while, too. When you travel during the weekend, why can't we go with you?" When he didn't respond, I answered the question aloud myself. "Because you don't want us around, do you?" When he didn't answer again, I walked away and shut myself in our bedroom. Minutes later, the front door slammed shut as he left for the airport. And we hadn't spoken since.

Honestly, I understood Beck's occasional trips during the work week, the ones he took solely for business, but I was annoyed when he traveled over the weekends because he did so for his own pleasure, without considering his family. He explained they were for the entertainment of his clients, usually to play golf, something he says they are hard pressed to do in the damp, often sunless Puget Sound area, even in the springtime.

According to Beck, a warm, sunny golf course was the perfect location to leisurely negotiate deals and mediate contracts, while his client was primed with endless amounts of alcohol, hearty expensive food, and the practiced hands of the local spa's beautiful masseuse. Their usual destinations were Palm Springs, Napa, and occasionally Hawaii, though tonight Beck had returned from Las Vegas. Lying beside him, my nose was assaulted by the mixture of his familiar cologne with the sharp aroma of tequila and women's perfume, a nauseating brew that repulsed me, though I ached for his embrace or even a simple touch. Rarely did I get either.

We spent way too much time apart to make for a healthy marriage. Even our fifteen-year-old son, Conner, felt the absence of his father, though he tried not to let on just how much it hurt that Beck would rather spend time away. They used to be so close, passing endless hours horsing around with each other, but as of late, Beck was rarely home, and I felt as bad for Conner as I did for myself. We were both lonely for him.

It hadn't always been so. We were very young when we first started dating and very much in love, but even after ten years of marriage, Beck had continued to call me three or four times a day. And when he came home each night, he kissed me passionately and told me how much he loved me, how much he had missed my face.

While Conner arrived early in our marriage, his birth only intensified our feelings for each other, strengthening the core of our union with the common goal of raising our child. But when the economy had begun its downturn, Beck allowed the financial pressures of his job as an IT consultant to worm its way into our private lives. He worried about sustaining the lifestyle we had become so accustomed to while residing in our well-manicured, upscale community on Seattle's Eastside.

Sammamish, Washington—or The Plateau, as it was often called—was heavily populated with the families of highly paid executives from Microsoft, Boeing, and Amazon. They settled here because the schools were some of the best in the entire state, while the geography offered unrivaled beauty and spectacular views of the many lakes, volcanic peaks, and even the Seattle skyline with the snow-capped Olympic Mountains nestled majestically across the Sound behind it.

I was so excited about relocating to Seattle's Eastside from the San Francisco Bay Area. We had made several profitable real estate investments while living in California, which now afforded us prime housing in an affluent area, but with the prosperity came a level of pretentiousness I had not foreseen. While I had made a few friends since moving here five years ago, mostly the parents of Conner's friends, I discovered I had little in common with most of the people who lived around me, and didn't care for them. I found them condescending and arrogant, and their overly-entitled children were spoiled, ungrateful, and often downright mean.

Before long, I grew isolated and lonely. Even Conner was unhappy and had requested a transfer to another high school in the district, but off The Plateau, where he felt the kids were more down to earth and less obsessed with material wealth. Beckham, in his quest to achieve everything that would brand him a success, focused so much on his job that he didn't notice what was happening between us. He was clueless about my depression, and that in itself made me even more detached and remote.

Beck had changed, too, and rarely ever confided in me. Our sex life was non-existent, though I know my aloofness was partly to blame. And now, I worried that he carried an additional cell phone, one he tried to hide. At first, he attempted to pass the clone off as his regular cell, but I confronted him with my suspicions.

"What's with the new phone?" I asked when I first made the discovery.

"What new phone would that be, babe?" he said as he texted a message, without even bothering to look up at me

"Um, the one in your hand...*dear*."

He snapped me a look like I was mentally unbalanced. "It's the same phone I've always had...*babe*."

"No," I said as I held up his old phone. "*This* would be the same phone you've always had. It's not broken, and it still has service. See?" I said, speed dialing my own phone.

Flustered when my cell rang out, playing his assigned ringtone, he stammered for an answer. "Oh yeah, that. Well, uh, it's nothing really. I just forgot to tell you about it. It's from one of my new clients. He wants unlimited access to me at all times," he explained, like I was stupid enough to accept his excuse as even remotely plausible.

"And he doesn't have that with your regular cell?"

"Hannah, I'm not going to argue with a new client and turn down his request. If this is how he wants to do things, then I'm fine with that. And since it's clients like him who keep a roof over your head, food in your belly, and expensive clothes on your pretty little back," Beck indicated with a wave of his hand, "well, I would think you would be fine with it, too."

Angry, he turned away and concentrated on his computer screen. In an effort to avoid yet another fight, something we'd been doing more often of late, I let it go, but I found it suspicious that Beck's new phone only vibrated in the evenings and then he wouldn't even answer it. He merely checked the screen to see who was calling. But I could set my watch by the amount of time it took him to find a task that needed his attention within ten minutes of each call. Apparently, he didn't think I noticed, and I seriously wondered what kind of idiot he took me for.

One evening, Beck carelessly left it on the kitchen counter and walked out of the room. Curious, I scrolled through both the call log and phone book, but there was not one single listing or entry. My nagging worries flamed obsessively at each red flag. Since he dismissed most of my accusations with the notion that I was delusional, I felt the only way to know for sure what was going on with my husband was to hire a private investigator. Avoiding an easily followed trail on my computer, I found Sam Tunney in the Yellow Pages and, after a lengthy phone interview, I hired him.

Sam, a retired Seattle police detective, was a grizzled, older man with heavily calloused hands and white hair, neatly combed back from a coarsely wrinkled forehead. His gray eyes appeared gentle yet keen, missing nothing as they darted around, evaluating every person nearby. His smile was easy though, and I liked him at once. Taking his lengthy list of referrals into consideration, I trusted he would do a good job.

Sam had an easy time digging up dirt on Beck. He followed my husband around for several weeks, documenting where Beck went and with whom he met. He snapped a lot of photographs, telling me they would be the proof I needed should I ever choose to dissolve the marriage. He even dug back into the last year of Beck's travels and interviewed people at the resorts where he had stayed while away on his many business trips.

After compiling a detailed report, Sam called me in for a meeting to discuss what he had found. We met at a small restaurant on Seattle's Queen Anne Hill where he primed my nerves with an ample amount white wine. With more than half a bottle beneath my belt, Sam spread dozens of photographs out on the table before me. As my eyes briefly scanned the images, I felt a lump settle in the pit of my stomach.

"Mrs. Maguire, it looks like your husband's had quite a few flings with women he's met at the resorts where he stays. This one here," Sam said as he slid several black and white photographs over the smooth table, "is a young bartender in Hawaii. Her name is Leila. She's kinda quiet. Keeps to herself mostly. But this one," another set of pictures slipped before me, "well she's a blackjack dealer in Vegas, and a mighty wild one, too, if I do say so myself. Her name is Julie. There's also Carla and Adrienne, both in Palm Springs." Two more photos were laid out for my perusal.

Except for the bartender in Hawaii, all the women shared a similar appearance: in their late twenties or early thirties and trim with fair skin and various shades of red hair. The lump in my stomach degraded into bile and moved up into my throat. I placed my hand over my mouth, worried I might be sick right there.

"But those relationships have cooled down quite a bit," Sam informed me. With a deft hand, he stacked up the pictures and moved them aside. He reached into his briefcase and pulled out a separate file folder. It was filled with more pictures. "Now this one here, she's the gal your husband is seeing right now and has been for quite a spell."

He fanned the photographs along the table. Some were black and white, but most were color. I reached out and lightly touched my fingers along the images.

"Who is she?" I asked, my voice quivering as the tears threatened to spill down my hot cheeks. Duly humiliated, my face flamed with embarrassment.

"That one there's named Erin, Erin Anderson. She works at a golf resort down in the Napa Valley. A real high-end, swanky spa kinda deal, you know. Mostly rich folk."

"Napa? But a lot of these pictures weren't even taken in Napa. I recognize this place," I said as I pulled out one snapshot. "That's Pier 39 in San Francisco. And this one here," I singled out another. "Look at the sign. They're at Heavenly Valley. Were they skiing?"

Sam bobbed his head. "Yes, ma'am, I'm afraid they were."

My mouth sagged open. We lived twenty minutes from the slopes at Snoqualmie Pass, but Beck had never once taken us up skiing, though Conner and I had asked numerous times. I threw the picture back down and poked through the others. Some were taken on the golf course, others at the beach. Every shot showed them living it up playfully, their arms often locked around each other. They were all taken from a distance which made it difficult to see the woman's features clearly. My fingers trembled at my lips as I scanned all the images.

Sam pulled out a few more color photographs. They were close-up shots of Beck and Erin Anderson. I gasped at the new pictures lying on the table. Staring back at me was my husband with a look of love and adoration for the girl next to him, a girl who, strangely enough, looked remarkably like me. I singled out one of the photos and brought it closer to inspect. I rubbed away the tears that blurred my vision and studied the face on the paper.

"Oh my God," I whispered, slowly running my finger along her profile.

Erin and I both had long, dark auburn hair, similarly textured with a natural glossy wave. Our eyes were both green, though different shades, but they were shaped roughly the same, as were our faces, both triangular with a sharp jaw and delicately pointed chin. Her mouth was different though. Her upper lip was considerably thinner while her bottom lip pouted unnaturally. Collagen injections would be my guess. And though she was slightly slimmer and somewhat more athletic in form, we were of comparable height and weight. Only one thing made us different: this girl was considerably younger, by at least ten years. This, in itself, was what upset me most, for I believed Beck had found a replacement for me, a new and improved model. Beck looked sincerely happy and in love.

Nausea rolled up from my stomach and made my head spin. In my hand was evidence of another life that Beck was leading, an affirmation that my life, as I had always known it, was about to change forever. I gathered up all the pictures and threw them into the folder. I grabbed my bag and pushed the straps over my shoulder with trembling ice-cold fingers then held out my hand.

"Thank you, Sam."

He shook it, looking at me with pity. "Mrs. Maguire, I'm real sorry—"

"No, no, Sam. It's okay. Really. I had a feeling this was going on. That's why I hired you." I gave him a brittle smile and pulled my hand away. "I have to go. You know…Conner, my son…he's…you know…I'm sorry. I really must go. Send me your bill when you're ready."

I escaped to my car where I cried for forty minutes. I kept glancing over at the folder lying on the seat next to me. My God, I was such a fool. I realized too late the mistakes I'd made with Beck, and that I had let him slip through my fingers out of negligence. Before all this, I never once suspected that he looked elsewhere for what he lacked at home, mostly because I had never thought of doing so myself. I felt as though the earth beneath me had evaporated, leaving me nothing on which to steady myself. My identity was obliterated into a million pieces and blown away. After all, who was I if not Mrs. Beckham Maguire?

My head was swimming. I could no longer just sit there with the evidence of Beck's infidelity beside me. I needed to figure out my next move. I wanted to have everything in place and planned out before he left me. I would need my own bank accounts and credit cards in my name only.

Of course, I thought about just divorcing him and sucking him dry, but I also wondered how this would all play out. I pulled out one of the close-up shots of Beck and Erin and stared at it. Would Beck really consider leaving his family for a younger version of me? Perhaps he would tire of this girl. Was there any hope of salvaging my old life, and did I even want that life, such as it was? How much did I really love him if I had allowed this to happen in the first place?

It was too much for me to just give up without really knowing where I stood. I figured Beck's loyalty to me correlated directly with how much he felt for this girl, or at least, how much she felt for him. I needed to see them together. I wanted to talk to this girl myself, to see if she knew about me and Conner, and find out what her intentions were. Maybe this was just a fling for the both of them, or perhaps I was being set up for a big fall.

Determined to protect myself, I drove home and scoured the Internet. I found and hired an attorney to help get my affairs in order, in case I did decide to file for divorce in the future. I also made arrangements for Conner to stay with a friend so I could take a short swing down to Napa, California. Beck was planning another business trip there over the weekend. I wanted to see for myself just how in love Beck and this girl really were.

And if given the opportunity, I would have a few words with her myself.

Chapter Sixteen
Hannah

Nervous tension coursed through me during the short flight from SeaTac down to Oakland, California. I couldn't help but think that I was somehow pulling at the very thread that would unravel my life. But no matter the qualms that plagued me, my resolve to see it through remained intact, so I rented a car and located the resort in Napa where my husband usually stayed and Erin Anderson was currently employed. Beck was supposed to return home in two days which gave me enough time to either find them together or question the girl alone. Either way, the next time Beck and I saw each other, all the cards would be laid on the table, and I would have to make a decision.

Armed with one of Sam's photographs, I walked around the lobby searching for Erin. Quite a few people turned and stared at me, which was unnerving, but I surmised they were employees who saw the strong resemblance between us. I checked the bar and restaurant but found no sign of her. Since I had made no headway on my own, I decided to check with one of the bartenders, a good-looking young man who barely looked old enough for the job.

I held up the photo for him to see. "Excuse me. Where might I find this woman?"

He glanced briefly at the photo then assessed me from head to toe, his attention freezing on my face. "You her sister?" he asked.

"No, I'm not."

"Are you family then? You look so much alike."

"Yes, I do realize that, but no, we aren't related."

"Oh, well then I'm sorry, but I can't give out any information."

"Why is that?"

"It's company policy," he explained as he wiped a towel across the bar. "We recently had a problem with an employee and someone who came looking for her here. The police were involved, and there was a bad scene afterwards, so policy now prevents us from giving out information. But if you'd like, I can get a message to her."

He threw the towel over his shoulder and began stacking glasses along a shelf above his head, but he never once took his eyes off me. I thought his offer over and decided against it. The bartender might tip my hand if he described me to her.

"Thanks, but that won't be necessary." With a wave and polite smile, I left the bar.

I walked back through the lobby, out the main door, and into the warm sunshine. Seconds later, a waitress from the bar approached me from behind and tapped hesitantly on my shoulder.

"Excuse me, ma'am?" she whispered. She took a small step back as I turned around. "I heard you inside talking to Jared. Would you mind if I take a look at that picture?" She raised her hand toward me and wiggled her fingers.

"No, not at all. Please..." I handed her the photo.

The girl looked back and forth between me and Erin's picture. "That is *so* weird," she said.

"Hmm, yes, I agree. So tell me, do you know her?"

She nodded. "Well, yeah, sure. Everyone here knows Erin. Some a little too well, if you know what I mean."

I raised a brow at her. "Do you know where I might find her?"

The girl looked around to make sure no one was watching or listening before she turned back. "Yeah, she's cleaning out her locker. She was just fired. Management is waiting to escort her off the property."

"Really? That's very interesting. Do you know why she was fired?"

The girl propped a fist on one hip and flipped her ponytail back over her shoulder as a false smile twisted a corner of her mouth.

"Well, she has some legal issues *and*," she said emphasizing the word, "she just got into a huge argument with a guest. It was pretty heated and really embarrassing," the girl— looking around carefully—delighted in telling me.

"Really? What happened exactly?"

The girl leaned in, like we were old friends sharing a sordid secret. "Well, her boyfriend, who, I might add, is a regular guest here, well, it seems he caught her with another guy. God, he was so pissed. You should have seen him. He screamed at her in front of *everyone*." The girl was positively giddy as she shared her news.

"Really? Umm…listen, would you mind walking with me for a few minutes? I wouldn't want to get you in any trouble for speaking with me, and I'd love to ask you a few more questions." I linked my arm through hers, reinforcing the image that we were good friends.

"Sure thing." She pointed in the direction in which we should walk to get away from prying eyes and ears.

"So what's your name?" I asked.

"Tracy."

After walking some distance, I stopped and turned to her. "Well, Tracy, I gather you don't like Erin very much."

"Is it that obvious?" she asked, and I raised one brow in answer. "Well, no, I don't like her at all, and I'm thrilled she's leaving. She's been nothing but trouble since she got here."

"Oh? How so?"

"Erin's a slut, always running around with the club's guests when she's off work. That guy I told you was her boyfriend? Well he's just one of many. That other guy was another. A new one. I'm just surprised it took this long for one of them to catch on. The hotel makes a lot of money off them and she keeps them...uh...satisfied, so they don't mind none. Hell, they practically pimp her out themselves, though I heard Erin got caught swiping credit card numbers from clients, and that a guest caught her and confronted her about it." Tracy looked distant for a moment, caught in a memory as she tapped her index finger against her chin. "There was a really bad accident and someone got hurt, like real bad or something..." She shook her head and turned back to me. "I don't know, but Erin was involved somehow. That's what I heard anyway. I'm telling you, that girl's nothing but trouble."

Hatred flashed like a light in Tracy's eyes as she rambled on. I was most interested in Erin's boyfriends. Knowing how often he was here, I bet Tracy would recognize Beck if I showed her a photo. I pulled my wallet out of my purse, selected a picture of Beck, and held it up for her.

"Tracy, have you ever seen this man?"

Recognition sparked within her as a smile spread across her face. "Yeah, that's the boyfriend who caught her, the dude who screamed at her earlier. He's here quite a bit." She handed the photo back. "Who is he anyway? I mean, you obviously know him so..." She shrugged.

"He's my husband," I informed her dryly.

"Oh my God, really?" She giggled then drew herself up short. "I mean, well, I'm sorry, it's just that... I can't get over how weird that is, you know, that you two look so much alike and all. I mean, he's your husband and her boyfriend? Kinda freaky, don't you think?"

"Yes, I do." I replaced the photo and held out my hand. She shook it with a hesitant grip. "Tracy, it has been a pleasure. Thank you so very much for your time." I smiled and turned away, but she caught my arm with her hand.

"Wait! You don't want to talk to Erin? Because I could take you down there. I'd *love* to see the look on her face when—"

"No, no, Tracy, please. I don't want her to know I was here just yet. You understand."

"Um, okay, sure." Tracy looked disappointed, but shrugged. "Whatever."

"Thanks again." I turned again to leave, but quickly turned back to ask one last question. "Say, Tracy? How long ago would you say it was that my husband and Erin had their little disagreement?"

"Oh, I don't know. Maybe an hour or so, I guess. He was really pissed when he left. I saw him check out of the hotel before the big fight so he might be on his way home...just so you know."

"Thanks." I turned away and walked through the parking lot.

I guess I had my answers. Beck was in over his head, and the girl was just having a little bit of fun at his expense. It was funny how everything changed in those moments I spent talking with Tracy. I climbed back into my rental car and looked through Sam's photos one last time, stopping on a close-up shot of Beck as he kissed Erin's cheek.

I flicked his image with my finger. I had only contempt for him now. The feelings I'd been carrying around with me the last few days soured all of a sudden, leaving a bitter aftertaste. I knew now why I'd never tried hard enough to save my marriage. I didn't really want to save it. I realized I was just having a hard time letting it go after all the years I'd invested. It was simply an old habit I needed to break, a bad one.

I snorted at the photo and shook my head. I was amused that Beck had caught his little girlfriend cheating on him. Serves him right, the bastard. I knew what I wanted to do. I was going to divorce Beckham. I would leave him, The Plateau, and all the ugliness of both far behind me. I pulled out my cell and called my attorney, waiting several minutes before her assistant put me through.

"Hi Sarah, this is Hannah Maguire. Those divorce papers you drew up for me last week? Yes, file them immediately, please. And I want full custody of Conner. Please see that it's taken care of today. Okay? Great. Thanks."

I hung up with a satisfied smile, feeling better than I had in years.

Chapter Seventeen
Tyler

I requested a meeting with Alexi to sort out the details of handing Erin over to Dmitri. He summoned me to a waterfront warehouse south of Market. As I stood waiting, his black Mercedes appeared out of nowhere, like a phantom emerging from the swirling fog. With his bodyguard remaining tucked away in the warmth of the idling car, Alexi emerged, stepping out onto the chilly parking lot with his standard grin.

I confirmed our previously discussed plans, and he promised his crew would provide any information and assistance I might need. I had only to ask. Alexi seemed quite smug that I would go to such extremes over the girl, but I assured him that it was not solely for revenge. I had an even greater issue motivating me now.

Dmitri would likely receive a large sum for Erin — blood money — none of which I wanted for myself. My terms were of a more personal nature, one that he certainly would not like or welcome. But I'd waited a long time for this opportunity, and I wasn't about to let it go.

"In return for the girl, I want Dmitri to release Nick from any further responsibilities within the organization. I want him out, Alexi. Completely," I demanded. "And I want his debt wiped clean."

He didn't have any reaction that I could see. He simply stared back with the same smile as always.

"And what if you cannot provide what you are promising? If we make arrangements for the sale and receive payment, there is no going back. You understand this, my friend?" he asked, his tone dripping with the implication that there would be consequences if I didn't hold up my end of the bargain.

I nodded. "Yes, I do."

"Well then, I need to speak with Dmitri and see if he is averse to the idea of letting Nick go. I am not sure he will be too receptive to the idea. Even with all the years of bad blood, he quite likes your brother," he said with a casual wave of his hand. "But I wonder, does Nick know about this little condition of yours?"

"No, he doesn't. And I don't want you to say anything to him about it. I need time to get him warmed to the idea. But he'll see reason…eventually."

Alexi chuckled and threw me a reproachful look. "I would not be too certain of that if I were you. You will hear from me tomorrow." Then with narrowed eyes, he scrutinized me. "You know, you look a bit out of sorts. This is a very delicate affair. I suggest you sober up before undertaking it." He began to walk away but turned back with a raised brow.

"I must say, I am a bit surprised by how you are handling the death of your beloved wife. Your brother once complained that you were rather hard on him after his accident a few years ago. And yet now, you take to the bottle like a baby, just as he did. It must be a family thing, eh…my friend?"

He laughed, turned away again, and waved two fingers in the air as a parting gesture. "Tomorrow then," he said, his shoulders shaking as he laughed and laughed.

My lip pulled up into an involuntary sneer of disgust as I watched Alexi climb back into his Mercedes. I wanted to believe it was a reaction to his accusatory tone, his smug grin, or my distaste at the mere sound of his voice, but I knew it was the message itself that had found its mark.

It shamed me to admit that he was right, that I was the very definition of a hypocrite. But as much as I recognized my shortcomings, it was not enough to deter me. There was no hope in my heart, no reason to stop my downward spiral and straighten out my life. The very realization only made me want to drink more. And I did, for the rest of the day and most of the night. I was surprised I even heard my phone ring early the next morning. I fumbled around blindly and knocked it off the nightstand before finally retrieving and answering it.

"Yeah," I ground out, wincing at the pain that tore through my head. I pressed the heel of my free hand against my brow.

"Good morning! Or maybe not, eh?" Alexi laughed as I moaned into the phone. "I am sorry if I have awakened you too early, but it might make you feel better to know that Dmitri has agreed to your terms and has already made a deal with a special client to whom he owes a favor."

I reached for a bottle of pills turned over on the nightstand and struggled with the cap. "Go on," I replied.

"This is Dmitri's best customer we are talking about here. *Very* wealthy. *Very* powerful. A man not to be crossed. And he expects his merchandise delivered within one week. One. Week.

Not a day more. You understand?   There will be no renegotiations of any kind, so do not fuck this up, my friend. Your life and that of your brother may very well lie in the balance if there is any trouble. You understand all this, do you not?"

"Yes, I do. Thank you," I offered as respectfully as I could, though it stuck in my throat to do so. I popped a small pill into my mouth and swallowed it dry. "I'll be in touch in a day or two," I said, returning my hand to my forehead and falling back onto the pillow.

I ended the call with apprehension, but I believed this to be my only opportunity to accomplish what I had failed to do years ago, to free Nick from the Russians' control, while also getting the revenge against Erin that my heart so ruthlessly craved.

Chapter Eighteen
Tyler

Nick and I spent the following day discussing how we would find Erin and bring her down into The City. I'd never actually seen her before and knew very little about her, only where she worked, though Alexi had promised me a photograph so I could easily identify her. My plan was to get acquainted with her schedule, locate her at work and follow her home, see if she lived with anyone.

I needed to determine the best way to grab her. It would be difficult to just nab her off the street or even out of her home. If she was single, perhaps I could try to pick her up at a bar and lure her away. I couldn't decide until I knew more about her, so I left to find her at work.

I arrived at the spa early on a warm spring morning. It was just as lavish as Jillian had described with a long, palm-lined drive that led uphill to the Mission-styled building. Glass and wrought-iron doors opened to a towering entry hall with a large sculpted chandelier and polished marble floor. Tuscan columns were set at steady intervals and led up to a long reception desk finished in burnished granite. It shone in the warm light of the stained glass rotunda some thirty-five feet above. And a gentle musical soundscape was piped into the voluminous space, creating the peaceful, Zen-like atmosphere. The place screamed of money, as did the clientele, fashionably dressed in high-end designer clothing. Not the kind of place in which I could ever envision Jillian.

I walked through the massive lobby and passed through another set of wrought-iron doors out onto a cobbled brick patio decked with iron tables and large market umbrellas. I offered a weak smile to several female guests who turned to stare, nodding politely as I passed. They were still craning their necks in my direction when I glanced back over my shoulder. Though I remained unshaved, I had showered and cleaned up reasonably well, dressed in khakis and a button-down shirt. My hope was to remain unnoticed, to blend in, but I realized I was drawing too much attention to myself.

I left the crowd behind and wandered the tastefully landscaped grounds until I found a large parking lot designated for the resort's staff. From there, I watched dozens of employees enter the main building through a basement level service door, but as far as I could tell, Erin was not among them.

I had only one photo that Alexi had forwarded to me through Nick. It was a grainy surveillance image of mediocre quality, but I could tell her features well enough to discern her from the others. I scrutinized everyone, glancing back and forth between each employee and the photo in my hand. I'd made no progress after loitering in the employee lot for nearly an hour, so I ventured back into the lobby from the main entrance. I walked around for a few minutes, scanning the fine art that adorned the stucco walls before I picked up a magazine and settled into one of the large club chairs that dotted the lobby. The entire area was visible: the reception and concierge, the entrances to the spa and pro shop, as well as the restaurant and adjoining bar.

I pretended to read or chat on my phone as I observed both the reception and concierge desks, the only places Jill had ever mentioned seeing Erin. Several of employees asked if I needed anything. With a smile, I explained that I was waiting on my wife who was still out on the golf course.

Though it was a busy place with people bustling about, toting golf bags over their shoulders or wheeling designer luggage behind them, the lobby was still pretty quiet overall, so I was startled to hear voices being raised in anger coming from the restaurant at the far end of the lobby. Their profane language echoed off the rotunda high above my head. I wandered over to see what the commotion was and casually took a seat at the bar. There were a number of people—both guests and employees— who watched the scene unfold in the restaurant. I turned to observe as the bartender settled a cardboard coaster in front of me.

"What can I get you?" he asked.

Though I was suitably inebriated from the half-empty flask in my car, the temptation was too great for me to just sit there and not order a drink.

"Cuervo Silver," I requested, "and a pint of whatever you have on tap." When he turned away to fill my order, I peered back over my shoulder at the spectacle playing out within the restaurant behind me.

A well-dressed man near my own age stood in front of a booth with a young couple seated at it. He directed his attention to the woman. She yelled back at him as he towered over her.

"Lower your voice," she hissed through her teeth.

"Who the fuck is he?" the man standing before her screamed, ignoring her command.

"Please, Beck, you need to leave. Now," she replied.

I couldn't see the woman very well until she pushed the man back from the table and stood up to face him. That's when I recognized her.

Erin Anderson.

I felt the blood drain from my face as my heart leapt within my chest. I turned back to the bar and slammed the shot of tequila then chased it with half the beer. With my palm flattened against the bar, I took a deep breath. My nerves were so taut, the sweaty glass of beer slipped from my grasp. It dropped onto the bar, sloshing frothy ale all over the counter. The startled bartender raised his eyebrows, silently asking if I wanted another. With an affable nod, I mouthed an apology then held up both vessels in an effort to cover my anxiety.

"I'm not leaving until you tell me what the hell you're doing here with *him*," the man shouted.

Erin's tone calmed as she tried to soothe him. "Please, Beck, it's not what you think."

"The fuck it is!" the man screamed.

Erin pushed Beck backwards as she tried in vain to console him. Her date, left seated at the table, sat quietly with a look of amused shock on his face as he watched the two bicker.

"*You* cancel *our* date and yet here you are with *this* asshole. And now you're telling me it's not what *I* think? You're a goddamn lying bitch."

It appeared the man had found Erin having lunch with a gentleman he believed her to be having an affair with. I gathered the angry gentleman must be Erin's husband since he wore a wedding ring.

"Beck, no, please. Just give me a minute to explain," she begged, though the provocative way she was attired spoke volumes as to her intentions.

She wore a dark red dress that clung to her alluring figure, barely falling to the middle of her shapely thigh. Glittering six-inch platform heels were strapped to her feet while expensive-looking gems adorned her ears, throat, and fingers. Her dark red hair fell loosely over her bare shoulders in long, thick waves, and though she was beautiful enough to go without, her face was slathered in heavy make-up. She looked like a high-priced call girl.

The resort manager, a tall, older gentleman with a balding head and well-dressed in an expensive suit, approached the two of them with his hands raised. "This is not the appropriate place for your conversation. I would ask you to take it elsewhere," he said in a hushed tone.

"Back off, Henry," Erin replied.

The manager's eyes grew wide then his mouth thinned as he rested his fists against his rotund waist. "That's *Mr.* Renton to you, Ms. Anderson. Get over to my office right now or you'll find yourself forcibly removed from the premises...for good this time," he said. His eyes burned with anger, following Erin closely as she stormed off. "And Mr. Maguire, I would like you to leave the restaurant, as well. I can have you escorted back to your suite, if you'd like."

They stared at each other for a tense moment before Maguire left the restaurant in an angry huff. Renton spoke to Erin's date, politely offering him the drinks and food he was sharing with Erin as compliments of the resort. With a nod, he turned back to the lobby and disappeared down the long hall after Erin.

I wanted to follow Renton and keep an eye on Erin, but thought better of it since they were still attracting a great deal of attention. I slammed my second shot then tossed the beer down my throat. I threw a twenty on the bar and left the same way

Maguire did. I followed him at a safe distance through the lobby, where he picked up his bag, then out through the parking lot to a rental with Hertz tags on the bumper. Maguire jumped in and sped off. I returned to my own car out back and drove around to the side, parking in the shade of a tall California oak. I hoped to catch my prize as she left from either the front lot or the rear.

Ninety minutes later, Erin walked out through the front door. I checked the photo one last time. She had cleaned up and changed into more conservative clothing, but there was no doubt in my mind it was her. I sneered and swore under my breath then tipped the flask to my lips. I drained the contents, seeking its numbing relief. Suddenly, a waitress from the bar jogged out through the front entrance. She chased after Erin and tapped her on the shoulder. Erin turned, and they spoke for a minute, but the waitress seemed uneasy, nervously scanning the area around them. Erin locked arms with her and the two strolled through the parking lot toward the rear of the building, chatting amicably along the way.

I couldn't hear what they were saying, but Erin looked surprised as the girl carried on. She pulled out her wallet and showed the girl what looked to be a photograph. The girl nodded and returned it to Erin as she continued to talk excitedly. Shortly thereafter, the two parted ways. Erin smiled as she walked back to her car out front where the guests parked. She pulled out her cell phone and made a call. I was surprised she looked so smugly satisfied, considering the fight she'd had earlier in front of her boss and fellow employees. She pulled out of the parking space and proceeded slowly through the lot. Not wanting to lose sight of her, I followed. She led me an hour or so south to the Oakland Airport where she pulled her car into the long line of rental returns then walked into the office, wheeling an overnight bag behind her.

I parked some distance away and jogged back toward the office to watch her. I was shocked to see her *and* Maguire, the man from the restaurant, arguing again in the middle of the rental office. Since Maguire had left nearly an hour and a half earlier, I thought for sure they had made plans to meet, but the posturing between them was completely different than it had been in the restaurant. Maguire appeared surprised to see her and very disturbed by her complaints. Erin was the one screaming this time. Though I couldn't understand what she was saying, her voice carried all the way out to the parking garage where it echoed off the concrete walls. Now *she* was angry, and *he* was sullen, like he'd been the one caught cheating instead of her. I'd never seen a couple who deserved each other more than these two.

Maguire ripped Erin's paperwork out of her hand and threw both his receipt and hers at the employee who stood behind the counter. The sheepish clerk looked concerned by the fighting couple. Maguire handed him a credit card and paid both accounts. He turned and grabbed his bag and Erin's arm, dragging them both out of the office toward the airport terminal. The clerk walked out from behind the counter and followed them out the door. He watched them with an open mouth as they walked away, still arguing back and forth.

I quietly entered the office from behind the clerk, walked up to the counter, and snatched the paperwork he'd left sitting there. One escaped my fingers and fell to the floor behind the counter, out of my reach. The clerk pulled the front door closed behind him and returned to the office. I spun around, avoiding eye contact, and pretended to lift some company literature off a kiosk. Then I turned and left the office before the clerk could notice the missing paperwork.

As I walked through the garage, I looked over the one receipt I'd managed to steal to see what kind of information I could glean from it. The name at the top was Beck Maguire's. It listed an address in Washington State, his driver's license, and two phone numbers. I stuffed the paper into my pocket and took off into the terminal after the bickering couple. Slipping into the line far behind them at the busy ticket counter, I listened as they quarreled over their plans to fly back home to Seattle. I wanted to follow them onto their flight, but it was more important that I talk to Nick and share with him what I knew. Perhaps we could use the receipt to find Maguire and Erin again up in Washington. I watched them proceed through the security line. They had finally stopped arguing, refusing to speak to each other at all. With nothing left to do, I drove home to find Nick and discuss our next step. Time was running out. We had to find Erin.

I needed that girl.

Chapter Nineteen
Tyler

Nick grilled me about everything that went down at the spa, as well as the Oakland Airport. He wondered aloud why Erin would be flying up to Seattle if she worked in Napa and most likely lived nearby. Working on a hunch, he called the spa and asked for Erin, hoping to get some answers. He used his considerable charm and chatted up the young woman who answered the phone. He listened silently for a few minutes then hung up and threw me an anxious glance.

"Erin was sacked today," he said.

"Sacked?"

"Yep, fired for inappropriate behavior and escorted off the property. Or so the lady said."

"Brilliant. So what'll we do now?"

"Well, we don't have anywhere else to locate her now except for the address on that rental car receipt." Nick picked up the slip and perused it before handing it to me. He paced the floor, deep in thought. "You said they both talked about going home. Those were their words. And their flight was headed to Seattle. I don't know, Ty. You seem to think they're married, but his name is Maguire and hers is Anderson. Something just doesn't add up." He stopped and looked at me. "I'm not sure what's up with them, but if Seattle is where they both said their home is, we don't have much choice. I think we should drive up as soon as possible. Take a look around. That's our best shot at finding her now. I don't want Alexi to think we've fucked this up before we even got started, you know."

I looked over the receipt and nodded, knowing it was the best plan, but feeling apprehensive about it. Nick considered me with doubt in his eyes, probably the same uncertainty I felt in my heart, not to mention the foreboding that sat like a rock in the pit of my stomach.

"You sure about this, Ty? I know I said all those things before, but if you're not—"

"No, you're right. I just want to get this over with as quickly as possible." I had no choice now, though Nick didn't know that yet. I hadn't told him about the deal Alexi and I had brokered with Dmitri. And while Dmitri had so far kept his promise not to tell Nick, he had called me twice already, a friendly reminder that the clock was ticking and that he was watching. And waiting. Like the sword of Damocles hanging above my head.

I slammed a fresh drink and grimaced. As the moment drew nearer and my determination grew weaker, my consumption of alcohol increased twofold. It dawned on me in that moment that I was gambling with our lives. Earlier in the week, it had seemed so clear, the sacrifice worth the uncertainty, but now that I was moving closer to my target—her life locked in my crosshairs—my resolve wavered. I was unsure if I could complete my mission. Maybe that was why I put Nick's future on the table, to make certain I would follow through, for Jillian's memory at the very least. I tried to swallow my fear and concentrate on the task, but I found my weakening confidence disconcerting. I chose to hide my disquiet from Nick and pushed forward.

Nick scoured through my garage, tossing two thin coils of rope, a knife, and some duct tape into a large canvas duffel bag. We took one more day to discuss strategy: where we would stay, how we would grab the girl, what we would do with her once we did, and how we planned on getting her back down to San Francisco, all without being detected. We walked through every scenario we could think of, the inevitable problems, and possible options. It certainly wouldn't be easy, and we were going to have to wait and see what the conditions were before we decided which plan would work best, but we felt certain we could complete our task and get Erin back to The City by Alexi's looming deadline, now a mere four days away.

When the time finally arrived for us to leave for Seattle, Nick shrugged casually, stuffed his wallet in his back pocket, and picked up his keys.

"Ready to go?" he asked, as if we were running a simple errand instead of planning to destroy a human life.

I nodded and hid my uneasiness behind a pair of sunglasses. As he left to start the car, I filled a bag with several bottles of liquor, because I knew full well that I would eventually need the extra courage. I paused at the front door and looked back into the home I had shared with Jillian, noting all the things that reminded me of her: her composition of photos artfully arranged on the walls and the pile of baby products heaped together in the corner. She was everywhere and yet nowhere.

I turned away and, with a great sigh, closed the door behind me.

Chapter Twenty
Tyler

My brother and I took shifts driving so we wouldn't have to stop for the night. Nick asked me to refrain from drinking any alcohol during the fourteen-hour drive, something I found especially difficult. Over the last few months, I'd never gone more than four or five hours without a drink. At that point, my hands would begin to tremble, and my heart would race. I would often break out into a cold sweat, and concentrating became a challenge. I even hallucinated a few times, jumping away from imaginary bugs as they skittered across the floor. Nick seemed immune to withdrawal. I suppose I had become a more hardcore drinker than Nick ever was. It was not something I was proud of, but I was resigned to it nonetheless, having no reason or motivation to change.

The weather grew increasingly worse as we drew closer to Seattle. The landscape turned to a lush overgrown green held to earth by heavy, steel-grey clouds leaden with rain which pounded relentlessly against the windshield. The sky lightened very early over the Puget Sound, and by five in the morning, the sun had risen fully behind the oppressive clouds.

"Welcome to Seattle," Nick said with biting sarcasm. "I hear it's sunny here less than two months out of the year. Can you believe that? Sixty days. I think I'd fucking kill myself if I had to live with the grey skies and all this depressing rain."

I laughed as I looked around at the tall trees that leaned in on the roadway from all sides, their height and breadth obscuring most of the sky. "Well, at least it's green here," I replied, "and with all the trees, you can barely see the sky anyway, so..." I shrugged.

He nodded in agreement as he craned his head forward to view the forested wetland around us. "It's kind of creepy, you know, the way you can't even see through the trees. You'd never know what's coming at you. And they have bears, coyotes and mountain lions all over the place up here, even in the residential neighborhoods. Fucking scary place. And depressing. And wet. How in God's name do they stand all this bloody rain?"

He shivered visibly, and I couldn't help but chuckle again. Unlike me, Nick was a true Aussie, raised in the blistering heat and scorching sun, his free time spent exploring both the bush and outback alike; that is when he wasn't surfing or trolling for girls along the sandy beaches of Melbourne. He didn't remember the dreary rain of London as I did. It was little things like this that exemplified the core differences between us. Though we looked very much alike, we couldn't be more different, right down to our accents.

"We need to go east up here on I-90," I said, pointing at the sign ahead.

Nick and I chose to stay in a small town just outside of Maguire's. Issaquah, Washington was nestled between several small mountains in the foothills of the Cascades just ten miles east of Seattle. It was a quiet bedroom community overloaded with teriyaki restaurants, two Starbuck's at every strip mall, and well-dressed, SUV-driving soccer moms who trolled about with their young children strapped into car seats while they gossiped through blue-tooth devices stuck into their ears. I watched the people venture about, doing their business. Even in the rain no one used an umbrella, and very few wore rain coats or even pulled hoods up over their heads. They simply ignored the spitting sky. I shook my head and chuckled in amusement as Nick pulled the car into a Motel 6 near the freeway.

"I'll go get a room," I said. "Why don't you grab us something to eat and bring it back. I want to go over the map, get an idea of where I'm going once I get up into Maguire's neighborhood." Truth was, I couldn't wait a minute longer for a drink. I needed one. My hands had been shaking for the last eight hours.

Nick nodded. "All right. I'll call to see which room you're in."

I grabbed the bag of alcohol, walked into the office, and secured a room. I opened the motel room door for Nick when he returned twenty minutes later. He tossed me my own bag of food then threw his car keys onto the small table where I had spread out a map. A bottle of tequila and a glass half full held it in place.

"I found Maguire's street," I informed him as I swallowed the contents of the glass, immediately pouring myself another. "It's only about five or six miles from here. Think I'll drive up and take a look."

Nick looked me over then focused on the glass in my hand. "Ty, you really need to slow down on that stuff and get some rest. We've been up twenty-four hours straight. I don't know about you, but I'm beat. " He yawned and stretched, emphasizing his point.

"Nick, come on—"

"No, Ty, *you* come on. I'm dead tired and need some shut-eye."

I looked at him closely, noting the dark circles under his eyes. "Right. Okay, well, maybe just a few hours."

I reached out and pushed him backwards, and he plopped into the middle of the closest bed. It squeaked in protest and bounced under his weight. He pulled out his fast-food breakfast from the bag still clutched in his hand, wolfing it down as he studied me.

"Ty, you look like shit," he mumbled with his mouth full of food. "Your eyes are all bloodshot. Why don't you go take a shower? And shave while you're at it. You look like a goddamn bum."

I ran my hand over my jaw and chin. I had remained unshaven for nearly two weeks, the grey in my beard a reminder that, as I grew older, Jillian did not, a motivating factor that helped keep my mind on task. I grunted a reply and turned back to study the map and eat my lukewarm meal.

Satisfied and weary, Nick folded a thin pillow up under his head and sighed. He was asleep in no time, snoring quietly. I had always envied how easy it was for him to fall asleep. After Jillian died, I craved sleep. It was the only place where I could see her, talk to her, and hold her in my arms. I could almost feel her there and breathe in her scent. But as time wore on and I drank more, I grew restless, and though I wanted to sleep more than almost anything in this world, it eluded me most days. Now was no exception.

I moved to sit on the edge of the other bed and stared at my brother lying opposite me. He was oblivious to the turmoil that raged inside me. I would keep it from him if I could. This was, after all, *my* battle, *my* demons that drove me foolishly into danger. As Nick slept, his jacket fell open at his side, exposing a gun strapped securely in a holster. I was shocked to see him carrying a weapon. I glanced back at his face, serene and youthful in sleep. I stood up and, leaning over him, pulled the gun from its sheath, watching his face for any sign of detection.

Sitting back down at the table, I held the gun in my hand and checked it for ammunition. It was fully loaded with the safety off. I looked down the barrel and along the sights before placing it on the table. It made me uncomfortable just having it in front of me, but at the same time it inspired a sense of confidence that had otherwise been absent, though anxiety continued to twitter restlessly in my stomach. I poured myself another glass of courage and turned my attention back to the map, noting the best route to Maguire's house.

As Nick lay sleeping, I hammered the rest of the tequila and started in on a six-pack of beer to wash away the sour taste. My head began to spin as I contemplated the table cluttered with the remains of my binge. It disgusted me, the way I drank, but it was the best company I had to ease my loneliness, and the bitterness I felt because of it. It was also the only buttress strong enough to bolster my resolve. I ignored the feeling of uncertainty and refocused on my goal. As I turned to Nick and studied his sleeping form, I made my decision to drive to Maguire's house, alone and without his knowledge. It would be better if he didn't know what I was planning. I stuffed the gun into my jacket pocket, grabbed Nick's car keys and the map, and quietly left the room.

My hands trembled as I climbed behind the wheel of Nick's Jeep. I closed my eyes and took several deep breaths, but it did no good. I threw open the door and puked onto the pavement of the parking lot, though whether it was from anxiety or the excessive amount of tequila, I couldn't be sure. I washed out my mouth with some bottled water then laid my head back, breathing slowly and evenly. Though my vision still danced about at times, my mind grew calm as I focused once again on the reason I was there. I started the car and drove off.

Maguire lived up in an area called The Plateau, a tall, narrow hill which rose steeply above Issaquah and the sparkling Lake Sammamish below. The forest was thick and impenetrable around the narrow, two-lane roads I traveled. Schools, lakes, and parks dotted the landscape, and deer foraged unbothered on the lush vegetation along the roadside. This was a community full of large, well-manicured homes. Expensive cars sat idle in the driveways while professional landscapers pruned the already neatly groomed trees and mowed the large parcels of plush, green lawn surrounding them.

As a young mother pushed a baby carriage along the sidewalk, I recalled Jillian asking for a jogging stroller, the one I destroyed in a fit of rage. I stared at the woman. Her face blurred, and Jillian's focused clearly in its place. Anger welled-up inside me again, burgeoning against the confines of my flesh. I looked around me, noting the level of affluence, and remembered the modest home we had tried to buy and the child we were supposed to have. All of it stolen from me through the careless disregard of a greedy woman who, in all likelihood, already had more than I could ever hope for. Tears stung my eyes, but I shook my head and tempered the anger down. I had a mission, and I vowed not to let my drunkenness or the rawness of my emotions turn me from it.

I found Maguire's house nestled in a large expanse of verdant, manicured lawn. A long aggregate driveway, edged with brick and lined with flowering trees and shrubs, snaked through it, while tall pines leaned over the elegant, custom-built home, expensively faced with real stone all the way to the roofline. I passed the house, turned around, and parked a short distance away in front of a pond rimmed with narrow evergreen bushes. From there, I could watch the house and not attract attention.

The only people about were a few landscapers, mowing and trimming for the wealthy homeowners, even in the dismal rain. They didn't seem to notice me skulking in Nick's Grand Cherokee. My head was pounding from the tequila I had downed, something which had been happening more often of late. From my jacket pocket, I pulled out the bottle of Nick's OxyContin I'd lifted from him weeks ago. I only took them now and then when the pain in my head was too much to bear. After waiting twenty minutes for the incessant throbbing to ease, I climbed out of the Jeep in search of the best and least detectable way onto Maguire's property. Luckily, there were no fences, which made it easy to meander from one property to the next. I glanced around to make sure no one was watching me.

The rain showered down in pale grey sheets and soaked me through in minutes. My wet clothes were heavy and uncomfortable, a dead weight that hung from my shoulders. I suddenly felt the endless hours I'd been awake added to the tequila and the pill I'd just taken. My head was spinning much more than I was used to, irritating me further as I walked through the pouring rain, hiding within the bushes and behind trees.

I watched Maguire's house for anyone inside but saw no one. Peering through the draperied windows, it appeared dark and empty. A security system control panel was mounted on the wall near the front entry, unarmed, its single green light holding steady. I walked all around the rear and sides of the house, keeping from the front so as not to be seen by the neighbors. I contemplated breaking in, as much to get out of the rain as to search around for information on Erin's whereabouts, but then a car turned into the long driveway and crept up toward the garage. The wide carriage door opened automatically, and a black, sporty convertible pulled in with Erin behind the wheel.

At the sight of her, months of rage and bitter loneliness blazed to fiery life inside me. It roared in my ears and pushed from behind my eyes, blinding me to everything else but her. I fumed, rooted nervously to the ground in panic as the garage door closed again, cutting me off from her. Blood pumped furiously through my energized body, rushing through my head with the sound of a fighter jet taking off. Adrenaline nauseated my gut as my brain swam with the dizzying effects of the booze and drugs.

This was it, my chance to claim vengeance for everything that had been stolen from me, for everything that ever gave me reason to live. Flashes of Jillian flickered in my head, memories of the day we met, our wedding, the night she told me she was pregnant. They passed through me so quickly, it left me breathless and disoriented. I sucked in large gulps of air in an attempt to still the temblor erupting from within me.

I recalled the last time Jill and I spoke, the fight we had that night, the words she screamed at me: *"You said everything would be okay, but it's not. You told me you wanted a wife, a child, a home. Well, this is part of that, and that woman has taken it away, but you won't even stand up and defend it. You won't defend us."*

Then I saw Jillian on the narrow table, her blood soaked through the sheet pulled over her battered body, and the tube still stuck in her throat. And, in my alcohol-fueled rage, I steeled my resolve, walked up to the front door, and rang the bell.

Chapter Twenty-One

Hannah

The house was a melancholy place, devoid of all souls save my own. I had already dropped Conner off at Beck's new apartment for his first overnight visit. He was staying with his father for the long Memorial Day weekend. I knew this day would be difficult, but I was still surprised by the intensity of it.

Since our separation two weeks prior, Conner had stayed solely with me. Beck had immediately filed papers to regain partial custody, and two days ago won limited visitation until the divorce was worked out in court later in the year. As much as I had come to resent my husband, he was Conner's father, and I had no place coming between them, so I allowed Beck to take him for the holiday.

I'd been crying off and on since watching Conner wave goodbye from the front entrance of Beck's tony apartment building. When I walked into the house, it felt so empty, so lifeless. It was difficult adjusting to Beck's absence. I thought I would be used to it, considering how often he was gone, but back then I always knew he would return. Now, on top of being lonely, I was alone.

I considered getting myself a cat, or better yet, a large dog to keep me company and make me feel safe, probably not very practical since I took Beck's beloved sports car away from him. I had the convertible BMW M6, a virtual two-seater, and Beck got the SUV, a more sensible choice since he was now living in Seattle's Belltown neighborhood. He caved, admitting the Beemer was too flashy for his new digs. I couldn't care less about the stupid car, one was as good as any other as far as I was concerned, but I enjoyed the fact that Beck was annoyed with me for pressing the issue with the lawyers. To be honest, I relished taking his favorite toy from him, at least temporarily, if for no other reason than spite. I tried to be an adult, even gave clemency great effort. I knew I should move forward with my life, but I wasn't quite there. Close, but not yet.

I turned on the TV to keep me company in the quiet, empty house. The rain snapped loudly against the windows in an irregular staccato as the wind picked up, blowing debris against the rear siding and making the tall trees sway and roar. The lights flickered indecisively but remained on. I wiped fresh tears from my face then jumped at the sudden peal of the doorbell. It was surprising since very few people ever traveled the long drive up to the house. The bell chimed again, and I called out, my voice shrill over the din of the storm outside.

"Just a minute!"

I walked to the front door, rested my hand on the lever, and looked through the peephole out of habit. I gasped when I caught sight of the strange man standing a few steps from the door. He was soaked through, even his heavy leather jacket. With both hands stuffed into his pockets, he shifted from one foot to the other, an angry scowl on his haggard face.

I didn't know him, but even if I had, I wouldn't have opened the door. He looked mean and quite incensed with his mouth pressed together in a thin line and his hawkish brow drawn down low over his eyes.

Alarmed, I pulled my hand away, jiggling the handle as I retreated. I backed a couple paces away from the door just as it exploded inward. The jamb splintered, and the door swung open, crashing violently into the wall. It ricocheted off the doorstop with a loud crack and bounced back toward the stranger who held out his hand to stop it.

I screeched in panic and jumped backwards, tripping on the steps directly behind me. The intruder pushed through the open doorway and pursued me to the foot of the stairs. Terrified, I scrambled to run, but he grabbed me from behind and yanked me back by my hair. I collided into his hard chest, crying out in pain. His mouth slid to my ear, his breathing labored and ragged. I smelled the sharp tang of alcohol on his breath. It was tequila, reminiscent of the nights Beck had come home late from business trips.

"Shut up," the man growled as he gave me a vicious shake.

Cold metal slid along the side of my face, and the barrel of a gun dimpled my cheek. I struggled against him. I kicked back at his legs and reached wildly for his arms as his fingers tangled in my hair. Fear crushed me. I screamed again.

"Shut the fuck up!" he roared.

But my fear was too intense. I continued to wail and fight against him.

A sudden pain and bright flash of light exploded through my head as he smashed my temple with the gun. Dazed, I slumped to the floor, his fingers tugging against my scalp before releasing their hold. Waves of nausea rolled through me as I crawled across the foyer. With the waterlogged sound of his footfalls behind me, I turned around and pushed my back against the wall. Warm blood trickled down the side of my head and dripped onto the wood floor. My bare feet smeared through it, sliding ineffectively as they sought purchase. I cringed against the wall with no visible path of escape.

The man reached down and wrapped his cold, wet fingers around my throat. He pulled me up along the wall. The length of his body pressed against me. His face lingered mere inches from mine. I stared at the cold anger that festered in his eyes. They were a startling shade of clear blue, made even more intense by the redness surrounding them. They bored into me with acute hatred of something familiar yet despised, confusing and terrifying me at once.

I opened my mouth to scream then flinched as he raised his hand. A loud snap cracked off the walls as he slapped me across the face. I fell back down to the floor, my blood splattering in abstract patterns across the gleaming hardwood beneath me. I clawed toward the door, an inch at a time, until the man pushed my backside with his booted foot. I sprawled face down. The tip of my nose grazed the small puddle of blood pooling beneath me.

"You're not going anywhere," he warned, "so don't even try. You'll only piss me off more than I already am."

I struggled onto my side and stared up at him. "Please, I haven't done anything. You have no reason to be angry with me."

He leaned down, grabbed me by the arm, and hauled me to my feet. He was calm and quiet as he whispered close to my ear. "I told you to shut up. I won't tell you again. Now, close that fucking door." He shoved me away.

I wiped the blood from my nose with my sleeve, turned for the door, and, with a trembling hand, pushed it shut, as commanded. The man walked up from behind and thrust me face first into the closed door, leaning into me with one knee pressed between my legs. His hand banded around my throat. He shook me hard once and murmured softly in my ear, his tone menacing in its warning.

"Consider this is a reckoning for everything you've stolen from me."

Though his voice was barely a whisper, I recognized a soft burr, an accent I couldn't quite place. It alarmed me and sent chills down my spine. I cried and raised my hands to my face. Warm, sticky blood congealed in my knotted hair, matting it against my head.

"Oh God," I cried.

The man laughed in my ear, jagged and harsh.

"You're calling on God?" he asked in disbelief. Then he snickered. "Forget it. There's no fucking way God can help you now."

With his hand still at my throat, he stepped back. He spun me around to face him and pushed me at arm's length. My back was pressed against the door. His brow was drawn into deep furrows as he peered at me with his fierce eyes, evaluating me somehow. Between the hostility and hatred, I could have sworn I saw a flash of uncertainty, a moment of doubt that clouded his focus. It was brief, and when I blinked it was gone. I shook my head. My tears and blood mingled and fell to the floor.

"What do you want?" I asked, my voice cracking under the pressure of his hand.

He snorted with a brittle smirk that pulled up at the corner of his mouth.

"What does it matter? You can't give back what you've already destroyed." His voice was quiet, but it seethed in a feral anger.

"I...I don't understand. What are you talking about? What have I destroyed? I...I don't even know you! Please—"

My words were cut off as his hold tightened around my throat. I reached both my hands up and grabbed hold of his wrist, trying with all my strength to break his grip. I looked into the man's eyes and saw a change, like something within him had broken, and the light that blazed in anger burned out. It turned into something else altogether. But it was too late for me to decipher what that was. My eyes fluttered shut. Blackness began to close in from all around, as if I were falling in slow motion down into a deep well. I believed it to be the moment of my death. I thought of Conner and what it would do to him if he were to find me, my body beaten and blood smeared across the floor and walls.

Just as my hands fell from his wrists and my knees began to buckle, the man released his grip on my throat. He grabbed my arm and pulled me with him as he surged toward the stairs. His gun nudged sharply against my ribs. I clutched at my throat, gasping for breath as pinpricks of light exploded behind my eyelids. I shook my head to clear my vision while he dragged me up the steps, stumbling, a trail of bloody footprints in our wake. His blows left me stunned, and my lungs labored to recover. I hadn't the strength to fight him as he forced me up the stairs then down the hallway.

He pushed me through the first set of doors, kicking them closed behind him. He released his hold on my arm and shoved me into my bedroom. I fell against the side of my tall poster bed and spun around to face him. My hands gripped the edge of the mattress behind me. The man stepped back and stuffed his weapon into his pocket then removed his soaked leather jacket. I stared at him, terror choking back my questions.

The man sneered at me and kicked off his boots. He pulled his t-shirt over his head then wiped it across his dripping face and hair. I sobbed, unable to tear my eyes away as he stood half naked in front of me. My entire body trembled. Now I knew what he wanted. This was the light that had changed in his eyes. He took a step in my direction. I backed away into the bed, cornered. No way to escape. My heart pounded and skipped. I felt sick. Another step closer.

"Are you afraid?" he asked quietly.

He took one more step. So close. I felt his heat. His expression grew even more intense. He scrutinized me, his hatred once again firm. Unmistakable.

"Tell me you're afraid." His voice was calm, hardly more than a whisper.

I shook my head. "Oh God, no, please don't do this. Please."

Begging didn't move him at all. I clutched my hands, drawn into fists, tight against my chest. I pressed them under my chin in a futile effort to protect myself from what I knew was coming.

His eyes swept over me, sizing me up, then locked onto mine. "You are, aren't you? You're afraid." A shadow of a grin played at the corners of his mouth. "That's good. You should be."

I held my hands up between us, as if that would protect me. "Please, don't. Please."

The hawkish scowl disappeared, and he laughed, but it was bitter and sharp, like a blade ripping across my soul. He sounded like a defeated man with nothing left to lose. A dangerous omen.

"I tried that, too," he said. "Begging, praying to God, pleading for mercy." He dipped his chin, and his brow shot up. "It doesn't help, I can assure you."

I stared at him, trying to discern his meaning. An odd mixture of emotions ran across his face. Uncertainty mingled with hatred, twisting together along his otherwise attractive features. I wondered how someone with such God-given beauty could choose such an ugly course. Surely someone so attractive would have many who offered freely what he was intent on taking from me forcibly.

Was this about hatred? Or was it power and control he sought? Maybe revenge as he implied? But for what? I'd done nothing. Could this be about Beck? Had he crossed the wrong person? Was this man a jealous husband? A jilted lover? His motive was completely lost on me.

"Why are you doing this?" I asked, my voice a choked squeak.

His brow furrowed as he bore down on me with his furious eyes. "Because I want *you* to feel a small fraction of the fear and pain you caused my wife—my *pregnant* wife—right before she died."

I stood up straighter, shocked. "*What?* That's insane. I don't know what you're talking about. I haven't done *anything* to *anyone!*"

His eyes widened in surprise for the briefest moment. Then they narrowed as he looked me up and down, appraising me. "How dare you? How dare you deny what you've done. You couldn't stop lying if your life depended on it."

"Because I didn't do anything! You've got your facts all wrong!"

His seethed through gnashed teeth. "*You miserable bitch!* You target innocent people, steal from them, destroy their dreams, mangle their lives. And for what? For *money? You're a pathetic whore!"*

I gasped at his accusations. "You're crazy. I've done nothing. *Nothing!* Now get the *hell out of here!"*

"I'm not going anywhere until you admit what you've done." He latched onto my throat with both hands, his expression mad with fury. "Say it. You killed my wife! *You murdered my child! Say it! Say it!"*

He dodged is head from side to side, bobbing and weaving as I clawed at his face. Even as blackness started to close in, my vision turned red, and my rage boiled over.

"Fuck you *and* your wife!" I croaked.

He jolted to a stop, his hands falling from my throat. He grabbed me by the arms and hurled me onto the bed. I kicked and twisted to get away, but he climbed on top of me. His knee wedged between my legs. He reached up under my dress and tore my underwear away.

"No, no, please! I'm sorry, *I'm sorry!* I don't know her, I swear! I don't know your wife! Please! *Listen to me! I don't know her! Please! Please!"*

My throat burned raw with fiery tendrils lacing through to my ears. I struggled against him with every ounce of energy I had. But his weight had me pinned. His other knee forced my legs apart. He fumbled with his jeans. Pushed them aside. I pounded my hands against him. Thrashed his shoulders and head. My nails raked across his flesh. He grabbed both my wrists. Pinned them above my head in one hand.

I was lost, completely under his control. I cried. Shook my head against the bed. My eyes shut tight. His hand grappled between my thighs. This was it. I knew what was coming. Yet I was powerless to stop it. I sobbed even harder.

His chest rose up as he readied himself. "Open your fucking eyes!" he yelled.

I obeyed. "Please, you can't do this! You can't!"

"You have to pay for what you've done," he roared, his face twisted in hatred.

My mind raced, searching for a way out, hunting for some way to connect with this man, to make him see me as human, to show me some small mercy. *Think, think!*

His wife. He was doing this for her, because she had died. She was pregnant. He lost them both, his wife and his baby! That was it. He had to see me as a mother, just like his wife!

"Please," I begged, "I have a child, a son! This will destroy him!" My body quaked with wracking sobs as I rocked my head from side to side. He was but a moment away from destroying me. "Please, please, he's just a boy. He won't survive this! It will kill him! You can't do this." Staring into his rage-filled eyes, I raised my head off the bed and screamed. "*I'm his mother!*"

The man startled as if physically shocked. He grew completely still. The rage blazing in his eyes melted away, replaced by what looked like...like...horror. He loosened his grip around my wrists then let go altogether, his hands snapping back to his chest as if touching my flesh had scorched him.

I dropped my head to the mattress and stared up at him through a thick film of tears. I pulled my hands in and wiped at my eyes with trembling fingers.

The man remained kneeling above me, just staring back, aghast, silent. His mouth was open, and his horrified eyes swept over me. He sucked in a large breath of air and pushed away with disgust tightening his brow.

"Oh God," he gasped with both palms pressed flat against the top of his head. "Oh my God! No, no..." He shook his head, and although he closed his eyes tight, tears began to escape, leaving glistening trails over the angular lines of his face.

I was struck dumb as *he* sobbed. Him. The intruder. *What the hell!*

"Oh God," he choked again. He yanked up on his jeans and pulled away. With the tall corner post at the foot of the bed behind him, he leaned back with his eyes still closed. He pressed a clenched fist against his mouth as if he were going to be sick.

"Oh God, Jillian," he cried, both hands now covering his face. "Please, forgive me. *Please...*"

He pulled one leg up and wrapped an arm around it. He laid his forehead down upon his knee, covered the top of his head with his hand, and wept as he rocked back and forth, crying and mumbling to himself. Then with a jolt that shook the bed, he slammed himself twice in the head with his fist and swore, "Fuck! *Fuck!*"

I backed away from him as far as I could, sliding onto my side and rolling up into a ball. Though relieved he had called off his attack, I feared the strange, erratic nature of the man in front of me. I cried noiselessly as I studied him, unsure of what to do.

My eyes swept back and forth between him and the door. I crept closer to the edge of the bed, painstakingly slow, so he wouldn't feel me. *Am I strong enough to make a run for it?* Every inch of me quivered in fear, exhausted from the battle. *This might be my only chance. Should I try to escape? Or will he fly into another rage? Try to hurt me? Rape me? Maybe even kill me? Oh God, what should I do?* I slid another inch closer, careful, cautious, then another, and another, my eyes pinned on the door. Until I felt him move.

He raised his head and, with his bloodshot eyes, looked over at me. He shook his head, his expression tortured with what looked like remorse and unfathomable regret.

"I'm...sorry. I didn't... I'm so sorry," he sobbed then let his head fall back onto his knee. He weaved his fingers through his hair and pulled it tight into both fists.

I didn't get it. I couldn't understand him at all. This angry man, filled with malice and violent intentions as he intruded into my world, now shook with contrition and sorrow? *Are you kidding me?* It was unreal. I was stunned and bewildered by his sudden transformation, and wondered the reason behind it. If he was truly sorry, he wouldn't hurt me again, would he? I slowly pulled myself up into a sitting position with my knees pulled in tight against my chest. I stared at him for a long moment as I worked up the courage to speak. I was terrified of provoking him, of having him lash out and continue where he had left off. But I needed to know the truth, to know why he had chosen me, what connection he thought we shared.

"Who...is...your wife?" I stammered.

His head snapped up, almost combatively, but though I flinched, I didn't back down. I was too angry.

"You answer me, godammit. *Who is your wife?*" I was surprised by the venom in my own voice. I screamed the words at him, my rage somehow outmaneuvering my fear. Pretty stupid, but then I never was very smart when I got angry.

He regarded me for a silent stretch of time, just as I had done him, with his jaw clenched tight. Then he leaned forward, his eyes narrowed in contempt. "Jillian Demetrio," he spat.

Confused, I shook my head. "I don't know that name. I've never heard it before. How could you do that to me? I don't know you. And I don't know your wife!"

He leaned forward, bent onto his knee, and grabbed me by my arms, his nose mere inches from mine and his eyes flitting back and forth. "That's bullshit! You knew her, Erin, all too well. You stole her identity, for God's sake! You took her life. *You killed my child!*"

He pushed me away in disgust and returned to the foot of the bed, his finger pointing at me in both accusation and warning: *Stay away, or else*…he seemed to say. His teeth gnashed together and his body trembled, barely under control.

My eyes widened as I fell back against the headboard. I gasped at the mention of that name, when it registered in my head.

Erin, he had said. *Oh my God. Erin.*

"What?" I squealed. "Did…did you just…call me…Erin?" I shook my head. "No. No, I'm… I'm not Erin. No, uh-uh." Though his lips pursed in an angry grimace, I pressed on. "Why? Why would you call me that? Erin who? You tell me her last name! Erin who? You tell me! *Tell me!*" I sprang at him, my hands clawing at his face and raking across his bare shoulders.

He grabbed my wrists and shook me. "You sick, twisted bitch!" He pushed me back hard into the headboard and pointed at me again. "We both know exactly *who* and *what* you are, *Ms.* Anderson. A filthy leech. A lying murderer!" He swung his fist wide and smashed it against the corner bedpost.

I pinned my hands to my ears, closed my eyes, and shook my head. "No, no, no! This is not happening. It's not happening." I looked back at the man. "Why? Why would you think that? I'm not Erin Anderson." I pressed my palm to my chest. "My name is Hannah. Hannah Maguire." Then I motioned toward the door." That…that…*whore*…is my husband's mistress!"

At first he looked at me in shock, as if I had sprouted a second head, but it quickly turned to anger. He leaned forward with that finger poking near my face. "Don't give me that shit!"

I stupidly batted his hand away. "No, *you* listen to *me*! I am *not* Erin Anderson. My name is Hannah Maguire. Hannah Maguire! That miserable whore, she's… She's having an affair with my husband."

"You lying bitch! You'd say anything to save to your pathetic neck. But you did it. You killed my wife. You're responsible for that accident. If you hadn't provoked her, she never would have pursued you. She's dead because of you, and you know it! Godammit!" For a brief moment, his rage-filled face crumpled into despair. "She was pregnant. Did you know that? Do you even care? You killed my child. *You killed them both!*" His face glowed a purplish red, and his whole body shook in outrage.

I leaned back with my mouth open. This man was completely mad.

"What are you talking about? You're insane! I told you. My name is Hannah Maguire. But I know her. I know who that woman is. She's having an affair with my husband. I had them followed. By a private investigator. And I have photographs to prove it."

He stilled himself and stared at me, contemplating my words, wondering about the possibility of his error. He grew worried. I saw it in his eyes, clear as day, the way his brow knitted together, deep chevrons that scored above the bridge of his nose. Then a V bulged down the center of his forehead, its apex terminating in the furrow. He lunged forward and tried to seize me again, but I scrambled across the blood-stained bed and fell to the floor.

"You're a lying bitch," he swore, maneuvering after me.

I crouched on the floor, cornered between the bed, the wall, and the man as he stood above me. I pushed away as far as possible and kicked out at him when he knelt down in front of me.

"No! Get away from me! Don't you ever touch me again!"

He rocked back and ran his fingers through his hair over and over, considering me with both apprehension and utter disbelief. At that moment, he appeared nearly as intimidated by me as I was by him.

"I'm *not* lying," I said, "I swear. You've mistaken me for someone else. You've got the wrong woman." I met his intense stare with one of my own.

His mouth hung slack. He knelt silently, his hands balling into fists atop his thighs.

"I...I don't understand. I...I saw you there. At that spa. You were having an argument with that prick, Maguire. And then I saw you again later in the parking lot with that waitress. You showed her a picture or something. I followed you all the way to Oakland. To the airport. I saw you *both* there. You *and* Maguire." He pointed his finger at me again and seethed through clenched teeth. "I *saw* you there! I *know* it was you!"

And then it dawned on me as I recalled that day, two weeks before, when I visited the spa down in Napa. He must have been watching me. He must have been watching us both—me and Erin—and thought we were one and the same. *Oh God!*

I shook my head. "No! I mean... Yes. That *was* me in the parking lot *and* at the airport, but you saw Erin at the restaurant. She had the fight with Beck. Not me. We look very similar, I know, but... That was Erin you saw in the restaurant. Not me. You've made a stupid, foolish mistake." Tears rolled down my cheeks again. "You were stalking the wrong woman, you goddamn bastard!"

He sprang back up onto his feet, and looked down at me, his eyes wild and panicked.

"Oh fuck, no!" He shook his head. "No, no, no, no, no. That...that can't be right."

He paced the small space between us, back and forth, over and over, mumbling to himself. Then all of a sudden, he stopped and peered back down at me. The same look of remorse and regret washed over him once more, but this time it was followed by fear. Acute and irrefutable.

"Oh my God!" he said as he stepped back from me, both hands resting atop his head. "Oh God, what have I done?"

He bent down and crouched on the balls of his feet then raked his hands across his face. With his chin tilted upward, he closed his eyes and whispered.

"What have I done?"

Chapter Twenty-Two

Tyler

I paced the floor around me, unable—perhaps unwilling—to process the reality of what I had just done—what I *almost* did—the severity of the mistake I had made, and the dire consequences that now faced me, my brother, and the wounded woman cowering in fear and humiliation in the corner. The reality was that through the hazy cloud of alcohol and pills, I believed delivering a degrading punishment would somehow empower me, fulfill my need for revenge, and expunge the hate, grief, and rage that filled me. I thought my mind might be rewarded with a sense of balance, my soul a thread of justice, and my heart a measure of peace.

But I despised myself for the act. Though I knew the woman must hate me with every fiber of her being, to the very core of her soul, I hated myself more. I was not the man I thought I was. The true measure of a man reveals itself during the darkest moments, and I had proven false to the man I always believed myself to be, to the man Jillian believed me to be. The fact that I had not followed all the way through didn't diminish the horror of it. I could not have sunk any lower had I taken a human life with my bare hands. *God, how did I get here? How could I have even thought of doing such a despicable thing?* I was an abomination, a monster far worse than Erin Anderson had ever been.

Even if I had dispatched the penalty upon Erin, rather than this woman, it still would not have accomplished what I sought. I could see that now, that my inability to accept my own guilt had robbed me of my humanity. And now, the actuality of my error in both judgment and reason lay broken and beaten at my feet. Whoever said vengeance is sweet was wrong. It's the thought of vengeance—filtered through memories that haunt and torment—that is sweet. Not the act itself. The act is vile and bitter. I felt physically ill as it filled me, as I realized what I had almost done, what I had, in fact, already done, the pain, fear, and humiliation I had caused.

I studied the woman as she sobbed on the floor, blood smeared and crusted along the side of her face. She stared at me with haunted eyes that bore through me with rage, hatred, and despair. I could relate. I had felt the same way and now abhorred that I was the source of all three. The man I once was wanted to reach out and comfort her, but I knew all I would accomplish would be to further terrorize her. Her dress was ripped, nearly torn from her body, and her legs were exposed and already showing signs of bruises. As I took a step closer, she raised her chin, but still pressed herself deeper into the corner.

"You keep back!" she screamed. "Stay away from me!"

"Okay, okay, I'm sorry. Just…calm down, all right? I won't hurt you, not any more." I made the promise, but realized how hollow my words must sound to her. I grabbed the blanket from the bed and held it out to her. "Here, take this. Cover yourself up. Please."

Instead of moving closer and scaring her further, I tossed the blanket at her. The blood on my hands flashed before me like a beacon at twilight. I held my hands up in front of my face, repulsed. I would have wiped the blood onto my shirt had I not been naked from the waist up. I turned, hunting for my discarded clothing, and put my t-shirt back on, though it, too, was stained. I pulled on my wet jacket and zipped it to cover the evidence beneath. A trembling sigh of relief escaped my lips, but I could not hide the true testament of my crime. With slow caution, I approached the woman again. Her frightened eyes followed me, round as saucers.

I knelt down in front of her, five feet away. "I'm sorry, your name?" I asked. "What did you say your name was?"

She sniffled. "Hannah...Maguire," she replied between hiccups. She wiped her eyes and nose with the blanket now secured tightly around her.

I offered her a feeble smile and gnawed on my lip. "Right. Hannah. Okay, um...good. That's good." I stared at her and sighed, unsure of the best way to proceed. "Look, Hannah, I... There are no words... I don't even...know what to say... What I've done...what I tried to do, it's...it's unforgivable, I know." I bowed my head, unable to look her in the eye any longer. "I can't even begin to explain...why I...what would make me... I have nothing that would help you understand. I don't understand it myself. I don't know where that came from, even with everything that's happened. I...I don't know what to say. I am so very, very sorry."

I looked back at her, hoping my regret was as plainly written on my face as it was seared into my heart. My throat constricted with the effort it took not to allow the sorrow and shame to overwhelm me. But I had to address her. The situation had become unbelievably dire. There was more at stake now than ever.

"Okay, so, um…Hannah…you mentioned that you had a private investigator following your husband, that you had pictures, right? May I see them, please? Whatever you have on the two of them together. I need to be absolutely sure. If you could get them for me, please."

She continued to glare at me silently from the floor.

"Where are they?" I requested more urgently.

She startled and poked a hand out from beneath the blanket, pointing to the room behind me. "They're…in the…closet. Back there…through…the bathroom."

"Right. Okay, good. That's…that's good. Um…would you get them for me, please?"

Again, she sat silently, not moving to get up or respond in any way.

"Please, Hannah, this is more important than you could possibly know."

She narrowed her eyes and stood up slowly, one hand pressed against her temple as she winced in pain. Her bare foot caught the edge of the blanket, and she stumbled forward. Without thinking, I reached out to steady her, but she lurched up against the wall, shrieking at me, her eyes wide with fear.

"No! Get away! Don't touch me!"

I pulled back and retreated a few steps with my hands raised. "Sorry! I won't hurt you. I promise. I won't hurt you." I stepped back farther, allowing her room to pass.

With her back turned away, she sidestepped around me, never once letting her eyes slip from mine. She retreated in reverse, each step slow and measured, all the way into and through the master bathroom where she stopped in the doorway of a large walk-in closet. Hannah spun around and disappeared into the darkness.

I followed her to the closet and flipped on the light, startling her again. She jumped and sucked in a sharp breath. I stopped in my tracks and raised my hands.

"It's okay. Take it easy." I even tried to smile, but it was a miserable attempt. "Now…if you could…the pictures, please."

She pulled a file folder out of a built-in dresser drawer. The file trembled as she held it out to me. I looked her in the eye, trying to reassure her that I meant no further harm. Without taking a step closer, I stretched forward and took the folder then gestured for her to return to the bathroom.

"Please, Hannah, go sit down."

She shook her head. "No way. I'm not going anywhere near you. You move first."

I chewed on my lip then said, "Okay, that's fair." With my eyes glued to hers, I backed out of closet and into the bathroom, stopping shy of the main door. "Okay, I'm all the way out here. It's your turn."

Her worried face eased through the open closet door and turned toward me.

"Good enough?" I asked.

She nodded, but only slightly.

"All right then. Come on out and have a seat, please." I gestured toward the large jetted tub.

She side-stepped across the carpeted bathroom floor, eyeing me warily every inch of the way. Her face screwed up as she lowered herself down along the edge. I winced at her display of pain, disgusted with myself. I dropped her gaze and lowered my head, my eyes pinned to the floor in shame.

I opened the file she'd given me and pored over the material in the folder. I read through a report prepared by the man she had hired. The descriptions noted numbered photographs which I studied intently. The people in the photographs were identified as Beckham Steven Maguire of Sammamish, Washington, age thirty-eight, and Erin Elizabeth Anderson of Petaluma, California, age twenty-four.

The pictures showed the two of them in a variety of locations. I stared at the images of Erin. There was no doubt that Hannah and Erin bore an uncanny resemblance, but with Hannah sitting so close, there was also no mistaking the differences. Erin was probably ten years younger than Hannah. Holding the evidence in front of me, I don't know how I could have made such a monumental error, even as drunk as I was. The magnitude of my mistake was astounding and crushed me anew.

"Oh my God," I whispered to myself. I was still looking them over them when I walked over to confront Hannah. Sighing, I shook my head and looked into her worried eyes. "Hannah, besides the obvious, this evidence provides me with a substantial problem." I wasn't sure how to explain the gravity of the situation and what my options were, especially without scaring the life out of her. "I've made a terrible—"

We both jumped when my mobile phone rang from inside my pocket. I kept my eyes on Hannah as I dug for it, glancing at the screen before I answered.

"Shit," I swore quietly to myself. I turned away and accepted the call. "Nick?"

"Ty, where the fuck are you? When I woke up, you were gone. And so was my gun. Did you take it?"

"Yes, Nick, I did. I'm sorry, but—"

"Ty, please tell me you didn't go up to Maguire's on your own."

"Yes, I did. Look, Nick, we have a problem." I looked back over my shoulder at Hannah. "A rather significant one. And I'm not quite sure what to do about it."

"Oh God, Ty, you didn't kill her, did you?"

"God, no. I did not kill her."

"Well, what is it then?"

"Well, um, there's...been a...mistake."

"A mistake? What does that mean, a mistake? What happened?"

"I don't have time to explain it right now. I'm kind of...busy. I'll tell you everything when I get back."

"No, Ty, I want to know what you're talking about. What mistake?"

"All right, Nick, please, listen carefully. I need you to call Alexi and tell him that I'll be delayed. Do *not* say anything else. Just tell him I'll be a few days longer than expected. Make up some excuse. Anything. I don't care. Just get him to extend the deadline, all right? I've got to figure all this out before I talk to him again myself."

"What is going on? You're scaring me, Tyler. You do *not* want to piss Alexi off, believe me. He doesn't trust you as it is. I'm sure he's having you followed, you know, to keep an eye on things, in case there's a problem. If you want, I can get some of the guys over there. Just one call to Alexi and—"

"No, Nick! Don't you say a goddamn thing. They can't come here! Not now!"

"Why not, Ty? What the hell is going on?"

"Nick, please just...just do as I ask, all right? I'll be there as soon as I can. We'll talk then. Don't worry about anything just yet, okay?"

Nick sighed impatiently. "Okay, but you better hurry."

I ended the call and turned back to Hannah who was fidgeting in her seat alongside the tub. What Nick had said about Alexi's men concerned me. I couldn't risk having them involved until I mediated a new arrangement with Alexi, one that involved only the repayment of funds. Dmitri had already been paid; his client was waiting. If they thought I was even slightly reluctant to turn the girl over to them, they would simply eliminate me, seize Hannah, and deliver her themselves. They wouldn't care who she was. Any girl would do. And with me out of the way, they wouldn't have to relinquish Nick either. They'd both be slaves to the Russians.

My God, what a mess!

"Hannah, I need to get you out of here...right away, okay?"

She shook her head. "No way. I'm not going anywhere with you. Just leave, please."

"Look, I know you don't understand. You're scared. You're hurt and angry. I get that but...I can't explain everything to you right now. It's urgent that we leave immediately, please."

"Why in God's name would I leave my home with *you*? I don't know you, and after what you've done..." She shook her head. "You're insane! Just get the hell out and leave me alone, please. I won't tell anyone what happened, I swear."

Hannah became agitated, alarmed by my urgency. As she stood up, a new course of tears erupted. She wiped at them with the blanket, smearing the dried blood crusted along the side of her face into streaks. I groaned inwardly as I scanned her appearance from head to toe, the blood and bruises, her ruined clothing. I grew more anxious by the minute. I couldn't take her out looking like that and risk drawing unwanted attention, and I didn't have time to argue with her.

"Find some comfortable clothing and change," I ordered. "Wash up first, you're covered in blood. Then pack a change of clothes and whatever personal items you might need over the next few days." I took a step closer. "We're leaving. Now."

"No, forget it. I'm not going anywhere with you." She stood her ground, her chin raised.

I reached into the pocket for Nick's gun. "Do as I ask, Hannah."

She hopped back and nearly fell into the tub. I reacted and grabbed her by the arms to steady her. She yelped out in fright and twisted her arms away, but I held firm though I tried my best not to hurt her. Fear swam in her eyes, and I lamented my harsh tone. I softened my voice as I eased her down onto the edge of the tub.

"Sit down, Hannah, please."

She squirmed and tried to pull herself free. I released my grip, reached for the washcloth on the towel rack, and dampened it under running water, squeezing out the excess. I crouched in front of her and pressed the cloth into her clenched hand. She stared at me through her fear, her stubborn chin thrust forward and her lips pursed in anger. I stared back, offering her my apologies, my sorrow, my remorse. Tears welled up, but I wiped them away before they could spill over. My throat tightened as I searched for the right words.

"I know what you must be thinking and feeling, Hannah, at least I can guess, but...I'm not the monster you think I am. Not really." I bowed my head once before finding the courage to look back up. "My wife, Jillian, she was pregnant. She died in a car crash, a preventable one caused by Erin Anderson and her reckless disregard. Since then, I've been driven to madness...with grief and anger. With loneliness. There's no excuse for what I've done, for what I...almost did. I realize that. Believe me, if I could take it all back, I would, but...now... Well, now I have no other choice than to rectify this."

"You can't rectify this!" she urged, her fist striking hard against her leg.

"I have to at least try."

"It won't matter what you do! You can't fix this. And you can't fix what you've done to *me!*"

"Perhaps...but I still need to try." I was uncomfortable looking into her eyes for very long. I softened my voice. "Now please, clean up, change, and gather your things quickly."

She took a ragged breath as I stood up and towered over her. As I turned to walk away, she released it. I looked back over my shoulder as she stood up from the tub.

"No. I won't do it." She gave me nervous shake of her head, but stood there unwavering. "Look, I'm...sorry for your loss and all. I can only imagine how...difficult it must be, but...you're crazy if you think I'm going anywhere with you. You should just leave. I won't say anything to anyone, I swear. I won't tell a soul, if you would just leave. Please. Just leave."

She stood bravely in front of me, clutching the damp rag and blanket beneath her chin. I walked up to face her, determined to remove her from further jeopardy no matter what it took.

"Hannah, I'm afraid this isn't voluntary. If I have to drag you out of here forcibly, I will, but I think you would be more comfortable in the long run with a few of your own things, so I strongly suggest you gather them. Now."

Still, she remained rooted to the floor, unwilling to cooperate. I didn't want to frighten her any further, but I needed her to understand that this was serious, that I didn't have time or the luxury of tolerating defiance in the face of danger. I closed the distance between us, grabbed her by the arm, and pulled her back into the closet. I shoved her toward the long rack of clothing and released her.

"I'm not going to ask you again. Change and gather your things. And wash the blood from your face. Do it now, or I promise, you will not like the alternative."

She studied me with narrowed eyes, her teeth clenched and visible between parted lips. She snorted a belligerent huff and reached for her overnight bag, never breaking her gaze on me.

"A little privacy," she snapped.

With a tip of my head, I left the bathroom. I paced the bedroom floor and checked my watch every sixty seconds. After five minutes had scraped by, I called out, "Come on, we have to hurry."

I heard her mumble a reply through the wall, and not a very nice one by the tone, but I couldn't blame her. I hurried her along one more time, but she kept silent, though I could hear the water running in the sink. When she emerged after another five long minutes, her appearance clean of blood and a packed bag in hand, she stood before me, trying valiantly to appear courageous, but I saw the lingering fear as she trembled.

"I'm not going along with this willingly," she explained, "but if you expect any cooperation from me whatsoever, I need some kind of explanation as to why it is so important, so urgent for me to leave with you. You owe me at least that much."

I acknowledged the fairness of her request with a nod. "I agree, but...it won't matter. You'll never understand."

"Let me be the judge of that."

"Right. Okay, um...well... I owe someone. In trade, that is. You might call it a debt, of sorts, and a rather large one, at that. And you—or Erin rather—were to be the payment of that debt, what I was trading. Now, with the current circumstances such as they are, I can't pay my end with the terms as they were agreed upon. But I assure you, my *friend* will not look favorably on this, and as he likely has associates nearby, he will certainly try to intervene to ensure repayment. At any cost.

"Hannah, this man, he's violent and extremely dangerous. Don't give me that look. I know what you're thinking. But what I've done, as bad as it was, is nothing compared to what this man will do should he get his hands on you. My brother and I have both experienced his abuse first hand. He holds absolutely no regard for human life whatsoever. Therefore, I can't guarantee your freedom, let alone your safety, if I were to leave you here alone. I need time to renegotiate a new settlement, one that doesn't include you, or anyone else for that matter. Though, at the moment, you might disagree, I am not the scariest monster out there. Not by half. And I don't want you further abused as an innocent caught up in my mistake. I can't undo what I've already done, but at this point, I have to try for a better outcome. You see my predicament, Hannah? This is very serious."

She nodded, but barely. "So then…what exactly were you trading me for?" she asked.

I sighed. "My brother, his freedom, maybe even his life."

With her chin now tucked close to her chest, she looked frightened as she stood before me, mulling over my explanation. She nodded again, like it somehow made sense to her.

"Tell me your name," she ordered.

"Hannah, we don't have time for—"

"We have time for your goddamn name. Now tell me."

"It's Tyler. Tyler Karras."

"Tyler?"

"Yes, but my friends call me Ty."

She narrowed her eyes again and tilted her head to the side.

"Hmm. So tell me…*Tyler*," she said, emphasizing the use of my full name, "how did you plan on using me—or Erin rather—in trade, as repayment for your debt? Because your explanation makes absolutely no sense. You cannot trade one person to pay for another."

She contemplated me while waiting for my response. She might be ignorant of the terrible things that happened in this world, but then again, I had been, too, at least before all this started. Now I had wisdom I wish I'd never gained. I hoped I could keep that from her, as well. But she wasn't making it easy. I placed my hands on my hips and sighed.

"That's a long story, and we don't have the time at the moment. So let's just say that I've made a serious mistake. Now, let's get out of here. I'll try to explain it all to you later. I promise."

"And why should I trust you?"

I paused and looked hard into her eyes. "Because right now, I'm the only one standing between you and certain harm. Good enough reason for you?"

She peered at me suspiciously. "For now."

Since she seemed to have no other questions, I picked up the folder containing the investigator's report and motioned for Hannah to lead the way. She gasped as she limped downstairs, scanning the horrific scene of her blood spread across the carpeted steps and hardwood floor of the foyer.

"Shit!" I cursed again. I took Hannah's arm above the elbow, felt her muscles tighten beneath my grip, and led her through the gore. "Where are your car keys and your purse?" I asked, glancing back over my shoulder at the unsettling mess.

Hannah directed me over to the built-in kitchen desk. I shoved her purse into her arms and grabbed the car keys.

"Give me your phone," I demanded. She rooted through her purse then handed it to me. I slipped it into my jacket pocket. "Where's the garage?"

Hannah silently indicated the way. She was spooked by all the blood, her face as grey as the stormy sky.

"I'm sorry, Hannah, but we need to take your car. I have my brother's and they'll recognize it for sure. No one knows about you, at least not yet, so they won't know your car. It'll be safer, for now anyway." I opened the door to the garage and stopped in my tracks. "Brilliant. You couldn't drive something a little less flashy?"

She cracked a slight smile, brittle as it was, then shook her hair from her face as she raised her chin. "It's Beck's. His pride and joy. I thought a little retribution was in order."

I matched her weak grin with one of my own. "Right. Good for you. And by the way...your husband? He's a real prick."

She threw me hard look. "Hmm. What is it they say? It takes one to know one?" Her mouth twisted and she turned back away.

I pressed my lips together and sighed. "Throw your stuff in the back. I'll drive."

Chapter Twenty-Three

Tyler

The main thoroughfare through Hannah's neighborhood was lined with expensive custom-built houses, each dressed to perfection with lush landscaping. Dream homes by any standard. Certainly by mine.

"Nice neighborhood," I commented, mentally tabulating the astronomical cost of such gentrified living.

"Hmm, yes...very nice," Hannah said absently as she stared out the windshield.

I glanced in her direction and raised my brow, questioning her noticeable bitterness. She glanced back with a dismissive shrug.

"I hate it here." Her eyes swept over me. "Now more than ever." She turned away and stared out her side window.

"Right." I shifted in my seat and tried to ignore her remark. "So, why is that? That you hate it here? I mean, most people would give their right arm to live in a place like this."

She folded her arms over her chest with a loud sigh. "You know, all things considered, I'm really not up for polite chit chat, so...if you don't mind..."

"Hey, I'm sorry. I know this is uncomfortable for you. It is for me, as well, but…we're going to be spending a great deal of time together over the next few days."

"So?" she said as she turned back to me. "What's your point?"

"So…we might as well make the best of it."

She chuckled, but it was bitter. "The best of it? Really? Are you kidding me? How the hell am I supposed to make the best of *this*?" She held her hands out.

"Well, you might start by being civil."

She barked another sarcastic laugh. "Civil? You're telling *me* to be civil? The man who nearly *raped* me?"

"But I didn't. Did I?"

"Only because I stopped you."

"You couldn't have stopped me if I was truly intent on doing it. I stopped myself."

"Because *I* made you see reason! If I had just laid there and taken it, you would have done it. Admit it. You were completely out of control."

My knuckles turned white as I gripped the wheel. But she was right; I was out of control. I had no excuse. Though I'd like to think I would have stopped on my own, I could never be certain of that. The thought of how close I had come to destroying us both was devastating. But that was difficult to admit out loud. I sighed instead.

"I am deeply ashamed of what I've done, but…you know I thought you were someone else."

"Oh, well, there's an excuse."

"All right, Hannah, I get it, I'm sorry. It's just… Look, my point is, ignoring each other or arguing all the time, it's only going to make things even more difficult than they already are. I'm only trying to make this, I don't know, not so…uncomfortable. It's not like I expect us to be friends or anything, but—"

"Oh gee, you think?"

"…but a little tolerance would be nice," I finished.

"Yeah, that's easy for you to say."

"None of this is easy for me! I realize my mistake—"

"Mistake? Is that all this is to you? A mistake?"

"No, that's not what I—"

"Like something you can simply apologize for and move on?"

"Oh for God's sake, Hannah, I'm sorry. I misspoke. What I meant was—"

"'*Oh, ma'am, I'm so deeply sorry I kicked your door down. I didn't mean to smash you in the face with a gun. And oh, that part where I almost raped you? My bad. It was all a big mistake.*' That what you meant?"

"Would you stop? Please. Give me one moment to think."

"Oh, so *now* you want to think."

"Godammit! Can't you see I'm trying here?. I know I don't deserve it, but just…bear with me; cut me a little slack, okay?"

She shook her head and turned away, holding silent for long pause. "Fine. Whatever."

I sighed and waited a moment then asked again. "So, tell me. Why do you hate it here?"

She peered back at me with narrowed eyes. "Why are so interested?"

I shrugged. "I don't know. I guess I find it hard to understand what you could possibly dislike about living in a place like this. It's what most people aspire to in your country, isn't it?"

"*My* country?"

"Well, anywhere, really. Everywhere. But here more than anywhere else, I suppose. So, what is it about this place? I'm just curious, because my wife would have given anything to live here or at least a place like this anyway."

She pondered her answer for a minute. "Yes...well...try as I might, I just don't seem to...fit in here. I wish I'd never left my little house back home." She kept her face turned away, disregarding me entirely.

"Back home? And where would that be?"

She sighed again. "Anywhere but here," she said under her breath, but then reconsidered. She turned to look out the windshield. "We moved up here from the Bay Area. All right? Satisfied?"

I smiled. "I live in The City...San Francisco. I've always loved it there. At least, I used to. Before." My smile faded away.

She continued to ignore me. The silence lingered uncomfortably between us. It was like being stuck in a crowded elevator with a bunch of strangers, on a slow crawl up a tall building, waiting for the door to open. Her fingers tapped restlessly against her knees, and she kept eyeing the central door lock mounted in the center of the dash. I worried she might try to jump out. I kept my left hand over the driver door locks, just in case. I searched for things to talk about, hoping it would ease the tension which seemed to swell as the seconds ticked by.

"You know, I don't think you should change who you are just because you've changed your address," I reasoned out loud.

"Is that so? Hmm. Strange, my husband doesn't agree. But then he was hardly ever home." Again, she eyed me with a contemptuous glare.

I focused back on the road, contemplating her character. She was not what I expected. Money obviously hadn't bought her any happiness. The silence settled in again, growing nearly unbearable as we both stared out onto the road before us. Five, six, seven quiet minutes ticked by, each one more unbearable than the one before

"Where are we going?" she asked, her mood a bit calmer and her posture more relaxed.

"Down the hill, off The Plateau. I have a room at a motel near the freeway. I need to see my brother."

"Your brother? Is that who you were talking to on the phone?"

"Yes, it was."

"Hmm, and what is he going to think when you tell him about me, I mean...that I'm not Erin?" Hannah looked at me with concern creasing her forehead.

I turned back to her again. Worry nagging at me, as well. "I don't know. I need to explain everything to him. He'll understand, I think." I faced the road. "I hope."

As I said the words, my stomach knotted up. Neither one of them would understand the quandary I now found myself in. I'd made the situation impossibly dangerous for us all. Dmitri would hunt us all down mercilessly. Nick, pleading ignorance, might be able to extricate himself, but I doubt he would step aside while Dmitri dealt with me.

And Hannah. God, when I thought about what would become of her, it made me sick inside. Of course, the obvious fix would be to find Erin and turn her over to them, but after all the pain and humiliation I'd caused Hannah, I found that I'd lost my appetite for that kind of revenge, or any kind, actually. I recognized the immoral road my bitterness had led me down, and I was hard-pressed to identify the man I once was within the villain I had become.

I reasoned the alcohol had clouded my judgment, but in reality, all it really did was dull my pain, making it impossible to empathize with the misery my actions would undoubtedly cause. I was no longer the man Jillian had loved and married. I was appalled at how low I had sunk as I drowned my grief in booze, malevolence pulling me down like an anchor.

I pulled into the motel lot and parked Hannah's BMW in front of our room. I fully expected Nick to throw the door open and greet me with anxious questions. That he didn't, concerned me.

"Grab your stuff," I instructed Hannah.

I was tense and nervous, in turn making Hannah wary. I unlocked the motel room door and slowly pushed it open.

"Nick?" I called out as I surveyed the empty room. I walked back to the bathroom and opened the door wide. "Nick?" I felt a moment of dread press down on me. I tried to shake it off, hoping he had simply left to get something to eat.

"He's not here," I explained. "He knew I'd be returning, so I'm sure he'll be back soon."

Hannah scanned the room from the doorway. Her face screwed up in disgust as she spied the beer and alcohol bottles strewn about. She looked up at me, her forehead lined with worry.

"Sorry for the mess," I said.

Embarrassed, I collected the bottles and threw them in the waste basket. The room fell into an uncomfortable silence. We glanced at each other, neither of us knowing what to do or say next.

"Why don't you throw your stuff down over there," I suggested.

Though she eyed the small table and chairs I'd pointed to, she dumped her purse and overnight bag down on the farthest bed and took a seat along its edge, her knees twitching and her fingers drumming. I gathered she was trying to stay as far from me as possible. I reached for the TV and switched it on to drown out the quiet. When I turned back toward Hannah, Nick burst into the room, startling us both. Hannah jumped up and cried out in alarm. Nick looked at me in relief before he focused in on Hannah standing near the rear corner of the room. He scowled at her with the same hatred I imagine must have been on my own face when I kicked in her door. Fear radiated from Hannah as she pressed herself into the corner. When Nick rushed toward her, I jumped over the bed and placed myself between them.

I pushed my hands against his chest. "Calm down, Nick!"

He strained forward with his eyes locked onto Hannah. "Get the fuck out of my way, Tyler." He struggled against me then twisted his body to the side, swinging his arm up and over, trying to break my grip.

I grabbed him by the arms and thrust him against the wall. "No, Nick, please, settle down. It's not what you think!"

He broke his focus on Hannah and frowned at me, confused and indignant.

"Not what I think? And just what the fuck is that, huh? That she drove your pregnant wife mad, ruined your life, got away with fucking murder?" He sneered at me. "You tell me exactly what I should *not* think, Tyler." With his hands tightened into fists at his sides, Nick refocused back on Hannah.

"Please, just listen to me, okay?" I pressed my forehead against my brother's and placed my hands on his face, trying desperately to get him to focus on me instead. "Nick, come on, please, look at me. Look at me!" I screamed, and his eyes finally locked onto mine. "I blew it, Nick. I've made a horrible mistake. That girl over there, she's not Erin. She's Maguire's wife, Hannah. This is all a terrible mix—"

"What are you talking about, Ty? Look at her." His eyes flitted back and forth between us. "That's her. That's Erin. Are you so fucking drunk you can't see that?"

He broke free, shoved me back a step, and moved to get by me again. I stumbled, still a little buzzed and clumsy, but jumped back in between them. Nick fumed, his eyes burning at us both.

"Nick, come on, stop. You're not listening to me!"

His face blazed red with rage as he pointed his finger at Hannah. "Jillian is dead, and that bitch is to blame. Don't you forget that, Tyler. Now get the fuck out of my way!"

"No, Nick, not because of her, I swear. Please, if you'd just let me explain."

But he wouldn't allow reason to break his focus. He struggled with me in his quest to get to Hannah. I pushed him back once more, but he lunged for me. I threw a desperate punch and connected with his jaw. Stunned, he flew back against the wall.

"Nick, stop." I stood before him with my fist raised as he held his injured jaw, glaring at me with shock and anger. "Listen to me." I slowly lowered my fist and straightened my stance. "I've made a huge mistake. That is not Erin. She's Hannah Maguire. She looks remarkably similar to Erin, I know but...this is not her. I have proof. Let me show you, okay?"

He gaped at me, hearing the words, but not yet believing them. I picked up the folder of photographs and held it open. Then I grabbed Hannah's purse from the bed and pulled out her wallet, removing her driver's license. I tossed it into the open folder and held it out to Nick. He took it, though he glared at me in challenge.

"Look that over carefully," I told him. "It was prepared by a private investigator hired by Hannah." I gestured back to

Hannah who was still cowering in the corner. "She's married to Maguire. That sick bastard is having an affair with a woman who looks very much like his own wife. I saw them both that day at the spa and mistook Hannah for Erin. This is all *my* fault, Nick. I followed the wrong girl."

Nick broke away and studied the contents of the file. He looked at the various photos and compared them to the ID then to Hannah who stood ten feet away. Comprehension washed over him as he discovered for himself the horrible misunderstanding. His shoulders slumped downward, his face melting into concern.

"Oh shit, Ty. Do you realize what this means?"

Hannah's breathing grew ragged as she measured the distress emanating from my brother. Nick let the folder and its contents fall to the floor as he raked his fingers through his hair. We locked eyes.

"Fuck! We're dead, Tyler. We're both fucking dead."

I shook my head. "Nick, please, don't do this right now."

He ignored me and started pacing the room. "Ty, you don't get it. You don't know them like I do. If you don't give them the girl, they'll kill us both...and then they'll take her anyway."

"Nick, please!" I looked back at Hannah and gestured toward the back. "Hannah, get into the bathroom and close the door. Now!"

Not wasting a second, she took off and slammed the bathroom door. I stepped toward Nick and lowered my voice.

"I know this looks bad, but...we have to stay calm. I can't handle her if she becomes any more hysterical. I've already...hurt her. Pretty badly, too. I lost control, Nick. Completely. I've... done something...or rather, I *almost* did something. Something terrible. And this poor girl, she's...she's innocent. She's done nothing wrong, yet she's paid a very steep price regardless."

Confusion crawled across his face. "What does that mean? What have you done?" When I didn't answer, he became angry. "Ty, what the fuck did you do? Tell me!"

I simply stared back, willing him to understand so I wouldn't have to speak the offensive words aloud. As he held my focus, a dim light of understanding sparked within him. With his mouth hanging open, he stepped back from me, as if I disgusted him.

"Oh God, Tyler. Tell me you didn't. You wouldn't." He shook his head and chuckled with a nervous smile, but it melted away as he stared into my eyes.

I reached out to him. "No, Nick, I didn't, but... I *almost* did. And I swear, I would have if..." I began, but I couldn't admit the truth, so I dropped my hand.

"Ty, most of that crap we talked about, they were just fantasies, to help you get through the pain. I mean, getting rid of the girl is one thing, but...doing that shit yourself? God! I can't believe *you*...of all people..."

"I told you. I didn't go through with it."

"No, but you almost did."

I stared at him, dumbfounded. "Nick, our plan was to deliver that girl to Alexi and Dmitri. They've already sold her, for God's sake. Just what the hell do you think was going to happen once they turned her over?"

He rushed forward and got right up into my face. "That's them, Tyler. They're fucking monsters. You're not. *You* don't do that kind of shit. Even *I* wouldn't do that kind of shit. What the fuck were you thinking?"

He turned his back on me and walked away, and I felt shame wash over me again. I had no response. I sat down on the edge of the bed and rubbed my hands along the back of my neck, shaking my head in despair.

"That's just it. I wasn't thinking. I never planned any of it, believe me. I only wanted to scare her, you know. I wanted her to know what it felt like, to be frightened, not knowing whether she would live or die. When I saw her and thought she was Erin, I just...just...snapped. I don't even remember making that decision. It's all a blur. And now it's too late. I can't take it back. All I can do is protect her until I can somehow make this right, somehow come to terms with Alexi and Dmitri."

He spun back around to face me. "Terms?" he asked with a short chuckle. "You're joking, right?" He shook his head. "Tyler, there's no coming to terms." He pointed toward the bathroom. "You deliver that girl unless you want us both dead."

I shook my head. "No way. That's never going to happen, Nick. I can't do that. You know it. I need you to call Alexi and let him know I have to speak with him before I drive back down there. Don't tell him what's happened. Just see if you can find out how much he was paid for the girl. I have all that money Jill and I saved for the down payment, and there's Jill's life insurance. I can repay him, with interest, if he wants. He won't be out a dime. Shit, he'll *make* money on this deal. A lot of it."

I tried to reason it all out, knowing full well how desperate it sounded. Nick shook his head again and backed away from me with his hands up.

"No way, Tyler! You're fucking mad. Alexi will never go for it. Dmitri's already made a deal. He can't back out now. We have no choice. We either deliver that girl or we find Erin and deliver her. There's no way we have the time for that now. We don't even know where she is, and we've got a deadline. Two days, Tyler. Two. Do you get that? They'll be gunning for us if we don't turn her over to them in two fucking days." He sighed and spun around in place, stomping his foot on the floor. "Godammit! We are so fucked."

"Just try, Nick. Please. Stall for a little time. I'll leave with the girl. We'll hide for a few days until I can work it out. Please, just call him. I need to talk to Hannah, try to persuade her to leave with me. I can work this out, I swear I can, but…I need your help. Please do this one thing for me. This *one* thing. Please."

Nick stared at me for a long moment then swallowed hard, finally nodding in agreement. I smiled in relief then walked to the bathroom door and knocked quietly.

"Hannah? May I come in?" I tried the handle but it was locked. "Hannah, unlock the door, please. We need to talk." There was no response. "Come on, open the door. Don't make me break it down."

"What if she escaped out the window?" Nick wondered aloud.

"Escaped? Come on, Nick, I'm not exactly holding her hostage."

"Yeah, well, maybe she isn't too clear on that point, Ty."

I panicked for a moment. "Go check out back and see if she got out," I ordered, waving my hand toward the front door. "Hurry!"

Nick ran out the front door and I turned back to the bathroom.

"Hannah, open this door or I swear to God, I'll kick it in." Still no response. Maybe she *had* escaped out the window. "Hannah! Open the door!"

I gave her only ten seconds longer then threw my shoulder into the door, splintering the frame and sending the door hammering into the wall. I saw her the instant I entered the bathroom, sitting in the tub with her knees drawn up to her chest and her arms wrapped tightly around them.

"For God's sake, Hannah, why didn't you open the door?"

She turned to face me. She was crying again. "What have you done?" she asked in a small, frightened voice before resting her forehead on her knees.

I stepped into the tiny bathroom and knelt down next to the tub. "I know what you heard out there scares you, but...I promise, I won't let anyone take you or touch you in any way. Hannah, please—"

"I don't think you can keep that promise," she said quietly as she looked me straight in the eye. "You've destroyed me...for good this time."

Her words cut deep. She was right. But it wouldn't stop me from trying.

"I'll do whatever it takes to get you home again safely. Whatever it takes, Hannah," I promised again, knowing that even if it cost me my life, I would pay to see it kept. And it very well might.

Nick burst back into the room, panting. "I couldn't find her..." he wheezed. "Oh, she's here. Good. Um, Ty, can I talk to you for a minute? In private?" He motioned with his head for me to follow.

I walked out to meet him. He looked nervous. Spooked. His hands were fidgeting, and he kept peering out through the drawn curtains.

"We need to get out of here," he urged. "I'm not sure, but I think they might be watching us. I thought I saw one of Dmitri's cars out there by the gas station. You take me back to my car then we can split up. I'll lead those guys away while you leave with the girl. Head to Cali on the back roads. Take it slow, and stay off the grid as much as you can. I'll take I-5 straight down and intervene with Alexi as best I can."

I grabbed his wrist. "No, Nick! You stay away from him. You don't need to talk to him in person. Just use your phone. I don't want him using you as leverage."

"Leverage? What are you talking about?" He wrenched free of my grasp and backed away. "Why would he do that?"

I groaned and ran my hand over my face. "Okay, look, I need to level with you about something, but...I don't want you to flip out."

He looked at me with suspicion narrowing his eyes. "What the fuck have you done this time, Tyler?"

"Well, when I negotiated this deal with Dmitri, I persuaded him to let you go, to forgive your debt, if I delivered Erin as promised."

"You did what?" Nick's face flushed red. "Bloody fucking hell, Ty. You have no right to stick your fucking nose in my business. I'm not some child to be taken care of." He paced back and forth across the room. "Godammit, Tyler! Do you realize what you've done? I'm a fucking dead man, for sure. Shit!"

I was so focused on getting him free that I hadn't considered the possibility of failure.

"The fact that you have to worry about your life is reason enough for me to want you out," I explained. "Can't you see that?"

"I don't need your protection. I know what I'm doing, and I know how to deal with these people. *You* have no fucking clue. They don't play games, Tyler. It's all about image and control. If you fuck them over, they'll take you out if for no other reason than you made them look bad. Something you should know better than anyone."

He sat down on the edge of the bed with his elbows on his knees. He ran his hands through his hair over and over. "This guy Dmitri was doing a favor for — the one who bought the girl — Sergeyev? He's fucking big time, from the goddamn motherland. You can*not* mess with these Russians, Tyler. They're mean fucks. For God's sake, I warned you. I told you this was complicated, that there were things you didn't know. What am I supposed to do to hold them off now, huh? What?" He looked at me like I had the answer, but I did not.

"Right. Okay then. Well…you're just going to have to stay out of sight until I can fix this on my own."

He jumped to his feet. "You *can't* fix this, Tyler, on your own or otherwise. That's what I'm trying to tell you. We are both dead. And that girl in there," he said, once more pointing towards the bathroom, "she's going to wish she was when they're finished with her. You think what *you* did to her was bad?" He shook his head. "Just get the fuck out of here, both of you. I don't even want to know where you're going."

"What about your car? I left it up at Maguire's."

He just glared at me. "Get out, Ty. Stay away from home. And stay the fuck away from me, too." He grabbed the keys to his Jeep, and left without looking back.

I ran around the room collecting all of our stuff, throwing everything into whatever bags I could find. I carried it all out to Hannah's BMW and threw it in the back. I returned and stood in the shattered bathroom doorway. Hannah was still in the tub; she hadn't moved an inch.

I reached my hand out to her. "We have to go," I said.

She glanced at my hand and shook her head. "No. I'm not going anywhere with you. I'm better off on my own. You're way too dangerous. You're drunk. You don't think things through, and you're going to get us all killed."

I stepped closer and offered my hand again, my expression stern. "Hannah, please don't mistake my regret for weakness or a lack of resolve. Now please, let's go."

When she still refused, I reached down and grabbed her arm, yanking her out forcibly. She gasped and struggled against me, but I held on tight. She protested as I dragged her through the door and closed it, pulling her along to her car. I pushed her in through the open driver's door and moved in behind her.

"Slide over," I ordered and closed the car door behind me. "As you might have discerned, this situation has become more complicated than expected. If we have any hope at all of getting out of this alive, you *will* do as I say. This is not a game."

"You're right. It's not a game," she screamed. "It's my life!"

"Yes, and it's in *my* hands. It's up to *me* to make sure you have the opportunity to live it!" I started the car and pulled out of the lot. I spied Nick walking alongside the busy road in the opposite direction. "I'm going to make sure we all do."

Chapter Twenty-Four

Hannah

In one moment of madness, my life had turned upside down. I was barreling down the freeway with a man I didn't know, who had beaten and nearly violated me then apologized for both as he wept over his dead wife's memory. I didn't know where we were going or if I would live to see tomorrow. He had intended to trade me in payment for some kind of debt, and though he promised otherwise, his life and that of his brother depended on him doing just that. I feared I was being delivered to the Devil at the very gates of Hell.

In what world did this kind of thing happen? I was trapped in a situation I could not navigate through, at least not on my own. The only person who might be able to help me was the very same man who had thrust me upon this road in the first place. My mind was spinning with fear and uncertainty. All I could do was trust my instincts and pray they didn't let me down. But was that enough?

The whole situation was spiraling out of control. The tension between the two brothers told me so. They were both scared and unsure of how to proceed. Tyler seemed committed to keeping me away from the men he'd been dealing with, but I wasn't altogether convinced that his remorse, as profound as it appeared, was enough to keep me safe. His brother seemed more than eager to sacrifice me in order to save his own neck. I had no idea what was going to happen or what they planned on doing to settle the dangerous dispute that loomed ahead. Tyler wasn't sharing any information with me. In fact, he wasn't talking at all.

As the silence grew heavy, I turned my thoughts to his wife. She was the root of all this. I was curious about her, about their relationship. He certainly seemed lost without her. I understood that, the rage he felt, the loneliness. I even understood his bitterness, of having everything that made you who you were stripped away. It's demoralizing to lose everything that defines who you are. Beck had cheated me out of that, of knowing exactly who I was—*Mrs.* Beckham Maguire— but I had contributed to it. I pulled away, was distant, remote. I shouldn't have been surprised; the signs were all there. This man, however, never saw it coming. Blindsided as he was, it's no wonder he chose the path he did. If I'd been given the opportunity, would I have given myself over to vengeance as he had?

I saw the regret in his eyes, the remorse that consumed him, and the pain of knowing his decision was more costly than he could have ever imagined possible. Down deep, I didn't *want* to believe he was a monster. I wanted to believe it was just a reaction to what life had thrown him. I knew only too well that life could change in the blink of an eye and take you down with it—hard—as it spiraled out of control. I was living, breathing proof. And so, I thought, was he.

I also knew weakness, the kind he had fallen victim to, which promised bittersweet numbness in the wake of extreme, debilitating pain. Grief can do strange things to the mind and spirit, like make you hate the one person you promised to love most. I understood it all too well, and I knew his experience was far worse than anything I had suffered. As close as he'd come, and as much as it frightened me, I would rather be raped a thousand times than lose the one person who meant more to me than life itself. There would be no meaning to anything if Conner were ever taken from me. I would collapse onto myself, just as this man had done. I understood it all perfectly.

Yet if I was to trust this man with my life, I needed to understand him—his character, not his motives. Most people don't stray too far from the core of who they are. Perhaps the severity of his reaction was the very measure of the love he held for his wife. Could someone who loved so greatly be a monster or simply be capable of doing monstrous things?

Then again, maybe I shouldn't believe him. Maybe this was all a con, part of his grand scheme, to make me believe he wasn't the monster he'd already exposed himself to be. So that I would trust him, go along willingly, even feel sorry for him. A loud voice in my head told me to fear him. It was screaming, flailing, jumping up and down, warning me to run. *Run, godammit, run!* That was the smart thing to do, wasn't it? To protect myself? You run from what tries to destroy you, what causes you pain. But there was something else there. I couldn't put my finger on it, but whatever it was, it made me believe him. No man could fake that kind of pain, that level of remorse and regret. And he wouldn't really need to, would he? I was at his mercy, after all. He had the gun. He had control. Yet he had begged for my forgiveness, and now he wanted to protect me from the very enemy he'd unleashed. Why would he do that if he weren't truly sorry, if he didn't want to save me? Why would he ask his dead wife to forgive him?

Yes, I agreed with the voice inside me. I did fear him, but my instincts were screaming, as well, telling me I had no better option than to trust him. In spite of everything he had done to me, my heart held a degree of empathy for him, telling me to be compassionate toward his tortured soul. *There but for the grace of God...*

I wouldn't fight him. I believed his need for redemption was the only thing that promised me deliverance. I closed my eyes and took a deep breath, giving myself over to whatever fate held for me.

What choice did I really have anyway?

Chapter Twenty-Five

Hannah

The longer we sat in the car together, the more uncomfortable it became. The silence was like a ticking clock, its volume so loud. It drove me closer to madness with each passing second. I needed to understand what was going to happen in the few days he said we'd be gone. I looked over at him, and though I know he must have noticed, he didn't turn to face me. His eyes were glued to the freeway. The fact that he tried to ignore me in the small confines of the car unnerved me even more.

I cleared my throat. "So, what's the plan?" I asked.

He broke his concentration on the road and glanced over at me. "The plan?"

"Yeah, your plan. Some kind of contingency. Surely you've thought that far ahead."

His brow rose high above his startling blue eyes. "No, I'm afraid not." He turned back to the road again. His jaw ticked repeatedly.

"Okay then," I tried again. "Where are we going?"

"Forward, as best as I can tell," he replied. I didn't appreciate his mockery and my expression told him so. "Sorry, just trying to lighten the mood," he added.

"Look, Tyler, all things considered, you can't expect me to just trust you. I need to know where we're going and what we're going to do once we get there. I think I have the right to know."

He studied me for a moment and agreed with a nod. "Yeah, you're right, you do, but…I don't have an answer for you. I'm inclined to head back to California."

"California. For God's sake, why? If that's where your brother's friends are, isn't that more than a little dangerous? Especially for me?"

"I won't let them get anywhere near you, I promise. But I can't ignore them either. We'll just take a longer route. Give Nick time to smooth things over a little."

"Your brother didn't sound too confident about being able to smooth things over." And I wasn't feeling very confident about letting either of them determine my future.

"Yeah well, I think he has more influence than he knows, and once his associates realize that bargaining will net them something, rather than nothing, they'll renegotiate. They're businessmen, after all," he said then paused briefly. "But you're right. We do need some kind of plan."

"Okay then. What is it? What's your brilliant plan? Because it's certainly not going back to California."

He shot me an exasperated look, and I was pleased I could get under his skin, even just a little.

"Well, first we need some cash." He looked over at me expectantly. "Like Nick said, we need to stay off the grid as much as possible. They'll know to be looking for me, so I can't use my bank cards. They don't know about you though. At least not yet." He cocked his eyebrow, as if willing me to understand his point.

"What does *that* mean? Surely you don't expect *me* to finance my own kidnapping?"

He flashed me a brilliant smile, his eyes sparkling with mischief. I stared like a moron and snapped my mouth shut, making a conscious effort to pull my eyes back into their sockets.

"Well, your husband anyway," he replied, still grinning ear to ear.

I spun around and focused blindly out my side window. "Yeah, right...my husband."

I wasn't an idiot. I knew he was purposely trying to manipulate me with his charm. But it didn't seem to matter much what I knew. I still had a visceral reaction to his smile, and as much as it irritated me to admit, it caught me a little off guard. I felt betrayed by my body to have even the slightest response to it, involuntary or otherwise. Of course, I would never let him see it, but it struck me then that good-looking men like Tyler knew exactly the effect they had on women.

It wasn't surprising though. Beautiful women were common; handsome men were not. But honestly, you couldn't even categorize Tyler as simply handsome. He was heartbreakingly perfect, every part of him, save his twisted soul. If I had met him under any other circumstances, I likely would have been drawn to him immediately. I imagine it probably drove his wife crazy the way women must have hit on him. It always bothered me when it happened to Beck, and, sadly enough, he couldn't hold a candle to the man beside me, at least not physically.

I stole a furtive glance, noting his eyes were surely his most interesting feature; that is when he wasn't scowling. They were the clearest, brightest, most intense shade of blue I'd ever seen, and when he smiled, they kind of crinkled up at the corners, radiating out toward his temples, like rays of sunshine on a child's drawing. It made him seem so approachable, something I found hard to swallow after the morning I'd spent with him. That, in itself, aggravated me to no end.

He had remarkable cheekbones, too, sculpted high and set widely apart with a slightly crooked nose between and a balanced brow above. Most women would kill for a bone structure like his, yet he carried it off with absolute masculinity. His jaw was strong with that scruffy, unkempt look many women found irresistible, something I was not altogether immune to. I swallowed hard at my musings, berating myself for being even remotely aware of his physical appearance. But I'd only seen him smile a few times, and then it was hardly more than a brittle smirk, so in all honesty, when he graced me with that last brilliant grin, I just couldn't help but be affected, much to my horror.

But more than anything, it was his fragility that struck me. Most of the time, his expression had been one of rage, remorse, or even fear with his brow gathered in an intense furrow. Like a raptor on the hunt, it made him appear dangerous, which, of course he was, but it also made him seem vulnerable somehow, and flawed, though not in a physical way. It was more emotional, as if he'd been beaten down by life, taken every punch yet still tried to stand.

That look of vulnerability tugged inexplicably at my heart. It made the mother in me want to run my finger over the wrinkle in his brow, to smooth it away and erase whatever pain had caused it. I knew I shouldn't, considering what he'd put me through, but for some reason, I felt very badly for this man. No one should have to endure what he had, and I realized that, though I was indeed his victim, I was also the victim of his tormentor every bit as much as he was. Erin Anderson had stung me twice over now. I would not let there be a third.

"Hello...Hannah? Did you hear me?" Tyler asked, interrupting my thoughts.

My face heated with embarrassment.

"You looked a million miles away. Did you even hear a word I said? We need cash first, then gas for your car. Maybe get some food for the road so we don't have to stop again. How does all that sound to you...as the financier, I mean?"

Damn, there he was again with that smile. I ground my teeth together.

"Would you knock that off?" I huffed.

"What?"

"You know what. All that...smiling. You can't charm me, you know. Do you do that on purpose, just to get your way?"

He looked indignant at first, with his mouth held open. But then he snapped it shut and looked away with a tiny smile playing at one corner of his mouth.

"No. Well...not for a long time, anyway. I didn't need to with my wife."

I snickered. "I bet."

"What? Is there something wrong? You don't like my smile?" he asked, genuinely surprised. "I find that...rather strange."

"Strange? Why? Do women make a habit of falling at your feet when you grace them with your smile?"

"No, of course not, but—"

"Good, because I damn sure won't." I wagged my finger between us. "This whole attacker, victim thing we have going on kind of ruins it for me, you know."

He shot me a heated look, another score for me. "Look, I don't expect you to understand. It's just that...well...Jillian... She loved my smile. Said it was my best feature, her favorite. That and my crow's feet," he admitted with a shrug. "Not that I ever really understood that."

His voice softened and his eyes took on a faraway look. I must admit, I preferred that look to the scowl he usually wore. He appeared content, maybe even a bit happy. I would have liked to preserve that look for a while longer, for my sanity's sake at least. He seemed less threatening that way, not quite so scary, and my nerves were grateful for it.

"What else did she like about you?" I asked.

He turned my way, studying my face for a brief moment before he turned back with a small sigh. "She rather liked my accent." He smiled to himself, just a touch. "I can't tell you how many times she told me that American girls loved a guy with an accent." He looked temporarily lost in his memories but then turned back to me. "Is that true? Do you American girls fancy men with accents?" He smiled, teasing me, but then he brought himself up short. "Oops, sorry. There I go again." He chuckled at my expense.

I folded my arms over my chest and turned away. We both remained quiet for a while, caught up in our own thoughts, but my curiosity was as restless as I, and though I was almost afraid to ask, I figured he might enjoy sharing a little about his wife. He was calmer when he talked about her, and I found I was less afraid of him when he was calm.

"It's obvious, you know," I said.

"What is?"

"That you loved your wife."

He nodded, pausing to swallow before he answered. "Yes, I did, very much. Still do."

"And what did you like about her...your wife? What was she like?"

Tyler turned to me again, that furrow settling in a touch before he turned back to the road.

"Well, Jillian was…beautiful. Joyful and kind. Impulsive. And rather restless at times, I'm afraid." He sighed as his shoulders relaxed. "She had such a fiery spirit, untamed. Opinionated, you might say, a bit of a hot-head. I suppose it got the best of her in the end." Then all of a sudden, he looked sad, wistful, and full of self-reproach.

"How so?" I asked though I was concerned about the melancholy turn in his mood.

Another heavy sigh, like the weight of his loss pushed the breath from his body.

"Knowing her as well as I did, I should have realized she wouldn't have been able to just let it go." He shook his head at the memories.

I wasn't sure what he was referring to. I didn't know the whole story behind his wife's death, and frankly, I was afraid to ask.

"I should have protected her better," he continued. "She went to Nick when I refused to intervene with the authorities, but I warned him off. So she tried to take care of it on her own…and it cost Jillian her life." He stole a quick glance at me again. "She paid for *my* failure, *my* mistake. That seems to be a pattern with me these days. A fact you know better than anyone, I suppose." His lips pressed together.

"Yeah, well…hindsight can be a real bitch," I mumbled. I was beginning to regret my line of questioning. I felt as if I had intruded on something personal, something that was really none of my business, though I suppose he had made it so when he kicked in my door.

"You'd think I'd learn," he whispered before falling silent again.

I felt bad that I had made him recall such unhappy memories. "Hey, I'm sorry. I never should have brought that up."

He kept his eyes on the road, his knuckles white as he grasped the wheel. "No, it's all right. You have every right to ask."

Silence settled over us again, more uncomfortable than ever. I turned away and nibbled on my fingernails, tearing the cuticles and making them bleed. One-by-one, I stuck them in my mouth to alleviate the self-inflicted pain. It was a good ten minutes before Tyler alerted me to a small strip mall just off the freeway.

"I'm going to pull up to that bank. We need money for gas and food." He threw me nervous glance. "We'll need to pay for a place to crash tonight, as well."

I hadn't thought about where we would sleep for the night. All my muscles went rigid, and I stiffened in my seat. A quiver pulsed through my stomach when I considered whatever arrangements he might provide. I hadn't considered many things before I allowed him to take me away. The gravity of my situation was weighing more heavily by the minute, and panic began to overwhelm me.

He parked the car and pulled up on the brake, turning the key until the engine stopped. I heard his voice as if from a distance, but my own felt choked off.

"Hannah?"

I couldn't make myself get out of the car. I just sat there as I moved closer to a full-blown panic attack. My heartbeat was loud in my ears, and the flutter in my stomach felt more like a bird than a butterfly. My door opened suddenly from the outside. Tyler reached in and disengaged my seatbelt. I gasped and strained against him when he took hold of my arm and pulled me from the car.

"Come on, settle down. I need you to withdraw some cash. Grab your bag," he ordered then reached past me and snatched my purse as I remained frozen. "Let's go, Hannah. Please don't make a scene. We don't need the attention."

He shoved my purse into my hands and guided me up to the ATM. I glanced up at him as I fumbled for my wallet, dropping it and my bank card to the ground. He reached down and retrieved everything then maneuvered me in front of the machine. He stood beside me with his hand at my elbow as I worked the keypad. My hands shook with anxiety, and I made several mistakes. Each time, I had to start over. And each time, Tyler sighed in impatience. I gave him the cash and waited for his orders. He directed me back to the car, opened the door, and nudged me back inside with an exasperated huff.

We drove down the street to the first gas station we saw. Tyler walked around to my side of the car, kneeling next to me in the open door. By his tone, I could tell he was more than a little annoyed at me.

"You need to relax," he said.

Yeah, like that's going to happen.

"Stay in the car while I fill it up. Do you want something from the market?" he asked as he gestured toward the little store centered in the gas station.

I gave my head a slight shake, but kept my eyes trained straight ahead.

"I'll be right back." Then he dipped his chin and raised his brow. "Please don't do anything foolish."

Even though he was pleasant enough, there was a modest threat to his words. I nodded, and he closed the door, but he remained standing in front of my window, contemplating me through the glass, his jaw ticking the whole time. When he swung away from fueling the car and walked toward the store, I turned to watch him. He looked back over his shoulder just as he pulled the door wide, making me spin back around. He was growing more tense and edgy, and I was the cause. I closed my eyes and breathed deeply. It wouldn't do me any good to make him uptight and angry. I jumped when he opened his door, climbed back in, and threw a bag of snacks in my lap.

"Ready?" he asked.

I could only respond with a nod.

He pulled onto the freeway again and reached into the bag for a bottle of water. "We'll keep to the back roads, but I want to at least make it over the gorge into Oregon before we stop for the night." When I simply nodded again, he sighed loudly. "All right, Hannah. What's wrong? What's changed all of a sudden? I can tell something's bothering you. Just tell me what it is so we can deal with it up front."

"Well...it's just I'm...a bit...worried...about stopping...for the night."

It was an awkward moment when he realized where my concern lay. At first, he pressed his lips together, but his impatience melted away before he turned to look me in the eye.

"You have nothing to worry about, Hannah. I promised I wouldn't touch you again. You have my word."

He stared at me in earnest and crossed his heart with his finger, but it was hard to ignore that part of me which feared him. I understood he felt only remorse for what he'd almost done, and I felt in my heart that he wouldn't touch me in that way again, but it was still difficult to disregard my anxiety.

"You believe me, right?" he asked.

I nodded, trusting my heart on this one, and praying it wouldn't let me down.

"Good," he said, smiling to make me feel more at ease.

But even with his efforts, it didn't take long for the strain to set in once again, increasing with each passing minute of silence. Small talk seemed out of place, but I could think of no other way to alleviate the disquiet. So I cleared my throat and searched for an appropriate topic.

"So, um...do you have any other family besides your brother, Nick?"

"No, actually, he's all I have left. Our parents died a few years ago, along with our little sister, Kim," he said, his shoulders sagging noticeably.

Holy cow! More dead relatives. It was like stepping into another tragedy. This poor bastard was surrounded by it, like a Shakespearian play.

"Oh...I'm sorry," I replied. "God, I can't seem to ask the right questions, can I?"

He chuckled slightly and reached over to pat my hand. I flinched at the contact, but if Tyler noticed it, he didn't let on.

"No worries," he said. "We all have our afflictions, right?" His faced screwed up a bit, but he continued. "My folks were wonderful people, and I miss them terribly. And except for the circumstances that took them from me, my memories of them are mostly happy."

I was curious about what happened to them, but I wasn't about to insert my foot into my mouth yet again by asking. I bit my lip to keep from doing so.

He peered over at me. "It's okay. You can ask," he said, seeming to read my very thoughts.

"All right then. What happened?"

"They were killed in a car accident a little over four years ago. Nick was driving, and though he was seriously hurt, he survived, so that would be the silver lining, I suppose."

"I'm sorry to hear that. God, your poor brother. How awful for him."

"Yeah, I feel responsible for that one, as well. We'd planned for Nick to pick them all up at the airport. They were flying in from Melbourne; first time in three years. Nick called me early that morning, said he was too tired and hung-over to drive. He was always shirking his responsibilities, and I got angry about it. I wouldn't let him back out, and he ended up falling asleep at the wheel.

"My mother and father died instantly, but Kim... Well, they told me she was brain dead, but it took me awhile to accept that and let her go. Eventually, I had to make that choice and turn off her life support. She passed quietly. Nick was seriously hurt and suffered through a very long and difficult recovery. Months of rehabilitation and physical therapy."

"My God. That's terrible."

"Yeah, he got a raw deal. But then it got even worse. He became addicted to his pain meds, and then later to booze. It was the only way he seemed to be able to make it through the day. I couldn't understand it back then, but I do now," he said, pausing with his own thoughts. "Anyway, I put him in rehab, but it didn't work out. Things kind of fell apart between us after that."

"Oh? How so?" I asked, surprised. They seemed pretty close, even in their criminal endeavors.

"Well, Nick got into trouble trying to finance his habits. He started running with a bad crowd. I tried to intervene, but all I got for the effort was a beating by his thug friends."

"Wow. What did your brother do?"

"Not a whole hell of a lot. Told me to stay out of his business. My wife agreed, so I relented."

"Oh, so you and Jillian were married for a while then?"

"No, we were together for several years, but we'd only recently married. Nick's accident happened just after we first met. That's part of the story, really. I was selfish. I had plans with her the morning my folks flew in, and I didn't want to change them just because Nick was too busy getting drunk the night before." He shook his head. "Story of my life."

Okay, now would be a good time to change the subject. I didn't particularly want to go down that road again. Everything I asked seemed booby-trapped with sentimental landmines. The subject of Jillian was different though. He liked talking about her. And though their story was bittersweet, he enjoyed sharing his time with her.

He told me how they met, and how he fell head over heels in love for the first time in his life. I heard about their wedding and honeymoon. But when he came to the part about Jillian's pregnancy, he was too choked up to share much at all. And while I knew their story didn't have a happy ending, I was astounded by how tragic it really was. Through it all, it was obvious how devoted and committed he had been to his wife, how much he loved her. They were like two halves making a whole; take one away and the other was incomplete.

"You know, as sad as your story is, Tyler, you were very lucky to have loved someone like that and know she loved you in return. A lot people never achieve that."

He kept his eyes on the road and nodded gently. "Right. When you put it that way, I guess I was pretty lucky," he admitted reluctantly. "You know, you'd make a good shrink." He glanced back over with a crooked smile. "Enough about me now. What about you?"

I snorted. "What about me?"

"Anyone else in your life besides your jerk of a husband?"

"Soon to be ex-husband," I corrected.

"Good for you, Hannah."

"Well, I do have a son, Conner. He's fifteen and a typical teenager, I guess. He's suffered a lot because of his father being gone so much. I try to make sure I don't come between them. It's hard though. Beck's such an ass. Conner's with him for the next few days. It's the first time since we split that Beck's had visitation. It was hard to let Conner go when I dropped him off this morning." Thinking back on it, I couldn't believe it had been less than a day since I had delivered Conner to his father. It felt like a lifetime had gone by.

"Now that you're divorcing, will you move out of that neighborhood you hate so much?" he asked.

"I'd like to. That place is more Beck's style than mine. I've only made a handful of friends, and only one good one, at that, so there's nothing actually keeping me there. And I really don't think I'd be missed anyway."

It was difficult to admit out loud just how lonely I'd been over the last few years, how there was not really anyone who would even know I was gone or might become alarmed if they happened to see the current condition of my house.

"Somehow, Hannah, I doubt that very much," he said with a genuineness that made me smile. "It seems to me that neither one of us has had the happy ending we want. What a pair we make." He chuckled then, but it carried more than a hint of bitterness. "Now, if you don't mind, I'd like to find a place to pull off the road and have a bite to eat, stretch my legs a bit. This car is a bit cramped for me. Does that sound okay to you?"

I agreed, and after a few miles, Ty turned down a gravel road just off the two-lane highway we were traveling. About a quarter mile in, he pulled over and parked. While he grabbed the bag of food, I pulled a small blanket from the trunk and spread it out on the grass under some trees.

222

Ty sat down and arranged the selection of junk food along the edge of the blanket, choosing what he wanted for himself. I leaned to sit down and grimaced in pain. Ty offered his hand in assistance, but I declined with a shake of my head. He studied me closely, his eyes tense and wary. My discomfort and bruised face seemed to make him uneasy. He turned away, but he couldn't ignore the issue. It was like a large elephant stuffed in a tiny closet, and he swallowed hard at its presence.

"Hannah, I can't begin to tell you how sorry I am," he began, keeping his eyes averted. "What I've done..." he said and sighed, "what I *almost* did... It's truly unforgivable. I am so deeply ashamed. I know it's not a valid excuse, but I was just so angry." He peeked up at me briefly then returned to stare at the blanket.

"After Jillian died, I just... I gave up. I allowed myself to drown in sorrow and alcohol — a great deal of alcohol," he admitted. "My brother and I would lie around the house, thoroughly wasted, and dream up ways to get even with Erin. It became a daily obsession, really, as pathetic as that sounds." He looked up and captured my attention. "Every day, I've been consumed with rage, bitterness, and hatred for that woman. I drank far too much, just to dull it all into manageable moments of time." He looked back down in shame again, shaking his head. "I still do. It's a real problem for me."

His hands trembled. He clenched them into fists to disguise it.

"It's been hours since my last drink — way too many — just before I came to your door. I'll need to..." he stopped short of finishing, the words difficult for him to say aloud. Then he sighed and continued. "I'll need to deal with that very soon," he said as he looked up at me once more. "On top of everything else, it's not a good time for me to cope with withdrawal. Do you understand what I'm saying?"

I stared into his eyes as I tried to comprehend his motive for sharing this with me. I broke away first, nodding in acceptance, but fearing what it would mean for me. I grabbed a small package of crackers, desperate for something else to focus on. As we ate in silence, Ty's phone rang. He pulled it from his pocket and looked at the display with concern.

"It's Nick," he said.

He stood up and walked away to conduct his conversation in private. I watched him closely as he spoke with his brother. When Ty looked over and caught me studying him, he turned and walked farther into the trees. It was easy to discern that their conversation had become urgent and heated, at least on Tyler's end. He was pretty agitated, raising his hand to his head and stomping his foot, but I wasn't sure if it was simply the conversation or if his need for a drink was exacerbating the situation. When he ended the call, he hung his head low. He put his hands on his hips and just stood there turned away from me as he collected himself.

He stomped his way back over to me and said, "Finish up, we're taking off."

"Why? We just got here."

"Just finish up," he snapped, and I couldn't help but flinch. He was instantly sorry, holding his hand out, as if to calm himself down. It was shaking even more than before. "Look, I'm sorry, but... We need to go." He put both hands in his pockets and stormed off to the car.

I stared after him, growing more concerned by the minute. I gathered up the food and blanket and stood up to walk back to the car when I thought I saw someone move through the trees about fifty yards away.

"Oh my God, Ty. Ty!" I pointed into the forest, "I think I just saw someone over there."

He ran over and scanned the area evenly, but didn't see anything. He reached down and picked up the bundle I'd dropped.

"Get in the car," he commanded.

He turned, took hold of my arm, and pulled me along, throwing the bundle into the open trunk. Then he forced me into my seat and slammed my door shut. He jumped into his own seat, started the car, and drove off, scattering dirt and gravel behind us as the tires spun. Ty glanced repeatedly in the rear view mirror, his paranoia all too evident. Maybe he hadn't actually seen anyone, but he believed it possible that someone was there, watching us. He seemed frightened by the possibility, and not knowing exactly what it was he feared scared me, as well.

"Ty, I need you to be completely honest and tell me what's going on. Why are you so upset? What did your brother say to you?"

He was reluctant to share, but my expression warned him that I was about to get difficult if he didn't. He threw me a sideways glance and groaned.

"Nick hasn't had any luck with his associates yet. They're being belligerent, and Nick is frustrated," he explained without really telling me much.

"Who are these associates of his, anyway? What kind of control do they have over him?"

He paused, searching for the right words. "Well, these people, they're not just some neighborhood street thugs as I implied. They're actually highly organized, more like a family than a gang, and I've had a run-in or two with them over the last few years trying to extricate my brother from their control. When

I told you I'd received a beating from them, I failed to mention that I injured one of their men. Apparently, a lost man is a great expense, or so Nick's boss explained to him. Guess it was his way of saying I was lucky to come out of it alive. Nick stepped in for me, I'm sure, said something to get them off my back, but you can't cross these people without expecting to somehow pay for it in the future, at their convenience, of course. I'm sure they think I owe them big time, just for letting me live.

"As an organization, they have their hand in just about everything: protection, prostitution, extortion, drugs, gambling. You name it, they deal in it. And to make matters even worse, they have their other hand deep in the pockets of some very wealthy, powerful men, and not just in San Francisco, either, but the entire state, the whole west coast, plus New York, Chicago, Miami, even overseas. They have considerable influence."

I stared at him, my eyes narrowing in concentration. My mouth fell open of its own accord, and I sucked in a long breath.

"Wait a second. Are you telling me you owe your debt to the mob?"

"Yes. The Russian syndicate, to be exact. And I have to find a way to repay them...without using you to do so, as I promised them."

"Great. That's just perfect. And what was supposed to happen after you traded me in?" I asked though I was frightened by whatever answer I might receive.

Ty took a deep breath and released a groan. "Erin, not you," he corrected, avoiding my question.

"Ty, please. Just tell me."

"Hannah, it won't do you any good to—"

I pounded my hand against the window. "Tell me, godammit. You owe me that much!"

He ran his fingers through his hair and sighed, apprehension tightening his expression. "Okay, okay. You're right, but...just try to stay calm, all right?"

"Fine. Whatever. Just tell me."

"Well, their cartel brings people into the country illegally. They smuggle in a lot of Russians, Ukrainians, Eastern Europeans, that sort. Many of them can't pay the entire price of admission, so to speak, so they're indentured into positions such as cooks, gardeners, nannies, whatever is needed." Ty hesitated and glanced over at me, which made me even more nervous.

"Human trafficking. I get it. I've seen it on the news. Keep going."

"Well, some of the women are indentured into...brothels and similar positions."

"What do you mean? Like sex slaves?"

"Yes. That's right."

I realized that this might be my fate and my body shook in abject horror. Bile rose up into my throat.

"Am I to be sold this way?" I asked.

"Yes, I'm sorry, but...as far as they're concerned, you already have been."

Chapter Twenty-Six

Tyler

I knew I probably shouldn't have told Hannah the entire truth, but I felt she deserved to know what we were up against. But perhaps brutal honesty was another mistake on my part, because she started to cry as she stared out the windshield. She sucked in her breath in gulping sobs, hyperventilating.

"Hannah, please relax. I won't let anything happen to you. You're safe. They won't get to you." I reiterated my promise, though to be honest, my confidence was not as firm as I would have liked.

Her hands trembled as she raised them to her face.

"Calm down. You have nothing to worry about, I swear."

"Pull over," she said breathlessly. She pulled at the handle, trying to open the door as I sped down the highway. The locks popped up automatically. One more pull and the door would open.

"Hannah, stop!" I grabbed her wrist to prevent her from tumbling out.

"Pull over! Stop the car, stop the car!" she screamed, banging on the window and clawing at the handle.

I slammed on the brakes and swerved to the shoulder as I held on to her wrist. She escaped my grasp when I shifted into neutral. Cars blew by with their horns blaring, veering to avoid hitting us from behind or swiping us from the side. Hannah managed to get her door open and tried to scramble out, but her shoulder got caught in the harness of her seatbelt and she landed on her hands and knees. She climbed quickly to her feet and sprinted away.

"Hannah! Stop!"

As the car rolled forward, I pulled up on the parking break then dashed out to chase her down. I caught her from behind, around the waist, thirty yards or so from the car, and pulled her off her feet. She flailed about frantically and clipped me on the cheekbone with her elbow. Momentarily stunned, I dropped her to the ground. She landed on her rear and skittered away backwards, crying out.

"Stay away from me, you sick bastard!" Hannah's eyes were filled with fear as she looked up at me from the ground.

I raised my hands up. "Okay, okay, I'm sorry. I won't touch you, I promise. Just stop, Hannah, please." I stopped moving toward her and bent down onto my knees.

She crab-walked even farther away.

"I'm sorry, Hannah, okay? Just stop." I stood, my hands raised high, and backed up until she finally ceased moving away from me. I lowered myself to my knees again and called out to her. "It's okay, Hannah. Nothing will happen to you, I swear. Please, just calm down for one minute."

"You bastard! How could you do such a thing? It's inhuman!"

"Please, Hannah, cars are slowing down. People are watching us from the roadway. This is dangerous. We need to get back in the car."

I looked repeatedly over my shoulder at the passing cars, worried that one of them might be Alexi's henchman. When one slowed down and turned off onto the shoulder, I stood up and walked toward Hannah, still on her backside with her hands propped behind her.

She kicked dirt and pebbles at me as I came closer. "Get away from me, you monster!"

"Hannah, we have to go. This isn't safe," I urged, my hand outstretched. I glanced back at the car now stopped just a few yards ahead of Hannah's BMW.

"Your lovely Jill would be so fucking proud of you!"

At the mention of Jill's name, rage filtered through me, and I snapped. I was on her in an instant, pulling her to her feet by her elbows, dragging her face to within an inch of my own. I gave her a sharp jolt.

"I would think knowing personally what a dangerous monster I really am would keep you from further pissing me off! Now get back into the goddamn car!"

Her eyes were wide with fear, but her lips were pressed together in anger. We stared each other in the eye for several moments before I released her and stepped back.

Sweat slicked my forehead, and my hands shook at my sides. I moved away and held out my arm, directing Hannah back to the car. She glared at me and brushed by without saying another word. I followed closely behind her, motioning to our audience that everything was fine. A man and a woman sat inside, their eyes bewildered and glued to my face. I'm sure my expression was enough to keep them inside their vehicle, but I didn't want to test the point. I feared they might have the urge to call the state patrol. Hannah and I got back into the car and I pulled onto the highway. We drove in silence for a good twenty minutes.

"We're stopping as soon as I can find a motel and store," I announced.

She didn't respond. She sat in stony silence, never even glancing my way. I was relieved when the Columbia River Gorge rose up before us ninety minutes later. Biggs, Oregon, a town so small it was hardly worth a blip on the map, rose up on the far side of a windswept bridge. I pulled into a motel parking lot heavily populated with semi-trucks. I stopped in front of the office, keeping the car and Hannah within sight as I checked in. The desk clerk stood up straight and pulled a burning cigarette from between his lips. He waved his hand in front of his face to clear the smoke and smiled a yellow-toothed greeting.

"Evenin'," he said. "What can I do for ya?"

"One room, two beds, if you have it."

He shook his head and the long thread of ashes at the end of his cigarette dropped onto the counter. "Sorry, buddy, only got a single queen left." He swept the ashes away onto the floor then tipped his chin toward the front door. "There's an event across the river tomorrow at the museum, and them windsurfers got some kinda' race or somethin'. We're almost full up."

I balled my hand into a fist. Hannah would no doubt believe I somehow plotted against her. I turned my head and spied her through the glass. Her eyes were trained on me in concentrated focus. Keeping my emotions in check, I doled out some cash and slid it across the scarred countertop.

"Whatever. The farthest room available then. Ground floor."

"I need a credit card for the security deposit."

I tossed Hannah's card across the desk. "Here, but don't run it through until I see you in the morning."

He nodded and passed me the paperwork to sign before handing me a key. I drove around to the room, relieved to see that it was not easily visible from the highway a hundred yards away. I opened the door and waited for Hannah to enter first, calculating her inevitable reaction.

She stopped short and whipped around to face me. "One bed? Really?" she said with her teeth clenched together.

"Sorry, it's all they had." I threw the bag of food on the table. "Don't worry. I'll sleep on the floor."

I didn't imagine for one minute that I would be sleeping at all, let alone on the floor, but I needed to reassure her I wouldn't be the big, bad monster again. She turned away in a huff and settled on the edge of the bed, her knees twitching back and forth.

"I'm going to walk over to the market across the road," I said. "I'll pick up stuff to eat for tonight and something for the morning. Is there anything in particular you'd like?"

Though I was trying my damnedest to be polite, she just shook her head, not even bothering to look my way. That irritated me, probably because I needed a drink, but still, she could have at least acknowledged my effort.

"Fine," I said. "Keep the door locked, your ass inside, and don't do anything stupid. Understood?"

I said this as much as a warning as to get under her skin. She snapped her head toward me and threw me a scathing look. I grinned and turned away, slamming the door closed behind me.

I breathed in deeply on my way to the market in an effort to cool my simmering temper. God, but she had a way of getting to me. I berated myself, knowing it was my own fault. I had put her in the position of having to defend herself. What else could I expect?

"I am such an ass," I said aloud as I entered the store, caught up in my own thoughts.

A woman chuckled as she passed by on her way out. I glanced at her over my shoulder, embarrassed. She turned and walked backwards away from me with a flirtatious smile spread across her face. I ducked in and behind the store shelves to avoid her lingering stare.

I moved around the store and selected an array of snacks to share with Hannah. The sale of hard alcohol in Oregon was strictly controlled by the government. Luckily, the one store in town was licensed to sell. I perused the liquor, selecting what I knew would get me through the night while not altering my mood too much. Tequila was definitely out, so I chose vodka and a six-pack of beer to chase it down. I paid for my purchases with Hannah's cash. On the way back to the room, I dialed Nick's cell to see if he had made any progress. The call was picked up after only one ring.

"Tyler, my friend, we have all been waiting anxiously for you to call."

I stopped dead in my tracks just outside the motel room door, my heart lodged high up in my throat.

"Alexi? What the hell are you doing with Nick's phone? Where's my brother?"

"Oh, why the rush? It has been longer than expected since we last spoke, has it not?" he asked, his meaning implicit.

"Where's Nick?"

"Ah, not to worry. He is out with some of my boys, handling a few errands. You know how it is, do you not?"

"No, actually, I don't. Why do you have his phone?"

As Alexi laughed, I pictured the same pompous grin he always wore. Hannah poked her head out from behind the window curtains and looked at me questioningly. She opened the door with the same expression. I walked through with my finger pressed to my lips, requesting silence.

"Tyler, as you may already know, Nick has been trying quite valiantly to arbitrate our deal, the one we shook hands on weeks ago, the same one I told you could *not* be renegotiated." Agitation crept into his usually calm voice. "You know Dmitri has promised the merchandise to a very important client, one who has already paid us, and rather handsomely. I was quite pleased to see Nick return, but disappointed when he said you were...delayed. You could have easily delivered the girl by now, yet you make us all wait in anticipation." He paused and sighed impatiently. "So I feel you might need some...reinforcement, so to speak, to compel you to complete our transaction."

I closed my eyes, my blood running cold. "Meaning?" I asked, only too aware that Hannah was listening.

"I think you know already, don't you, my friend?" Alexi laughed again. "Yes, of course you do. When you are ready, we will make a trade. Nick for the girl."

He disconnected the call.

I sank onto the edge of the bed, the shock settling into my already overloaded brain.

"Well? Who was that?" Hannah asked. "Your brother?" She watched me closely, waiting for an explanation.

I could barely muster a blank stare in return. I couldn't let her know what had happened. She'd freak. I had to play like nothing much had changed yet. I broke away and moved to the table where I placed the bag.

"Um...yeah. That was Nick. He's, um... He's...taking care of things." I removed the six-pack, grabbed a bottle, and cracked it open, draining it in one long pull.

Hannah shot me an uncomfortable look. "You think that's a good idea?" she asked.

I sighed in blessed relief then said, "Well, if you'd like me fully functioning, then yes, it's a grand idea."

I pulled out another bottle, popped the cap, and held it out to her. Hannah declined with a shake of her head. I wiggled the bottle and smiled at her, knowing it would elicit some kind of response.

"Oh come on," I said, "it's just one six-pack between the two of us. I insist...please."

Surprisingly, she accepted the bottle, returned my smile, and took a sip to appease me. I sat down at the small table and patted the chair next to me. Hannah, though somewhat reluctant, joined me. I pulled everything out of the bag, except for the vodka, and placed it on the table. I selected a deck of cards from the stash and shuffled.

"Care for a game of poker or maybe twenty-one?" I asked. "Rummy? Go Fish? Old Maid?"

I fanned the cards in front of her, my very best smile, however false, plastered upon my face. I wasn't above manipulating her as I needed. I was turning over all the implications of Nick's predicament while still trying to remain calm for Hannah's sake.

Hannah snorted in resignation. "Sure, how about some poker?" she said and smiled. It was pure and genuine and changed her entire face, lighting it up from the inside out. I was captivated by how lovely she looked when she appeared relaxed and happy. I found it difficult to take my eyes from her face and the sudden spark in her bright green eyes.

"What?" she asked when I continued to stare.

"Nothing. Let's play."

Though I was distracted by Alexi's ultimatum, I tried to concentrate on the cards and relax with Hannah for a while. We played several hands of Texas Hold'em, wagering outlandish bets with the goldfish crackers I'd bought. She was quite the card shark and hustled me out of every goldfish I possessed. We shared a sandwich and chips and washed it all down with the beer. Hannah was enchanting when she loosened up. While I hoped it was my charming company, I realized it was most likely just the alcohol.

Much to my surprise, I enjoyed playing cards with her, even with all the worrying about Nick and what I was going to do to get him back without giving up Hannah. After three beers, I caught her staring at me. With a bashful smile, she turned away. If I didn't know any better, I would say it almost felt like flirting, but again, it was probably just the beer. She was getting very tired. Her eyes drooped and her attention slipped away.

"You look wiped, Hannah. You should probably get some sleep," I said, though I hardly wanted to let her go yet. "Why don't you go get cleaned up and hit the sack? I'll be over on my side of the room all night, I swear." I raised my hand and crossed my heart.

She offered me an anemic smile then headed off to the bathroom. I cleaned up the table and spread the map out to examine. Hannah came out of the bathroom, dressed in sweats, and climbed into bed.

"You know, the car has a GPS," she offered.

"Yeah, I know. I just need to get a clear idea of where we're going in my head," I said as I tapped my temple. "I'm kind of a Luddite, I guess."

She twisted her lips into a semblance of a smile. "Oh, well, goodnight then," she added.

"G'night," I replied.

She lay down and turned away from me. I sat there for a long while, staring at her back. When I thought she'd relaxed into sleep, I spoke out softly.

"I'm very sorry, Hannah. For today. For everything." It was no more than a whisper, spoken more for me than for her, but after a moment, I heard her respond.

"Okay."

It was just one word, but it was like being pierced through the heart. One bittersweet, heartbreaking moment that underscored the differences between us. She had the ability to be compassionate, to forgive even the most unforgivable offense. As much as I needed to believe that she might actually forgive me, it nearly destroyed me that she genuinely seemed willing to do so, because I certainly was not worth forgiving.

When I heard her even, steady breathing and knew she was asleep, I pulled out the bottle of vodka, not so much because I needed it to calm my nerves or chase away the ghosts, but more because I felt contemptible and beneath Hannah's company. I couldn't keep the tears from stinging the backs of my eyes as I poured glass after glass, feeling the Devil fill my soul.

This time, the hate and rage were not directed toward someone else, but at myself, where it truly and ultimately belonged.

...

I paced the floor for a couple hours, trying to come up with a plan to save both Nick *and* Hannah. I spent more than a small amount of time propped up against the wall watching her, studying her face, so beautiful, so peaceful in sleep. I knew I shouldn't be watching her without her knowledge, but I missed having that kind of beauty near me. Having it so close, yet knowing it was not mine was a bitter pill, but I felt as if I'd been pulled back through time, back to when Jillian was still alive. I was unbearably lonely, and, at that moment, Hannah filled me in ways Jillian once had. It was difficult to turn away from something as alluring as that. With all the turmoil inside me, it was calming to just sit and stare at her.

Eventually, I closed my eyes in the darkness, leaned my head back against the wall, and, for the first time in more days than I could count, I fell asleep. It seemed like only seconds later when Hannah cried out. I was on my feet and at her side in a heartbeat. I tried to wake her with a gentle tap, but she continued to thrash about in her sleep. It took a long moment for her to come fully awake, and when she did, she screamed and pushed away from me.

"No. Get away. Don't touch me!" she wailed.

I jumped back with my hands raised. "Whoa! Easy now. I'm not going to hurt you."

She sat up and pressed herself back against the headboard, her eyes wild and confused.

"Hannah, it was just a dream. It's okay. You're safe."

She looked at me, mistrust pulsating with every ragged heartbeat. It took great effort for her to suppress her fear. Both hands trembled as she raised them to her mouth.

"I'm sorry," she said. "I'm okay. I'm okay. I'm okay."

It felt like if she said it enough times, she might actually believe it. She eventually calmed down enough to lie back in bed, turning away from me once more. It took a great deal more time before she relaxed enough to fall back to sleep. The whole time, I sat at the small table, my eyes fixed on her back. My head felt ready to explode with renewed throbbing. I was completely exhausted, running on nothing but on fumes.

When I finally heard Hannah breathing slowly and evenly again, I poured myself one more glass and pulled out the vial of OxyContin. I slipped a tiny pill into my mouth and washed it down with the vodka. I closed my eyes, laid my head in my arms on the table, and waited for the world to mercifully disappear.

Chapter Twenty-Seven

Hannah

A gentle tapping on my shoulder urged me awake. The weight of someone pushed down on the edge of the bed beside me. The fog of sleep that lingered heavily in my brain dissipated as if a strong wind had blown through. My eyes flew open and searched through the darkness.

Tyler was sitting next to me, looking distressed with his finger pressed up to his lips, asking me to keep silent. He had the gun in his hand with the barrel raised up as he pointed toward the door. I was instantly alert and on edge.

"Gather your things quickly and put your shoes on," he whispered then stood and backed away.

With my heart thumping, I slid out of bed. I tried to be soundless while the panic rose inside me. I stuffed my few belongings into my bag then searched for my shoes. From the window, I glimpsed a thin shaft of light as it knifed through the gap in the draperies. It shimmered onto a clear bottle standing empty on the table, refracting into a kaleidoscope of colors.

My attention flew to Tyler. He stood near the door with his back pushed up against the wall. He caught me studying him, and I knew the moment he closed his eyes against me that he'd been drinking, and heavily. The hairs on my neck and limbs stood at attention, like tiny needles piercing my skin from the inside out. It was a warning, a neon sign buzzing with electricity, glowing red in the black of night. How could Tyler protect me if he was drunk? I took several calming breaths and crammed my feet into my shoes without untying them.

The front door knob rattled. Someone was trying to enter. Ty backed away in my direction and pushed me toward the rear of the room. With a sudden blast, the door exploded inward. A man dressed in black stood silhouetted in the light pouring through splintered frame. He held a gun in his hand and lowered it in our direction. There was a quick flash and a muted thwack as dust exploded from the wall near my head.

"Hannah, get down!" Ty screamed as he pushed me to the floor.

Explosions of light and sound were tossed back and forth, an exchange of bullets between the gunman and Ty. Tyler fell back on top of me, his gun still raised in his hand. Then the gunfire ended, as quickly as it began. A sulphurous odor weighed heavily in the wispy cloud of gun smoke hovering in the air.

Tyler jumped to his feet, his weapon trained on the intruder's head. He stood over the wounded stranger who moaned and writhed on the floor. Ty kicked the gun from his hand then picked it up, holding it up to the light streaming through the open doorway. The shape was abnormally long, as if it had a silencer attached to the barrel. A sure sign this was no simple robbery. The intruder struggled to his knees, blood dribbling from his mouth as he cursed in a foreign language. Tyler took a step back and pointed the gunman's own weapon at his head.

"Don't do it," he warned, though the gun trembled in his hand.

The man pulled a knife from his boot and surged forward in a quick blur. Ty jumped back, turned his head, and fired a single round, all in the same instant.

A red mist sprayed onto the wall behind the intruder while a small trickle of blood oozed from his forehead. He fell over onto his side, his body convulsing in jerky spasms. Brain matter lay in globs amid the torrent of blood draining from the back of his head, staining the tattered carpet beneath him.

I gasped at the sight of the man being killed, though I knew in all likelihood he had come looking for me. Ty, who was strangely calm, turned to face me. He met my terrified gaze and ordered me to grab my things. We both charged around the room, picking up our meager belongings. Stepping over the body of the now dead gunman, we dashed out the door and scrambled into the BMW. The tires screeched as we retreated from the motel parking lot, heading south onto the darkened highway.

Though we were both breathing heavily as we made our escape, we remained otherwise silent. My body hummed, my muscles charged as if a current buzzed through me. I began to shake all over. I clasped my hands tight between my knees and breathed in deep through my nose and out through my mouth. Tyler was still as a starfish. For a while, the adrenaline kept him focused on the dark and winding road ahead, but as time distanced us from the ugly scene we'd left behind, his driving became erratic. He groaned in pain, wincing as he ran his hand over his right shoulder.

"Oh my God, Ty. Are you hurt?" I asked, frightened at the possibility. "Pull over! Pull over right now!"

"No, I'm fine. We can't afford to slow down now." His eyes rocked back and forth between the road and the rear view mirror. "I don't know who else might be behind us."

"Oh, for God's sake, it won't matter who's behind us if we crash. Now pull over." I was alarmed at the difficulty he had controlling the car, and terrified that he might be more seriously injured than he was letting on. "Tyler, please."

He relented and took the next turnoff, checking the mirrors for anyone who might be pursuing us. Satisfied that no one followed, he turned right and drove down an isolated roadway for several miles until I urged him to stop. Finally, he pulled over and cut the engine.

"Do you need help getting out?" I asked as I climbed from the car and headed for the trunk.

He didn't answer, just climbed out on his own, though he drew in a deep breath and clenched teeth.

"Come back here so I can take a look," I ordered. I opened the small toolbox built into the trunk lid and pulled out a flashlight. Ty's leather jacket was torn and stained near his shoulder. "Okay, let's get that coat off you."

He grunted and grimaced as I pulled the jacket away from the injured area. When it was free, I threw it into the trunk and reached for the first-aid kit.

I grabbed some gauze pads and alcohol. "Your shirt, too," I added.

He eased out of his shirt gingerly. I gasped when I saw the claw marks crisscrossing his chest and trailing over both shoulders onto his back. Swallowing hard, I ignored the damage I'd inflicted the day before and examined the new wound on his arm. I moaned in distaste, sickened by the gore. It was ugly and bleeding more than I was comfortable with, but it appeared to be only a flesh wound, the bullet tearing clean through. As I cleansed it with the alcohol, I looked hard into his eyes.

"What were you thinking back there, drinking that entire bottle of vodka? I'm depending on you to keep me alive and out of the hands of those men, *as promised*," I stressed, pulling tightly on a strip of gauze I had wrapped around his injured arm.

He winced and reached for his shoulder. "Ouch, that hurt."

"I can't count on you if you're drunk, Tyler. You need to pull yourself together, for God's sake."

He looked at me sheepishly, but his chin jutted outward. "I think I did all right back there, all things considered," he replied as he pulled his shirt back on.

"We were lucky and you know it," I threw his jacket back into his face.

A small bottle fell out of one the pockets and rolled along the ground. Its contents rattled inside the plastic container. I bent down and picked it up, examining the label in the light of the trunk.

I sucked in a large breath. "OxyContin?" I hurled the bottle at his head. "My God, pills *and* booze? What the hell is wrong with you?"

He looked down and bit his lower lip. I packed everything back up and walked to the driver's side where I turned back to Tyler.

"Hannah, please, let me expl—"

I cut him off with a raised hand. "Just shut the hell up, Tyler, and get back in the goddamn car."

Chapter Twenty-Eight

Hannah

I found my way back to the highway and turned south toward California. The eastern sky was just beginning to brighten as the sun started its lazy ascent. Tyler laid his head back against the seat with an exhausted sigh and turned his face away from me.

"Hannah, I'm sorry. I know you find it hard to understand. I don't have a good explanation for you. I can only tell you that, after Jill died, I just...couldn't handle it. The loneliness, the grief, it overwhelmed me, and I retreated, into myself, into the darkness of my own head."

He paused for a long moment. I had never heard anyone sound so tired.

"Nick understood what I was going through. Only too well. I don't think he could stand to see me suffer, so he offered me the only thing that ever worked for him. He brought me a bag filled with bottles of alcohol, and we sat around the house, drinking, day after day. It dulled the pain enough that I could go for moments at a time without remembering why I was even drinking in the first place."

He peered back over at me. Our eyes met, and when I saw the pain in his, my resolve to stay angry evaporated.

"Look Ty, I feel badly for you, really. I'm trying to understand where you're coming from, but drowning in booze and numbing yourself with drugs won't make it better. It just delays the inevitable. And, at least for the time being, I really need you alive." I smiled weakly.

He nodded, completely missing my subtle attempt at levity. "I'll try, Hannah, but... Withdrawal is hard, even under the best circumstances." He turned away again. "I know I'm weak. I'm embarrassed to say so. I'm in my own private hell, and no matter how hard I try, I just can't seem to find my way out." He sighed again and his eyes fluttered closed.

I drove for over a hundred miles out in the middle of Nowhere, Oregon, with Tyler asleep next to me. The lines that usually creased his brow were erased. I hoped that he could rest dream-free. In the quiet moments alone, I thought about the last twenty-four hours. I had not spoken to Conner since I'd dropped him off at his father's. I wondered if he had missed me last night, if he had tried to call to say goodnight. I couldn't remember a night in which I had not been there to tuck him in or kiss the bridge of his nose. I reached for Tyler's jacket draped over the center console and rummaged through the pockets until I found my cell phone. I turned it on and waited for the icons to appear.

There were six missed calls: five from Conner and one from Beck. They both left messages asking me to call them back. Conner sounded worried while Beck seemed rather irritated, which told me they had remained at his Seattle apartment. No way he'd be that calm if they'd seen the house the way I'd left it. I was relieved that Conner had been spared the anxiety of knowing his mother was missing, but frustrated that I hadn't yet been missed. It was probably best though that nobody else was involved or in any danger. I turned the phone back off and slipped it into my purse, vowing to call Conner at my first opportunity. I didn't think Ty would mind, but I also didn't want him around when I talked to my son.

I glanced over at Tyler and wondered about him, especially what he was like before the nightmare of his wife's death had robbed him of his happiness. That kind of pain can change a person, both physically and emotionally. Had he once been a carefree soul? Did he smile easily and often? Was he warm and affectionate with his wife?

I was curious about Jillian, too. I knew his wallet was in his jacket, so I rooted around hoping I might find a photograph of her. Keeping an eye on the road, and Tyler in case he woke up, I pulled out his small photo holder and held it up to the early morning light. The first picture was an old family portrait with Tyler and Nick, and with who I assumed were his parents and their sister. Ty looked about seventeen or so, while Nick was perhaps seven or eight. Kim was a tiny infant in her mother's arms. They all looked happy and at ease.

Flipping the plastic page over, I found a photo of a much younger Ty—just barely a man—and his adolescent brother. It was a candid shot of the two of them with their arms locked around each other's shoulders. They were both smiling or perhaps laughing in playfulness as they hammed it up for the camera. I sighed, imagining the moment.

The next picture was of a stunningly beautiful young woman with long dark hair and enormous eyes fringed with impossibly long lashes. She had a radiant smile with lips shaped liked Cupid's bow and perfectly straight, white teeth set between two dimpled cheeks. She was at once both a sultry beauty and the wholesome girl-next-door. Every man's dream come true.

I was dazzled by the spark in her lively eyes, a mischievous glint. This had to be Jillian. What man wouldn't be in love with a woman like this? I sighed and turned to the last photograph. It was a portrait of both Tyler and Jillian. They looked happy and in love. I stroked my thumb across Ty's face, noting how striking his eyes were, azure blue flashing in the camera's light. His every emotion was written in those eyes. They were both beautiful and made a remarkable couple. I could only imagine the children they would have borne had she lived. It was a tragedy. Erin had ruined so many lives.

As I returned the holder to Ty's wallet, I found two more photographs slipped in behind his cash, both worn and frayed, as if they'd been handled often. The first was a grainy black and white image, nearly unrecognizable until I rotated it around. Jillian's name was typed at the bottom, along with the date it was taken. It was an ultrasound snapshot. I gasped softly, the photo shaking in my hand as I realized I was looking at an image of Jill and Tyler's baby, likely the only one ever taken. I wiped at the tears blurring my vision and carefully slipped the photo back where it belonged.

The last picture was actually a series of black and white photos running vertically down the narrow cardstock. It was the kind taken in one of those booths often found at cheesy tourist attractions. Jill and Ty were fashioned around each other in various animated poses. They looked playful, at ease, and committed all at once. It was as if I could see into their connected soul. They could have been entwined in their bed and it would not have been any more intimate. Just looking at it made me uncomfortable, like I was intruding on their private moment. I blushed and quickly returned the photo to its proper place.

I sighed deeply thinking of Ty's loss, of the woman he loved, his soul mate, his very life. I missed loving and being loved that way. I wondered how much more both he and I stood to lose in the coming hours and days. I understood him a little better after seeing his pictures, and I appreciated a measure of his pain and loss. And I felt awful that he should have to live every day so overwhelmed by it. There was no way I could ease any of it, but the urge was there, nonetheless. I was still angry at what he had done to me, as I was still fearful of his unstable nature, but I understood what drove him, and I trusted that he truly wanted to make things right again.

Whether he would be able to do so was another matter entirely.

Chapter Twenty-Nine

Tyler

The sun had risen considerably when I woke up to Hannah parking her car at a roadside café. I jumped in my seat and reached for the gun in drowsy confusion.

"Sorry. I need a bathroom break," she explained as she pulled up on the brake.

I wiped the sleep from my eyes. "Right. Good idea," I agreed then yawned.

"How are you feeling?" she asked. "Is your arm bothering you?"

I rotated it around, testing it. "No, it feels okay." I gave her an appreciative smile. "You'd make a good nurse."

She rolled her eyes. "First a shrink and now a nurse."

She did return the smile though before she eased out of the car. She walked into the café and back to the ladies' room while I held back to scour our surroundings. Satisfied we were safe for the moment, I walked toward the men's room and reached into my pocket for my mobile.

I'd put both of our phones in my pocket, so I was surprised when I only found mine. Since I was sure I hadn't dropped it, I could only surmise that Hannah had removed hers while I slept. I retreated a few steps and stood just outside the ladies' room door. As a patron walked out, pulling the door wide, I spied Hannah inside with her cell in her hand and her fingers working the display. I pushed through the open door and entered as another woman was coming out of a stall. She threw me an annoyed look.

"Excuse me," the woman grumbled. "I think you have the wrong room."

Hannah, who had her back to the door, spun around. "Ty!" she exclaimed.

"Hannah," I said dryly, my eyes locked onto hers.

The woman's attention was drawn back and forth between the two of us. I could only imagine what she was thinking as she examined the bruising on Hannah's face. I continued to hold Hannah's gaze, my brow raised with an unasked question.

The woman looked concerned for Hannah and seemed reluctant to leave us alone together. "Is everything okay here?" she asked.

Hannah stood there staring back at me with a devilish spark in her eye. "I don't know. What do you think, Ty? Is everything all right here?"

I wasn't sure whether she was being humorous or warning me not to interfere with her phone call. I kept my eyes trained on her and returned her exact grin.

"Yep," I said, my lips popping at the end, "it's all good."

The woman kept peering back and forth between us as she walked out of the restroom, finally leaving us alone.

"What do you think you're doing, Hannah?" I asked.

"Calling my son. You have a problem with that?"

"No, though I question why you felt the need to hide the fact." I took a step closer and held out my hand. "It's safer to use the pay phone out in the hall. If they've identified you through your license plates, I don't want them to have another way to track you down."

She huffed at me and turned her phone off then placed it in my hand. I slipped it into my pocket, turned, and walked back out into the hall. A few minutes later, Hannah followed, stopping to use the pay phone. I stood on the other side of the wall and listened in on her conversation, just to make sure she didn't volunteer any important information or call the cops. Sure enough, Hannah dialed her son and explained why she hadn't called him earlier, that she was out of town and her phone had died and she'd forgotten her charger.

It was a plausible excuse, and I was glad I didn't have to intervene. She told him how much she loved him and to behave, all the things a good mother tells her child. She whispered a bittersweet goodbye before she replaced the handset. Wiping away her tears, she walked around the end of the wall and spied me leaning against it with my arms crossed over my chest. I gave her an embarrassed smile though I was unconcerned she'd caught me.

"Hungry?" I asked.

She sighed, her own smile a forgiving one. "Starving."

We sat down and shared a pleasant breakfast together. The food was hot and decent, and made up for all the junk we'd been snacking on. We both worked to keep the mood light. Neither of us brought up our current situation. She was curious, and I was happy to answer her many questions, if for no other reason than to prove I wasn't always the miserable bastard I now appeared to be.

"So where exactly are you from?" she asked. "You have a weird accent I can't quite place. Is it English or Australian?"

"Well, aren't you perceptive," I replied. "Actually I'm British, born in London. But my family immigrated to Australia when I was twelve. Then I moved to the States about ten years ago, so my accent is a bit...muddled, or so I'm told." I sat back in my seat and dropped my gaze to my hands on the table. "Or *was* told, anyway. By my wife." I glanced back up at Hannah.

With her lips pressed into a sad smile, she looked me in the eye for a long moment then moved judiciously on to another subject, grilling me about my childhood and young adult years.

"If you missed London so much, why did you move to the States instead of returning to England?" she asked.

"Well, I'd planned to, but I fell in love with San Francisco while traveling and couldn't tear myself away. Later, Nick followed me, and though I was a bit resentful, I didn't want to leave. I had a thriving business building and remodeling homes. I'd made some good friends. And then I met Jillian."

I found it difficult to continue as I remembered that time. My throat grew tight as the memories sifted through me.

"Not too long after that, Nick had his accident, and life changed considerably for us all." I finished with a bitter grin. "So, tell me more about your son."

Hannah's face lit up when she talked about Conner, and she laughed, which was a sound I'd not heard from her. It was captivating, just as she was, and it made me smile and laugh, as well. Enjoying the moment with her took me back to a happier time, when Jill and I used to dream of our family together.

"You know, you remind me of my wife in some ways," I remarked.

Hannah looked surprised with her lips parted and eyes wide. "Oh? How so?" she asked.

"I don't know, your spirit, perhaps. Your independence and sense of compassion. Those were some of the things that made her beautiful to me. You share that same kind of beauty." As Hannah stared back open-mouthed, I felt the need to clarify. "Not that you look like her, but..." I reached for my wallet and pulled out the photographs we'd taken last year at Pier 39. I handed it to Hannah. "You do share the same fearless nature. She had a fire in her. I've seen the same in you."

She stared at the photo with a melancholy smile. "You both look so happy." she said then handed the photo back. "It's easy to see how much you adored her."

I held it in my hand and ran my finger over Jill's image. I imagined all the times I'd run my finger along the side of her face, tipping her chin up so I could kiss her, and I smiled at the memory.

"I still do," I whispered as if speaking to Jill. "That will never change." I shook my head and returned to Hannah. I replaced the photo and took out some cash before putting my wallet away. "We'd better finish up and get back on the road." I dropped the money on the table in front of her. "Would you mind paying the bill? I still need to use the men's room."

"Oh...sure. No problem."

"Thanks. I'll meet you back at the car then. Just keep the doors locked."

I excused myself and used the facilities. I poked my head out the rest room door and spied Hannah as she was leaving the café, and, because I knew she was out of earshot, I decided to try Nick's phone again. I was surprised, but greatly relieved, when I heard my brother's voice on the other end.

"Nick! Oh, thank God. Are you all right? Alexi hasn't hurt you, has he?"

"Tyler?"

Goosebumps sprang up along my arms at the rough sound of his voice. "Yeah, Nick, it's me. I was worried about you. Alexi answered your phone when I called last night. He wouldn't let me talk to you." I waited for his response, but there was nothing. "Nick? You still there? Are you okay?"

"Ty...I'm...I'm so sorry, brother."

I grew concerned. Something wasn't right.

"Nick, what's wrong? Where are you?"

"Ty, this is all my fault. I tried to take care of it, but I've just made things worse." He sounded like he might be crying, a rare thing for my little brother.

"Nick, it's all right. Just tell me what happened. Are you hurt? Where are you?"

"Ty, don't come after me, okay? This is my responsibility now. I don't want you to come looking for me. I'm so sorry. You don't know half the shit I've done, Ty, so please, don't—"

"Nick, what are you talking about? What's going on?"

I was frightened for him. Alexi must have done something to him, hurt him somehow. Nick sobbed into his phone. I'd never heard him so desolate. Even after his accident, he never fell apart like this.

"Nick, stop crying. Calm down and tell me where you are," I commanded.

"No. You can't come here, you hear me? It's not safe for you here. Don't come back down here looking for me, Tyler." His voice broke when he used my name.

"For God's sake, Nick. Why not? Just tell me what happened," I asked gently this time.

"I can't, brother. I want to. I need to, but...I can't."

"How am I supposed to help you if you won't tell me what's wrong? Please, Nick. I'm sure it's not as bad as you think."

"No, Ty, it's worse. I fucked up. I fucked up bad. You have no idea."

"I would if you'd tell me what's going on. Please. You'll feel better. You know you will. You always feel better after you talk to me, right? Come on, Nick. Let me help you. Please. Just tell me."

"Oh God, Ty. You never knew it, but...I was getting even with you. I was pissed when you came down so hard on me after the accident, even though I knew you were right, that it was my fault. But I didn't care. I just wanted to get back at you for putting me in that position in the first place. Do you see? Can you understand now?" He cried even harder.

"No, Nick. I don't understand at all. What does that have to do with anything?"

"I was such a fucking disappointment, wasn't I, Tyler? I could always see that in your eyes."

"That is *not* true."

"And you, you were always so perfect, weren't you? The perfect son, the perfect brother, the perfect husband. You never did anything wrong. Not like I did, huh, Ty?"

"Nick, what are you talking about?"

"I was just as devastated as you were when Jill died. I loved her, too, Tyler. Just like you did. But you didn't know that, did you?"

"*What?*"

"You couldn't see what was right in front of you."

"Fuck you!"

"I could have helped her, Ty."

"Stop, Nick. Please."

"I could have saved her—"

"Why are you doing this?"

" —and she wouldn't have died."

"Shut the fuck up!"

"But you didn't trust me. You never do. You didn't think I could help. Because I'm just Nick, the fucking screw up, right? *Right?*"

"No, Nick, come on. Please. Don't do this."

"Well, Ty, I proved you were just as fucked up as I was. You got hooked on booze, too, didn't you, brother? It helped you through. Made it all a little more bearable, didn't it? Well, you can thank *me* for that. *I* manipulated *you*, for once, and you went along for the ride, like I knew you would. I brought you down, made you no better than me, so you could see I wasn't such a loser after all, that I wasn't a bad guy. I knew you could be weak, too, Tyler, just like me. I dragged you down on purpose, brother. God help me, I did it on purpose." His confession complete, he finally broke down, sobbing uncontrollably.

My hands turned ice cold, and there was a sinking feeling in the pit of my stomach. I didn't know what to think or say. My mouth just flapped open and closed like a beached fish. I was utterly stunned. When a couple of guys entered the men's room, I pushed by them and ran out the back door of the café.

"I'm so sorry, Tyler. Do you see now? This is why I don't want you to come after me. You were right all along. I just get in the way. And that's just the half of it. You don't know, Ty. You just don't know. You're better off without me."

I felt like the earth had been blown out from underneath me. I leaned against the back wall of the café and slid down to the ground, running my hand over my head again and again as I tried to clear out the confusion of Nick's confession. I couldn't respond. I could only sit there listening to Nick sob and apologize.

"I'm so sorry, Tyler. Please don't hate me. I couldn't stand it if you hated me."

I couldn't find my voice to reassure him. I remained still and silent.

"Are you still there?" he asked. "Tyler?"

I suddenly realized I didn't care what he'd told me. It didn't matter to me one way or the other what he'd done or why. He was my brother, and I needed to get him back alive.

"Nick, where are you? Please, just tell me so I can come get you."

He was perfectly calm now. "No, I don't want you to, Ty. It doesn't matter now. I don't need your help anymore."

"Don't be stupid. We can work this out, you'll see. Just tell me where you are."

But he said nothing.

"Nick, I'm not angry, I swear. You're my brother. I could never hate you. I understand how you must have felt, and I'm sorry. I love you. I need you to let me help you, please, just one more time. Like the old days. I can fix this. Haven't I always? Just tell me where you are."

"No, not this time, Tyler. You can't fix this. Not this time. It's gone way beyond you and me now."

"Nick, godammit, tell me! *Where the fuck are you?*"

I heard a lot of rustling noises and then what sounded like the phone being dropped on the floor. I could make out Nick yelling. He was angry and scared. And there were other voices taunting him, laughing at him. I didn't know what was happening, but it didn't sound good, and I feared Nick's life was in serious jeopardy. I yelled his name into the phone over and over to no avail. He was gone, though the line remained open.

Suddenly, another voice broke over the line. "Tyler, I think it is time you brought the girl in, don't you?"

It was Alexi. The mere sound of his voice made me shake with impotent rage.

"Alexi, you fuck. If you've hurt him, I swear, I will hunt you down and fucking kill you."

Alexi chuckled softly. "Well, Tyler, I am not hiding so there is really no need to hunt me down, as you say," he explained, sounding oddly light-hearted. "Feel free to come see me anytime. I welcome an end to this most tiresome affair, as I am sure your brother does. Just bring me the girl and all will be settled. No hard feelings. I promise."

It sickened me the way he behaved, like this was just some simple act of bartering, one human life for another.

"Alexi, please. I know Nick must have told you. I have the wrong girl. She's not just merchandise to be traded."

"Ah, but you did not feel this way some weeks ago. Did you, my friend? No, you sought revenge. So you shall have it." I could almost see the grin on his face as he spoke.

"There's no revenge to be had, Alexi. I'm telling you, I have the wrong girl. You must understand. I can't turn her over to you."

He laughed again. "Well then, you have a significant problem, as does Nick, so I suggest you either find the right girl or bring the one you have, because your brother is running out of time. Tick-tock."

"Alexi, please. What does Nick have to do with any of this? This is between you and me. He can't make up for my mistake."

"Perhaps not, but you chose to involve him in what should have been a simple transaction. And now you have gone rogue and left your beloved brother out to dry. No matter. I cannot have dogs like the two of you make fools out of me and Mr. Chernov, now can I? No, I think not. So you have until tomorrow to decide which it will be, the girl or your brother.

Now, I like your brother. I really do. So for his sake, I hope you make the right decision."

That was it. I was trapped. I couldn't just let Nick die, but neither could I turn Hannah over to Alexi. Once Hannah and I got down into The City, I would make arrangements for her to return home, and I would meet Alexi alone. If I had to trade myself for my brother, I would, gladly. No one else would pay for my sins ever again.

I sighed, my defeat all too bitter. "Where do you want to meet?" I asked.

"Very good." His tone was smug and satisfied. "Come to Dmitri's Tea House on Geary near 25th. You know it?"

"Yes, I know it. I should be there tomorrow morning."

"Make sure that you are, my friend." And the line went dead.

I fell back against the building and slid to the asphalt, my elbows on my knees and my head in my hands. That *was* it. I'd played my hand and lost. Alexi knew it and was no doubt enjoying his victory while awaiting his spoils. He had us both now, me *and* Nick. I just prayed Dmitri would accept me in my brother's place, that I, alone, would be enough. I would turn over everything I had to appease him, but I wasn't sure, even with all my savings and insurance money, that it would be enough. He wanted the girl, any girl. He expected one, demanded one. What would they do to us when I returned empty-handed? The walls were closing in. I could see no way to escape.

I stared blindly at the pavement between my feet, trying to come up with a plan when my hands were pulled out from beneath my head. Hannah was kneeling in front of me with her brow puckered in distress. I hadn't even felt her wrap her fingers around my wrists and pull.

"Ty, what are you doing out here?" she asked. "I've been looking for you everywhere. Didn't you hear me calling?"

I gazed back at her with a blank stare, my jaw slack.

"What is it?" she asked. "What's happened now?" Her face was creased with tension, worry pulling the outsides of her brow down

I stared at her for a long time, as if I could somehow find the solution in her eyes. I offered a feeble grin then turned my hands and grabbed hers, squeezing her fingers between my own. I released one hand and stood, helping her up with me. I smiled again, this one a little more encouraging than the last.

"Forgive my moodiness, Hannah." I ran both hands over my face. "Ah, damn, I could really use a drink." She was just about to rebuff me for the remark when I threw her a reassuring glance. "No worries," I said. "I'll be good, just for you."

I touched her elbow and escorted her back to the door. She hesitated for a second, unsure of my change in mood. She knew something was wrong and that I was trying to hide it from her. I could see her anxiety growing into full-blown alarm.

I smiled once more and dipped my head. "Don't worry, Hannah. Everything's fine. I'm just tired. That's all."

I opened the door with a gesture for her to precede me. She shook her head and passed through.

"I'll drive," I said as she walked by.

With an exhausted sigh, I followed in after her.

Chapter Thirty
Tyler

Grateful now to have such a high-performance vehicle, I shifted the BMW into seventh gear and sped down the highway as fast as I dared, alert for the highway patrol. I tried to keep a casual smile plastered on my face. Hannah was too perceptive, and I didn't want her to worry about what I was thinking, and especially what I was feeling. I fiddled with the radio, trying to find some music amid all the static.

"What kind of music do you like?" I asked.

"Hmm, well, alternative mostly, but I have an assortment on my playlist."

"Your playlist?"

"Man, you are a Luddite, aren't you?" She reached into my side pocket and pulled out her phone. She attached a small wire to it and powered it up.

"What are you doing? Turn that off!" I commanded.

"Oh relax, it's on airplane mode. There's no signal, just power." She made selections as she ran her finger over the colorfully lighted display. "See?" She held it up for my inspection. "I keep all my songs on here," she explained as music filled the car.

It was soothing, if a bit melancholy, and I enjoyed it. Hannah tapped her foot and hummed along with the song.

"30 Seconds To Mars," she announced.

"Thirty what?" I asked.

"30 Seconds To Mars," she said again, like I should know what she was talking about. "This is Hurricane, my favorite song."

I gave her a blank stare, not recognizing the group or the song.

"You know, the band...with Jared Leto, the movie star. *Panic Room, Alexander, Requiem for a Dream.* Any of those ring a bell?"

I shook my head.

"Never mind," she said with a wave of her hand. She continued to sing along quietly for another minute, all the while peeking over at me with another one of her expressions I couldn't quite read.

"So I don't watch movies very often. Something wrong with that?" I asked.

"No, it's just... This song, you know. It kind of got me thinking."

"Yeah? About what?"

"Well, the lyrics," she said with a shrug before reciting them. "*'Tell me would you kill to save a life...would you kill to prove you're right?'* They've often made me wonder, what would make a good man do something...you know, really awful, like kill or whatever. And well, now...I guess I have my answer, don't I?" She peered at me like she'd just received all of God's wisdom. As if she could read me through and through.

263

"Hannah." I paused, unsure of what to say. "It doesn't really matter. There's no excuse for what I've done."

"No, no. You misunderstand. I'm not looking for an apology. I'm just saying that... I think I get it, you know. I think I...understand. You, that is. I think I understand why. I mean, I'm not saying it's right or anything, but..." She shrugged again. "I get it. That's all."

I couldn't find an appropriate response, so I just nodded and returned my attention back to the road ahead, feeling both humbled and humiliated.

"Oh, and um...there is one other thing," she added, her bottom lip pulling down like she was unsure whether to ask or not.

"What?"

"Well, while I was looking for you at the café, a couple of people said they saw you on your cell." She said it like an accusation.

I arched an eyebrow, uncertain of her point. "So?"

"So, why is it all right for you to use your cell when you said it was unsafe for me to use mine?"

I sniggered. "Look, I don't know if any of Alexi's men are near or not. If they were and I called from a payphone, it would pinpoint our exact location."

"Okay, but why isn't it safe for me to use my cell?"

"Because I don't want them to have a conduit directly back to your son," I replied, wary of how she might respond.

As expected, Hannah sucked in her breath, instantly alert, panic spreading across her face. "Oh my God, is that really possible? Can my signal be traced back to Conner?"

"Possible, yes, but unlikely, I think. I'm just trying to cover all the bases. I don't want to take any chances. Though they know I have the wrong person, I don't think they actually know who you are. That's the whole problem. Your identity and Erin's are intertwined and confused because of your husband."

"What about that man back at the motel? He probably saw my car. He might have given someone my plate numbers. Maybe they've traced the car to Beck. Now you're telling me I shouldn't be worried about Conner being with his father? They could both be in trouble."

"Hannah, try to stay calm, all right? You just talked to Conner and he was fine. There's no reason to suspect they would be interested in your son, or your husband, for that matter. We'll just keep calling from time to time to make sure nothing has changed."

My suggestion seemed to appease her as she thought it over.

"Okay, but in the meantime, what exactly is your plan?" she asked. "I need to know where we're going, what we're going to do."

I couldn't look her in the eye and lie, so I kept my eyes on the road. "I'm working on that and will let you know when I have it figured out."

"That's not good enough, Ty. This is my future in jeopardy, and maybe my family's, as well. What are you hiding from me? I know something happened back at that café. I saw it all over your face. You're scared. Why won't you just tell me what's going on?"

Why? Because *I* didn't know what was going on. I had no idea what might happen.

"Ty, answer me."

I didn't know if Alexi's men were still on our tail.

She touched my arm. "Tyler."

I didn't know if we'd been setup, if we were walking into a trap.

"Tyler, I'm talking to you."

I didn't even know if Nick was still alive.

She drummed her fingers along my bicep. "Tyler, what's *wrong* with you?"

What could I tell her? There was nothing I knew for sure.

"Why are you ignoring me?"

I wasn't ignoring her. I wanted to reassure her, to make her feel safe.

"I need to know what's happening, Ty."

But I didn't have an answer. Not one. I couldn't think with all the noise.

"Tyler! Why won't you tell me?"

"Godammit, Hannah! You don't need to know right now, all right? When the time is right, I'll tell you everything."

She gaped at me with her mouth open then snapped it shut and crossed her arms over her chest. "Yeah, well, it'll be too late once you've fed me to the wolves!"

"I told you I wouldn't do that."

"Well, I don't know if I believe you. Why should I after what you've done and the plans you've made?"

"Hannah, please, just drop it already."

"No, I think I have the right to know exactly what's—"

"Shut the hell up, will you. Good God!"

"Don't you dare talk to me that way. I'm not your wife."

"No, you're not. Not even fucking close."

"Yeah, well, thank God for that or I'd be dead already, wouldn't I?"

That was it, strike three. The rage burned through me again like wildfire through a eucalyptus grove.

"Fuck, fuck, *fuck!*" I pounded my fists against the steering wheel with each curse. "God damn you, Hannah! God damn you!" Angry tears blurred my vision.

Hannah clasped her hands over her mouth. "Oh God, Ty, I'm sorry."

"Why, Hannah? Why would you *do* that? Why bring her up?" I wiped the back of my hand across my damp cheeks. "You know what that does to me, godammit." I struck my fist against the wheel twice more. "*Godammit!*"

"I know. I'm so sorry. I shouldn't have said that. I didn't mean it. Really. I didn't. I'm just... I'm so...so frustrated."

I took deep breaths to calm myself and swiped my sleeve across my eyes and beneath nose. Everything was crumbling around me — *everything* — and I was completely helpless to stop it. It was as if my life were caught in a current, drifting further away from shore, away from home and everything familiar to me. I was hopelessly lost.

I shook my head. "What am I doing?" I asked myself. "What the bloody hell am I doing?" I screamed the second time, as if to wake myself from a bad dream. I bit my lip to stop myself from sobbing. But it didn't work.

Hannah looked over at me and put her hand on my wounded shoulder. "I don't know, Ty, but I might be able help if you would just let me in and tell me what's going on. You wanted me to trust you, and I did. Now I'm asking you to do the same."

Her words reminded me of my last conversation with Nick; how desperately I wanted to help him, and how he wouldn't let me. I sighed, feeling defeated all over again. Then I dried my eyes one last time and sat up as straight as I could.

"All right. Fine. Have it your way. Once we check in to a hotel, I'll tell you everything. I hope you're right. I hope you *can* help me figure this out. Because God knows, I can't seem to do it on my own."

Chapter Thirty-One
Tyler

It was early in the evening when we pulled up to the valet entrance at the upscale Four Seasons Hotel in San Francisco. As I jumped out of the car, an attendant opened Hannah's door and offered his hand. The valet handed me a claim ticket then placed Hannah's bag on the curb.

"Will you be staying with us tonight, ma'am?" the valet asked Hannah.

"No," I jumped in before she could reply. "We're just meeting some friends for dinner."

Hannah threw me a confused glance. I tipped the valet, grabbed Hannah's bag, and escorted her into the hotel. The lobby was elegant with walls finished in contemporary paneling and adorned with modern art. The crisp white marble floor was dressed with thick area rugs bordered by elaborate patterned tile. A considerable step up from the last place we'd stayed. But Hannah ignored it all, her eyes pinned on me.

"Why did you tell him we wouldn't be staying?" she asked.

There were people all around so I leaned in close to whisper. "Because I don't want your plates associated with our room. No loose ends. It's safer that way."

She finally looked around, soaking in the richly decorated interior with awe. "Why are we even staying at such an expensive place anyway?"

"Again, it's safer," I explained as I scanned the lobby. "They have better security, lots of cameras, plenty of staff twenty-four-seven. It would be much more difficult for an intruder, like the one we had last night, to get past all that."

I smiled down at her, hoping my precautions made her feel safer. I reached for Hannah's hand and led her into the lounge, back to a table in a dark corner. Perhaps she saw the perspiration along my forehead or felt the way my hand trembled and put two and two together, because she resisted and pulled against me.

"Ty, I don't think this is a good idea."

"Oh, come on, one drink won't hurt. Besides, I need to observe the lobby."

She wasn't too excited by the idea, but she sat down with me anyway. "Okay, but only one drink, something light, then we go check in."

A cocktail waitress approached our table, smiled a polite greeting, and placed napkins on the table in front of us. "Good evening, folks. What can I get you tonight?" she asked, looking briefly at Hannah before her eyes settled on me. Her smile broadened and she winked.

I glanced back over at Hannah. Her eyes were shooting daggers into the woman's back.

"Coffee, black," I ordered without even looking up at the waitress. "And you, Hannah?"

Her irritation turned to surprise. "Um…yeah, same for me, thanks."

The waitress scribbled on her notepad with a muffled humph. As soon as she left, Hannah smacked me on the arm.

"Ouch! Watch the shoulder." I wagged my finger at her. "Remember, I took a bullet for you."

"You're a jerk!"

"What? Would you rather I order something stronger?"

"No! And that's not what I'm referring to and you know it." She looked away for a moment then turned back with a soft shake of her head. "I bet that happens all the time, huh?"

"What's that?"

"That waitress," she replied, tipping her chin toward our fleeing server.

I shrugged. "What about her?"

"Oh, come on, Ty, don't be coy. She was flirting with you. That is so rude. For all she knows, I could be your wife."

I chuckled again, a memory of Jill having a similar reaction rushing through me. "Yeah, my wife used to get pretty upset when that would happen."

Hannah sat back in her seat and crossed her arms over her chest. "I bet." A crooked smile pulled up on one side of her mouth. "I hate to think about what your poor wife must have put up with having you around."

I leaned my elbows on the table and steepled my fingers under my chin. "You might not believe this but, I wasn't such a bad chap. She didn't seem to mind so much."

Hannah stared at me with only a tiny smile remaining. "No, I don't imagine she did." Then she sniffed and looked away.

I studied her as she scanned the people milling around us. I thought back to when I was younger, when I enjoyed the attention I received from women like the waitress. But then Jillian came along and the flattery turned to subtle embarrassment. It was damn awkward to sit next to the woman you loved and be flirted with by strangers.

We lingered in the bar for about an hour, watching people come and go. We made a game out of choosing guests and, by their appearance, guessing where we thought they came from or what they did for a living. We mimicked their posture and spouted made-up lines of dialogue as entertainment. It was a childish game, good for a few laughs, and it gave me the opportunity to look out for any of Alexi's men. Hannah seemed relaxed and comfortable, given our circumstances. It was nice to see her smile and hear her laugh.

I patted her arm. "Stay put while I get us a room," I said as I rose from the table. "I'll be back in a few minutes."

I used my own credit card to secure the room. Now that we were in San Francisco, I didn't want there to be any connection to Hannah. It was bad enough that her car was in the garage and that anyone might see it. With two card keys in hand, I returned to the bar and picked up Hannah's bag.

"Ready?" I asked, offering her my arm.

She looped hers through mine and accompanied me through the lobby to the main elevators which whisked us up to our suite on the seventeenth floor. I handed her one of the card keys and she opened the door. Hannah looked pleased as we entered the suite. It was large and elegant with contemporary furnishings done in shades of silver, pewter, gold and greyish-blue. The view out the expansive windows was magnificent and looked out onto Yerba Buena Gardens. I escorted her to a separate room and deposited her bag on the luxurious king-sized bed.

"You have your own bedroom. No monsters allowed," I joked in bad taste. She swatted at me again, but I maneuvered out of the way. "A little more like what you're used to, I hope," I said as she walked around the suite examining everything.

She didn't look up, just ran her hand over the furnishings and replied, "More so than the last one."

Given her tone, I thought I might have insulted her with that last remark, but she continued her tour and didn't act offended. I walked over to the small dining area, well-appointed with a chic table for four.

"We can order in tonight," I suggested. "Something good to make up for all the bad food we've endured."

She caught my eye. "Breakfast wasn't so bad."

"The company was good, at least," I added, hoping to make her smile again.

It worked. Hannah flashed me a charming grin.

"Ty? Since we're settled in, would you mind if I went for a short walk? When we drove in, I saw a little shop a few doors down that I'd really like to visit. It's been so long since I've been in The City."

I shook my head hesitantly. "I don't know, Hannah..."

"Oh, come on. It's busy out on the street, and it's only three doors down, at most. I need to get some fresh air and stretch my legs, have some girl time...you know, *alone*."

I wasn't very comfortable with the idea, but she was persistent.

"I'll wear a hat and dark glasses," she added, trying her best to twist my arm.

I still didn't like it, but she'd been a pretty good sport, all things considered. And I didn't think even Alexi would snatch her off the street in this neighborhood. Still, I wasn't willing to take that risk.

"Well, perhaps just down to one of the shops in the lobby, as long as you stay where there are plenty of people. And here, bring your phone, just in case." I held out her cell. "Keep it off unless you absolutely need it."

She was disappointed at being restricted, but didn't argue.

"One hour," I reminded her as she headed for the door a few minutes later, her hair pulled up and her cap and glasses in place. I was relieved to see that she appeared unrecognizable. "Hannah, would you mind if I ordered dinner for you?"

"No, that sounds good. And since Beck's paying, go ahead and make it something decadent," she suggested. "But Ty? Please...be good. Okay?"

"Right-o, Mum," I said with a salute.

Hannah shot me a look of warning with her head tilted to the side and her hand on her hip. She posed just like my mum when she reprimanded me as a young boy. Both the image and the memory made me chuckle.

When Hannah left the room, she took all her energy with her. It was remarkable how much calmer I was when she was near. I walked to the window towering above the city streets and scanned for Alexi or his car, but I was too far away to discern anyone on the busy roads.

I turned on the wide-screen TV and scanned the cable news to see if anyone from the Seattle area had been reported missing. When the news proved clear, I surfed through the other channels, trying to find something to divert my attention, but I was too restless with Hannah gone and couldn't sit still. I searched the satellite radio stations until I found one that played alternative music, Hannah's favorite. I listened to it for a while and found the tunes to be rather angst-ridden and melancholy, too much for my present mood.

I gave it great effort, but I couldn't keep my attention from the mini bar. I looked at my watch and noted it had been nearly eighteen hours since my last drink. Every last minute of those hours twisted through me like a knife. My hands were trembling worse than ever, and I swallowed hard, breaking out into a cold sweat at the sight of all that alcohol. It was no use trying to deny myself when it was all I could think about. I grabbed two tiny bottles of Jack Daniel's and a cold can of Coke and mixed them in a tall glass with some ice. I consumed the contents quickly, relief filling me and quieting the building tension.

After wrapping the empty bottles in paper, I stuffed them into the waste basket then rearranged the remaining liquor so it didn't look like any were missing. I even brushed my teeth. I'd rather not have to deal with Hannah's accusations, should she take notice. The guilt I felt at resorting to such measures was tempered by the easing of my stress. I needed to be calm. It would be impossible for me to sort out all the issues with Nick and Alexi, not to mention Hannah, without some kind of external reinforcement, and I accepted that for what it was: pure weakness.

After washing out the glass, I refilled it with another soda and drank it down just as fast. The caffeine hummed through my veins and picked up my spirit. I looked over the menu from the hotel restaurant and selected dishes for each of us, as well as an indulgent dessert to share.

I felt much better when Hannah returned fifteen minutes later with a tall bag in her hand and a welcoming smile on her lovely face.

Chapter Thirty-Two

Hannah

After being confined to a car for so long, it felt good to be out and walking around. Though I was restricted to the hotel, I welcomed the small taste of freedom. I strolled through the few shops off the lobby, but felt too distracted to really focus on shopping. My thoughts were consumed by Tyler alone in the room with a fully stocked bar so close at hand. We couldn't afford another night of his heavy drinking.

An idea had been brewing for a few minutes before I finally decided to act on it. I knew it would be difficult, if not impossible, for Ty to go too long without something to drink, but I hoped that weaning him off the hard stuff would be an acceptable option. Wine was much weaker, yet very relaxing, so I picked out a bottle of fine Merlot to share over dinner and returned to the room.

As soon as I walked through the door, I noticed a difference in Ty's demeanor. Suspicious, I scanned the room, but all I saw were a couple of soda cans left on the coffee table. There was no evidence that Tyler had had a hard drink, so I took his good mood at face value and enjoyed it for what is was.

"Wow, you seem in good spirits," I commented.

"Caffeine on an empty stomach," he replied with a wide grin. He glanced at his watch and tapped the crystal. "Speaking of an empty stomach, I ordered dinner a while ago. It should be here momentarily."

"Good, I'm starving."

As if on cue, there was a knock on the door, and a voice called out "room service." We both laughed over the timing. I crossed the room to answer the door, but Tyler stopped me and pushed me behind his body. He peeked through the peep hole then cracked open the door and peered through. He sighed slightly in relief and pulled the door wide, allowing the waiter to roll his cart inside.

"Good evening," he said cheerfully. "May I set your meal up for you in the dining room?"

Ty nodded his approval. "Please," he said and gestured toward the table.

The waiter quickly set the table for two, settling the artfully arranged dishes between the silverware then lighting two tall candles in the center. "There you go, folks. Enjoy your meal."

Ty thanked the waiter, signed the tab, and slipped him a few bills before he showed him out. He turned to me and rubbed his hands together. "Let's eat, shall we?"

I held up one finger. "Wait, I have something else for us." I retrieved the bag I had left on the entry table and pulled out the bottle of wine. "I thought this would be nice to have with our meal. I thought it might...help, you know, with your cravings...at least I hope so...while not being too strong, of course." I shrugged at Ty's shocked expression, reasoning with him as he had with me the night before. "It's just one bottle between the two of us."

He stuffed his hands in his pockets and peered down at the floor. "Thanks, Hannah."

He smiled, but it didn't reach his eyes. Inwardly, I wondered why, but let it go.

I walked over to the low buffet in the dining room and pulled out two glasses and a cork screw, and handed them all to Ty then opened the draperies so we could enjoy the twinkling evening cityscape.

When the bottle was opened and the glasses half-filled, we sat down to enjoy our meal. We kept the conversation on lighter topics while we ate, sharing our entrees with each other. The food was tasty, and we finished nearly everything, the wine included, before we dove into the tempting dessert. When I thought he was relaxed and comfortable, I changed the subject of our discussion.

"Okay Tyler, you promised to tell me everything once we were settled in. So now it's time. Spill."

He choked on his food and wiped a linen napkin over his mouth. "Can't I have a few more minutes to finish my meal?"

"I think you've had long enough."

"Hannah, why do you want to ruin our nice dinner?"

I knew he was just stalling for time and gave him a sharp look. I sat back in my chair and folded my arms. "Ty, it doesn't matter if it's now or an hour from now. You *are* going to tell me everything, even if I have to get you drunk to do so."

He coughed again, threw his napkin down onto the table, and pushed his chair back. "Why are you so determined to run headlong into danger?"

I lowered my eyes to the table, my anger simmering just beneath the surface. "I'm not running headlong, Tyler. I was unceremoniously *pulled* in, without my consent. And while I understand the circumstances and have, more or less, forgiven you for your…mistake, I might remind you that I haven't forgotten it.

"I'm not exactly here of my own free will. And I resent your patronizing tone, especially since I'm willing to help you clear up your mess without involving the authorities. I could have called the police, you know, back at the café or even downstairs in the lobby while you were checking in, but I didn't because I'm trying hard to trust in your word. Even after everything you've done. So, once again, I think you owe me."

The grin was wiped from Tyler's face while he pondered my words. He looked me square in the eye and held it there for a moment before dropping his gaze uncomfortably. Pushing his chair clear of the table, he stood up and gently took my hand.

"Come join me on the sofa," he requested.

He escorted me over and motioned for me to take a seat. We both sat sideways, facing each other squarely. He reclaimed my hand in his own and began.

"First, I want to reiterate how sorry I am for all that I've put you through. For the pain and fear I've caused. That is not who I am, and I have no excuse to offer that would be reason enough to have attempted such an unspeakable thing. No matter the situation, what I did was wrong, and I know that. I am deeply ashamed."

Ty grew agitated as the regret washed over him again. He could no longer look me in the eye, and he was losing control over his emotions, his face twitching in self-disgust.

"Ty, I told you I understood. You don't have to rehash all—"

He shook his head and raised his eyes back up to mine. "Please, Hannah, let me finish before you offer me absolution."

He dropped my hand and turned away from me, sitting straight along the edge of the sofa. With his elbows resting on his knees and his fingers steepled between his nose and upper lip, he struggled to find the right words. Unable to sit still, he stood and paced the floor.

"Hannah, I've explained that you—by proxy, of course—have a price on your head, that you'd been sold already. I've been trying to get you out of this deal, but these people Nick and I are mixed up with are reluctant to renegotiate. They've already received payment from their client and are just waiting for me to deliver you to them. I've explained to Nick's boss, Alexi, that I'd made a mistake, that I had misidentified you, that I had the wrong girl."

Ty shook his head and kept his eyes pinned to the floor.

"From the beginning, Alexi knew I was intending retribution against Erin, and since he would directly benefit from it, he was only too willing to accommodate me, but essentially, he doesn't care about the reasoning behind the plan. All he cares about is that I owe him his, uh...merchandise. Merchandise he's already sold and been paid for. He only cares about closing the deal. I told him I would repay the price his boss, Dmitri, had accepted, with interest, and he could refund the money to his client. But he's not willing to do that. Nick said it's not about the money for Dmitri, it's about power. They can't allow themselves to be screwed with, to look weak."

He stopped pacing, stuffed his hands in his pockets, and stared out the window.

"I told Alexi I would never turn you over—an innocent girl—to be used that way. At this point, I couldn't even do that to Erin."

Tyler's focus wavered and he choked up. He looked down at his feet and continued, his brow knitted tightly together.

"We argued over this point for some time without coming to an agreement, so Alexi felt... He felt it...necessary to secure some kind of...insurance policy — leverage, you might say — to compel me to complete the deal by our prearranged deadline."

Tyler dropped his hands to his sides and tightened them into fists. He glanced over his shoulder and looked me in the eye.

"Hannah, Alexi has my brother, and he will kill him if I don't comply."

I sucked in a large breath and my mouth fell open. "Oh God, Tyler, I'm so sorry." I stood and took a step toward him.

He raised his hand to stop me. "I was allowed to speak with Nick this morning before we left the café. He told me not to go through with it, not to bring you in or to even attempt to help him. He said that...that he was...willing..." Ty paused, pressed his lips together, and swallowed hard. "He said that he was willing to pay with his life."

A single tear spilled from the corner of his eye. The anguish there was unbearable to see. I was dumbfounded. Just the day before, Nick had been all too eager to turn me over. I wondered what had changed so drastically that he would offer himself up in my place. I walked over and faced Ty.

"Why, Tyler? Why would Nick do that?"

He turned away and paced the room again. "I wondered about that myself. He wasn't very forthcoming with me, at first, but...Nick eventually confessed something. I still can't believe it though."

Tyler's tenuous control over his emotions unraveled even further. Tears streamed down his face and his chin quivered. He looked ready to implode.

"Apparently, Nick has been harboring a great deal of anger and resentment toward me since the deaths of our parents and sister four years ago. He felt I blamed him, and thought he was irresponsible and weak for getting sucked into drinking and drugs. He thought I was disappointed in the man he'd become."

Tyler paused and tried to gather himself, but failed. "I think... I think he hated me for it."

Ty could barely speak. He cried, his shoulders shaking with pent up emotion. I reached out to comfort him, but he pulled away.

"No!" He bowed his head and raised his finger, asking me to wait. "Last winter, when Jillian discovered Erin Anderson had stolen her card and assumed her identity, she became frustrated by the authorities' unwillingness to prosecute. She even asked me to help, but I advised her to wait it out. With nowhere else to turn, she approached Nick and asked for his assistance. But when I got wind of their plan, I reprimanded Jillian and forbid Nick from getting involved, a decision I regret, because if I had just let Nick handle it, then maybe Jillian would still be alive. But... But I..."

Tyler completely fell to pieces. He grabbed the back of the sofa with both hands and doubled over, resting his forehead against them, sobbing uncontrollably. It was heartbreaking to watch, especially since I felt so incapable of comforting him. Still, I reached out and touched his shoulder, but he shot up and backed away with his hands in the air.

"No. Don't fucking touch me. I'm...poison! I make bad decisions and destroy everything I touch. Can't you see? I chose to ignore Nick, and now my parents and sister are dead. I forbid Nick to help Jillian, and now she's dead. I pulled Nick into this mess, and now look what's happened. And you, Hannah. God, look at what I've done to you."

He took a long pause, but still could not gather himself together.

"Now, no matter what I do, someone will get hurt. Someone may die. One way or the other. What am I supposed to do now, Hannah? What?"

With a renewed effort, he began pacing back and forth across the room, shaking his head.

"No, I can't. I can't do this. I can't make that choice. I've already ruined Nick's life. I've ruined *your* life. This is impossible. I can't do it. I just can't."

And then he froze and tilted his face upward with his hands atop his head.

"*Godammit!*" he screamed. "How do I fix this?"

Tyler slumped his shoulder against the wall and slid down to the floor onto his knees where he wept into his hands. My heart broke for him, cleaved in two. I walked over and knelt down in front of him. I captured his face in my hands and pulled his head to my shoulder, whispering his name while I soothed him. Inconsolable, Ty placed his hands on my shoulders and tried to push me away.

"No, Hannah…"

"Shush, Ty, shhh. It's okay, it's all right." I leaned back and kissed his forehead and cheeks, shushing him over and over, like a mother to a distraught child.

"Don't, please," he pleaded as he pulled back.

He shook his head while I stared into his tortured eyes, seeing for the first time all the tragedy embodied there. I saw more pain than I thought any one person could ever contain. I was desperate to ease it in some way, but I had no idea how. It was a purely instinctual reaction to lean in and press my lips to his. I pulled back and looked at him again, but the torment still twisted his features, and tears continued to spill down his cheeks. His head fell back against the wall, and his lips parted as his hands fell away.

I moved my whole body into his and wrapped my arms around his back, my cheek pressed against his chest. He rested his hands along my waist and dropped his face into the crook of my neck and shoulder.

"Hannah, please...don't..." He sounded broken, irreparably so. A man at the very end of his rope.

"It's okay," I said over and over as I held him. I cried, too. I couldn't help it.

His body quaked with wracking sobs as he finally wrapped his arms around me, pulling me in tight, his longing for human compassion outweighing his need to distance himself. He cried out for his parents, then his sister, and lastly, for Jill and their lost child, insisting each death was his fault. He called out for Nick, hopeless as to how he might save him and bring him back alive. And he apologized to me, for being too focused on revenge, for being drunk and careless with my life. He piled each of us onto his shoulders and tried to carry the load, the burden way too much for one man to bear alone.

With no other way to comfort him, I held him close for a long, long time, until his sobs finally ebbed and his muscles relaxed from exhaustion. He had no fight left in him. I pressed him back onto the floor and leaned closely over his chest with my face above his. His hands were raised, lying slack on the floor next to his head, like an infant asleep in its crib. I reached out and braided my fingers through his, pressing my palm flat against his hand.

As he lay quietly beneath me, I ran my thumb over the tense furrow dividing his brow. I stroked the wrinkle and eased it away, just as I had yearned to do. His mouth fell slack, and the last of his tears glistened in the soft light. I cupped my hand to his damp cheek and slowly leaned down, my lips barely grazing his mouth. I moved my head slightly from side to side and let the tip of my tongue stroke his parted lips.

There was a tentative response as he finally seemed to surrender. He sighed and closed his eyes then tightened his grip around my fingers. He lifted his free hand and weaved it through my hair, pulling me in gently and returning my kiss. It was guarded at first, unsure, slow and tender. Then his body stirred beneath me, a desperate hunger rising to the surface like a drowning man gasping for one last breath. His arms coiled around by back, hands splayed across my skin, fingers curled with nails that bit into my flesh, as if he couldn't pull me in close enough, tight enough.

He needed me, to heal him, to want him. And in that moment, I did. I wanted him, just as much as he wanted me. It had been so long since I'd felt desired by a man. I realized then just how empty and lonely I had been, and not just for the last few months either, but for years. Ty wasn't the only one desperate for human touch. My body quaked in urgency, and I cried. My tears fell and mixed with Tyler's and streamed down his temple. We shared our quiet anguish, stirring our pain to bloom into a frantic kind of passion.

I needed him to know that he could be forgiven, that I could be the instrument through which he could ask for forgiveness: forgiveness from his wife for letting her down, from his brother for not being there when he needed him, from his parents and sister for their preventable deaths, and lastly, from me, for everything he had done. He needed forgiveness more than he needed air in his lungs.

He would never be able to forgive himself until he asked for it from those he loved, from those he had hurt most. I had learned over the last few months that holding onto pain, anger, and resentment only consumed the soul, leaving nothing but bitterness, preventing one from moving on. I was trying my best to forgive so that I could be released from all that. At some point,

Ty would need to let go and forgive, as well. He would need to forgive himself *and* the woman who had taken everything away from him. I would show him it could be done, to forgive the unforgivable. I would give that to him. I would show him that there was still hope—for him, for me, for Nick. For all of us.

It was my turn to take control. I removed Ty's clothes and then my own. I ran my hands over him, marveling at his masculine beauty. He was so perfectly formed, broad shouldered, hard and trim, and massively muscled. Completely flawless on the outside, yet so terribly damaged within. I was overcome with my need to comfort him, to show that I had forgiven him. To show him that he could do the same. Lying beneath me, I saw that he was ready, and so was I.

I gave myself over and made love to Ty on the carpeted floor. I straddled his glorious body with my own and pulled his face up to meet me. He held me about the waist, his lips pressed to the hollow at my throat, and my cheek along the top of his head. His despair, still raw and palpable, made our joining all the more poignant.

In the long moments we held each other, we became one. One spirit, one body, one soul with one purpose. We each cried out, both in pain and in tortuous pleasure, holding on while our bodies shook in fierce release. It was the single most bittersweet moment of my entire life. One I would remember and cherish forever.

We remained locked together until our breathing calmed and our heartbeats returned to normal. I loosened my grip on his shoulders and leaned back, smiling down at him tenderly. He looked up and smiled, too, ever so slightly. Tears still sparkled in his vivid blue eyes. He shook his head almost imperceptibly, and with a tremulous sigh, his chin fall to his chest.

"Ah, Hannah…that doesn't exactly make it any easier for me now."

I sighed in return and touched my hand to his cheek, still damp with his tears. I raised his head up so he could look me straight in the eye. And then it all became clear. I smiled.

"Don't worry," I said. "I have an idea."

Chapter Thirty-Three

Tyler

I stood in the middle of the room and pulled my clothes back on, staring in horror and fear. "No way, Hannah. There's no bloody way in hell."

She glared at me with her arms crossed over her chest, her fingers drumming against her bare skin. "Why not? It just might work."

I couldn't believe she would ask me such a stupid question, but then again, her suggestion had been far worse. I crossed the room and touched my hand to her cheek. With a sorrowful smile, I pulled her in close, resting my chin on the top of her head.

"You are a silly, brave girl. And I...appreciate...your generous offer." I kissed her forehead then pulled back to look her in the eye. "But that will never, ever happen." I turned and walked away, trying hard not to let my anxiety get the best of me yet again.

"Do you have a better idea then?" she asked.

I looked back at her in wonder. "Come on, Hannah. *Any* idea would be better than that."

She huffed and stomped her foot. "But you said this Dmitri character made a deal with a client who would most likely just keep me for himself, right? So then don't you think it would be easier for you and Nick to rescue me from that man's house, than it would be for you, all alone, to save Nick while he's hidden somewhere among all those thugs with guns? It would be suicide to attempt that, Tyler, and you know it."

"I'm not discussing this with you."

Terrified of the way she was thinking, I turned away again, but she closed the distance and faced me, undeterred.

"Tyler, I can do this. I know I can."

I grabbed her by both arms and got right up into her face.

"No, Hannah. You *can't* do this, and you won't. You think I have any way of knowing for sure where they might take you? You think Alexi was *ever* honest with me? For God's sake, you could just as easily end up in a whore house, maybe even sent to another state or country. No way would I ever risk your life like that, Hannah. No way. You'd never survive, not for one blasted second."

She stared at me with eyes round as the moon, momentarily frightened into silence. Then her stubbornness kicked in, and her chin jutted out.

"What about your brother?" she asked. "How the hell do you plan on rescuing him?"

I stared her in the eye for a long moment then let go and pushed her away.

"Don't you worry about Nick. He's my problem. Not yours. I'll figure everything out on my own, without your help."

In all honesty though, I didn't know what to do about Nick. I was resigned to the idea that I would have to throw myself at the mercy of Alexi and Dmitri, that they would allow me the chance to somehow repay them, even if my very life was forever beholden to them. The only chance I had of that working was if I cut all ties with Hannah and sent her away. I was convinced that Alexi didn't know who she really was. During our last conversation, he told me to find the right girl or bring the one I had, like one was as good as any other. He didn't care. Nick had only spoken to Alexi about Erin. He never shared the information from that rental car receipt. Alexi couldn't know about Beck Maguire, or Hannah. We never saw any of his men back in her neighborhood, so if I made sure she got out of town safely before I met with Alexi, he would have no choice but to settle with me alone. His prize would be long gone. He would never find her, and I would never tell.

Convinced that was my only option, I pressed my lips together and brushed by Hannah, but she caught my arm and spun me around.

"You can't just dismiss me, Ty. I deserve a say in my own future."

I shook my head. "That's just it, Hannah. *This* is not your future."

There was no way I could take the chance of having her wait for me at the hotel. Not now. Not with her cavalier attitude. I didn't know whether they knew to come here looking for her. For all I knew, I might not even make it back alive. She'd be alone and defenseless. The best and safest thing for me to do would be to buy Hannah an airline ticket back to Seattle. I could arrange to have her car shipped straight home. As long as she was gone before I left to meet with Alexi, there would be nothing he could do.

With my decision made, I ran my fingers along her cheek and up under her chin. "You're future's at home, Hannah, in Seattle with your son, and no matter what it takes, I *will* get you back there." I tapped the end of her nose with my finger and walked away, but I heard her sigh impatiently in reply.

Given her response, I had a strong feeling Hannah was going to be difficult and refuse to go if she feared for my wellbeing. I would have to tell her that I'd managed to swing a new deal after all, that Nick would be released, and together we would repay Dmitri the money we owed him. I would tell her that she was safe, and that we no longer needed her.

I was at odds with myself about sending her away. I didn't understand my feelings for her at all. I was deeply touched by the way she had so willingly given herself to me, to ease my pain, to show that she had forgiven me. But allowing myself to make love with Hannah had further complicated an already unmanageable situation. I realized, with great remorse, everything she had forfeited, and yet she still offered herself to me as a source of comfort. I was bewildered by her sense of compassion and her ability to forgive, especially when all I had ever shown her was my own selfish need for revenge.

I came to accept that I must break our strange bond and part ways, and because she seemed reluctant to do so, I would push her away. I would make her *want* to leave, whether it was by way of anger, fear, or simply hurt feelings.

I would cast her aside to save her.

···

Later, I approached Hannah, trying my best to appear casual and confident.

"Tomorrow, I'll meet face to face with Alexi and Dmitri, and I'm positive we'll be able to work out an acceptable deal."

She looked at me, a single brow raised in suspicion. "That's odd. You didn't seem so sure *earlier* this evening."

I blanched inwardly at her remark. "What happened between us, Hannah, that was a moment of weakness, nothing more, brought on by the wine and my regret at having involved you in this mess. It won't ever happen again, I assure you."

Hurt flashed across Hannah's face, and I saw my opportunity to drive the necessary wedge between us, to start the process of getting her back home where she belonged.

"I'm sorry, Hannah. I don't want to hurt your feelings, but I need to focus on Nick right now. His confession this morning hit me at my core."

"Confession? What confession?"

"That's what I was trying to tell you earlier. Nick admitted to seizing the opportunity to bring me down a peg when I was having a difficult time adjusting to Jill's death. He said he purposely got me abusing alcohol as retribution for all the slights he imagined I'd paid him, to show that I was just as weak as he'd been when he started using. To prove that I was no better." I saw the fury rage within Hannah as she took in this bit of information.

"Why would your own brother do that to you...at your lowest moment? That's unfathomable."

I raised my hand to calm her down. "It's okay, really. It's put everything into perspective for me, and it's the one reason why I'd never even consider risking your life to help Nick. We got ourselves into this mess, and we can damn well get ourselves out.

"I've known these Russians for several years now, and I've dealt with them on my brother's behalf before. They know Nick is impulsive, and that I'll always be there to step in for him. Dmitri is a businessman, after all, and all he needs is money—albeit a lot of it—to see the deal through. Blood spilled in retribution would garner him nothing. I'm certain I can get him to see that much."

I watched Hannah closely. She seemed to accept what I told her at face value. Offering her a solution that didn't include violence appeased her, calming her fears on my behalf.

"Well then, what's going to happen to me?" she asked.

"For now, I want you to stay put and out of the way until I've worked out all the details."

"And what details would that be?"

"Don't you worry your pretty little head. It's getting late. You should get some sleep. I'm going out for an hour or so. I'll try not to disturb you when I get back."

I was purposely dismissive, as if I were trying to distance myself from her after our tumultuous union earlier this evening. Making her think I regretted making love with her was a sure fire way to do that. My words and attitude plainly hurt her, and I hated myself for doing it, but I believed it was the only way to disentangle myself from her quickly.

"Be a good girl and stay put." Without another look, I turned and headed out the door.

Chapter Thirty-Four

Tyler

For my plan to work, there were several items I needed to attend to immediately. I visited the concierge who helped make arrangements for Hannah's flight back to Seattle. She printed off the electronic ticket and placed it in a small envelope. I also had her make arrangements for a Town Car to pick Hannah up at the hotel and drop her off at the airport in time for her flight in the morning, paying extra for a personal escort up to the security gate.

Next, she helped me locate a shipping company. I made arrangements with them to pick up Hannah's BMW at our hotel and ship it to her residence on Seattle's Eastside. The bill of lading was faxed to the concierge. I had her put all the paperwork for the airline ticket and shipping into a large manila envelope. I scratched Hannah's name across it with a thick black marker and handed her the key to Hannah's car.

Lastly, I needed to find a quiet, private corner to make another phone call to Nick, or Alexi, since I wasn't sure who would answer. I was prepared for either, so while I was disappointed, I wasn't surprised when I heard Alexi's voice. His tone was more serious than it had been the last two times I'd spoken to him. I think he was tired of playing games.

"Tyler, my friend, so good of you to call." He addressed me with his usual sarcasm, his concise articulation aggravating me more than usual.

"Alexi."

"I hear you are nearly back in town. I hope the girl is well. We need her in top form, after all. I cannot afford damaged goods, you understand."

I was relieved he didn't know we'd made it back into San Francisco yet. I was a little surprised though, knowing he was probably watching us from a distance. I couldn't rely on him telling me the truth. As long as Hannah stayed put, she would be safe until I saw her off to the airport. After that, I would be face to face with Alexi, and he would have to deal with me alone.

"She's fine," I answered. "Now put my brother on the phone."

"In a moment. First, I want to make arrangements to meet—you, me, and the girl."

"Not so fast, Alexi. I need to speak to Nick before we get down to business."

He barked a command in Russian, snapping his fingers impatiently. Loud voices called out in the background as Alexi handed the phone over.

"Tyler?" It was Nick. His voice was even rougher than before, thick and garbled.

"Nick, are you all right?"

"Ty, remember what I told you—" he began but was cut off. He yelled out from far away. "Stay away, Ty. Don't come here. Don't come looking for me!"

Then his voice faded away altogether. It killed me inside to hear him calling out so desperately and not be able to come to his defense. It was difficult to control my temper when Alexi returned to the phone.

"You see, my friend, your brother yet lives, but I think he could use your help. I suggest you bring the girl and meet us at the tea house. Nine a.m. sharp. And Tyler...this is your last chance to make it right, so do not fuck it up. For your brother's sake."

Alexi hung up before I could say anything else. I glanced at my watch. I had nine hours left to lay the ground work and get Hannah away from the hotel. It was time for me to go back to our suite and get started. I prepared myself by ordering six shots of tequila at the hotel bar. It was enough to set me on edge, yet not so much that I was overly impaired, given how much alcohol I normally consumed. I downed all six shots quickly then ordered a bottle of beer to take back up to the room.

It was dark and quiet in the suite. Hannah had gone to bed, as I'd suggested. I was hesitant about taking the next step, nervous even, but I had little choice. I stood in the doorway to her darkened room and stared over at her resting form. I walked over to the bed and stood next to her. She was sleeping on her side, turned away from me with just a sheet pulled up to her waist. It was easy enough to tug the sheet away from her body without her feeling it. Hannah lay exposed to me, with only her undergarments covering her tempting curves.

I allowed my eyes to roam over the alluring silhouette of her body, recalling the sweet moments we had shared earlier. My pulse, already accelerated with thoughts of my plan, quickened even more as the heated blood rushed through me. My muscles were taut, and I grew hard with desire. I wanted nothing more than to climb into bed beside her and repeat it, to show her that I could be just as giving as she had been. But, as aroused as I was, I knew I could never go there again. I would have to be satisfied with the precious memories she had given me.

With a reluctant sigh, I took the end of the cold, sweating bottle of beer and touched it to the side of her bare leg just above her knee. I slowly swept the chilled vessel up her thigh, over her hip, to her waist, and along her ribs. She startled awake with a quiet gasp, turning to look back over her shoulder as I loomed above her in the dark.

"Ty?" she called out in sleepy confusion.

"Mm. How lovely you look, Ms. Maguire," I taunted her menacingly then returned the bottle to my lips for a long pull.

She drew a sharp intake of breath. "Ty, what are you doing? Are you drunk?"

She tried to pull herself up in bed, but I swung my leg up and over her. I straddled her body at her hips and knelt down on the bed, pinning her in place. When she attempted to scoot out from under me, I pushed her back down by placing the bottom of the bottle against her chest, just below her chin. She shivered in fear while I leaned down to stare at her with a devilish grin.

"Oh Hannah, relax, it's just one beer," I pulled back to take another drink, "to wash down a few shots."

The fear in her eyes was plain, even in the dim city light outside the window. Her soft voice trembled as she spoke. "What's wrong? Why are you drinking again?"

I chuckled. "Why should there be anything wrong? I'm just...reliving old times." I smiled and continued to stare into her frightened eyes.

"Ty, please. Get off me."

She pushed against my chest with a half-hearted effort. I leaned down farther and pressed my lips against hers, kissing her until she was breathless. I sat back up and finished the beer then threw it against the wall where it crashed in a loud spray of shattered glass. Hannah jumped with a sharp yelp, her hands cupped against her ears.

I looked back down at her and slowly ran my hand up her arm, along her shoulder, and up to her throat, where I allowed it to linger. Very gently, I wrapped my fingers around the silken column of gleaming pale skin. My other hand entwined in her hair. I pulled my face to within an inch of hers and gave her a gentle but quick shake. She screamed out my name as the first tears began to roll over her temples. She pressed her eyes tight against me and wrapped both her hands around my wrist.

I gave her one more sharp jolt. "Open your eyes, Hannah!"

When she complied, I lowered my mouth to hers and kissed her slowly, drawing my tongue over her lips then plunging into her mouth. She didn't fight me at all, though I could feel how frightened she was as her body tensed and trembled. I pulled myself back and stared into her panic-stricken eyes, laughing softly at her fear.

"How well do you think you know me, Ms. Maguire? I mean, we've spent nearly every second of the last few days together, shared the most intimate of moments, the threat of death looming over our heads. You've seen me at my barbaric worst. My most broken and vulnerable. You've heard my pathetic tale of lost love and family betrayal. But you don't *really* know me. Do you?" I paused and held her gaze. "No," I laughed bitterly, "you don't know me at all."

I released my hold on her throat and pushed away. As I swung up off her, I grabbed her by both arms and forced her up off the bed with me. I wrapped my arms around her back, pinning hers to her sides while my mouth rested near her ear.

"That fear you feel right now, Hannah? I suggest you remember it well." I loosened my hold, pulled back, and looked her in the eye, then I kissed her again, one last time, tenderly at first, and then with all the hunger and desire I had for her. I left her shaking, stunned, and silent.

I pushed back from her and walked away; throwing onto her bed the manila envelope I had stuffed into the back of my waistband. I hesitated in the doorway and peered back over my shoulder. Hannah stood there alone in the dark. The tears in her eyes sparkled with the reflection of the city lights. Her arms were drawn up and pressed in front of her chest with her fists tucked firmly under her chin like a frightened little girl.

I was struck still in my tracks. That was exactly how she looked only two days ago, just before I pushed her down onto her bed and savagely tried to rape her in a haze of drunken retaliation. The image of that morning lingered in my mind then merged into the one before me now. The sight of this poor broken woman, abused for my base need for revenge, left me shaken and nauseous. *All the more reason to see this finished.* I clenched my jaw tight to keep myself from running back to her, from wrapping my arms around her and begging for her forgiveness yet again.

"You're going home in the morning, Ms. Maguire. Make certain you're ready," I said then left the room.

I heard her collapse back onto the bed, crying quietly. I left her confused and frightened, angry and betrayed, and, worst of all, hurt, but it was for the best.

For her, at least.

Chapter Thirty-Five

Tyler

As the sky blushed early the next morning, I returned to the hotel lobby and paid the bill of all current charges, with my own money, not Hannah's. Once back in the suite, I could hear Hannah in the bathroom. I seated myself in one of the large living room chairs and waited for her. She finally emerged, freshly showered. Her eyes were red and swollen with pale purple shadows marring the porcelain contours beneath them. I felt a moment of regret for my deceitful performance last night, but my resolve was firm, and if she was angry and hurt, or better yet, afraid, then she could leave me behind without looking back, and remember me as nothing more than a bad experience.

"All packed?"

Startled, Hannah came to an abrupt halt before me. She glared at me for a brief moment then looked away as she searched around the room.

"Yes," she replied, her tone bitter and flat.

"Then what are you looking for?"

"My car keys," she answered without looking up.

"Don't worry about it. You won't need them."

With a loud sigh, she hitched both hands onto her hips and glared at me. "Excuse me?"

"I said you won't need them. You're flying home. I've already had your car shipped back. Didn't you look in the envelope I left for you last night?" I asked, but she refused to respond. "All the arrangements have been made. The bill of lading for your car is in there, your boarding pass, plus all your cash; I even paid back what we spent. And a Town Car is waiting downstairs to take you to the airport. I've already spoken to the driver and given him precise instructions. He's bringing an assistant to escort you all the way to security. So you're all taken care of."

Hurt blossomed across her face yet again, but she smoothed it over with an icy stare. "You don't control me anymore."

I chuckled at her remark, rose from the chair, then walked over and stood in front of her. Although I loomed over her, and she couldn't hide the alarm in her eyes, she stood up to me without backing down, her chin raised defiantly. Though not surprised, I was duly impressed with her bravery, but I was dismayed that I would have to continue with my charade. I reached down and took her hand, turning it over to kiss the inside of her wrist.

"Oh, Ms. Maguire, I beg to differ," I said with cool confidence and a hint of a smile pulling up at the corner of my mouth.

Hannah ripped her hand from my grasp, pulled it back then slapped me hard across my face. The noise cracked like a whip off the walls. She took a step back and bore into me, contempt burning in her eyes. "I guess you were right. I don't know you at all. Goodbye, Mr. Karras."

Hannah stormed back into her room and grabbed her bag, purse, and the manila envelope. She returned a moment later and paused at the front door. She turned back to face me, as if she had something else to say.

"Hannah, I'm—"

She held up her hand with her index finger singled out. "No. It's *Ms.* Maguire now. Isn't it?"

I pressed my lips together and sighed. "I'll escort you down to the car."

"That won't be necessary. I think you've done enough already." Though her tone was bitter, she looked at me with what I could only call longing in her eyes.

I gazed back and felt my heart soften, my resolve slip. I wished I didn't have to do this, but I had no choice, so I hardened my expression and tipped my head at her.

She turned away and slipped through the door.

Chapter Thirty-Six

Hannah

I wasn't even through the door yet before I started crying again. I thought I'd cried away all my tears last night, that I had none left to shed, but they came back just the same. I felt deceived. I was angry that Ty had allowed me to comfort him as I did, offering him my forgiveness for every despicable thing he'd done to me, only to cast me aside as if it meant nothing, as if I were but a distraction to his real problem.

I was confused by the way his mood always seemed to shift from one extreme to the other. It was as if he had two personalities: one mean and manipulative, self-serving and hateful, the other tender and caring, remorseful and loving. I had come to care for the latter and despise the former. More than anything, Tyler had frightened me, and the tentative trust I'd held in him was gone.

Having all those feelings didn't lessen the pain I felt at leaving. I still hadn't sorted out the strange pull he had on me, and I was embarrassed, even horrified, that I could have any tender feelings for him at all after everything he'd put me through. But there was something there, as strange as it was, and right now it hurt more than I could bear.

I exited the elevator and crossed the lobby to the auto entrance where brightly colored taxis and sleek limos lined the curb. I looked around for some sign of who was to take me to the airport and noticed a tall gentleman in a black suit and tie. He leaned casually against the side of a polished black Mercedes and held a sign with "MAGUIRE" written neatly across it in bold letters. I walked up to him with a wan smile, my heart still aching and my nerves raw.

"I'm Hannah Maguire."

He tipped his head and grinned. "Going to the airport, ma'am?" he asked with a heavy European accent.

"Yes, I suppose I am."

With a courteous nod, he opened the door. I climbed in and sat down. My nose wrinkled at the aroma of fresh tobacco. The driver took his seat and looked back at me in the mirror.

"I should have you at your destination shortly, ma'am," he informed me in his awkward, clipped tone.

As he locked the doors, a slight chill ran through me, and I couldn't help but feel trapped somehow. I shook it off though, telling myself it was just the past two days of fending off attackers that had gotten to me. I leaned my head back and closed my eyes, determined to relax.

Soon this nightmare would all be over, and I would be back home where I belonged.

Chapter Thirty-Seven

Tyler

It was done. There was no going back, no matter how I felt about Hannah. I hated to see the pain in her eyes, knowing full well that I'd put it there yet again. Though it would haunt me forever, I would accept it, because she would be better off without me in the end. But still, I felt her absence acutely. Just having her near helped me stay calmer than I would otherwise, so with her gone and the task of facing Alexi and Dmitri ahead of me, I was a jumble of nerves. There was no putting it off though. I had just over thirty minutes to get to Dmitri's Tea House in the Outer Richmond. I flagged a cab and gave the driver the address.

When I arrived, Alexi's black Mercedes was parked in front of the restaurant. I nodded at the tall man leaning against it and pulled open the restaurant door. He followed me in, close on my heels, the strong smell of cigarettes preceding him. Two more large men with side arms bulging beneath their jackets met me as I entered. One put a hand out to stop me while the other patted me down for weapons.

As they searched me, I strained to see into the darkened room, looking for exits, additional men, and anything I could use as a weapon, should the need arise. The guards found nothing and let me pass, though I felt their eyes trained on me as if I had a bull's eye painted on my back. Alexi's voice called out from the private banquet room in the rear.

"Ah, Tyler, my friend, come," he said, oozing a polite charm. "Come and join us. Please, back here."

I crept cautiously through the main room and into the next, spying Alexi with two other men seated at a table, each expensively dressed in a finely tailored suit and tie. Sitting next to Alexi was Dmitri Chernov, a heavy-set man whose age was prominently mapped out on his markedly creased face. Though I had never met him in person, he was well-known in The City, repeatedly featured in the San Francisco Chronicle, sometimes in the crime section, but most often in the society and political pages. Across from him was a third man I did not recognize.

Four more intimidating men held watch directly behind them, their shoulders crammed together awkwardly around the small table. Everyone scrutinized me, each set of eyes looking me up and down deliberately. Only Alexi had a broad grin plastered to his face, accompanied by a measured glean which glowed in his eye. I walked up and stood in front of their table. Alexi gestured to the empty seat directly across from him.

"Sit, please. Have a cup of tea. It will refresh and energize you." With calculated civility, he poured me a cup then slid a creamer my way. "Earl Grey and milk for the Englishman, eh, my friend?" He winked and smiled, but it was anything but friendly.

I had the uneasy feeling I was being maneuvered somehow, like a bait dog being forced into the pit. I remained silent and took my seat next to the stranger who glared at me without an ounce of humor. Dmitri had a similarly sour look.

With a sharp clap of his hands, Alexi brought my attention back to him.

"Tyler, we are all surprised that you do not have the girl with you. Why did you not bring her as I asked?" Alexi's grin turned serious. Contrary to what he'd said, he didn't look surprised, and that had me worried.

"She's in a safe place. Don't worry, you'll get your merchandise once I've seen that Nick is well."

Dmitri and Alexi turned to each other and shared an amused look and a remark spoken in Russian. I found both disconcerting. They were entertained by my discomfort. Dmitri looked over at his men and gestured with a snap of his fingers. Two of them jumped up and disappeared into the kitchen, returning a minute later with Nick. His flannel shirt was torn and open, his jeans splattered with blood. They dragged him roughly by the arms, both of which were fastened behind his back. He couldn't even walk on his own. I jumped up out of my seat as they hauled him into the room. The remaining two guards popped up. One stood in my path while the other restrained me from behind, both my arms locked in a full Nelson hold.

"Oh my God, Nick!" I called out, straining to lift my head and shoulders so I could see him. The goon standing in front of me whipped his hand up to my throat. His fingers dug into the flesh around my windpipe.

One of the men holding Nick grabbed a handful of his hair and pulled his head up. When I caught sight of his bruised and swollen face, my stomach flipped, feeling as though it had lurched up into my mouth. My heart raced, the adrenaline giving me increased strength as I struggled to break free, but the massive guards were unyielding and easily held me in place. The one behind me yanked me back and the other punched me in the stomach. The grip on my arms gave way, and I fell to the floor, doubled over in pain, certain I would puke all over Dmitri's clean tile.

"Ty? What are you doing here? I told you not to come," Nick cried out as I rocked on my knees, fighting the overwhelming nausea.

"What about our deal, Tyler?" Alexi asked. "We had an agreement. Why have you not held up your end of the bargain?"

"I had...the wrong...girl. I told...you that," I ground out through the pain.

He walked over and stood above me with an angry sneer. "Well, that is not my problem, now is it...*my friend?*"

I leaned back on my heels, my arms still wrapped around my belly, and looked Alexi straight in the eye. Even as sharp spasms coursed through my gut, I couldn't keep the smirk from twisting at my mouth.

"It is now," I replied.

Alexi glared down at me, his nostrils flaring and his face red with rage. He gave a curt nod, and his henchmen pulled me back up. They raised their fists and pummeled my head then kicked my body with their booted feet as I slid back to the floor. They were skilled at their craft, expert professionals who knew precisely how to hit a man, inflicting as much pain and damage as they could in as few blows as possible. I felt my nose and several ribs break simultaneously. Thick blood filled my mouth and choked off my airway. I coughed to clear it, causing knife-sharp pain to shoot through me like a spear. I was seized by it with every ragged breath. I rolled into a ball and lay still as a stone as warm blood pooled on the floor around my face. Satisfied with their work, Alexi called his men off with a bark.

They left me moaning and writhing on the bloodied floor. I gasped for air, but could only manage to pant in small wet breaths that wheezed and crackled through dense clots of blood. I hacked and spit to draw in just enough oxygen so I wouldn't pass out, but the room spun and tilted at odd angles regardless. Stars of vertigo swirled through my head, which felt rent in two, the pain churning into wave after wave of nausea. I beat my fist against the floor, a weak effort to deal with the pain and keep myself from throwing up.

Alexi pushed me over with his foot and bent down close to my face. The casual smile was finally gone. An enraged sneer took its place, distorting his neatly groomed face with contempt.

"You think this is my problem, do you? Well, my friend, you would be wrong, *very* wrong., and you are about to find out just how wrong you truly are." He straightened his back, turned to his men, and roared, "Take them to the cages!"

I screamed in agony as Alexi's praetorians hefted me up and dragged me toward the kitchen.

"No, Ty," Nick wailed as I passed him. "Alexi, Dmitri...please. Don't do this. Please!" he begged. "We had a deal. You *promised* me. You said I'd be enough. You swore!"

I didn't know what Nick was talking about, but both Alexi and Dmitri cackled in reply. I was hauled outside and thrown into a waiting van, its rear doors flung open wide. Nick toppled in behind me, and the doors slammed shut. The engine roared to life and the van sped away.

Chapter Thirty-Eight

Tyler

Nick and I were tossed about the van as it threaded erratically through city traffic. Every sharp turn and pothole hurt like hell. I tried in vain to stay oriented and figure out where we were going, even as I drifted in and out of consciousness. Though we traveled a good distance, I was certain we were still in San Francisco. We drove alongside of a long industrial building—a warehouse from what I could tell from the rear door windows—stopping in front of a partially opened roll-up door where several men were stationed, waiting for our arrival. The van doors were thrown open, and both Nick and I were pulled, feet first, out into the numbing fog.

I looked around and tried to get my bearings, but the mist was too thick to see much of anything. From the rhythmic hum and click of tires droning above my head, I assumed we were south of Market at the waterfront directly below the Bay Bridge. The warehouse was strategically located; no one would ever hear us scream.

With a sharp squeal and thundering bang, the rolling door was slammed shut just after we passed through. The warehouse darkened into a murky gloom. Alexi's men dragged us across a great expanse of empty space. The staccato click of their heels echoed in a seemingly endless repeat. We paused at a tall barricade of chain-link fence set back into the farthest corner of the warehouse. The guards unlocked a gate and swept us through then locked it again behind us, metal grinding and clanging against metal, resonating off the hard walls as if in a prison.

At the end of a long, fenced corridor, we moved through another locked gate and into a wide, circular opening some twenty-five feet in diameter, the perimeter of which was more chain-link fencing, roughly eight feet high. Within the walls of the circular fence were gates with numbered placards above. Each gate had a secure lock and opened to a cage about ten feet square. Capping the top of the cages was a galvanized steel ceiling which served as a second floor above. A railing stood along the inside perimeter of the second deck to prevent anyone from falling onto the concrete floor of the circular arena below.

Two of the gates leading into the cages were unlocked and opened. I was dragged in and dumped onto the floor of one, the gate and lock quickly secured behind me. Nick was pushed face-first against the other gate in the adjoining cage. The hand of one of the men pressed against the back of Nick's head while another cut away the zip-tie that fastened his hands. With unnecessary force, they pushed him through the open gate, closed, and locked it. Nick hobbled over to the fence separating our cells, his fingers weaving through the web of metal between us.

"Tyler, are you okay?" he whispered. "Look at me, Ty. Talk to me."

With a grunt, I rolled onto my back and looked over at him with my one eye that wasn't swollen shut. I tried to move closer to Nick, but the pain in my ribs was sharp and relentless.

"Nick...where...are we?" I grunted, still breathless.

"Dmitri's fight cages. This isn't good, brother. We're in deep shit." He shook his head and rattled the chain-link. "Why did you come for me, Tyler? I told you not to. Now we're both going to have to fight tonight," he cried out, his voice anxious. "You need to pull yourself together."

I pushed my body backwards with my feet, sliding across the smooth concrete floor until I felt the cinder-block wall rise up behind me. I rolled and twisted my body until I could sit, propped up against the wall in the corner next to Nick's cell, where I moaned in pain. Nick slid over and knelt next to me, the chain-link an impenetrable barrier between us.

"Nick, what is this place? What do you mean by fight cages?"

"It's kind of like dog fighting. Crowds gather on the walkway above to watch the fights below."

"And what, they want us to fight each other?" I asked.

"No, not each other. Other men will be brought in like we were."

"Who? And why?"

"Guys like us who owe Dmitri something they can't or won't pay."

"But what's the point? How the fuck does Dmitri benefit from this?"

"It's for sport. For gambling. Dmitri will make money on every wager, whether for or against us." Nick's face was pinched with fear. "This is serious shit, Ty. These are often fights to the death."

I rolled my head against the wall and cursed.

Chapter Thirty-Nine

Tyler

About eight hours later, the pain had eased enough that I could move around, though my head still felt as if it were split down the middle. The swelling had lessened around my eye, and it was getting easier to breathe without feeling like a knife had been slipped between my ribs. Hunger began to gnaw inside me, and a thirst so great, my throat felt as dry as a sandy desert.

Nick and I whispered to each other through our cages. We cautiously searched every inch of our cells, but they were both sturdy and free from defect. We tried to come up with a plan to escape. It didn't look very promising with all the armed men Alexi had posted. While we waited, Nick explained how the fights worked, giving me advice on how to survive. He'd spent the last two nights forced to fight here. He relayed, in great detail, how he had beaten his opponent into unconsciousness the first night. However, last night was different.

"He was tough," Nick said, "a lot bigger than I am, and he wouldn't go down. I thought I was a dead man, Ty. I knew if I didn't kill him, he would kill me, plain and simple."

The memory tormented him. He sat crumpled up with his knees pulled into his chest and his arms wrapped tightly around them as he rocked back and forth. He stared into space, his eyes wide and haunted, and his brow furrowed as he worried his split lip with his teeth, gnawing at the blood congealed within the deep cuts.

"I just went nuts," Nick recalled. "I tore into him like a fucking madman. I didn't let up, even when he was on the ground, barely moving. I stomped on the back of his neck." Nick shook his head, disgusted at himself. "It snapped like a dry twig, and the guy slumped into the floor, like he was melting. I stood over him, watching his blood puddle up. I was shaking so hard, I could barely stand. And the crowd above was screaming and cheering, everyone patting each other on the back, high-fiving, and fist-bumping." Nick held a pained expression, his brow drawn tight and worried.

I looked him in the eye to offer him my support and experienced a moment of profound discovery. Even though Nick had grown into a man, I continued to think of him as a boy. But as I looked into his eyes, I saw that he looked old, as if he had aged twenty years in the last three days alone. What I saw was guilt and a lonely tiredness, a willingness to give up, to believe that nothing was worth the effort any more. That look, that lack of wanting more, frightened me. He was tired of trying to keep up with me, with what he thought I wanted him to be. It was the saddest look I'd ever seen in a man's eyes, and I knew I was the cause.

Uncomfortable with my probing, Nick broke away and stared at the floor. He weaved his fingers through his hair. "I can't do it again, Tyler. I won't make it."

"Yes, you can, and you will. If you have to, to survive, you *will* do it again. We have to get out of this alive, Nick...together. Whatever it takes, okay? Promise me."

He nodded, taking in a ragged breath as he wiped away his tears.

Suddenly, the gate from the long corridor just outside the fighting arena opened, and Alexi and Dmitri walked through. They stood before my cell, each with their own brand of smug satisfaction.

"So, just whose problem is it now, Mr. Karras?" Dmitri asked with a snide grin on his fat, ugly face. He waited patiently for me to answer.

"It's my problem, Dmitri. Mine alone," I replied, trying to placate him for Nick's benefit. I was worried about my brother and would do anything to keep him from fighting again.

Dmitri smiled and turned to Alexi, mumbling a few words in their native tongue. They both laughed at some inside joke I wasn't privy to. "I don't think that's entirely true," he said as he glanced over at my brother.

"Okay, our problem, then," I countered, my temper and control wearing thin. "But let *me* take the blame, okay? Not Nick. This is my deal. He has nothing to do with it."

Dmitri shook his head. "You are wrong there, I'm afraid. Nick has everything to do with this. More than you know, apparently. Perhaps you are too proud to see the truth. Or too blind. Either way, you are not grasping the big picture here." He signaled to one of his men who stood on the railed walkway above the cages directly across from us.

A sick feeling settled in my stomach, and it wasn't caused by the beating I'd taken earlier. Dmitri was capable of terrible violence and enjoyed playing sadistic games. I pulled myself to my feet—snarling in pain—and walked over to the gate to get a better look up onto the walkway above.

An unknown fear clawed along the edge of my mind. Before I could decipher what it was, two men walked out from a doorway on the back wall. They pulled a woman along with them. She screamed and fought like a stray cat. Her head thrashed back and forth, and her legs kicked at her captors without effect. Together they hauled her up against the metal railing. One of them pulled the hair at the back of her head and, with a sharp yank, settled her down. I jumped up to the front of my cage and pulled against the fencing, nausea rising from the pit of my stomach.

"Hannah? Oh God, no. Hannah!" Terror surged through me. I heard her whisper my name before the men yanked her backwards the way they had come. I shook the confines of my cage, screaming her name over and over. I looked back at Alexi and Dmitri, still standing before my cell, noting their satisfaction had turned into unmitigated amusement. "I'm going to fucking kill you both!" I shouted. "Do you hear me? You're dead! *Dead!*"

Dmitri brought his face up close to mine. "You hold onto that anger, Mr. Karras. It might just save your life. You live through this and perhaps you will even see your debt paid off tonight."

"And the girl?" I seethed.

He just laughed at me. "You Karras men, always the heroes, eh?"

"The girl, Dmitri! What about the girl?"

"Ah, well, she is just gravy for me at this point, I'm afraid. Like whipped cream with a cherry on top." He laughed. "Isn't that what the Americans say?"

"What are you talking about? What does that mean?"

315

He shrugged. "A little payback for old sins. You should forget her. She is out of your reach now. Though you never know, you just might see her again very soon," Dmitri taunted before he turned on his heel and walked away.

"No, Dmitri! No!" I slapped the quivering metal fence. "Dmitri, let the girl go, please! She has nothing to do with this! Let her go! Dmitri! *Dmitri!*"

I screamed until I was hoarse and the words felt like burning sandpaper grinding along my throat. I fell to my knees and wept in despair, calling out for Hannah again and again.

In the cell next to me, Nick lowered his head in silent defeat.

Chapter Forty
Tyler

Two more hours passed. Physical and emotional exhaustion overwhelmed me. My whole body shook with tremors, and I was covered in sweat. My heart raced, and though I knew it was from my need for a drink, my anxiety over Hannah's welfare made it much worse. Nick and I both sat quietly in our cages. I thought about what Dmitri had said, and wondered what he meant about seeing Hannah later. I was sure he had said it to taunt me, as if I might not like what I would see. That frightened me beyond words. I was terrified to think about what she might be going through while I sat there waiting. I prayed she wouldn't do anything to further anger them. Not knowing was driving me mad and had my gut tied in knots. I had to get free. I searched for the means, but found nothing. I was trapped, left to contemplate a dismal future.

"Nick, what did Dmitri mean when he said I might see my debt paid off tonight...if I lived?" My voice was a raspy whisper.

"Well, not everyone is forced to fight. Some do it just to pay off their debt. For everyone, a percentage of what you owe is automatically wagered in your own favor, like a personal incentive. If you win, it's deducted, but if you lose, your debt is even greater, that is if you survive. And although at least ten percent is automatically pledged, you can choose how much more of your debt you wish to wager in favor of yourself. If you stake the entire amount on one bout and win, your debt is paid in full. But I have no idea how that would apply to either of us. Dmitri doesn't seem to want our money. I think he's just fucking with us now."

"And these fights, who determines who wins or loses?" I asked.

"Ty, there's usually no doubt as to who loses."

"Right." I closed my eyes and shook my head in utter disbelief. "What is this, ancient Rome? It's fucking barbaric." It sickened me to be forced to participate in such depraved conduct, but I realized I had succumbed to such behavior months ago when I put myself on this path of vindictive retribution. It was my own fault. "And what am I supposed to do about Hannah?" I asked.

Nick sighed heavily. "Tyler, she's gone. There's nothing you can do about it now. You need to forget her and let it go."

I sent him a cold stare then turned away. "Like I could," I said, more to myself than to Nick. "I don't know how he even got his hands on her. I bought her a ticket home. Had a car pick her up and take her to the airport."

"Alexi had someone watching you from the time you left Washington. He never trusted you, Tyler. He told me so. They were going to get her one way or another. I don't think she ever had a chance. And whatever deal you made concerning me, well, I doubt Dmitri ever intended on honoring it."

I thumped my head against the wall behind me. "God, I'm so fucking stupid."

"Ty, you need to put all that out of your mind now. Focus on surviving. If we're lucky, we might get out of here tomorrow."

"Tomorrow? Hannah will be God knows where by then. I have to get out tonight, Nick. It's her only chance."

He gave me a weak smile of encouragement then laid his head back and shut his eyes.

Chapter Forty-One

Tyler

Late that evening, the thrum of voices grew louder as the gallery began to fill with men and a few garishly dressed women. Their heels clanged and clattered against the metal above our heads. They spoke excitedly about the night's bouts and their wagers. Four more men were escorted up the long gated corridor and placed in the remaining cages along the perimeter of the arena floor. I studied them closely, trying to determine each man's possible weakness, as well as his strength.

One of them was just a kid, maybe eighteen or nineteen at most, and scared witless. There was something about him, something oddly familiar, though I couldn't place it. He was tall, but thin, with lean arms and a hollow beneath his narrow chest. He reminded me of Nick when he first got mixed up with Dmitri's crew. He paced the floor of his cell with his arms wrapped around his chest, nervously eyeing each of us. The rest of the men appeared to range in age from the late twenties to early forties, and none too happy to be there. They were sizing us up, as well. A couple of them spouted off about how Nick and I both looked the worse for wear. They called us pussies and declared us easy to put down. Except for the kid, they all seemed to purposely pump themselves up for the fight.

The crowd above was getting rowdy, and pushing matches broke out. Alexi and Dmitri joined the mob at the head of the gallery where they both stood up to the railing. Alexi motioned to one of his men, who rang a loud bell, calling everyone to order. With a wave of his hands, he summoned all to be quiet. When the room settled down, Alexi greeted the crowd.

"Good evening, my friends. Thank you all for coming. It should prove to be a most interesting evening, I am sure. As some of you may already know, we have several ways to wager here tonight. You may merely choose to bet on a winner or a loser at the given odds, or you may wager on the length of time you think either opponent might last. You may also bet on whether one man lives or dies."

Loud cheers erupted at this last point. Alexi raised his hands and quieted everyone down.

"Mr. Chernov, as host and sponsor of tonight's event, will take his cut off the top of each wager. The balance goes into the pot and the odds are configured. All bets must be made before the fight begins, except for the death wagers which can be made for the duration of the bout, until one fighter falls. After each fight, all accounts must be paid in full before wagering again or leaving for the night. You will be checked at the door, my friends, so please, do not attempt to leave without settling your account.

"The match-ups are determined at random by picking numbers from a hat. Each number corresponds to the number on the outside of the fighter's cage." Alexi focused his attention on me, glaring down with malevolence. "There are no exceptions to this rule."

Nick and I shared worried glances.

"Now for the match-ups," Alexi called out. He pulled one number out of the hat then another, and held them up to the crowd. "The first bout will be between fighters number three and six."

The crowd roared anew as Alexi's men unlocked the gates to the cages, and the two fighters emerged. One of them was the young kid. He walked slowly out of his cell and looked up at the screaming crowd. Loosening his grip around his chest, he lowered his arms to his sides, but the worried frown remained. He turned to look at his opponent, who had already strutted out and was waving his arms up and down to get the mob further excited. He was cocky and sure of himself as he circled the kid standing in the center of the arena floor. The older fighter looked to be in his late twenties and had at least forty pounds on the kid, all corded muscle that rippled beneath the heavily tattooed flesh of his arms, neck, shoulders, and back.

"You have ten minutes to place your bets," Alexi yelled aloud.

Suddenly, the gallery looked like the floor of the stock exchange as the gamblers, with slips of paper shaking in their raised hands, screamed, while bookies snatched eagerly at their orders. Below the chaos of the mob, the two fighters circled each other around the arena floor, wary of the guards who shouted orders to keep their distance. The tattooed man raised both fists in the air, opening and closing them three times.

Nick turned to me and said, "That's the signal. He just bet his entire balance."

I snickered. "Guess I would, too, if I were him. That kid won't last thirty seconds."

Nick agreed with a solemn nod and glanced up at the timer on the wall. It counted down the minutes until the fight was to begin while the crowd grew louder and more rambunctious.

As soon as the timer hit zero, the bell rang out. The older, larger fighter ran toward the kid, who backed up defensively, his hands raised up and one leg bent to protect himself. The tattooed man tackled the kid and pummeled his head and body with his meaty fists. When the man slowed to catch his breath, the kid lashed out and landed a solid hit to the man's throat, knocking him away with a sickening croak.

In a quick flash, the boy jumped up and turned his body at an angle. His arms flexed, lean muscle rippled, and his hands shaped into blades near his hips. When Tattoo charged at him again, the boy threw a forward kick, followed by an undercut punch — martial arts style. The man went down hard, falling into his own blood splattered on the floor. The kid stood over him for a moment, until he was satisfied the man wasn't going to get up, then he moved away and looked up into the gallery. The crowd erupted into a clamorous roar of unexpected enthusiasm.

Tattoo pulled himself up onto his hands and knees, but not for long. With a running start, the kid launched a savage kick into his ribcage. The man rose a foot off the floor before rolling across it, his blood spiraling outward as he spun like a top. Cheers from the audience rose in a deafening roar. Early on, the odds seemed stacked against the kid, so those few who had wagered for him stood to make a lot of money should he win, while most of the crowd would likely lose a large sum.

After nearly a full minute, Tattoo staggered to his feet. He planted them wide with his knees pulled inward so he wouldn't fall over. The boy allowed him to hold steady for only ten seconds then hurled himself into a rapid roundhouse kick. The man's head snapped back on his neck, and he fell to the arena floor, limp as a child's ragdoll. His eyes rolled back into his head, and blood poured from his mouth and nose. The assembly bellowed all at once, and brawls broke out. Down below, the boy paraded around his victim with his arms held high. He raised his face to the crowd and screamed as the bell rang, ending the short-lived match. Then the kid turned to Alexi and Dmitri and, with both hands, pointed at them with a devilish smile.

"Damn," Nick swore, his eyes wide and his brow shooting upward.

"Don't kid yourself, Nick. That boy's a hustler," I offered bitterly. "Dmitri's pawn, no doubt."

Nick's mouth hung open as he stared at the kid, his brow gathered with intense concentration. "Huh. Yeah, maybe," he said, a spark igniting in his eye. "I know that asshole. And so does Dmitri." He shook his head with something akin to a grudging respect, like he'd been proven less clever, less devious. "Maybe nothing's what it seems after all, huh?" Then he dropped his chin to his chest. "Dmitri. Fucking bastard."

I looked at him, puzzled by his comment. "What is it? What's wrong?"

He shook his head. "Nothing. Nothing at all."

"How do you know him then? Who is he?"

"Just a nobody who thinks he's going to be somebody someday," he replied, pressing his lips together and waving me off.

But something had changed in him. I just didn't know what it was.

Meanwhile, on the catwalk above, markers were distributed to those few who had won. There were angry jeers leveled at the boy who still circled around the floor in a victory lap while Alexi's henchmen dragged the battered, still form of the beaten tattooed man away. With a final yelp in conquest, the boy was escorted off the arena floor.

It took nearly twenty minutes for the gallery to settle down, but my anxiety blossomed while we waited for more names to be called. The bell rang again, signaling the start of the next match-up. Alexi selected two more numbers from the hat. This time, Nick was chosen to fight. My heart tumbled, and nausea rolled through me.

I weaved my fingers through the chain-link between our cells. "Nick?"

He looked over at me, his forehead wrinkled in doubt. With a weak smile, he raised his chin, trying to be brave for my benefit. "No worries. I got this. I know what I have to do now. *I'm* going to take care of things for once in my life. My last gift to you, brother."

"What are you talking about? What do you mean, *last* gift?" I pointed my finger at him. "Don't you do anything stupid, Nick, you hear me? You made me a promise."

With a soft chuckle, he smirked, another one of his crooked smiles. But his eyes were different somehow. Resigned. Like the day he and Alexi had made their deal at the hospital.

"I've made a lot of promises, Tyler, but there's only one I need to keep now."

"And which one is that, Nick? Huh? You tell me. Which one?" I trailed after him as he meandered through his cage.

He ignored me and took a deep breath, releasing it in a loud whoosh as his shoulders sagged.

"Nick, you fight, you hear me? Don't you give up. You do this for me, okay? You promised."

He looked me in the eye, calm and composed. "Someone has to appease the gods."

"Not you, Nick! Not you!" I beat my fist against the fence, making it sway and quiver. "You promised, Nick! *You promised!*"

But he turned away and walked to the gate.

"Godammit!" I spun around and slammed my foot into the concrete floor.

Nick waited as a guard worked the lock, facing his opponent across the arena floor, the oldest of the remaining two. As they were both released, I got a good look at his adversary. He was an old Joe, but well-muscled, and he seemed too eager. Nick, though young and strong, was weary from fighting the last two nights, and his injuries made him more vulnerable.

The timer was reset, counting down as the crowd made their wagers. His opponent circled Nick around the floor. Nick threw me an anxious glance. A foreboding darkness lingered in his eyes. My stomach was already tied in knots at the thought of having to watch my little brother take a beating. Now I worried about whatever Nick was planning, and I thought for sure I would puke. *Appease the gods? What the fuck does that mean?* I tried to take strength from the knowledge that he had won his last two bouts, but that hope was only a glimmer.

The bell rang, and the fight began. Nick's opponent ran toward him at full speed. He swung his fists with animated ferocity. Nick took evasive action and avoided the initial throws. But that only worked for a few seconds until he was bowled over by a head butt to his stomach. He flew backwards five feet. His head slammed hard against the concrete floor. While Nick lay stunned, Old Joe straddled his chest. He threw blow after blow to Nick's head.

I pulled hard on the chain-link fence, calling out to Nick, over and over. He couldn't hear me above the crowd. I screamed names and insults at his opponent in a frantic attempt to distract him. He heard me and turned my way. A scowl distorted his face. He climbed off Nick and trudged over to my cell, threatening me and kicking at the barrier between us. I stepped back, but continued to taunt him, hoping to give Nick enough time to recover and stand up. Nick slowly shook off his disorientation, stood up, and stumbled around the arena.

My attention flashed to Nick for a split second, breaking the tenuous spell I had over his opponent. Old Joe turned back toward Nick and tried again to head butt him at his midsection, but Nick saw it coming and side-stepped at the last moment. The man ran headfirst into one of the galvanized steel poles that framed the cages. Stunned, he fell onto his hands and knees.

"Go, Nick, go! Get him," I yelled as I slapped at the fence. "Tear him apart! This is your chance. Lay him out! *Do it, Nick! Do it now!*"

Still dazed, he stumbled over to the man. Old Joe lay bleeding profusely from the top of his head. He kicked the man in the chin, rocketing him over and onto his side. Nick stepped after him and kicked him again, this time in the ribs. Joe doubled over in pain and tried to roll away. Nick slowly regained his senses, the roaring crowd motivating him, urging him on. He pulled his leg back once more, aiming for his adversary's face, but Joe reached out and grabbed Nick's foot. He bent his ankle around over 180 degrees. Nick twisted over his opponent and fell to the floor, but Joe held on firmly. He continued to twist Nick's foot, using his momentum to snap his ankle. Nick's shrill scream reverberated over the roar of the stunned crowd. I froze in helpless agony and watched Old Joe take advantage. He stomped on Nick's ribs then kicked his head repeatedly, as if punting a football.

I yelled for Nick to move, to get out of the way, but he was hardly able to cover himself between blows. I glanced up at Alexi and Dmitri. They returned my look with smug grins. I begged them to stop this madness. I banged against the chain-link in frustration as the man relentlessly punched, kicked, and stomped on my baby brother, until Nick stopped moving altogether.

While Old Joe raised his arms above his head in victory, I kept my eyes pinned on my brother. Nick jerked a few times then lay still on the cold floor, alone in a growing puddle of his own blood. My body shook in absolute terror. As the crowd roared, aroused beyond reason, Alexi motioned to his men. One removed Nick's bloodied opponent from the floor while the other checked on my brother.

The guard stepped over his back, careful of the large pool of blood. He pulled Nick's head up by the hair with no response. He rolled him over, and though Nick's eyelids appeared already open, he pulled them back even farther, one at a time. Then he felt for a pulse, first at Nick's wrist, and then at his neck. The guard looked up at Alexi and shook his head before he turned to stare over his shoulder at me with a look akin to pity.

I stared back, frozen in place, unable to breathe. I whispered, "No...Nick...no, no, no." I looked up at Alexi and Dmitri in the gallery above. "Let me out...*please!*"

With a flick of his wrist, Alexi motioned to his man standing over Nick. He walked over and unlocked the gate to my cage. I scrambled out, ran over to Nick, and knelt down beside him. I removed my t-shirt and gently scooped his body into my arms, wiping away the blood that covered his face. His sightless eyes stared past me. The fear was gone; they were finally at peace. My eyes brimmed over with tears as I spoke quietly to my fallen brother. I pulled his head up under my chin and held him tight as I rocked him back and forth.

I had failed him. Nick was dead because of my poor decisions. Because I needed revenge. Because I was selfish. I'd traded my soul for the chance to get even, bartering with the Devil with a life that was not my own. Two lives, in fact. Both forfeit for my own base satisfaction. It was incomprehensible. I had lost everything. My entire family was wiped out: my parents and sister, my wife and unborn child, and now my brother. Even Hannah was lost to me. And I was responsible for each one of them. A shrill scream escaped from the very deepest part of me, a wail of utter desperation, of annihilating failure. I was no longer a man simply broken.

I was destroyed.

Chapter Forty-Two

Tyler

The crowd quieted down as they watched me cradle the body of my dead brother in my arms. They moved in unison up to the railing and wrapped their hands around the metal bars. Those behind them leaned over their shoulders, craning their necks for a better look. I scanned their faces one at a time, searching for a shred of humanity among them, but there was none, not one ounce. As the once rowdy audience stared silently at us on the bloody arena floor below, Dmitri directed two of his men to see to me. They loomed over my shoulder and requested that I move away from Nick.

I pulled Nick's body in even closer. "No! Back off! Keep the *fuck* away!"

They glanced back up at Dmitri who nodded. I struggled against them, twisting my body from side to side as I held tight onto Nick with all the strength I could muster, but they grabbed me by the arms, pinning one behind by back as they peeled me away from Nick. Two others dragged his lifeless body away, a bloody trail in its wake. I labored to break the binds that held me back until I caught Alexi and Dmitri chuckling above. Then I composed myself and stared murderously in return.

"So help me God, I will fucking kill you both," I said calmly.

Dmitri cocked an eyebrow and snapped his fingers, directing Alexi to let the last fighter out of his cage. I tore my eyes from Dmitri and turned to the fighter approaching me. We were of similar size and weight, evenly matched. I felt him sizing me up as he paced around.

"Place your bets, gentlemen...and ladies, of course!" Alexi called to the quietly humming crowd.

Again they erupted into a frenzy of activity. Dmitri peered down at me, and I stared back in a bloody rage. My opponent walked near, taunting me while I was still held in place.

"Hope you're tougher than that pussy brother of yours," he snarled, his Russian accent thick and coarse.

I flashed him a hard stare, calm and focused now, intent on revenge. I felt the change as it coursed through me. My despair rapidly evolved into a cool, but full-blown fury. I would begin with my adversary, and move on to whichever of Dmitri's men got in my way before I finally reached Alexi and Dmitri themselves. Though the noise of the crowd had intensified, I tuned it all out and concentrated solely on my new path, the new target of my vengeance.

The timer rang, bringing an end to the betting session, and commencing the fight. The men holding me back released their grip and set me free. I stood up straight and faced my opponent square on. He snarled insulting epithets and danced around me with his fists held up like a boxer. He lunged and threw a punch, a glancing blow to my chin. I stumbled back then raised my fists.

I pushed the Russian's arm around as he swung at me again. My fist sliced through the air and connected firmly with his sweaty face. Blood spurted from his nose, though he was only slightly stunned. He spun back around and, with surprising speed, ran headfirst, square into my chest. The impact knocked me backwards onto the floor. I used his momentum to hurl the Russian up and over my head, into a flying somersault behind me.

I scrambled to my feet and readied myself again. My opponent was fast as well, advancing on me with his fists swinging. He connected another blow, this time to my already broken nose. I was stunned for a fraction of a second. Blood flowed freely from us both. When the Russian swung his fist again, I twisted away, spun around, and booted a kick to the center of his back, followed by a blow to his head. He fell to his knees on the concrete, dazed and confused. I backed away and looked up into the gallery where Alexi and Dmitri stood.

Next to Dmitri stood another man. I recognized him as the third man at the table at Dmitri's Tea House. He sneered at me with hatred, though I didn't even know him. He exchanged words with Dmitri then turned away, roughly pulling a woman out from behind him. He grabbed her by what looked like a leather collar bound around her neck. Her hands were secured behind her back. And though her hair was a tangled mess covering her face, I knew instantly that it was Hannah.

My heart skipped a beat in terrified dread. The man jerked back on the collar, forcing her head up. To my horror, Hannah's face was swollen, covered in angry scrapes, cuts, and bruises. She looked down at me, and I recognized the defeat in her dead, expressionless eyes before she turned her face away in humiliation.

"Hannah," I whispered, taking a small step in her direction.

They'd dressed her in whore's clothing that revealed bruised flesh and bloody streaks trailing down her legs. I gasped just as my opponent grabbed me from behind. He spun me around and landed two punches directly to my battered face. I wobbled back a few steps, shook my head, and stood straight up to face him. Rage, black as night, coursed through every cell in my body.

I took three steps forward and swung like a madman. I struck blow after blow to the Russian's face, ribs, and abdomen. I kicked at his knee and snapped it backwards. He fell to the floor, screaming. But I kept moving forward as the fury and hatred swept through me like a virus. I stomped on his ribs. They crackled beneath my foot like bubble wrap. I kicked him hard in the head. His neck snapped, breaking with an audible pop. He was dead before his body even settled to the floor. Without a moment's hesitation, I sprinted over to the cages directly below Hannah. Before anyone even knew what I was doing, I climbed up the chain-link fence and pulled myself up and over the metal railing. The crowd whooped in unison and drew back.

I came to Hannah's captor first as he peered over the rail and crushed his windpipe with one swift blow to his throat before any of Dmitri's men even knew what I was doing. I grabbed him as he flailed and stumbled backwards then threw him, head first, over the railing and onto the concrete floor eight feet below, all while the crowd screamed and surged to the exits, blocking Dmitri's guards from my path. Dmitri caught my eye, his lips pressed tightly together. Alexi and his men pushed Dmitri from the side, urging him to flee. They both glanced at me over their shoulders, caught in the tide of a panicking sea of people and the small army of guards that swelled against them.

Off to the side, Hannah stood frozen in fright. I pushed her up against the wall at the far end of the gallery, away from the hysterical crowd. Then I turned to the railing and kicked it repeatedly, over and over, until a bar loosened and became disjoined at one end. I grabbed it and pulled hard until it broke free. I swung my makeshift weapon wildly at Dmitri's men as they descended upon me with their guns drawn. They seemed reluctant to shoot into the terror-stricken crowd swirling around us.

I ducked from grabbing hands and reaching arms and swung the metal bar against their skulls, one after the other. One man went down at my feet, his head split open like a ripe melon. Another staggered against the rail. I kicked him high in the chest. He tumbled backwards, falling to the arena floor, his face frozen in a grotesque mask of fear as he anticipated the lethal landing. I turned back to Hannah for a moment as she crouched down on the floor. She stared at me in shocked disbelief.

"Hannah! Go...run and hide. *Go, go, go!*"

She scrambled along the wall to a doorway and passed through. Men streamed all around her, jostling her about. I feared she might fall since her hands were still fastened behind her back. I lost sight of her as she was swept along in the human current and enveloped into the darkness of the warehouse.

Satisfied she had escaped, I turned back to settle the score with Dmitri. He was dutifully protected by a small group of his disciples. In a fury blind to all else, I swung my club at the closest attendant. He crumpled to my feet, but locked his arms around my ankles. I stumbled, off balance, and was grabbed from behind and lifted off the ground, my arms pinned to my sides. The anchor at my feet gave way, and I kicked out, connecting with the man's throat in a grotesque yelp. I flung my head back and felt my captor's nose crush beneath the back of my skull. He released me, his hands reaching for his bloody face. Rotating in his direction, I wheeled my weapon with everything I had. The impact left a deep impression in the side of his head. I pulled hard, repulsed by the wet sucking sound as the bar came free from the yawning groove.

I made similar work of the man still at my feet, as well as two more of Dmitri's men. No one was left to challenge me. With the immediate danger gone, I scanned the gallery and spied Alexi's back as he fled with Dmitri a short distance ahead.

I caught Alexi first and cracked my weapon along the back of his head. He fell forward onto the ground. With a dazed look, he peered back at me over his shoulder. Terror had erased all evidence of his usual grin, and his mouth grew wide in fear. I was glad he knew he was about to die at my hands. I sneered in vindictive delight and heard Alexi's frightened shriek in response. As he scrambled away on his hands and knees, I rammed the metal rod into his back like a sword. He wanted a gladiator, and I was only too happy to oblige.

Without even waiting for him to die, I pulled the bar from Alexi's twitching body and ran after Dmitri. Two more of his thugs advanced on me, but neither could open fire with the handful of people still surrounding us in curiosity. One raised the butt of his pistol and whacked me over the head. I fell onto my back, blinded for a moment by my own blood, but even from the ground I kept fighting. I swept the bar along the floor and felt it crack against the man's ankle. He fell beside me, crippled with pain, cursing and screaming. I swung the rod in the direction of his voice and made contact with his skull. Lights out. With a quick swipe of my arm, I cleared the blood from my eyes then looked up. The second man stumbled over his accomplice, arms flailing for balance. As he fell towards me, I aimed the rod up underneath his chin, embedding it deep into his skull.

Panting and covered in blood, I pulled myself out from underneath their bodies then pushed through the few who remained on the walkway. With the bloody metal rod still in my hand, I scrambled down the stairs, three at a time, in search of Dmitri. I ran through the darkened warehouse, roaring his name, pushing myself through the crowd as they fled through the exit. Tires screeched as cars sped away.

Finally, I spied Dmitri twenty yards ahead. He was being assisted by one of his few remaining men, the same man who'd been waiting outside the Tea House. He and Dmitri sprinted for the Mercedes, or at least as fast as a nearly three-hundred-pound man could sprint. He clambered frantically into the car and locked the doors as his driver revved the engine to life. I reached the vehicle just as it started to move. I gave chase and bashed ineffectively at the windows before it sped out of reach.

I stared after the vanishing car, stomping in rage, deeply disappointed to have missed my opportunity to snuff the worthless life out of Dmitri Chernov. Breathless and bleeding, I dropped the metal bar and leaned over, resting my hands on my knees, my heart thrashing within my chest. I took a moment to catch my breath, and promised myself I wouldn't rest until I had settled the score with Dmitri.

My priority now was to find Hannah. I prayed that she'd found someplace safe to hide within the warehouse. I picked the metal rod up off the pavement and ran back into the building. There were a few men still walking around the expansive space. I raised my weapon as I approached them. I must have presented a frightful specter: half naked, covered in blood and gore, a bloodied weapon in my hand, and a fierce rage in my eye. Their eyes grew wide and their hands flew up, backing away before turning and running.

When I saw no one else in the building, I called out Hannah's name and searched through the warehouse racks and pallets. I wanted to scream for her, but I was afraid to draw attention from anyone who might still remain unseen. I moved as far away from the arena cages as possible, hoping Hannah would have thought to do the same. All around me were tall racks that held large mechanical parts. I hissed Hannah's name over and over, praying she would recognize my voice and reveal herself.

I thought I heard some shuffling and low sobbing. I stopped and held myself still, listening in concentrated focus for the source of the noise. Advancing slowly, I made my way through the maze of shelves until I found Hannah crouched in a dark corner, shivering. I covered my face in relief and hurried to her side. She shrieked in terror and turned away.

"Hannah, it's okay. Shhh, it's just me."

I leaned down and knelt next to her. She sobbed uncontrollably, and her entire body shook. With great care, I folded her into my arms.

"You're safe now, Hannah. You're safe. No one will ever hurt you again. I promise. Shhh. It's okay. It's okay."

I held her for a long time, until her sobs eased and the tension in her body lessened. When she was finally quiet, I pulled back and looked into her eyes. I smoothed her tangled hair back from her face and placed a few chaste kisses along her forehead.

"Hannah, let me untie your hands, okay?"

She nodded and turned so I could assist her. I worked at her binding, but the knot was pulled too tight.

"I need to cut it off, all right? Wait here."

I searched around until I found something sharp enough to cut through while still small enough to slip under the rope, close to her wrists. It took several minutes, but when I finally sawed through the bindings and freed her arms, Hannah immediately wrapped them around my neck. Mine found their way around her trembling body, holding her tight against me. My fingers entwined themselves into her hair, and I rested my face in the crook of her neck and shoulder.

"I'm sorry, Hannah. I didn't know. I never should have let you go."

Hannah nodded, selflessly offering me absolution yet again. I leaned back and searched her eyes to see if she really meant it. I put my hands on her cheeks and kissed her forehead, then her cheek, and lastly, her mouth, very tenderly. When I pulled back, my hands slid to her neck where the offensive collar still rested.

"Hannah, can I cut this thing off you?"

She nodded again. I made short work of it and threw it aside as if it burned me. She gave me a tentative smile.

"All right now, we need to get the hell out of here, but..." I found it difficult to say the words. "They killed Nick, Hannah. They took him away. I can't just leave him here. I have to find his body."

She bowed her head, her eyes sad. "I know. They threw him into the van as they were bringing me out," she said. "I'm so sorry, Ty. I know how hard you tried to save him."

I nodded. "I should go see if the van is still here."

I helped her stand, and we ran to the rear door, back near the cages. The white van was still parked there. We peeked in through the passenger side window and spied the keys in the ignition. Looking at each other, we had the same thought.

"Get in," I urged.

As Hannah jumped in through the passenger door, she turned and glanced into the back where Nick's body lay cold and still. Hannah and I shared a long, sad look before I started the vehicle and sped away.

Chapter Forty-Three
Hannah

By some miracle, some grace of God, I was saved. I released a shaky sigh, laid my face in my hands, and cried. My fate had changed so abruptly, and in such a short span of time, I scarcely knew what to believe. From the relative safety of Ty's protection, to the living hell of captivity, and back again in mere hours, I survived what I felt sure was to be a lifetime of sexual servitude.

It hadn't taken me very long to realize I was not being driven to the airport, as Tyler had planned. Terror filled me as I was delivered to the sadistic Mr. Sergeyev instead, his gaze silently assessing. I glared back at the man who considered me his personal property—bought and paid for—to do with as he wanted. There was no hope for me. I was condemned.

I was thrown into an empty utility room with nothing but a dim light overhead to illuminate the blood-stained mattress lying on the floor at my feet. They left me there by myself for nearly an hour while I imagined all the horrible things that awaited me. I cried, huddled in the corner, terrified and sick to my stomach.

Suddenly, the door was thrown open, and the monster, Sergeyev, stood silhouetted in the harsh light pouring in from behind him. He was eager to assert his authority. I wasn't prepared for what he did. I endured it, as much as I wished I could simply curl up and die. He purposely tried to rip my humanity from me, making me beg for mercy then refusing to grant it. Fighting only served to further arouse him, so I learned to submit quietly. But this, in itself, enraged him, so I found a place in between.

I shook my head and closed my eyes, determined to banish the humiliating memory of my submittal, of thinking that Ty had played some part in my kidnapping. He saved me…again. Tears of relief streamed down my face.

From out of nowhere, sirens began to wail, and the lights of squad cars flashed in the night before us as Tyler and I raced to escape the carnage of the warehouse. Dozens of police cars stormed along the waterfront and poured onto the wharf.

"Bloody hell," Ty bellowed. "Who called the cops?"

We passed the regiment of police cars and turned westward into The City. Tyler kept his worried eyes alert to the rear view mirror, and ran his fingers through his hair. He glanced over at me for the first time since we'd left, scanning my appearance in the undulating streetlight. He tipped my chin up with his finger and swallowed hard. I tugged at my meager clothing, trying my best to cover up. His lips, split with bleeding cuts, tensed into a thin line as he surveyed the dried blood, scrapes, and bruises that covered me from head to toe.

"Good God, Hannah. You need to go to the hospital."

I shook my head. "No, please, not yet! I need some time." I looked away, shame washing over me as the excitement of our narrow escape receded. But I felt his eyes on me.

"Hannah—"

"No, Ty, please," I pleaded, turning back. "Just a little while longer. I'm begging you."

He nodded reluctantly and turned back to the road. "Fine. For now," he said. "We can go to my place. Get cleaned up. I'll find you something to wear. It'll give me some time to figure out what to do about Nick."

He remained quiet for several minutes, though his lips moved as he silently debated our next move. Finally he sighed and met my gaze.

"Hannah, I don't think there's any way we can keep the police out of this now. I'm going to have to tell them about Nick. About Alexi and Dmitri, and my own involvement in all of this. There's just no way around it now."

His eyes swept over me, studying my injuries. "You *will* need to go to the hospital, and when they realize the..." He stopped abruptly and shook his head, his jaw ticking in angry frustration. "...extent of your injuries, they'll call the authorities. They'll want to know what happened." He turned back to the road when the traffic light turned green. "Eventually, the police will link us together with all that's happened since that first night in Oregon. We've left a long trail, easily followed: the ATM, your credit card, our trashed motel room, and Dmitri's dead man. It all leads back to us. And now...all this."

We stopped at another light, and he glanced back at me again. "They'll put it all together, Hannah. You need to figure out what you want to tell them, how much you want them to know," he said, his tone very serious, "especially about me," he added. "I'm willing to confess my part in all this, and suffer the consequences."

I shook my head hard. "No, Ty, please. I don't want them to know. Please."

"Hannah, we can't hide the evidence at your house. They'll make assumptions. They *will* figure it out."

"No! We…we can…make the evidence appear to support something else. They'll already know about Dmitri's man at the motel, right?" I didn't wait for his response. "Well, then, we…we can say that you came to my home to see me, thinking I was Erin, but I explained everything to you, showed you the PI report and photographs proving I wasn't and…and when you were leaving, Dmitri's man burst in and…and attacked us both. We'll tell them we managed to escape in my car. They can think he was after you because of Nick, that he followed you to my place."

I rambled on, frantically trying to mold the evidence to support my story.

"Ty, you have a history of rescuing Nick and…and he has a history with Dmitri and Alexi. They sent that man there to find Nick, and you and I were collateral damage. That guy is dead. They'll never know the difference. Never!"

I urged him to believe it could work. But Ty shook his head, undeterred.

"No, Hannah. Think about what you're doing. They'll trip us up. It'll never work."

"Yes, it will, Ty. It will! If you just stick to the story. They'll never know what happened between us. I don't want them to know. I won't tell them. I can't."

Tyler stared at me, disbelief written across his bruised face. "Why, Hannah? Why, in God's name, would you do that? Why protect me after everything I've done?"

I didn't know how to respond so I looked away. A horn honked at us from behind, and Ty drove forward, his eyes sweeping back and forth between the road and me.

"Hannah, you can't shoulder this all alone. You shouldn't be burdened with this at all. I've put you through hell. It kills me to think of what I've done, how I've hurt you, the danger I've put you in. My God, I'll never forgive myself. And neither should you. I'm not worth it. This is all my fault. My responsibility. And I should be made accountable!"

"No, no, no! Please. You'll be arrested; you'll go to prison. I don't want that. Can't you see?" I screamed, my fingers pressed tightly against each temple.

"Why not, Hannah? I don't understand."

"I don't know," I yelled. "I really don't." I looked back over at him and sighed. "I know I should be angry, Ty, that I should hate you. I *should* want justice. I know it. But I don't."

I shook my head and turned back away again. It was so difficult to face him as I realized the intensity of my feelings and admitted them out loud.

"I shouldn't want to be with you, Ty...but I do. I can't help how I feel." I sighed and closed my eyes for one brief moment. "I want to do what feels right...for me," I murmured and returned my focus back to him. "And this feels right, Ty. It really does. I can't explain why. It's just...that...I get it, you know. I understand how you feel. Your grief. Your loss. That you drink to dull your pain. I even understand your impulsiveness, your need to take back control, your desire for vengeance. I get all of that. What I don't understand are my own feelings. I'm trying to make sense of why I feel this way, of what I feel for you."

Unable to look at him one second longer, I focused on my hands in my lap. My tears refused to be held back.

"What you did to me, Ty...it was...brutal. You terrified me. Hurt and humiliated me. You took something away, destroyed my sense of peace and safety. That can *never* be put back or made whole again. I know this. I *feel* this." I pressed my hands to my heart. "But, in the time since then, after everything we've been through, you've given me something else. You could have just left me behind with that man at the motel. You could have simply turned me over in Erin's place. It would have been so much easier for you if you had. But you didn't. You took responsibility for your mistake, for what you did. You protected me, even though it cost you everything, what little you had left. That's something *I* can never give back to *you*."

"My God, Hannah, you owe me nothing. It's insane for you to think—"

I threw my hands over my ears and shook my head. "Stop! I know, *I know!* You think I'm crazy. Maybe I am, but before all this, I was isolated and unwanted. Unneeded. Except for Conner, I didn't feel tethered to anyone. Not physically. Not emotionally. There was nothing. *I* was nothing. And now, for the first time in so long, that's changed somehow. I feel more alive when I'm with you. I feel that I'm somehow needed, that, like a missing piece to a puzzle, I'm meant to fit into some small space in that hollowed out place inside of you. That place left empty and barren by the deaths of your parents and your sister. By Jill and by Nick. If I can help make *you* whole again, then maybe *I* can be, too. And I need that, Ty. I need that more than you could ever know."

My embarrassment, which had at first rolled over me like an armored tank, ebbed, leaving something new in its place: fear. Fear of being rejected, for having feelings that were irrational. There's no way he'd be able to understand what I felt and why. I couldn't look at him, for I knew he must think me a lunatic.

Ty pulled the stolen vehicle into the driveway of the home he and Jillian had shared and cut the engine. His shoulders quaked, and his hands trembled at the wheel, but he stared straight ahead, his eyes focused on something distant, something elusive and unreachable.

"I don't know what's going to happen, Hannah. I feel responsible for you. Nothing I say or do will ever make up for what I've already done." He lowered his eyes and his brow knitted together as he spoke. "I've come to care a great deal for you. Perhaps it's all been brought on by the extreme circumstances, I don't know, but...I can't help but wish that...we could have known each other under normal circumstances." Ty turned to meet my gaze. He looked unsure, uneasy with his thoughts. "I don't have a good feeling about what will happen next. What the authorities might do. They're going to draw their own conclusions based on all the physical evidence and what we tell them."

"Then we tell them *my* story, Ty, just as I said. It's close to the truth."

"No, it's not that simple, Hannah. The evidence —"

"It *is* that simple, Ty. You owe me this; you said so yourself. Do this for me, please. I don't want anyone to know. What happened stays between us. *Everything* stays just between us. All right?"

He stared at me for a long time as his judgment warred with my request. Finally, he nodded acceptance. "Right. Okay. Just us then."

I couldn't help but sigh. "There *is* something there, Ty. Between us. I don't know what it is, but I feel it. And I know you do, too. I can see it in your eyes."

He reached for my hand and held it firmly between his own. "Yes, Hannah, there *is* something there, but we might never find out exactly what that is or who we could be together. Don't you see? After we leave here tonight, we might not get to see each other again for...God knows how long. Maybe never. So I want you to know that I'm sorry. For everything. I've come to care for you more than I thought I could possibly ever care for another person. Especially a woman. I want you to be happy, Hannah. You deserve to be happy. To be loved again."

His eyes glassed up, glistening in the soft glow of the streetlights. I smiled at him and nodded, too choked up to speak.

He sighed, wincing as he raked his hands over his battered face. "All right then, we should go get cleaned up and changed."

He looked back at his brother's body, his face somber and remote, and then stepped out of the van, locking it securely behind him. Ty led me into his home. I could see Jillian everywhere: in photos, the furniture, the draperies, even the paint. I felt like I was violating a sacred place just being there. It made me very uncomfortable, and I think Tyler could see how awkward it was for me. He directed me to follow him into his bedroom.

"I'll look through Jill's things and find something for you to wear," he said almost in a whisper.

"Maybe just some sweats."

He nodded silently and sorted through his wife's closet. With hands that continued to tremble, Ty laid the clothing and some undergarments on the bed and gave me a plastic bag for the clothes I had on, informing me the police might want them. He showed me to the bathroom and drew a warm bath in continued silence then pulled a couple of large bath towels from the linen closet.

"There you go. I'm going to grab some clothes for myself and use the guest bath down the hall. If you need anything, just yell." He left and closed the door behind him.

I wandered around the room, examining Jillian's things: her perfume and makeup, her hair products and jewelry box, even her hair brush with Jill's long dark strands still entwined in the bristles. I was surprised that Ty still had everything out, like he hadn't touched a thing since her death. It felt like a shrine, a place of worship, and I was an interloper who didn't belong.

I undressed and threw the soiled clothing into the plastic bag. When I caught a glimpse of myself in the mirror, I gasped and turned away. I looked down at my body, remembering each moment as I fingered the cuts and bruises. A lump grew large in my throat. I stopped my probing and moaned.

I stepped gingerly into the tub and winced as the hot water stung my angry flesh. The heat seeped into my aching muscles, urging me to relax. I washed my hair then added bubbles to the water and began erasing all the bloody evidence. I was sure the police would not appreciate my efforts, but no amount of evidence would ever be necessary. Sergeyev was dead. He was at God's mercy now, and I hoped God showed him as much charity as Sergeyev had allowed me. My injuries would be enough indication of my assault, and my testimony would fill in the gaps, if it even came to that.

As I scrubbed away the blood and grime, I slowly shed the many layers of self-protective armor I had blanketed around myself. The degradation and self-loathing at my submittal rose, like steam from the bath water, and I began to cry. I needed to cast off all the pent up resentment, all the powerless rage and fear I felt while in Sergeyev's hands. And Tyler's too, I suppose, since he had been the first to nearly violate me, however remorseful he was now.

I needed to leave it all behind me forever. I stopped scrubbing and sobbed into my hands. I ran through every moment of the last few days, the last few hours in particular. I imagined my tears were enough to fill a deep pool, and that I had the power, the strength, to press Sergeyev's head beneath the surface, to drown him while he fought against me, as I had against him, and to flush him away with the all dirt and debris that was my assault. I cried until the bubbles disappeared, until the bath water grew cold, until everything slipped away, freeing me as much as I could possibly be free.

A gentle knock at the door startled me.

"Hannah, may I come in?" Ty asked, his voice unsure.

I ran wet hands over my face to conceal my tears. "Um...okay."

With a deep pain aching in my side, I pulled my knees up and wrapped my arms around them as I sank deeper into the cloudy water. I looked at Ty sheepishly as he entered, embarrassed that he might have heard me weeping. He dimmed the lights and leaned back against the counter's edge. His fingers grasped the tile so tightly his knuckles turned white. He kept his eyes cast down at his feet as tremors quaked his shoulders every so often.

"Are you okay?" he asked quietly, glancing in my direction for a brief moment.

I nodded.

"Good. That's good. Umm...would you rather be left alone?" Another quick glance.

I shook my head no.

"Okay then. Good. That's good." He bobbed his head in approval and swallowed hard.

He glanced over once more, and I saw a flicker of emotion I could not place. All the sadness, regret, and loss still lingered there, painfully so, but there was something else, as well. A deep longing perhaps. A bitter understanding of what lay ahead. He looked as though he wanted to say something, but whatever it was, he kept it to himself, turning away as he bit nervously along his lower lip.

"So um...the water... It must be getting cold," he said. "Are you ready to get out?"

"Um, sure…I guess."

Ty retrieved one of the large bath sheets, unfolded it, and held it up to me in invitation before looking away. As I stood up and stepped over the tub's edge, he enveloped me snugly into its thick warmth, wrapping his arms around me like a cocoon. I leaned into him and rested my cheek against his chest. Tyler tipped my chin up with his finger and raised my face up to meet his. He gazed into my eyes like he was searching for my soul. Then he kissed me, so warm and tender, and I finally felt safe and protected.

It was the last place I should have felt either. It was unbelievable how things had changed between us. After everything he had done to protect me since that first awful morning, I felt he had redeemed himself, as best he could anyway, and at that moment, I was in the one place I wanted most to be.

I desperately needed to feel like I could be loved and desired as a woman, despite my ordeal. That there was more to me than what I had endured.

I rested my head against his shoulder and nestled into him, allowing him to hold and comfort me.

Chapter Forty-Four

Hannah

I dressed in Jill's fashionable warm-up suit and joined Ty in the living room, the bag with my soiled clothing in hand. He smiled warmly, though he looked worried.

"Are you ready?" he asked.

"As I'll ever be, I guess."

"And do you know what you're going to say?" When I nodded, he raised an eyebrow. "Are you absolutely sure that's how you want to play this, Hannah?"

"Yes, I am, just like I told you earlier."

With a frustrated sigh, he shrugged. "Okay then, let's go."

He kept pretty quiet on the way to the hospital, sharing with me only what I might expect once I got there. "I'll take you to the triage nurse. She'll probably question you before your examination, so be prepared. While you're being examined, I'll see if they can help me with Nick. It'll all be out of our hands after that. Okay?" He searched my eyes for reassurance.

"Okay," I replied, suddenly unsure, because right then it hit me, what I might be facing when I entered the hospital. As the adrenaline wore off, the pains in my body grew more intense.

I knew I might be more seriously injured than I thought. I had to be checked out. I couldn't risk otherwise. But they would know as soon as they examined me exactly what had happened. The law would require them to call the authorities. A more forensic exam would be requested, possibly even expected. They might try using guilt tactics to convince me to comply, "to protect future innocent victims," they might say. I decided I wouldn't comply, no matter what they said. But that could snowball into something altogether different, something I would have no control over, especially once the authorities were involved. Beck would likely be contacted; Conner might find out. Suddenly my plan seemed risky and full of holes, landmines that could explode in my face. But what choice did I have?

None. None at all. I was committed.

We rode the rest of the way in silence. Tyler never once looked over at me, even as he kept glancing back over his shoulder at Nick's body. The tremors that wracked his body became more frequent and violent. His jaw clenched as tears threatened to spill over onto his bruised cheeks. And the tension rolling off him as he gripped the wheel was palpable. I think he feared losing control all over again. I understood, only too well.

Fifteen minutes later, Tyler pulled the stolen van up to the ambulance bay of the emergency room at St. Mary's. He peered back for one last glance at Nick before he walked over to my side and opened the door, helping me out of the vehicle. His hand seemed to vibrate as he escorted me into the hospital.

The triage nurse looked at us with our battered, swollen faces, and hers registered alarm. "Oh my," she said directing us to some chairs. "Please, both of you, have a seat."

"Thanks, but I'm fine. If you could just see to Hannah," Ty bid the nurse. "I do need your help with something else, though. My brother, Nick...he's...he's dead and...his body is outside in that van," he admitted as he pointed toward the doors.

The nurse looked even more startled. "Are you sure?" she asked.

"Yes. Quite," Ty replied with some difficulty.

"Oh, well, I'm sorry then, but I'm required to call the medical examiner's office, and the police, as well," the nurse informed Tyler. "At this point, the coroner is the only one authorized to move your brother's body."

Ty nodded in understanding. "While you see to her, I'll be outside with the van until the police arrive." He turned, kissed me on top of my head, and touched his shaking hand to my cheek. "I hope to see you soon, Hannah," he whispered. His eyes were both worried and sad.

I touched the hand he placed against my cheek and held it as he backed away, his arm outstretched, until he finally stepped beyond my reach.

Chapter Forty-Five

Tyler

The first cops arrived with their lights flashing in the dark. Tires screeched to a halt just a few feet away from where I leaned against the van. I pushed off and stepped toward them as they approached, their hands resting on the butts of their holstered guns.

"Stop right there, sir," one of them ordered. "Put your hands on the back of your head and turn around."

I turned slowly and did as he asked. He restrained my hands against the back of my head and pressed my face into the side of the van. My whole body trembled against the cool metal.

"I'm the one who asked you to come," I said. Even my voice quivered.

"Just a precaution, sir," he said as he patted me down. He kicked at my feet for a wider stance. "Do you have any weapons on you?"

"No, nothing."

"Am I going to be stuck with any needles if I search your pockets?"

"No."

He removed my wallet and tossed it to his partner. I grunted in pain as the officer's hands pressed against my ribs and along my back, twisting my arms uncomfortably. When he was satisfied I was unarmed, he asked me to sit down on the curb while he and his partner talked to the coroner who had just arrived.

The scene became chaotic and crowded in a short span of minutes, with uniformed officers, medical examiners, and weary-looking detectives dressed in cheap, wrinkled sport coats all meandering around each other. And all the while, the lights of numerous emergency vehicles continued to pulse: red and blue, yellow and white, out of sync, over and over as the service radios crackled with activity. With the exception of one uniformed officer stationed close behind me, the rest of the personnel all spoke amongst themselves, often turning to look or point at me, but so far, I'd been asked very few questions, just my name, address, and my relationship to the deceased.

The back door of the van was opened, and everyone descended on Nick's body like flies on a carcass. My breathing rose in short, quick spasms, and I began to hyperventilate. The investigator's camera flashed in slow, deliberate succession, whirring and clicking over the quiet hum of the expanding crowd. One of the detectives pulled me up by the arms and ordered me farther away. I did as he asked, but kept my attention on the van and what they were doing with Nick.

There were several detectives on scene who watched me closely, one of them a dark-haired woman who spoke in hushed tones to the man who had asked me to move. She eyed me suspiciously then turned away and walked into the emergency room. My heart faltered when I saw the coroner zip Nick's body into a black bag and load him onto a gurney. I bit the back of my hand, squeezed tight into a fist to stop it from shaking, and pressed my eyes closed.

I couldn't stand to look anymore. I bowed my head and wrapped my hands around the back of my neck as nausea rolled through me in waves. I feared I would throw up at any moment. They loaded Nick's body into their van, slammed the doors shut, and pulled away. I couldn't hold the tears back any longer. They spilled down my face, falling silently to the asphalt between my feet, as my shoulders shook with both withdrawal and sorrow. My brother—the only person I had left in this world—was gone. And ultimately, I was to blame.

The toes of a scuffed pair of loafers came to rest near my feet, and from above my head, a voice called out my name. Not ready to face anyone just yet, I chose to ignore him, but it was one of the weary detectives addressing me, and he refused to be disregarded.

"Mr. Karras," he barked again.

I raised my head. "Yes," I replied, my voice still hoarse. I swiped at my eyes, stood up, and shook the outstretched hands of two police detectives.

"I'm Detective Paul Stevens and this is Detective Chris Avery," one of them said, indicating his tired-looking partner next to him. "We have some questions we'd like you to answer."

I nodded, trying to be cooperative. "Yes, of course." I wiped my sleeve across my eyes and coughed, wrapping my arm around my body as my ribs screamed in protest. The detectives looked me up and down, though neither of them reacted to the bruises and cuts all over my face, or the tattered flesh across my knuckles, other than to glance briefly at each other.

"There was no identification on the deceased. You said he was your brother?" Stevens asked.

"Yes, my younger brother, Nicholas Karras."

"And how did you come to be in possession of his body?"

I sighed in exhaustion. "That's a very long story."

Stevens pressed his lips together in impatience. "How about the condensed version for now."

I was so tired. My hands and voice both trembled as the DTs ramped up in the wake of my withdrawal from alcohol. "Well, we were both taken against our will and forced to fight for our lives like dogs." I paused for a moment and looked back and forth between them. "Nick didn't make it." I said curtly, becoming defensive knowing how it must sound to them.

"But you did, Mr. Karras?" Stevens asked with mock amazement.

"Right. Very astute of you, Detective."

I figured I should only answer direct questions and then only as briefly as possible. They weren't going to understand until I was given the opportunity to fully explain, something that wasn't going to happen in the hospital parking lot at two in the morning.

"And you somehow managed to free yourself from your kidnappers and bring your brother's body here?" Stevens shot back at me. By his tone, I didn't think he believed me.

"Exactly."

"Well, who killed your brother, Mr. Karras?"

I shook my head. "I don't know his name, and ultimately, somebody else is responsible for Nick being there. For killing him."

"And who might that be? Or do you not know his name either?"

I looked them each square in the eye and sighed. "Dmitri Chernov."

"Dmitri Chernov?" Avery repeated. He glanced over at his partner and chuckled. "As in the Russian Mafia?"

"Yes. That's right."

They looked at each other with more than mere surprise. It was almost gleeful the way their eyes lit up when I confirmed Dmitri's involvement.

Avery nudged his partner with his elbow, leaned close, and said, "That warehouse south of Market." Stevens nodded silently. But their joy was short lived as we were interrupted by two more men, both of whom were expensively dressed in designer suits and imported leather shoes buffed to a crisp shine. With their air of superior authority, I immediately took them for federal agents, and I was proved right when they each flashed their identification at the detectives.

They asked Avery and Stevens to step aside for a moment then seemed to share some unwanted news with the local boys, for the detectives became instantly indignant, their arms flapping about in frustrated discourse. It seemed the feds were about to step on their delicate toes. Of course, it wasn't good news for me either. The involvement of the federal government would only make this more difficult. I had taken the oath of allegiance when I was naturalized nearly eight years ago, and had even married a U.S. citizen, but being somewhat ignorant of U.S. immigration law, I feared for my status, especially since Jillian was dead.

The FBI shut down the whole show at that point. When the detectives returned, one of them handcuffed me, while the other read me my rights. I was arrested on suspicion of murder, a trumped up charge, no doubt, just to get me in for further questioning. I figured it might play out this way. I knew I would have to give them my story at some point, but I didn't know what they were aware of yet as far as Hannah was concerned, so I was worried about tipping my hand too soon.

I was booked, fingerprinted, and photographed, then dumped handcuffed into a small interview room and left to stew by myself for over two hours, shaking and sweating in a hard wooden chair. I imagined insects running across the floor at my feet, a sure sign that my withdrawal was in full swing. I breathed in deep, closed my eyes against the hallucinations, and tried to focus on Hannah. I desperately wanted to ask about her, but I had no idea whether they'd made the connection between us yet.

One of the federal agents entered the tiny room and took a seat without a word. He was tall and thin, with dark blonde hair, and long fingers. He had that gaunt look of an Eastern European, with large sunken eyes, a sharp nose, and thin lips. Detective Stevens followed him in, removed my restraints, and threw a file folder onto the table in front of me. He took a seat and opened the file, revealing arrest records for Nick. I jumped in my seat as a cockroach skittered out from between the pages and scurried toward me along the table's edge. The men traded stares with each other over my reaction. I breathed in deeply to slow my heart rate, which continued to race, as much from the situation I now found myself in as it did from the delirium tremens and hallucinations that plagued me. Stevens looked me over, surveying my symptoms with a measured stare.

"DTs, eh?" he asked, as if he knew only too well from personal experience.

I gave him a rueful smirk. "Yep."

Stevens glanced again at the agent sitting next to him who indicated that the interview should continue regardless. Stevens raised his brow in doubt, but complied.

"Okay Mr. Karras, we've been busy looking into your brother's past. You might already know that his arrest records here in San Francisco go back nearly four years — mostly petty stuff — but his file does note his suspected involvement in quite a few auto theft incidents attributed to the Russian *vory v zakone*, or thieves-in-law, as they like to call themselves. You, on the other hand, well...we've found nothing on you at all, not even a parking ticket, though there are a couple of unsigned complaints with your name on top. Interesting you never pressed any charges. Wonder why that is?" Stevens said as he peered above the rim of his glasses.

"Your point?" I asked.

"Well, we'd like to know how an upstanding citizen such as yourself became involved with your brother's criminal activities, and just how you managed to get on the bad side of Dmitri Chernov."

Stevens leaned back in his chair with his hands on the back of his head and his elbows stretched out to the side. My one good eye shifted back and forth between both men before I decided to play their game.

"I don't know anything specific about my brother's activities, though I tried to extricate him from Dmitri's influence. I suppose that's how I first got on his bad side, as you say."

"What was your relationship like with your brother," he asked.

"I loved him, obviously. Why else would I risk my own life to protect him?" I countered, annoyed at his combative tone.

"And how did Nick feel about *that*?" Stevens asked, his demeanor becoming more challenging.

I was pissed, on the verge of losing my temper. My whole body shook like a malaria patient. I was strung out and on edge. It had been nearly thirty hours since my last drink. I had no hope of getting another. I regretted not taking the opportunity while I was home earlier, though at the time I had debated with myself whether or not I should.

"Look Detective, I haven't slept in...God...I don't know how many days, and in that time, I've had the living shit kicked out of me. Twice, in fact. So why don't you just save us all the

THE MISTAKEN

time and ask me exactly what it is you want to know instead of dancing around."

"Fine, Mr. Karras. Tell us, please, how you got involved with the Russian Mafia, and why your brother is lying dead in the morgue," Stevens asked as he pointed his finger against Nick's file on the table.

I sighed, wiping my hands over my face in exhaustion. I told them the story of Nick's accident, the deaths of our family, his injuries, recovery, and subsequent addiction. I related how Nick turned first to petty crime to support his habits, then to armed robbery which led to the involvement of the Russians. I explained how I'd tried, in vain, so many times, to pull my brother away from their influence, even going so far as to injure one of Dmitri's men, something for which he took great offense. I told them how I was lured to Dmitri's Tea House to see my brother, who'd been injured while forced to participate in human dog fights because of my transgressions against them.

Neither one of them seemed surprised when I shared the details of my evening in the cage, or of watching my brother crushed beneath the boot of a brutal animal, all at the whim of a rapacious madman who benefited financially from each blow. I felt as though they knew it already and were simply waiting for me to confess my participation. The federal agent, who had remained silent up to this point, finally addressed me with a steely gaze.

"Mr. Karras, I'm Special Agent Maksim Sidorov with the FBI. I am very familiar with Dmitri Chernov and the Russian syndicate here in San Francisco. I have been investigating Chernov for well over two years now, including his involvement in the *Solntsevskaya Bratva* and *vory v zakone*," he said with a perfect Russian accent, "and all of his connections in Little Russia and beyond. I attended the fights tonight at the warehouse. I saw

361

what happened to your brother. And I saw you, as well." His implication was clear.

My eyes danced between the two men before settling on Sidorov. "Bloody hell! You were there?" I jumped up to face him, knocking my chair over backwards and pushing the table forward as I leaned towards him. "What the fuck is wrong with you? Why didn't you stop it? How could you allow that to continue after the first fight?"

I stepped out from behind the table. Detective Stevens was surprisingly quick as he bowled me up against the wall behind me, his forearm crushing my throat. I ignored Stevens and glared at the agent across the small room. Detective Avery burst in and grabbed me by the arm. He bent it behind my back and spun me around to face the wall. I resisted both men as they worked to subdue me, twisting my head to look back over my shoulder at Agent Sidorov.

"You goddamn son of a bitch! You could have prevented this, but you just sat there and watched with the rest of those fucking animals. You let my brother die! How could you do that? *How?*"

"Calm yourself, Mr. Karras!" Sidorov shouted over the detectives who were mumbling threats in my ear. "There was nothing I could do. I was deep undercover and couldn't reveal myself. You saw how fast your brother was taken down. I left the building and called for backup when I saw how badly your brother was injured, but it was too late. There was nothing I could have done."

"That's fucking bullshit! If you knew about Dmitri like you said then you should have known what could have happened. You never should have allowed those fights to take place in the first place."

"Mr. Karras, the few times I'd been allowed to attend the fights, there had never been anyone killed. I was trying to gather the evidence to bring Chernov down, to stop those fights, as well as his other activities. I didn't expect anything like that to happen. I'm very sorry, but there was really nothing I could have done at that point. I had no choice but to see it through."

"Fuck you! There's always a choice. You just made the wrong one." I struggled against the two detectives who pressed me against the wall. "Get the fuck off me!"

They ignored me and pressed even harder. "You gonna calm down, Karras?" Avery asked.

I was bruised all over, and too many of my ribs already felt broken without them smashing me against the concrete block wall. I stopped straining against them and slowly relaxed. "Yes. Now let go of me."

The two men eased up and backed away. I wrapped both arms around my body, closed my eyes, and leaned my forehead against the wall, waiting for the pain to ebb.

"Do you need medical attention?" Sidorov asked, sounding more annoyed than concerned.

I considered it; I knew was in pretty bad shape. But Hannah's claw marks and the bullet wound in my shoulder would likely bring about a whole round of questions Hannah would rather I not answer. So I gritted my teeth and declined. "No, just...just give me a minute."

I dragged my chair back to the table and sat down. Sidorov and Stevens did the same while Avery leaned his shoulder against the wall behind me with his arms crossed over his thick chest. Everyone was quiet for a few minutes while I pulled myself together.

"Like I told you," Sidorov began, "I was deep undercover. I'd already spent well over a year establishing a relationship with

Chernov's people. Nobody knew I was with the Bureau. As far as they were concerned, I was just another invited guest, there for a little entertainment and friendly sport.

"When your brother went down, I left to call for backup, but I still had to protect my identity. I went outside. A few of Chernov's goons were standing guard nearby. I made it seem like I was going out for a quick smoke and a phone call. Next thing I knew, people were streaming out of the building. By the time my backup and the SFPD arrived, most everyone had already fled. But there was quite a mess left back inside, wasn't there, Mr. Karras? I want to know what happened in there. So, what can you tell us about the seven dead men found at the warehouse after you fled?"

I stared at him without acknowledging what I knew. Frankly, I was surprised there were only seven. "Sorry. I don't know what you're talking about."

"Hmm, is that so? So you have no idea how the last remaining fighter ended up with a broken neck, or how Alexi Batalov might have sustained a cracked skull and a lethal stab wound to his back?"

I squeezed my bruised hands together to subdue the tremors and shook my head, never letting my eyes fall from Sidorov's. "Nope, none at all."

"And the five sizable men known to be Chernov's body guards? No idea how they died either?"

"Can't say that I do, Agent Sidorov, but karma can be a real bitch, don't you think?"

I couldn't keep myself from throwing him a challenging smile. Sidorov and both detectives scowled at me, the same exasperated look drawn across each face.

"And what about Hannah Maguire?" Sidorov tilted his head to the side. "What can you tell us about her? How did she acquire her injuries?"

My smile faded, and my heart sank. I bowed my head in regret and humiliation and closed my eyes against all three men.

"We know you escorted Ms. Maguire into the emergency room earlier. We also know she was assaulted, suffering considerable injuries and —"

My head snapped up. "What injuries exactly? Is she okay? Will she be all right?"

Sidorov smiled, happy he'd found vulnerable spot. "Are you family, Mr. Karras?"

I looked at him, confused. "Family? No. No I'm not, but...she and I have —"

Sidorov interrupted with a dismissive wave of his hand. "Then I'm sorry. I can't give you any details."

With a sigh, I lowered my head to my hands clasped tightly on the table. Sidorov must have felt sorry for me, though he huffed in exasperation.

"She's been admitted, but she'll recover," he offered.

I looked back up at him. "Thank you," I replied, grateful for his mercy. I relaxed and leaned back in my chair.

"So, how do you know Ms. Maguire?" Stevens asked.

"That's another long story."

Sidorov threw his pen down onto his notepad then folded his arms across his chest. "By all means," he said.

I told them about Jillian, the circumstances surrounding her death, and the woman I believed responsible. I explained how I started drinking heavily afterwards, wallowing in my misery, looking for some kind of retribution. I told them Nick and I had decided to find Erin Anderson and confront her, if for no other reason than to have some kind of closure, but we had inadvertently misidentified Hannah as Erin because, not only did they look alike, but Erin was also in a relationship with Hannah's husband.

Sidorov's brow shot up. "You're joking."

I shook my head and continued. I thought about Hannah and what she wanted me to say if it came down to it. If it was just about me, I would have confessed everything, but Hannah didn't want that, so I fought the urge and related exactly what she'd asked me to.

"That doesn't make sense, Mr. Karras. Why would she leave with you, a man she didn't even know and who was obviously involved in a dangerous situation?" Sidorov wondered aloud.

"Well, I apologized for that, and told her she could be in danger if she stayed there alone, that I didn't know who else might have been watching me. She was a loose end; she could identify the man who had broken in, possibly tie him back to Dmitri. Hannah was frightened, and I guess she would rather have taken her chances with me than with Dmitri's men. That's it."

"That's hardly *it*," Sidorov said. "We have the two of you on surveillance video at a bank ATM over seventy-five miles away near Cle Elum, Washington. Ms. Maguire appeared to be very upset. While you seemed to be...oh, I don't know, in control, I'd say."

"Of course she was upset," I answered, the lies coming much easier. "She'd just been through a traumatic experience, and neither one of us knew what to do. I was simply trying to...help her out. That's all."

Sidorov offered me a slight smile. "Ah yes, the Good Samaritan. Such an interesting way to look at it." He shook his head and rifled through his legal pad, checking his extensive list of notes. After a brief pause, he looked up and said, "And what happened in Biggs, Oregon exactly?" His eyes returned to the pad and pointed to a particular line. "It seems you registered in *your* name and secured the room with *her* credit card." He looked up from his notes, his brow drawn up in question. "Though you forgot to pay in cash as you promised the clerk, that is, before you gunned down a man in your room and fled...again."

"No, I paid him cash. I just asked him not to run her card through. I was afraid Chernov's goons might be following us. And they were. That was Dmitri's man at the motel, the same one from Hannah's house. He broke in and fired his gun, even pulled a knife. I just fired back in self-defense."

Sidorov smiled like a cat with a canary. I'd stepped into his trap, admitting I'd killed the intruder. "I see," he said. "And where did you get the gun?"

"It was Nick's. He gave it to me for protection before Hannah and I left."

"Aw, that's touching. But while he was shot in the stomach with a gun we have not yet recovered, the victim was actually killed by a round to the head, and we believe the gun used to kill him belonged to the dead man himself. I'm curious how that happened." He sat back in his seat, his pen tapping against the legal pad. "Tell me, whose prints will we pull off that gun, do you suppose? Yours, by any chance?"

"Yes, most likely. After I clipped him the first time, I took his gun away to protect myself and Hannah, but even injured, he attacked me again. Like I said, he pulled a knife. So I shot him. His gun proved to be much more effective than mine."

Sidorov stopped writing and looked up from his notes. He clasped his hands and rested them on the pad. "My, my, you have an answer for everything, don't you?"

I shrugged. "Just telling you how it happened."

"Is that so? Well, then, tell me why Dmitri Chernov wanted to kill you and your brother?"

I shook my head and offered him a weak smile. "I don't know exactly. It seemed to me like an overreaction to a mere disagreement, but those Russian boys are serious about their work, and they hated me for coming in between them and Nick." I shrugged again.

Sidorov smiled, like he didn't believe a word I said. "Why were you and Ms. Maguire at the Four Seasons here in The City," he persisted, skipping from one incident to the next in what I was sure was an attempt to trip me up.

Another casual shrug. "Just a place to decompress before I met with Dmitri about my brother."

"What about your brother?" He referred to his notes once more. "You said earlier that you left him back at the motel in Issaquah, Washington, correct?" He peeked up at me.

I nodded. "Right."

"What happened to him, then? How did he end up in Chernov's cage?"

"Nick drove back here to try to talk sense into Dmitri, so he would call off his dogs. But it didn't work," I said, the anger and bitterness seeping back into my voice. "Agent Sidorov, earlier tonight, Nick told me that he'd fought his first bout two nights ago, and that last night, he was forced to fight again. Besides being a mess physically, he was pretty upset about it. He thought he might have killed the poor bastard, but he felt he had no choice. It was either kill or be killed, something you, in your two years of investigation and being undercover, should have known before going into that warehouse. If you had, we might not be here tonight, and my brother might still be alive."

He ignored my comment and stared hard at me with his chin jutting out and his lips pressed tight, like I'd struck a nerve. "And what about Ms. Maguire?" he countered.

The tic in my jaw began to work as I stared back. "What about her?"

"Well, you said she was under your protection, yet she turns up at the hospital, beaten and raped. Brutalized even."

I gasped at the insensitive way in which he revealed the details of Hannah's assault.

"You do know what that means, don't you, Mr. Karras?"

I couldn't look at him, I was so disturbed and angry. "Yes," I answered under my breath.

"*Do you?*" he asked again more urgently.

"Yes!" I screamed, lifting my head and staring him in the eye.

He leaned forward and raised his brow. "Well then, I'd say your services leave a lot to be desired. So tell me what happened? How did she end up like that?"

I clenched my hands together to keep from lunging across the table, but I think Sidorov was purposely baiting me, so I leaned back in my seat and cooled my temper before I spoke.

"Since both Nick and I were all Dmitri really wanted, I arranged for Hannah to fly back home. I arranged for her car to be shipped back to her home, then bought her an airline ticket, and hired transportation to the airport and an escort to see her through to security. We said our goodbyes, and she left. Afterwards, I took a taxi to Dmitri's Tea House out on Geary, as we had arranged, but it was evident pretty quickly that he wasn't interested in anything I had to say."

Agent Sidorov stopped writing and looked at me above his glasses. "How so?" he asked.

"Well, two of his men beat the shit out of me, threw me and Nick into a van, drove us to that bloody warehouse, and dumped us each in a cage. Then they made me watch as some fucking thug beat my brother to death," I said, glaring contemptuously at him for asking. "Afterwards, I was... forced...to do something...something I never thought I'd ever do to another human being." My eyes flitted from one man to the next as I gauged their reaction.

All three men stared back, silent, waiting. I remained stone quiet for several uncomfortable moments before I pulled myself together and finished.

"I didn't know that Dmitri had gotten to Hannah at the hotel. I didn't know until right before the fight began. They paraded her out on the gallery for me to see. It was...distressing, to say the least." I shook my head, and my jaw flexed in silent rage. "Hannah didn't tell me what had happened, and I didn't ask. I could tell just by looking at her." I paused again, trying to calm the fire that burned inside me as I remembered Hannah standing on the walkway above the arena.

"They brought her there for no other reason than to get to me, Agent Sidorov." I turned away, unable to look him in the eye. "And it did," I admitted with a nod. "It got to me."

For a few moments, all I could hear was Sidorov scratching notes on his pad. Then he placed his pen down and sighed through his nose. "Did you kill all those men, Mr. Karras?" Sidorov asked directly. He paused and waited for me to respond. "It would be...understandable if you had, to save your own life, to save Ms. Maguire."

I couldn't respond. I just sat there looking at my hands resting on the table. I felt Sidorov staring at me. After a few silent minutes, he began to pack up his things.

"All right, that's all for now. An officer will be in shortly to escort you to your cell. We'll speak again sometime tomorrow." He glanced at his watch and huffed. "Or later today."

My shoulders sagged and I let out a long breath, relieved that he wasn't going to push me any further. I caught his arm as he passed me on his way out.

"Agent Sidorov, if it's at all possible, would you find out how Hannah is doing and let me know...please?"

Sidorov hesitated then nodded before he left.

Chapter Forty-Six

Tyler

I spent a difficult night in jail. Violent tremors wracked my body and didn't even begin to ease until the following noon hour. At that point, I might have been able to hold a spoon and eat my lunch if it weren't for the nausea that tightened my belly, or the imaginary insects that continued to startle me as they crawled out from my food. I think I was on my seventh straight day without meaningful sleep, but I couldn't be sure. The pounding that had been hammering around in my head the previous four days had ramped way up in the last few hours, but thankfully began to mellow as the tremors faded to a slow simmer. The only thing that made the morning bearable was the news I received from Sidorov: Hannah was resting comfortably and would be all right.

I was allowed to shower, and I shaved for the first time in nearly three weeks. My grey beard—which aged me considerably—was replaced by the cuts and bruises beneath. I hardly recognized my reflection in the mirror. As I looked myself in the eye, I no longer saw the man I used to be. He was gone. I was afraid I would never see him again. In his place was a shell, a ghost. And I cried knowing I had thrown everything away.

I was escorted back to the same small interview room late that afternoon. Only Agent Sidorov was in attendance when I arrived. He stood and greeted me with a firm handshake, ignoring the soft quaking of my hands and the beads of perspiration across my forehead and lip. He took a seat and got right down to business.

"Did you receive my message about Ms. Maguire's condition?" he asked.

"Yes, I did. Thank you."

"You're welcome. Now, Mr. Karras, taking into consideration all that you've been through and all that you've most likely done yourself, the Bureau has decided to offer you a deal."

I snorted. "And what if I don't like your deal?" I asked, unsure if I should be grateful or not.

He pulled back in his seat. "Well then, the Bureau would have no choice but to prosecute you on multiple charges of murder and interfering in an investigation, as well as kidnapping and conspiracy charges. All of which would be federal, of course, each very serious with severe penalties. At best, you're looking at thirty years. Worst case? Well, let's just say that kidnapping across state lines with bodily harm is a capital offense." With his brow raised, he gave me a tight-lipped grin.

"Right," I replied stiffly. I was no fool. Without Hannah's cooperation, I knew the kidnapping charges probably wouldn't stick, but the others had me worried. "What's your offer then?" I asked.

"You may not have heard yet but, Dmitri Chernov was arrested early this morning. After two years, we feel we have a significant case against him for illegal gambling, tax evasion, extortion, human trafficking, and even federal murder. Given your insight into his organization over the last few years, as well as personally witnessing the events that took place last evening, we would like you to provide testimony against him at both the evidentiary hearing and at trial."

I was about to interrupt when Sidorov raised a finger, delaying me a moment while he finished.

"In exchange for your testimony, we will withdraw all current charges against you and offer you the government's services within the witness protection program, including a new identity, relocation, job training and placement, as well as protection, of course. But I must warn you, you will have to cut all ties from your current life, and you will not be allowed to contact anyone from your past. Since your immediate family is all…deceased, I imagine it will be easier for you than most." He paused, gauging me for a reaction. "So, what do you think, Mr. Karras?" He smiled, like he was doing me some great favor.

I stared at him for a long time then sat back in my seat. "I think I should consult with an attorney."

"Well, that would be your prerogative, of course, but I urge you toward haste. Mr. Chernov's attorney is currently working to get him released on bail," Sidorov explained then paused for effect, "from the same unit where you are being held. I'm not sure which is more dangerous for you: Chernov here in jail or out on bail. You *should* be safe in here, but I can't guarantee that. You know how it is. And I can't guarantee that bail won't be granted either. As you know, Chernov is a man of great influence and an even greater propensity toward violence. It seems he has quite the vendetta against you. So the faster we make this deal, the quicker we can get you out of here and make you safe."

"What vendetta?" I asked. "He got what he wanted. Nick's dead. What more could he possibly want from me?"

"Oh, quite a bit more," he said. Then he tilted his head, looking a bit confused. "You don't know? Your brother never shared your father's secret?"

"My father? What are you talking about? What does he have to do with any of this?"

"Everything, apparently. Our sources have determined a link between your father and Dmitri Chernov."

"That's insane. My father had never even stepped foot in San Francisco before the day he arrived here, the same day he was killed in a car accident. He didn't know Chernov."

"It seems he did, Mr. Karras. Chernov came to the U.S. by way of London some eighteen years ago, two years after your father unexpectedly moved your family to Melbourne."

"So, what does one have to do with the other? I don't see a connection."

"Three months before your family relocated to Australia, your father testified in court against one Mikhail Chernov on murder and racketeering charges. Chernov was convicted and sentenced to twenty years in prison. Unfortunately, he didn't get the opportunity to serve that sentence. He was murdered by a rival within the first month of confinement. Mikhail's younger brother, Dmitri, held your father responsible and put a contract out on his life, but your father had already disappeared. Not long afterwards, Dmitri and his younger half-brother, Alexi Batalov—with whom he shared a mother—came to the U.S. and set up shop in San Francisco's Outer Richmond District. You can imagine their surprise when, seventeen years later, your brother, Nick, fell right into their lap."

I shook my head. "No, there's no way. I would have known about this, about my father."

"What do you remember about the months before you left England?" Sidorov asked. "What was life like at home?"

"It was fine. I mean, there was nothing different. Not really. My father was just stressed about his job, that's all. He was an accountant with a big firm in London. Then all of a sudden, he took a promotion and we packed for the move. My mum was upset, at first. She didn't want to leave, but once we did, she never looked back. In fact, she never...she never..." I stopped and search my memory. "Oh God, she never did go back. Not once. Even to visit her family. My father wouldn't allow it. And when I finished at university and told him I was returning, he forbid me. Said it wasn't safe. I never even thought to question him about it. Oh my God, all those years. He never said a word."

"And what about your brother?" Sidorov asked. "Nick never said anything to you about Dmitri and Alexi knowing your father?"

"No, never. Not once. He couldn't possibly have known. Nick would never have gone to work for them if he had."

"Are you sure about that? He wasn't forced to join their ranks?"

"Yes, well...I mean, he had no choice. They forced him in, but it was to pay off his debt from the robbery. At least, that's what he said, or what he intimated anyway. He said it was... He said..." I paused again, rooting around my head for my brother's exact words. "Bloody hell. Nick said it was more complicated than I knew. Oh my God, he knew. He knew, and he didn't tell me." I laid my face in my hands. "Oh, Nick. My God. What did you do?"

"When Nick robbed that store, he brought them right to your door. I have a feeling, once Nick knew who they were and what they wanted, he tried to protect you—from them, from the "sins" of your father, so to speak. An eye for an eye sort of thing. Only it was first born son for first born son. And Nick stepped in. Am I right, Mr. Karras? Did your brother sacrifice himself in a last bid attempt to appease Dmitri Chernov and Alexi Batalov for the death of their oldest brother?"

I thought about the possibility and wanted to toss it out of hand, but there were too many things Nick had said that clicked into place. When we spoke on the phone and I begged him to let me help him. *"I'm so sorry, Tyler. Do you see now? This is why I don't want you to come after me. You were right all along. I just get in the way. And that's just the half of it,"* he'd said. *"You don't know, Ty. You just don't know..."* And then right before his last fight at the cages, he'd said, *"No worries. I got this. I know what I have to do now. I'm going to take care of things for once in my life. My last gift to you, brother."* I pleaded with him to fight, but he said, *"Someone has to appease the gods."*

It was true. My God, Nick *had* sacrificed himself for me. Tears flooded my eyes and poured over my cheeks.

These last few years, I had been so hard on my brother. I had shunned him for his weakness, for his addictions, for choosing to serve Alexi and Dmitri in order to repay *his* debt, for offenses I thought *he'd* committed. But I'd been wrong about so many things, like Nick's culpability for the accident that killed our parents and sister, for preventing him from helping Jillian. And now this.

All this time, Nick had been protecting *me*, and he'd done so in a way that would keep me far from the danger that he subjected himself to every single day. I would never be able to thank him, to acknowledge all that he had forfeited in order to protect *me*, the older brother who believed he'd done so much to take care of his younger, irresponsible sibling.

The truth was too much to bear. The shame of it crushed me.

Sidorov tapped his fingers on the table. "I'm sorry, Mr. Karras. I thought you deserved to know. I realize it doesn't make it any easier, but perhaps it will help you make your decision. Dmitri Chernov deserves to rot in prison for the rest of his life. And you can help put him there. I can't offer you protection—in here or on the outside—unless you help us out."

I swallowed hard at the threat and turned my thoughts in another direction. I wasn't the only one at risk here. Nick may have inadvertently brought Dmitri and Alexi to my door, but I had tossed Hannah into the mix in my quest for vengeance. I wiped the tears away and leveled my gaze at Agent Sidorov.

"What about Hannah?" I asked. "Will she be offered any kind of protection?"

"Well, Ms. Maguire might be useful if we were looking at secondary kidnapping charges from when she was taken from the hotel, and I certainly haven't dismissed that notion, but as it stands now, she has very limited knowledge about Chernov himself. The man who allegedly assaulted her was among the dead at the warehouse, so obviously there's no need to prosecute on those charges."

I pounded my fist on the table. "That's bullshit! Chernov had to have known. One of his men took her. And she was assaulted on his property, while he was there. Surely you can find some way to implicate him!"

"Mr. Karras, Ms. Maguire has been highly traumatized, and any testimony she provides will be open for a difficult cross examination, so if I can avoid it, I'd rather not subject her to that, especially if it isn't a charge we would likely get a conviction on."

I couldn't fault him for that. I'd rather Hannah not have to relive anything either. I nodded in resignation. "Will she at least be safe, from Dmitri, I mean? He won't go after her, will he?"

Sidorov shook his head. "I doubt it. She can't tie what happened to her back to Dmitri. His attorney would know that. And, therefore, so would Chernov. He'd only be further jeopardizing himself if he went after her."

I sighed in relief. "Well then, what will happen to me if I do accept your deal?"

"You will be taken into federal protective custody and arrangements will be made for your living accommodations during the testimonial process. When the process is complete, probably within a year or so, you will be permanently reassigned a new identity and relocated to a secure location of *our* choosing. Of course, all this hinges on the amount and value of the information you provide."

I contemplated his response for a moment, unsure of what to do. "Do you feel you have a good case against him? Will Chernov be convicted?"

Sidorov looked at me earnestly. "We have a number of witnesses to various aspects of the investigation, and there are many charges being leveled against Mr. Chernov. We feel confident that we can convict on at least a few, if not all charges. But of course, there is no guarantee. You need to consider that when making your decision."

I deliberated over everything Agent Sidorov had told me. It wasn't going to get any better for me than this, and though I did deserve to spend time in prison for all I had done to Hannah, I didn't think I deserved it for killing Alexi or Dmitri's other men, especially considering all they had done to Nick. After everything he'd given up for me, Nick deserved some kind of retribution on his behalf. And only I could provide that for him.

I had only one real concern and that was Hannah. I didn't want to be whisked away without having the opportunity to speak with her one last time. I needed to explain everything myself and tell her why I would likely never see her again. Given all she'd confessed to me regarding her feelings, my leaving might prove difficult for her. I needed to be the one to break the news, to beg her to understand the impossible quagmire I now found myself in.

"Agent Sidorov, I would accept your terms with one small condition."

He raised his brow at me and removed his glasses. "What might that be?"

"I'd like the opportunity to speak with Hannah, in person, one last time before I'm taken into your custody."

He shook his head. "Ms. Maguire will be remaining in the hospital for several more days and, I'm sorry, but she cannot be moved to accommodate your request."

"But surely you can move me to her location."

"That would hardly be prudent."

"Still, I insist on this one condition," I asserted, sitting back in my seat. "I can't just vanish forever without expressing my..." I paused with my head bowed, reflecting on all the things I would like to tell to her. "...without expressing my regret. I have much to say of a personal nature. Please, Agent Sidorov, I beg you to consider this one request. And then I'll give you my full focus and attention."

He sat there contemplating me for a long moment. "I'll have to clear this with my command, but...I'm fairly confident something can be arranged."

I smiled weakly. "Thank you. Then I accept your deal."

We both stood and shook hands.

"Good. A contract will be drawn up within a couple of hours. After you sign it, I will see to the arrangements of your request. Good day, Mr. Karras."

He packed his briefcase and left the tiny room.

Chapter Forty-Seven

Tyler

A few hours later, I signed the agreement with the FBI. Detective Stevens informed me that the San Francisco Police Department had dropped all charges, and I was free to leave into federal custody. Afterwards, I was escorted through the booking area and into a waiting SUV, the windows tinted black as pitch.

Agent Sidorov and his partner drove me back to St. Mary's Medical Center where we arrived at the rear of the main building. Sidorov got out and spoke to a hospital administrator who gave him specific instructions on how to proceed. Both agents were tense and on edge. They searched the area thoroughly with their guns drawn while I waited in the car. Sidorov pulled me from the SUV and placed me between him and his partner, escorting me into the hospital through a service entrance.

They pushed me to the rear of a freight elevator and stood ready at the doors, blocking my view. I was accompanied up to radiology and a dressing room where I was given full scrubs and a surgical mask to change into. From there, they hustled me into an MRI room where they conducted another diligent search.

When they were satisfied we were alone, they directed me back to the equipment terminal which stood quiet in the dim light.

"Wait here, Mr. Karras," Sidorov said. "We'll be in the next room if you need us."

I thanked them both and sat down to wait. My heart pounded in anticipation, both at being able to see Hannah again, as well as dreading what I was going to have to tell her. I waited fifteen minutes until an orderly pushed a wheelchair through the door, calling out Hannah's name before departing. I looked across the darkened room toward Hannah who craned her head over her shoulder at the fleeing orderly.

"That guy's weird," she commented to herself. Then she turned her attention my way. She watched me, but, in the darkness, did not recognize me with the mask covering my nose and mouth. "Hey, I don't think I need another scan already," she said impatiently. "I just had one last night, for Pete's sake. Could you recheck my doctor's orders before you begin? I don't want to be charged for an unnecessary test."

I walked out of the darkness, removed the mask, and bent down in front of her wheelchair. The whites of Hannah's eyes grew wide, and a slow smile spread across her bruised face.

"Tyler," she burst out, grimacing in discomfort as she tried to stand.

"No, Hannah. What are you doing? Sit back down before you hurt yourself."

I turned around, grabbed a plastic chair, and slid it up close in front of her wheelchair. I sat down and took her hands in mine, kissing them both several times.

She stared at me with a bright smile, though bewilderment lingered in her eyes. "Why are you here?" she asked. "How did you get here? What happened to you?"

"Whoa, slow down," I said as I smiled back warmly, hoping she would appreciate it. I couldn't help but lean in and kiss her on her mouth, just once. As I pulled back, I looked at her and she still had her eyes closed, as if she expected something more. When she opened them, she looked at me so sweetly. And my heart shattered.

"How are you, Ty?" she asked with genuine concern.

"I'm okay, all things considered. And you, Hannah, how do you feel? Are you on the mend?" I touched my hand to her cheek, stroking her bruised flesh with my thumb.

She laughed softly as she covered my hand with hers. "Yeah, I'm on the mend. Guess I have a lacerated liver or something. They want to keep me here for a few more days. But I'll live." She shook her head, her eyes caressing my face as worry wrinkled her brow. "My God, look at you. You have two black eyes. Is your nose broken?"

I mugged my chin up for her and gave her my very best smile, knowing fully how much she would appreciate it. "Yes, but doesn't it make me more ruggedly handsome?"

We both laughed at my poor attempt at humor.

"Yes," she replied. "Yes, it does, if that's even possible." She reached out and slowly ran her fingers along my jaw. "I've never seen you clean-shaven. That's a good look for you." She turned serious then and the grin disappeared. "What happened, Ty? I've been so worried."

I looked down at the floor uneasily before returning to hold her gaze. "Well, for starters, I was arrested by the police. But then the feds showed up, and they were very interested in my case, so…" I shrugged.

Hannah's eyes grew wide again. "The feds? Like the FBI? But why?"

"Well, it seems one of their agents was at the fight, working undercover. He was the reason all the cops showed up as we were leaving." I bowed my head. "He asked me a lot of questions...about Nick, about Dmitri and Alexi." I swung my eyes up to meet hers again. "And about you, Hannah."

She gasped. "About me?"

"Yep. I was backed into a corner, so I gave them the story you suggested. I'm not entirely sure they bought it, but they were very interested in my...participation in their investigation."

Hannah's eyes narrowed. "Investigation? What does that mean exactly?"

I expelled a ragged sighed as sadness overwhelmed me. "Hannah, they've offered me a deal."

"What kind of deal? What could they possibly want from you?"

"Well, I either help them by testifying against Dmitri, or...they charge me with multiple federal murders, conspiracy, interfering in a federal investigation. Even kidnapping."

"Kidnapping?"

"Yes, Hannah. Kidnapping you."

"What? No! They can't do that. Not without my—"

I jumped up from my seat. "Hannah, this is the U.S. federal government we're talking about. They can do whatever the hell they want, and I have very little choice in the matter." I stopped and sighed, frustrated that I continued to allow my emotions to rule me. "I'm sorry." I sat at back down and took her hands in mine once again.

"Look, I didn't want this...any of it. I've made some very poor choices. I've tried to make up for it as best I can. I didn't count on becoming so... I mean, I didn't go looking to become...involved. But, for whatever reason..." I struggled to find the right words, but my throat was tight with emotion I couldn't control, no matter how hard I tried. "For whatever reason, Hannah, you and I...we seemed to...need each other. It was incredibly intense, but...it was...artificial. It wasn't...real. No relationship formed under those circumstances can survive the day to day of normal life. We are too different. We would never work. It could never last."

Hannah stared back at me, her eyes glassy. She sat up straight and ripped her hands from my grasp. She tried to wheel herself away, but I caught the arms of her wheelchair and held her in place.

"Wait, Hannah, please. Let me explain—"

"What are you doing here, Ty?" she whispered, searching my eyes for the answer.

I stared back, willing her to understand. "I had little choice. I took their deal."

She pulled on the wheels, trying her best to break free.

"No, Hannah, wait. Please, listen to me."

She stopped struggling and looked me hard in the eye.

"I will testify for them. And in return, they'll protect me by giving me a new identity and relocating me. I'll get training, a new job, whatever I need to start a new life."

"And your old life, Ty? What about that?"

I sighed, my attention back on the floor by my feet. "It's over. I have to cut all ties and move on. I don't have any family left. It shouldn't be too difficult to start over."

I looked back up at her and the tears I tried so hard to hold back spilled over.

"God, Hannah, I don't want to do this. You must believe that. I don't want to hurt you again. I've done that too many times already. Every time I hurt you, it rips away a piece of me. There's so little left of the man I once was. I don't even recognize myself anymore. I can't afford to misplace one more part of who

I really am. Can't you see that? You told me how you understood so much of what I've been through. Please, tell me you can understand this."

She nodded while tears rolled down her cheeks, swallowing hard before she spoke. "Yes, of course I can understand."

"Hannah, I'm so sorry. I hope someday you can forgive me for this, as well." I held her face between my hands. I kissed her forehead, then each side of her tear-stained face. And then, lastly, her mouth, once, tenderly. I pulled away and looked into her sad eyes for a long moment then kissed her again, long, slow, and desperate. When we parted, Hannah wouldn't even look at me. She kept her head bowed. I kissed her crown and stood up.

"Goodbye, Hannah. Please take care of yourself, okay?" She only nodded, refusing to speak or even glance up at me. "Okay," I said once more and walked out of the room.

I stopped just outside the door and heard her sobbing quietly. I walked to the next room and knocked. Sidorov opened the door and I stepped just inside with the door cracked. I watched the orderly return and take Hannah away. It felt like my heart had been ripped from my chest and taken away with her.

Despondent, and destroyed all over again, I walked out of the hospital the same way I came in, into the custody of the FBI, who — without even allowing me to bury my brother — swept me away to a new life.

Chapter Forty-Eight

Hannah

Too restless to lie still in my hospital bed one minute longer, I rose and paced the cold floor of my private room, mulling over Ty's every word. I should have asked him to stay. If I had, perhaps he would have reconsidered. While he might have guessed how I felt about him, I never actually told him straight out. And now he had made the decision to leave. I'd never be able to see or talk to him again. If I'd told him how I really felt, maybe he would have stayed. We could have fought those charges together, but I never made the offer, and now my regrets were mounting.

As I wandered around aimlessly, the police detective who had tried to interview me as I was being admitted knocked on the open door of my darkened room. I snapped out of my trance and looked up. She smiled politely and walked in to re-introduce herself. I pushed myself back into the shadows.

"Good evening, Ms. Maguire. I'm Detective Michelle Simmons with the SFPD. We met when you were first brought in to the emergency room. I know that must have been very difficult for you, and you'd like nothing more than to forget, but perhaps you remember me?"

"Yes, Detective, I do." Though she held out her hand, I remained standing in the dark, trying my best to hide my bloodshot eyes and the tears that refused to cease.

She dropped her outstretched arm. "May I come in?"

"Oh, um…yeah…I suppose."

"Thank you. I hope this is a good time. We didn't get to speak very much before and I need to get a formal statement from you." She pulled a chair from the corner and sat down, a small notepad and pen in hand. It looked as though she planned on staying awhile. "The status of this case has changed considerably since you were admitted," Simmons reported.

"Changed how?"

"Well, as I believe you may already know, this case is now under federal authority. The SFPD is cooperating with the FBI on your end due to the multijurisdictional police investigations."

"On my end? I don't understand."

"Ms. Maguire, after you were identified last night, a local investigator was sent to your residence. The front door appeared damaged, so the detective entered on suspicion of a crime having been committed. He found quite a bit of blood. Your husband was contacted. He and your son said they had only spoken to you once in the last few days prior to the incident here in The City. They said that was unusual and that they were concerned. Your home was determined to be a crime scene, and your local police department would like to know what happened. So, if you wouldn't mind going over it with me, I could send them and the FBI your statement and get this whole thing wrapped up."

My mind spun at warp speed. *Oh my God, Beck and Conner know! Conner must be so scared. What else has happened? What have the police uncovered? Where is Tyler, and what has he told them?*

My heart instantly ticked up to a frenzied pace, beating so loud I was sure she could hear it. The rush of adrenaline made me nauseous and light-headed. I tried to hide my nervousness. I had to control the interview. I needed her to trust me, to believe me. I sucked in a deep breath and released it, slow and measured. Turning away from Detective Simmons, I walked over to the large window on the far side of the room and focused on the lush green of the park below.

"My husband and son...are they all right?" I asked.

"Yes, Ms. Maguire, they're fine. I believe they're on their way and should be here quite soon, in fact. So I'd like to get this wrapped up. Why don't you tell me what happened."

I sighed, and, with my back still turned on Detective Simmons, I shook my head.

"Just start at the beginning," she said.

I took another deep breath. "Well...I had just dropped my son off at his father's apartment. My husband and I had recently separated, and Conner was spending the holiday weekend with him. I hadn't been home for more than a few minutes when I heard the bell ring."

I became quiet and lost in my thoughts as I inwardly recalled seeing Ty for the first time. I leaned my shoulder against the window frame and gazed down at Golden Gate Park, stretching westward for several miles before me. I had never felt such consuming despair in all my life. I wrapped my bruised arms around myself, hoping it would somehow hold me together and keep the fragments of my heart from escaping the broken shell of my body.

Detective Simmons asked questions from behind me, but I couldn't focus on what she was saying. I tuned her out. I couldn't face reliving everything in order to answer her questions, especially when she broached each one with suspicion. I rolled my head against the window as I looked down, willing the tears to stop. I wished I could push through the glass and escape. I wished the detective would go away and leave me in peace. I wished that I could erase the last week of my life.

No.

I wished Tyler would come back to me again. To save me, to hold me, to hurt me. Anything to have him near me once more. I felt so twisted to want that, but I couldn't deny what was in my heart, what I wanted down deep inside.

"Ms. Maguire, I realize this is difficult, but we really need to continue with your statement. If you would just sit back down and focus on the timeline, we could get through this much easier."

We? Easier? Are you kidding me? She had no clue, and if I were to confess everything, she'd probably have me committed. But maybe I deserved that.

"Ms. Maguire? Would you please come back and continue? Ms. Maguire?"

I pulled my head away from the glass, sighing with the amount of effort it took, and wiped away the tears. "Yes, Detective, just...give me a moment."

I turned around to face her and walked into the soft light. As our eyes met, she winced in regret. That made me feel even more violated, as if she saw the stain I carried, like it was written all over my body, all over my face. I wondered what she was thinking. She knew who I was, where I lived, and the bloody trail left behind there. Would she guess the real reason before I gave her my version of the story? What could I tell her to alter her suspicions? The truth was not an option. I vowed to keep that to myself and twist the facts to serve me better, to serve *him* better. She would never understand. Ty certainly didn't. Nobody would. Least of all me.

"Why don't you lay back down in bed and rest while we go over all this?" Simmons asked. "I think if you were more comfortable, you might get through it easier, all right?"

I walked around the bed, clutching the rails for support. I sat on the edge and pulled my legs up under the rough sheets. Detective Simmons' eyes grazed over my body, her lips pursing at the bruises and scrapes covering my limbs. She turned her head away and steadied her emotions before she looked back up with a false smile.

"Okay, you left off when you heard the doorbell ring. What happened next?"

I laid my head back and recalled the morning that had changed the course of my life forever. I told her very little, only what Tyler and I had agreed upon, that he had shown up at my door, thinking I was Erin, and I had straightened him out. I described how a strange man had broken in and attacked us both before we escaped in my car; how he attacked us again at that Oregon motel; and how Tyler had saved us from certain death. I took her all the way to the moment I was kidnapped by Dmitri's man and delivered to his home. When I was finished, Detective Simmons peered at me through narrowed eyes as she tried to decipher whether I was being honest or not.

"So you went willingly with Mr. Karras? You weren't taken forcibly from your home...without your consent?"

I sighed and shook my head. "No, Detective, I was not kidnapped. I went willingly with Mr. Karras. We drove to San Francisco, and after he informed me that he had straightened everything out, he bought me a plane ticket home and arranged for a car to take me to the airport." I hung my head again, remembering the true course of events, even as I chronicled the lies. "That was how I was taken by Dmitri's man, while I waited for a ride to the airport. *They* took me, Detective Simmons, *not*

Mr. Karras. He tried his best to protect me, to keep me safe. If it weren't for him…well… I don't want to think about what might have happened, what would have become of me."

"So what happened after you were taken from the hotel?"

I turned away and stared into the darkened room. "I can't get into that, Detective. It was…humiliating and…degrading. The man responsible is dead and no amount of justice can be gained. So I have no desire to discuss it…with you or anyone else. Ever."

Simmons eyed me curiously. "What about Dmitri Chernov's role in your kidnapping and assault? Don't you think he deserves a measure of justice?"

I was tired of her questions, sick of discussing it. I didn't want to think about anything associated with the last five days of my life. I cocked my head to the side and looked straight at Detective Simmons.

"Right now, I'm done with all of this. I just want to go home. It's the FBI's problem now, right?" I asked and she nodded. "Well, then, let them worry about Dmitri Chernov. I'm finished. With everyone…including you, Detective. So if you wouldn't mind, please close the door on your way out."

Detective Simmons huffed and gathered herself up. "Okay. That's all for now, but I'll be in touch, Ms. Maguire."

"Actually, Detective, I would rather you weren't. You may speak to my attorney, if you must, but otherwise, I prefer to be left alone and never speak of this again."

"That's fine, Ms. Maguire, but the FBI wants answers. If you don't talk to me, they might show up asking all kinds of uncomfortable questions. Is that what you want?"

"What I want is to be left alone. Goodbye, Detective."

I closed my eyes and turned my head away, effectively ending the interview and praying for an end to this episode of my life.

Chapter Forty-Nine

Tyler

Eight Months Later

I stood outside the door of the federal courthouse on Market Street in San Francisco and looked around at the city I'd called home for nearly ten years. A comforting flood of familiar intimacy overwhelmed me. Even on this chilly winter afternoon, with the sky a steel grey and threatening rain, I realized how much I had missed this beautiful city by the bay. Just a few months ago, I'd been longing for the cool, foggy days of summer and the warm, sunny days of autumn here in The City. I'd spent last summer living — or maybe hiding would be more accurate — in Chicago, where the heat and humidity had nearly driven me mad.

In October, when the FBI had detected a threat against my life, I was allowed to travel back to Melbourne, Australia, escorted by my own private special agent, where I marked what would have been my first wedding anniversary alone in a small, sparsely furnished apartment, courtesy of the United States government. It was there I could remember Nick best, as he was as a boy, unbound by the complications of physical pain and chemical dependence, carefree and unbridled, his eyes worry-free, and his laugh spirited.

I needed to remember him that way, before my actions changed the course of our lives. I had always been so hard on Nick, my way of keeping him at a distance, of breaking free of my family. And all he had ever wanted was to be close to his big brother. I never saw the sacrifices he'd made for me. I was too preoccupied with my own life, my own anger and resentment.

He was everything I was not, but believed myself to be. I never *was* that man I saw in the mirror. My disgrace at coming to terms with that was unbearable. But in the end, Nick had taught me something: that family meant acceptance without judgment, forgiveness without condition, and love without expectation. That all we are is who we surround ourselves with and let into our hearts. Those were hard-learned lessons.

I took a lot of time to reflect back on my life over the last year and all that had happened, especially since I'd last spoken to Hannah late last spring. I vowed never to allow myself to be ruled by my emotions again, a promise I should have known I could never actually keep. It just wasn't in my nature, I guess.

Now that I was back on American soil, I yearned for the familiarity of home and the tenderness of loved ones, neither of which I currently had. It was difficult to be here and no longer feel at home. Even still, it was wonderful to be standing in San Francisco again.

I loved its rhythm and vibrancy, the eclectic mix of cultures, and the endless possibilities to entertain and explore. Mostly, this was the only place where I'd felt connected and truly happy. I longed, with every fiber of my body, to feel connected like that again. But, although I had once called this home, and I could not imagine living anywhere else, I knew now that it was not the actual place, but rather the people in my life that had made me feel that way. And now, without Jillian and Nick here to hold onto, I felt like a kite with its string cut, flying wildly in the breeze, not knowing if I would return to earth, and, if I did, where I would land and what condition I would be in.

It was disconcerting to be among all that was so familiar yet feel that the heart that beat within my chest was not actually my own. I was lost, like a child separated from a parent in a large crowd. Not alone, yet quintessentially lonely. I needed to find home again, and now that so much had changed, I felt it might actually be possible to do so.

Eight months ago, when I thought I had no other choice, I turned my back on my own life and identity. I left my brother to be buried by strangers. I said goodbye to Hannah and broke her heart, hoping she would move on more easily and forget me. It was stupid of me, though, to think that I could put her out of my thoughts and move on. The longer she was apart from me, the more I felt pulled toward her. Until now, I'd had no hope of ever reconciling with Hannah.

That frame of mind was not ideal as I detoxed myself from all the booze and pills. It took many difficult weeks of drying out and counseling to learn to be clean and sober again, and then many more to remember and reconcile with the man I used to be.

With Herculean effort, I came to terms with the monster I'd become. I took emotional responsibility for nearly raping then kidnapping an innocent woman, for exposing her to danger so extreme she very well could have died or, at the very least, lost her freedom and any sense of her humanity.

Even the lives of Dmitri's men, which I took in defense of Hannah and myself, weighed heavy. It was impossible not to measure Hannah's life, or even my own, in greater balance than the lives of those I took, but just as Nick had joined Dmitri's crew under duress, I had no way of knowing who those men were, why they had chosen that life, or the loved ones they had left behind because of my actions. I faced down each and every facet of that monster and vanquished him forever. Then I worked hard every day to carve out a new man who could somehow straddle the world I'd created between.

Afterwards, I spent months preparing and testifying at every hearing prior to Dmitri Chernov's trial. I had returned to San Francisco this week to finish up, countering Dmitri's accusations against me with the story Hannah had sworn me to tell. I was assured by the federal prosecutor that I was more believable, but testifying to the lies bothered me nonetheless. I was still on the stand completing the last of my promised testimony when Dmitri suffered a mild heart attack in the court room. He clutched frantically at his chest as sweat popped from his ashen face. The courtroom erupted into loud chaos when the bailiff jumped to Chernov's side, grasping his arm as he settled Dmitri onto the floor.

He was taken by ambulance to San Francisco General, at the government's expense, where a procedure to unblock an artery was being undertaken when he suffered a major stroke. Dmitri lingered for several days with tubes and wires attached to his withered body in an attempt to keep him alive, so that he might face the justice he so richly deserved. But fate had intervened, and Dmitri died early yesterday morning. While I hoped he burned in hell, I decided it best to never think of him again.

I turned my thoughts to my future instead. And it was *my* future again, not an assumed one. There was no threat against me anymore. Over the last few months, Dmitri's organization had collapsed without clear leadership, and its members had moved on within the broad confines of the *vory v zakone*. I was free again.

I raised my face up into the cold breeze, closed my eyes, and imagined what my life would be like now, where I could find my heart again. I knew the answer to that already. I would follow the echoing heartbeat to the Puget Sound and up to Seattle's Eastside, where I knew Hannah still lived.

"Yo, Karras!" a loud voice rang out.

I opened my eyes. It was Agent Aaron Moody. "Aaron, I'm glad you came. I wanted to see you one last time and thank you for all you've done."

"Hey, man, it's my job," he said.

But I knew it was much more than that. We'd spent a great deal of time together over the last eight months after Moody was assigned to protect me. He told me about his family, the high school sweetheart who had become wife, and about his three kids. He also explained how his folks had been murdered during an armed bank robbery when he was still in law school, and how that had motivated him to join the FBI.

I shared parts of my sad story, as well, about my parents and sister, my wife and child, how Hannah and I had grown close, how we'd clung to each other in our most desperate moments. With so much of our lives laid bare between us, Moody and I had come to think of each other as great friends, and so, when the trial was discontinued after Dmitri's death, Agent Moody did me two great favors.

First, he pulled a great deal of strings and had Nick's body disinterred from The City's cemetery, allowing me to bury my brother next to my parents, sister, and Jillian. I was grateful they all now lay at rest together, and it gave me great peace to know that Nick no longer lay lost and forgotten. I ordered a new monument engraved with all their names and an empty space at the bottom for my own someday.

After a great deal of professional therapy and personal reflection, I'd finally found a small measure of peace regarding all their deaths. It was a matter of understanding why I had become so rigid in my values, and accepting accountability for my role in their lives, knowing that I could have, and should have, chosen a path less selfish. I held everyone to a standard I felt *I* deserved, while not looking hard enough at myself and realizing where I fell short.

I accepted all my shortcomings and forgave myself as best I could. I had to let Jillian go, and Nick, too. I needed to move on. It was the only way I could survive.

To that end, Agent Moody had found out where Hannah was currently living. Against orders, I had tried to contact her, but she'd moved, and her phone numbers were disconnected. I asked Moody if he could provide that information for me, and he did so, against agency protocol, because he knew, almost better than I did myself, just how much Hannah meant to me. Moody was a romantic, a sucker for a happy ending.

"You've done much more than your job," I replied.

Moody clapped me on the shoulder and shook my hand. "The FBI appreciates all your hard work and patience, my man. It's too bad it didn't all work out."

"Oh, but it did," I argued. "That bastard is exactly where he belongs."

Moody snorted a short laugh. "I'd like to think so. Anyway, you take care of yourself, you hear? Stay in touch," he said. "And good luck. I really hope you find what you're looking for, man." He waved goodbye as he walked down the sidewalk, away from the federal court house.

I smiled at his back and turned northeast up Market Street to the Embarcadero BART station which I knew would take me to SFO, San Francisco International Airport. In a little more than three hours, I would be in Seattle and one step closer to the beat of my heart.

Chapter Fifty
Hannah

It was a very cold day, but, thankfully, it was sunny and dry, a minor miracle for the Seattle area in January. I dressed in several thin layers, easily shed when I eventually warmed up. I planned on a two-hour run up at the Tradition Plateau trailhead on Tiger Mountain. Though the hike up was steep, once up on the main trail, it was mostly flat and firm.

I loved to run in the forested wetland. It was so densely green with pine and fern, the smell so fresh and earthy. It helped clear my head and calm my soul, and though there were always other hikers about, it was never crowded.

It was mostly a safe place to hike, walk, or run, but there had recently been an incident where a man had used a stun gun in an attempt to incapacitate a female conservation corps worker tending to a trail. She fought back and escaped unharmed, but now trail users were urged to travel in groups. That wasn't an option for me this day, but I wasn't going to let it stop me. I kept my head up, my eyes on the trail ahead, and let the rhythm of my footfalls hypnotize my mind into a relaxed state.

This was where I worked out all my anxieties and problems. I'd spent too many hours to count up here, sorting through all that had happened to me in the last year. The time alone helped me change my life in so many ways since returning home from California, allowing me to rebound from what surely would have destroyed me.

After I fully recovered from my injuries, I made myself a bucket list of sorts. My plan was to take back control of my life in every way possible. I would not let my past define who I was or who I would someday become.

My first matter of business was to hire a new cutthroat divorce attorney. I was not out for blood so much as I was making up for lost time. I was determined to get everything that was legally coming to me after seventeen years of marriage, especially after the last five had been spent in anything *but* wedded bliss. After a little light digging, and with Sam's original report in hand, it was determined that while Erin Anderson had been his only long term affair, there were many more women with whom Beck had had repeated relations over a number of years.

I considered each of these women to have a monetary value because Beck had spent company time and money on them, and if his employer were to ever find out, not only would they fire him, they would require that he reimburse the company for every penny he could not physically account for. I had my husband backed into a corner, and he was forced to reckon with me for every slight and dalliance, especially for Erin, whom he continued to see occasionally, against my objections, and with the knowledge of all the damage she had done, to us, as well as to Tyler and Jillian Karras and their unborn child.

Beck managed to display a fair amount of guilt, not so much over his infidelities, but rather because of what he believed

I had suffered. I never shared the details of what had happened, not in San Francisco, and certainly not at our home, but he had culled a small number of facts from the police reports, as well as the medical billing, for which he was required to pay. Beck not quite knowing everything, yet enough to feel guilt over, put me in a rather advantageous position, and I was not above milking it for all it was worth. He owed me that and much more.

I was also determined to change my living situation. After getting the house in the divorce, I sold it for a nice profit and moved to Olde Town, a section of Issaquah nestled at the very foot of Tiger Mountain. I bought an older, modest little bungalow with a picket fence surrounding the large lot, and a huge garden out back.

My new neighbors were friendly and warm, always available for a borrowed egg, help with composting, or putting Christmas lights up on the house. We shared our family histories while sipping coffee over the fence or rocking gently back and forth on porch swings as we listened to coyotes bay in the night.

We watched each other's children and organized block parties during national holidays. And when someone new moved into the neighborhood, we all rallied around them, bringing them food, information on local services, or just a welcoming presence so they knew they were part of a real community where every member cared for and protected one another.

Conner enrolled at the local high school and was much happier with kids who placed greater value on true friendship than on material wealth. When he turned sixteen, he passed his driver's test and acquired his license, and when his father offered to buy him a new car, perhaps a BMW of his own, Conner insisted on something a bit more practical. I couldn't have been more proud.

It was a peaceful, meaningful, and bountiful life Conner and I shared in Olde Town, and I would not have been happier anywhere else, though I often worried that Ty would not be able to find me should he ever come looking. But that was just wishful thinking. I knew he never could.

I also decided to concentrate on my physical, as well as my mental health. I took up walking which turned into running. With Tiger, Cougar, and Squawk Mountains all within a few miles of home, I often ran on the many trails frequented by the locals. I took up kickboxing at a local women's club, and though I was no expert, I could effectively defend myself now that I was strong and healthy. I enrolled in design classes at the local college and worked part-time at a small studio in town.

I felt good about every aspect of my life, save one. Because I was so busy, I didn't allow myself much time to feel lonely, but late in the evenings when my mind was quiet, I felt the empty space around me all too keenly. I continued to fantasize about clear blue eyes invitingly wrinkled at the corners smiling down upon me, hard-muscled shoulders to hold onto, and a finely shaped mouth to rest my lips upon. I shook my head and chastised myself for useless daydreaming. Why could I not move on from that part of my life? I sighed and accepted that only time would heal the ragged edges of my heart, though thus far, the calendar had done very little in the way of reparation.

Undoubtedly, the most satisfying part of my life was, at first, a shock, and then a major hassle, but when I realized the opportunity I was being offered, I attacked with the full fury of a woman wronged. Erin Anderson had made a poorly calculated mistake when she used her relationship with Beck to assume my identity. She had a fake ID made with her photo and my information. From there, she was able to forge other documents, gaining access to my accounts and stealing from me.

I'm sure she believed that our resemblance was of some aegis against detection, but unless Beck had confronted her with my accusations, Erin could not have known my connection to Jillian Karras, or my determination to see her answer for her past transgressions. When I noticed the activity on my accounts, minor as they were, I did some digging. I smiled to myself, knowing that if I played it right, I could gain enough evidence to put Erin behind bars for quite some time. And while Ty would never know, it gave me a good amount of satisfaction knowing I had secured a measure of justice for his wife and child.

I moved most of my money around so as not to be available to Erin, but I also left one account open and well-stocked with money I borrowed from Beck. I obtained fraud insurance to protect myself, notified the credit agencies, and waited for Erin to go too far, which she did, of course. I gathered all the evidence I had of every instance of fraud and theft and presented it to the King County District Attorney, who shared it with the federal boys in Seattle since Erin had used my identity across state lines while traveling back to the San Francisco Bay Area. She even deposited a large chunk of cash, drawn by check against my account, into one of her very own down in Napa. It was a tidy operation and yielded ample proof of her deceit.

Realizing the futility of fighting all the evidence, Erin copped a plea. She was convicted of multiple state charges and received a cumulative sentence of six years in state prison, only half of which she would likely serve. But she was also indicted on federal banking charges and was currently awaiting trial. If convicted, she would likely serve an additional five years in a federal penitentiary. The institutions she had stolen from were seeking financial restitution, and the fines levied by the state were astounding. I was content with those numbers and slept soundly at night.

I thought of all I had accomplished, especially healing myself emotionally from what certainly should have destroyed me. What could have devastated my son had he lost his mother. I smiled to myself as I ran along my favorite trail, relishing how far I had come. I kept my pace even and steady, though I felt a prick of nervous tension. I observed the other hikers around me and was aware of one who seemed to watch me closely, keeping pace with me, though he was well ahead on a nearby trail.

Though my ordeal was eight months behind me, I was still wary of strangers. There were many coiling paths up here in the forested wetland, and although they all meandered about in different directions, winding through the trees like a serpent, they all joined together up ahead at the trailhead marker. Our paths were destined to cross, and, with so few people around, I wasn't sure how best to handle it. I was tense and ready to strike as he drew closer. I stared straight ahead and visualized using my well-practiced kickboxing moves against the man, should the need arise.

I thought I could probably outrun him, and that maybe that was the better choice since he looked to be fit and strong, though he was still too far away for me to get a good look. My heart thudded painfully in my chest, more out of fear than exertion, as I pulled ahead in a full-out wind sprint. The man fell behind on his trail as it bent over toward mine. I was breathing hard, and my heart beat so loudly I could scarcely hear anything else. I wasn't able to keep the pace up for very long though, and he started to gain on me.

I decided my best option was to catch him by surprise with a kick to the head or chest. So, as the stranger nipped at my rear flank, I dug in my heels in an abrupt halt. I spun around backwards and released a powerful roundhouse kick. I screamed a shrill "kiyai" as I made contact with my pursuer's chin. His head snapped sideways, and his entire body was thrown into a flying spin. He landed with a loud thud on the firm earthen trail beside me.

Panting heavily while my heart pounded against my sternum, I stood above him in a fighter's stance, ready to unload my fury, but the man moaned as he rolled face down on the trail. He mumbled incoherently as he pushed himself onto his hands and knees, shaking his head to clear it.

"Good God, Hannah!" he exclaimed. "Bloody hell!"

My breathing hitched at the sound of my name and the familiar voice of my dreams. Blood roared in my ears as my heart pounded even harder. I remained at the ready, standing over him, confused, excited, and terrified all at once.

I pulled myself up straight and gasped in shock as I stared at Tyler, who rolled over onto his backside, his legs splayed straight out in front of him. He fingered his chin gingerly, opening and closing his jaw while he tested its function.

"Man, you're dangerous," he said as he looked up at me with one eye closed and his mouth held open awkwardly. "This isn't exactly how I imagined our reunion. But I guess I had it coming." He smiled with a wince and winked at me.

"Ty? What... I thought... Why..." I stammered. "I...I don't understand. Why are you here?"

He chuckled. "You asked me that the last time I saw you."

"Well, I hope you have a better answer this time," I replied. I held out my hand, and he accepted, allowing me to help pull him to his feet.

"I think I do," he said with a grin.

He held firmly onto my hand even as I tried to pull it away. He raised it to his mouth and kissed the top first then he

Nancy S. Thompson

turned it over and kissed the inside of my wrist. I stared silently, open-mouthed, my eyes wide like a lovesick schoolgirl.

"Chernov is dead. It's all over. I'm free," he said. "I had to find you, to see you again, hear your voice. Look into your eyes. I need to know if I have a chance with you, Hannah."

I couldn't find my voice. I just continued to stare at him.

"I can't move on unless I know for sure, one way or the other, how you feel about me. You've never, for one moment, left my thoughts. And after all these long, lonely months, all I can think about is you. My heart belongs here, Hannah," he said as he placed his palm over my chest, "and I can't live another day without knowing if you can feel me there, in your heart."

I bowed my head to hide the tears that collected and threatened to spill over. I didn't know what to think or how to feel. He had done this to me before then cast me aside, twice in fact. I didn't think my heart could tolerate a third. I looked up into his eyes and searched for the truth.

He bent closer and whispered. "Forgive me, Hannah, please. I can't take back what I've done, but I can spend forever making up for it, if you'd just give me the chance." He paused and kissed me softly. "Tell me you feel me there, Hannah, in your heart. Please tell me you feel the same way," he begged with his hand still resting gently against my chest.

I nodded as I gazed into his beautiful blue eyes. "Yes, Ty. I've felt you there every second of every day, and it...it hurt so bad knowing that I'd never see or talk to you again. I've missed you so much. And now that you're here, I don't think I could take it if you left me again."

Ty crushed me in his arms like he couldn't hold me tight enough, like he was trying to step right into my skin along with me. I buried my face in his shoulder and cried, breathing deeply of the scent I could never seem to get out of my mind, thinking

408

that the moment was better than any I had ever imagined. And I had imagined it at least a thousand times. I felt his shoulders quake as he cried the first happy tears I'd ever seen him shed.

We held each other for a very long time, each afraid of ending the moment. Finally, Ty pulled back and put his hands on my face, holding me still as he leaned in and pressed his lips against mine. His kiss increased in urgency and depth as we each laid claim to the other. The moment so tender and intimate, it embarrassed a couple of hikers as they passed us on the trail.

"Get a room," one of them snickered as the other giggled.

We looked each other in the eye and held each other's gaze without a word until Ty smiled and said, "You know, that's a pretty good idea."

I laughed. "Yes. It's a very good idea. Let's go." I pulled back and took a step away from Ty then turned back and raised my hand out to him. "Coming?" I asked.

He took my hand in his and kissed it once more. "You couldn't keep me away," he answered with a wide grin that reached his eyes, crinkling them at the corners like small suns brightening the world.

He held my hand as we moved slowly down the sun-dappled trail, disappearing together into the lush green forest of pine and fern.

CPSIA information can be obtained at www.ICGtesting.com
Printed in the USA
BVOW040358190612

293052BV00001B/11/P